NO HIDING PLACE

Megan didn't want to initiate a suit against a great city hospital for AIDS infection because she knew it would be an agonizingly difficult case that she couldn't afford to lose.

Megan didn't want an opponent like defense attorney Frank Parks, who would use every twist and trick of the legal trade to sway a jury—yet she had no choice but to beat him at his own trial game.

Megan didn't want to know that the devastatingly attractive surgeon who was her perfect lover was a far less than perfect human being—and that Frank Parks had a dangerously seductive side outside the courtroom.

Megan didn't want to believe that the serial killer whom she knew only from newspaper headlines might be someone who knew her all too well.

But if Megan didn't want to die, she would have to replace her desperately clung-to doubts and deadly fears with terrifying truths. . . .

ACTS AND OMISSIONS

D0596613

ACTS AND OMISSIONS

NANCY KOPP

A SIGNET BOOK

SIGNET
Published by the Penguin Group
Penguin Books USA Inc., 375 Hudson Street,
New York, New York 10014, U.S.A.
Penguin Books Ltd, 27 Wrights Lane,
London W8 5TZ, England
Penguin Books Australia Ltd, Ringwood,
Victoria, Australia
Penguin Books Canada Ltd, 10 Alcorn Avenue,
Toronto, Ontario, Canada M4V 3B2
Penguin Books (N.Z.) Ltd, 182–190 Wairau Road,
Auckland 10, New Zealand

Penguin Books Ltd, Registered Offices:
Harmondsworth, Middlesex, England

First published by Signet,
an imprint of Dutton Signet,
a division of Penguin Books USA Inc.

First Printing, September, 1994
10 9 8 7 6 5 4 3 2 1

For my parents,
Rudy and Wanda Kopp

ACKNOWLEDGMENTS

Special thanks go out to the following people for helping make publication of this book a reality: Dona Chernoff, for being the most supportive agent an author could have; Joan Sanger, for her invaluable assistance in restructuring the manuscript; Hilary Ross, my editor at Dutton Signet, for making the nuts and bolts process of launching a book so painless; Joan Bedner, Pat Prisk, and Georgia Weis, for their friendship and their encouragement; and Terri Crocker and Judy Gundersen, for getting me started.

Prologue

If Chet McCloskey hadn't been so damn softhearted, someone else would've discovered the body.

The middle-aged Chicago truck driver had run his early morning route thirteen days in a row and was looking forward to having the next day off and being able to sleep in long past his usual three A.M. wake-up call. He had just finished eating some leftover pizza, and was settling back in his easy chair with a bottle of beer, when the phone rang.

It was his old buddy and fellow driver Rocky Generro, sounding frantic. His wife had been rushed to the hospital with a ruptured appendix. She was going to be okay, but Rocky wanted to spend the next day with her. He hated to ask on such short notice, but four other relief drivers had already turned him down. Could Chet possibly take over his route tomorrow?

McCloskey protested. He was beat. He had other plans. Wasn't there anyone else? No one. Generro pleaded. It was a short route. Chet would be done long before noon. Wouldn't he reconsider? Oh, all right, McCloskey grumbled. He'd do it. He wished Rocky's wife a speedy recovery, then finished his beer, let the dogs out to do their job, and went to bed. Three o'clock would come all too soon.

The stop at St. Michael's Catholic Elementary School was midway through Rocky's route. St. Michael's was a three-story, red brick structure in a solidly middle-class neighborhood about two miles south of Chicago's Loop. McCloskey had finished unloading the cases of bread, hamburger and hot dog buns, and assorted sundries which the cafeteria workers would use for that day's luncheon, and had just started backing his truck out of the alley next to the school when he caught a glimpse of something sticking out from behind a Dumpster straight ahead of him.

What was that? McCloskey squinted. It looked like red fur. Must be a dog. Maybe a collie. He stopped the truck, flicked on his bright lights, and squinted again. Yup, it was definitely some kind of animal.

McCloskey was anxious to finish the route and head home for some badly needed shut-eye. But then he thought of Lady and Tramp, the two fat cocker spaniels that eagerly awaited his arrival home every afternoon, and decided what the hell was a few more minutes. This must be his day to play Good Samaritan. He put the truck in park and reached under the seat for his Coleman flashlight. With the truck's engine still idling, its headlights pointing toward the Dumpster, he opened the door, eased his bulk out of the seat, and slowly began to walk forward, shining the flashlight in front of him.

It was a chilly morning in late April, and a light covering of ground fog gave the beam of light an eerie glow. McCloskey tucked his red-plaid flannel shirt into his khaki-colored work pants and snapped his red quilted vest shut over his gut. Not knowing whether he might confront a sick or wounded animal, he began to speak in soothing tones as he approached.

"Are you hurt, boy? It's all right. Let's take a look at you. Just lay still. That's a good boy."

When McCloskey reached the side of the Dumpster, he cautiously directed the light toward the red fur and blinked hard, trying to bring the sight into better focus. "Oh, Jesus!" he gasped, recoiling in horror. "Oh, God, no!" What had looked like fur was a shock of auburn hair. On the ground in front of him was the body of a woman.

McCloskey broke out in a cold sweat. His first impulse was to run, but he suppressed it. Better make sure she was dead, although there didn't seem to be much question about that. Stepping forward again, he nervously leaned down to get a better look.

She was lying on her back, her arms close to her sides. Trembling, McCloskey focused the flashlight on her face. She was very young, no older than twenty. Her eyes were closed peacefully, as though she had merely decided to lie down on the pavement and take a catnap. Her face was pale and lightly freckled, and even in her present state, McCloskey could tell she was definitely a looker. Her long shiny hair was pulled back into a low ponytail held by a green bow. It was the end of the tail that had first caught his attention.

Slowly moving the flashlight's beam down her body, McCloskey saw that the white skin of her neck was badly bruised. She was wearing a green wool pullover sweater with a brown cotton turtleneck underneath. The sweater and turtleneck had been slit open from her collarbone to her waist. The clothing had been parted, and her breasts were exposed. There was a great deal of blood pooled on her chest and on the ground next to her. McCloskey felt his stomach roll, and for a moment he was sure he was going to vomit.

The girl's green-and-brown plaid skirt had been pulled up around her waist, and the crotch of her white filmy panties had been ripped, revealing a tuft of curly reddish hair. The flashlight beam lingered there a moment. Her legs were slightly spread apart. There was blood caked on her upper thighs and a lot more blood under her bottom. She was wearing green knee socks and brown loafers. One shoe was upside down about two feet to her left.

Swallowing hard, McCloskey bent down farther and slowly stretched out a shaky hand to touch her cheek. She was cold and already slightly stiff. She had probably been dead for hours.

McCloskey straightened up and took a deep breath. Although he was not a religious man, he glanced across the street to where the steeple of St. Michael's was illuminated by a spotlight and quickly crossed himself before hurrying back to the truck. He heaved himself inside and for a moment just sat there, paralyzed. He took several more deep breaths, jammed the truck into reverse, and backed it out onto the street. He was so shaken that he didn't bother to check for traffic and had a near miss with a white Pontiac, whose occupant leaned on the horn and gave him the finger. With tires squealing, McCloskey sped three blocks north on Halsted until he found a pay phone from which he called 911.

By the time the first streaks of daylight were beginning to break through the fog, the police had nearly finished securing the crime scene.

The senior officer on hand, Detective Lieutenant Mike O'Riley, Chicago Police Department Homicide Division, stared silently at the body as the department photographer clicked off shot after shot. As he gazed at the lifeless form, O'Riley's pulse quickened with the dual sensations of anger and sadness that he always felt at homicide scenes. Even after thirty years on the force, murders still bugged the hell out of him. Whenever he was confronted with a new victim, particularly one this young and pretty, he wanted to make sure the bastard who did it never got the opportunity to inflict similar harm on someone else. Maybe that's why he'd stayed in the job so long. The pay and the working conditions were sure nothing to write home about.

At age fifty-eight, O'Riley's five-foot-ten-inch frame remained lean and hard, his eyes clear and deep blue. As he continued to watch the team of officers efficiently go about their duties, he unconsciously rubbed his right thigh. The damn thing was numb again. In his third year on the force, he had been wounded while making an arrest for armed robbery and had been left with a slight limp that was only noticeable when he was tired or rundown. This morning's call had roused him out of a sound sleep, and he hadn't been able to do his normal five miles on his stationary bike. As a result, his leg had seized up. He'd have to try to find time for some exercise when he got home.

O'Riley ran one hand through his closely cropped hair. It had been a flaming carrot color in his youth, but in recent years had faded to a duller rust mixed liberally with gray.

Shit! I'm getting too old for this, he thought. He

rubbed his right hand over his bristly cheek—he hadn't taken time to shave—and shrugged. He wouldn't be getting these predawn calls much longer. In a little over three weeks he'd be retired and the city's endless round of murders and mayhem would be behind him. The only thing he'd have to worry about then would be if the fish were biting and if he had enough bait. Maybe he'd join one of those health clubs where he could use the sauna and whirlpool. That would be good for his leg. Hell, maybe he'd finally be able to quit smoking once he got out of this rat race.

Detective Greg Jablonski, a tall, blond man of thirty with two years' experience in Homicide, was bent intently over the body. When he straightened up, O'Riley asked casually, "Well, what do you think, Gregarious?"

O'Riley noted with amusement the slight clenching of the younger man's jaw. He knew Jablonski hated that nickname, so he made it a point to use it now and then. It helped keep the kid humble. "I'd say she died sometime before midnight," Jablonski responded.

O'Riley nodded. "What else?" he asked as he turned and began to walk toward the school, with Jablonski following close behind.

"There's bruising around her neck. She was probably strangled till she was unconscious before he started carving her up."

"Go on," O'Riley prompted, shoving his hands into the pockets of his blue jacket.

Jablonski looked back at the body. "Two massive wounds to the chest that probably killed her, and some minor abdominal cutting. Also, we've got definite signs of sexual assault."

"And does any of that look familiar?" O'Riley asked.

Jablonski nodded. "It sure does. The whole shebang is just exactly like what happened to that school teacher they found on the south side in early March. Plus, the two women look enough alike to be sisters."

"What'd you say?" The hair on the back of O'Riley's neck stood on end.

"I said we've got an unsolved prior by the name of

Julie Santini who could be this girl's twin," Jablonski explained patiently. "If you didn't already know that, why were you baiting me with those dumb questions?"

O'Riley shoved his hands deeper into his pockets. " 'Cuz the answer I was fishing for is that this girl looks just like a Jane Doe we found off of Pulaski three weeks back. I didn't know anything about Santini."

Jablonski's eyes widened, but before he could reply, a uniformed patrolman standing near them spoke up. "I couldn't help but overhear," he said. "There was another girl that bought it over on Clark on Valentine's Day that was a dead ringer for this one, if you'll excuse the pun."

O'Riley could feel his blood pressure soar. "Shit!" he spat. "What's wrong with the goddamn communications in this department? You mean this is the fourth one with the same MO and nobody picked up the similarities till now? Jesus! What are we, still in the Stone Age?"

Jablonski's eyes grew wider. "Four of 'em." He emitted a low whistle. "Sounds like we got ourselves a repeater."

O'Riley looked at the young detective and frowned. "Wipe that shit-eating grin off your face," he ordered crossly. "Discovering we might have a serial killer on the loose isn't exactly something to celebrate."

"I guess that depends how you look at it," Jablonski countered brightly. "It'll sure be one hell of a career boost for the guy who cracks this one."

Jablonski's intense ambition and eagerness to rise in the ranks of the department at a meteoric rate had rubbed many senior officers, including O'Riley, the wrong way. But now that O'Riley was getting out, he found the younger man's unabashed enthusiasm rather amusing. "I hope you do crack it, Jablonski," he said, removing his right hand from his pocket and rubbing his thigh. "And after you do, I hope you get promoted to superintendent. All I know is that it ain't gonna be my problem."

At the sound of rapidly approaching footsteps, both

men turned. A young patrolman jogged toward them. He stopped short, out of breath, and swallowed hard.

O'Riley looked at him closely. According to the patch on his jacket, his name was Larson. The kid's face was white as a sheet. He must be a rookie. It took a while before you got over the feeling you were going to puke when you looked at a corpse. "What's the matter, son?" O'Riley asked kindly. "Did you find another body?"

The young man shook his head. "No. No, sir," he stammered. "But I found a witness a couple blocks over on Halsted, an old guy who said he was walking his dog around eleven last night when he saw a man running from this direction. He said the guy was really pumping, like he was either chasing somebody or being chased himself."

O'Riley's countenance brightened slightly. "Good work, Larson. Can the witness give us a description?"

Officer Larson swallowed hard and nodded. "Yes, sir. He said he was tall, over six feet, had dark hair. . . ." His voice trailed off. "And he said he was wearing a policeman's uniform just like mine. He said he figured it was an officer in pursuit of a suspect, so he didn't think anything of it."

Shit! O'Riley thought, clenching his jaw. He gave the young patrolman a quick pat on the back. "All right, Larson. Get your witness to come down to headquarters later this morning to give a signed statement."

"Yes, sir." Officer Larson hurried off.

"What do you think of that?" Jablonski asked.

O'Riley rubbed his forehead. "I don't know what I think. I'll tell you after we get a statement."

"Yeah, but what's your gut reaction?" Jablonski pressed. "Do you think it could be a cop?"

"Right now, I think it could be anybody . . . including you," O'Riley answered curtly. He looked over at the school's parking lot. "It looks like some of the teachers are starting to arrive. Better get inside."

As Jablonski walked toward the school, O'Riley looked at his watch. It was nearly seven. Soon the sidewalks would be dotted with St. Michael's students

arriving for morning classes. He had instructed
Jablonski to remain behind to explain events to school
authorities. O'Riley's oldest grandchild attended third
grade in a westside suburb. Kids were so impression-
able. He wished there were some way to spare them
the sight of the yellow crime scene banners and the
chalk marks delineating where the body had lain.

On the other hand, kids were exposed to so much violence on TV that this might not even faze many of
them. Hell, some of 'em would probably find the idea
of a murder on school property to be real exciting. He
scowled. The world had sure changed since he was
young. And he couldn't say it was for the better.

As O'Riley was contemplating the degeneration of
American youth, Dr. Randall Packard, the assistant
medical examiner, walked up to him. Packard was a
tall, stocky man in his late thirties. He had dishwater-
blond hair and wore dark brown horn-rims. He was
thorough and intense. In O'Riley's opinion, Packard
was one of the best ME's he had ever worked with.

"All finished?" O'Riley asked.

Packard nodded and pulled his tan trench coat
around him. "I've got everything I can here. We're
ready to take her in—that is, if your people are finished."

O'Riley nodded. "Any ideas on time of death?"

"I'd say probably around ten," Packard replied.

O'Riley nodded again, then put his hand on the
doctor's arm. "When you get back to the office, I'd appreciate it if you'd check some files for me."

"Sure thing," Packard replied, pulling a pen and pad
out of his pocket. "Which ones?"

O'Riley quickly explained what he'd just learned
about the three unsolved homicides. "I'd like your fast
and dirty opinion on whether the knife used on any or
all of them seems to match this one's wounds," he concluded.

Packard raised an eyebrow. "Think we've got a repeater?"

"Dunno yet. I hope not, but let's talk after you've
looked at the files and done the post on this one."

"Will do," Packard said, slipping the pen and paper back into his pocket.

"Thanks, Randy. I appreciate it."

O'Riley turned and walked silently back to his car. Jesus! he cursed to himself as he got behind the wheel. A serial killer . . . maybe a cop. It was a hell of a way to start the morning. He lit up a cigarette and inhaled deeply. The sensation of blowing smoke toward the windshield was oddly comforting.

As he headed back to headquarters, O'Riley's foul mood began to lift. He reflected that sometimes the fates were kind. His retirement couldn't be coming at a better time. He mentally ticked off seventeen more working days in which he planned to do nothing more strenuous than finish up some paperwork. As he'd told Jablonski, this mess was going to be somebody else's problem.

Strong, steady hands lifted the large scrapbook from its niche on the shelf. The book was filled with heavy black pages, the kind on which older family members used to paste newspaper clippings of births, wedding announcements, deaths, and other significant community events. The left side had two punched holes with a black cord laced through them. The cover was made of heavy cardboard stock in a dark rose hue.

Such a pretty color. Ashes of roses, Grandmother called it.

Gently open the book's cover. There are so many entries already. Flip to a clean sheet.

Pick up a white calligraphy pen and slowly, painstakingly, begin to write at the top. Take your time. Artistry can't be rushed. There. Isn't it lovely? "She makes a swanlike end, Fading in music." The Merchant of Venice, *Act Three, Scene Two.*

The young woman had been a musician. At least she'd been carrying sheet music. What an amazing coincidence that had turned out to be, since the verse had been chosen long ago. Seeing the sheet music merely confirmed that her death had been preordained. But of course you knew that all along, didn't you? A bit of the sheet music would have made a nice momento for the scrapbook. What a pity you didn't think of that sooner, before you disposed of her belongings. Oh, well. No matter. There would be more than enough clippings to fill several pages.

Starting a scrapbook has been such a good idea. It gives you so much pleasure to study the other three sections of clippings, one for each young woman. And each is headed by a verse. All Shakespeare, of course. It has to be Shakespeare.

Admire the writing once more. Very nice. Flip through the rest of the book. So many empty pages. So many more lovely verses to recite. Which one should come next? No need to hurry the decision. There is plenty of time. Close the book and reverently return it to the shelf.

PART ONE

CHAPTER 1

"Megan, I asked you here today to let you know that the partners have voted unanimously to invite you to join the partnership. While we realize this is a year earlier than you'd normally be eligible, you've done such outstanding work that we decided it would be foolish to make you wait another year."

"Thank you, Michael. I appreciate the vote of confidence."

"So you accept?"

"Of course."

"That's wonderful! The other partners will be so pleased. Now in addition to a fifty-percent increase in your salary, you will also receive eight weeks of paid vacation, a second full-time secretary, and a company car. Let me think. Am I forgetting something?"

"What about a new office? The one I have *is* rather small."

"An office. Of course. As you know, we *are* a bit short on space at the moment, but I'm sure we'll be able to come up with something suitable. I know! Why don't you take *my* office. I spend so much time traveling that I really can't justify having something this lavish."

"Really, Michael, you are too kind."

"Nonsense. Nothing's too good for you, Megan."

Megan Lansdorf's daydream was interrupted by a clock chiming the hour. She glanced impatiently at her watch. Damn it! Where was Mike Gillette? She'd already been waiting for fifteen minutes. How could she get the good news about her partnership if he didn't show up?

Megan's green eyes darkened a shade in irritation. She gave her shoulder-length brown hair a toss, got up from the blue leather chair, and walked to the window. Looking east from the twelfth and top floor of the World War I-era building, she had an unobstructed view of the old Water Tower, one of the few survivors of the 1871 Chicago fire. Behind it, the facade of the behemoth John Hancock Center glistened in the sun. Traffic on Michigan Avenue, she noted, was lighter than usual for nine o'clock on a weekday morning.

Megan turned around and cast a critical eye over her surroundings. She was an associate at Barrett, Gillette & Stroheim, a thirty-five-person law firm specializing in plaintiff's personal injury actions. The office belonged to name-partner Michael Gillette, and he had summoned Megan to an eight-forty-five meeting. Gillette was a forty-six-year-old powerhouse who, along with his former University of Chicago Law School classmates, Messrs. Barrett and Stroheim, had founded the firm fifteen years earlier.

The original goal of these former 1960's radicals had been to be in control of their own destiny—rather than having to be at some senior partner's beck and call—while at the same time taking worthy plaintiffs' cases that more conventional firms might reject. After a couple of slow years, in which the three young partners had used up their available credit lines at local financial institutions and borrowed all they could from families and friends, their luck had turned when they won a large verdict for a child who had been severely burned by an exploding water heater.

That case had established their reputation as competent plaintiffs' lawyers, and they started getting referrals. The firm had grown dramatically in the last ten years and now consisted of fifteen partners, including four women and two blacks, and twenty associates.

Megan had joined the firm five and a half years earlier, as a University of Chicago Law School honors graduate. As she continued to scrutinize the office and its lavish furnishings, she nodded with approval. Gillette had exquisite, though eclectic, taste. The dark blue leather of the chesterfield sofa and two wing chairs was a perfect match with the shade of blue in the antique Sarouk carpet that graced the center of the room. The custom-made mahogany desk and built-in bookcases shone with a hand-rubbed finish. The walls were covered with lithographs by Miro, Picasso, and Chagall.

I wouldn't mind having this office, Megan thought. She smiled. While Gillette wasn't likely to pack up his belongings and vacate to make room for her, by next year at this time she might have something nicer than the dinky associate-sized office she now occupied. She adjusted the buckle of the black leather belt she was wearing with her blue linen dress. At a slender five-foot-four, suits made her look even smaller than she was, so the bulk of her working wardrobe was composed of dresses. Her eyes were large and expressive, and she had a small beauty mark to the lower right of her full, slightly pouty lips. Megan had turned thirty a month earlier, but without makeup, in jeans and a sweater, she could pass for eighteen.

Barrett, Gillette prided itself on providing its associates with a more nurturing environment than was generally found at larger firms. Young attorneys still worked long hours, but were given more hands-on experience and client contact than their large firm counterparts. The result was that associates were able to hone their legal skills more quickly and were considered for partnership after just six years, as opposed to the eight- or nine-year-partnership track in place at other firms.

Barrett, Gillette had devised a unique test—a sort of rite of passage—to determine if a senior associate was suitable for partnership. The test was to give the associate carte blanche in the handling of a major case. Ideally this meant that the associate would take the case to trial and act as lead counsel. Partnership decisions depended less on whether the associates won a big verdict than on how they handled the pressures that led up to the law suit's resolution. Over the years, several young lawyers had decided the stress of big case management was too much for them, and had left the firm to find more laid-back employment.

Megan suspected this was the day Gillette would inform her of her partnership test assignment. In the twenty-four hours since he had set up the meeting, she had mentally gone over her four largest cases dozens of times, wondering which one the partners had chosen.

Each of the cases had its own pros and cons. It was unlikely she'd be assigned a discrimination suit filed by minority faculty members at the University of Illinois who claimed they had been unfairly passed over for tenured positions. The case was rather mundane, and Megan suspected the partners would prefer to give her something more challenging.

An action against a local hospital filed by patients who'd contracted the AIDS virus through surgical procedures performed by an infected doctor featured four clients whom Megan genuinely cared for, but the case had a major downside as well: the lawyer heading the hospital's defense was the biggest asshole Megan had encountered in her years of practicing law. Her blood pressure shot up just thinking about having to deal with him. Luckily, the partners were well aware of her feelings, and she was sure they wouldn't stick her with that one.

A civil rights action filed by prisoners at a federal penitentiary claiming inhumane conditions of confinement was okay, but it necessitated many trips to central Illinois where the prison was located. Megan had gotten her fill of rural life as a child, and if she had to do a lot of traveling, she preferred jetting to more exotic climes, not driving two hundred miles past corn fields.

There was no doubt in Megan's mind which case she wanted. A suit against an airplane manufacturer on behalf of the estates of fifteen people who had died in a commuter plane crash was by far her favorite, partly because it was so technically demanding. She was proud of how much she'd been able to learn about aeronautical engineering concepts. Besides, she'd been working on the case for over two years, and it just wouldn't make sense to expect someone else to have to retrace her steps. Yes, the plane crash was the only logical choice the partners could've made.

She continued to gaze out the window, tapping her foot impatiently. "All things come to those who wait" was one of her father's favorite sayings. When she was a child, Megan's dad, an English professor at a University of Illinois campus downstate, was forever imparting such words of wisdom. Megan's brother, an aeronautical engineer, had taken those lessons to heart. He was easygoing, slow to anger, quick to forgive those who did him an injustice. Megan was just the opposite. She had a short fuse and thrived on conflict. Her father had said law was the perfect career for her because it was the only job he knew where she'd actually get paid for being combative.

Megan returned to the blue leather wing chair and sat down again. Her stomach started to growl. The two chocolate chip cookies and three cups of coffee she'd had an hour earlier just weren't sticking with her. When she finished talking to Gillette, maybe she'd pop down to one of the restaurants in the lobby of the building and grab something more substantial.

She picked up a copy of the morning *Tribune* off the edge of Gillette's desk and noted with dismay that the murder of eighteen-year-old Mary Collins, the daughter of a city sanitation worker, was still front-page news. It had been a week since her mutilated body had been found, and there were no suspects in custody. Megan's fiancé played handball with someone in the medical examiner's office, and there were rumors that Mary's killer was also responsible for several other deaths. The thought of a cold-blooded killer on the loose was unnerving. Megan hoped they caught him soon.

Megan casually glanced down at her engagement ring with its three-carat diamond flanked by baguettes in a platinum setting from Tiffany's. She was meeting her fiancé, a plastic surgeon, for lunch on the ninety-fifth floor of the Hancock Building to celebrate her official assignment to the airplane crash case. She could hardly wait. Although Paul was something of a health food nut who drank sparingly, he'd suggested they really splurge and have a bottle of champagne.

As Megan flipped through the rest of the paper, Michael Gillette breezed in. He was average height but carried himself with such authority that he appeared taller. He had light brown, curly hair and dark eyes. He was always impeccably dressed, and today was wearing a hand-tailored, gray pinstripe Savile Row suit with a Turnbull & Asser shirt, and a yellow Hermés tie.

"Sorry I'm late," he said, sitting down behind his desk. "I got hung up in a partners' meeting. Anything interesting in the *Trib* this morning?"

"Not really," Megan said, folding the paper up and setting it back on his desk. "Mike Royko is on vacation this week, and apparently none of us did anything brilliant enough with any of our cases to warrant reporting."

Gillette chuckled. Megan looked sweet and demure, but you never knew what was going to come out of her mouth. In her second month on the job, she'd been sent to take her first solo depositions in a multimillion-dollar products case. She'd walked into a room full of male attorneys, and the oldest one—a crotchety, white-haired old geezer renowned for his sexist attitudes—had greeted her by saying, "Well now, young lady. Whose secretary are you?"

Without batting an eye, Megan had answered brightly, "I'm the plaintiffs' attorney. And you must be a work release patient from the sheltered workshop. I think it's just wonderful that this law firm believes in hiring the handicapped."

The room had dissolved into laughter, and the start of the depositions had been postponed for half an hour while the offended gentleman had stormed off to his office to call Megan's superiors. Gillette and his partners still joked about the incident from time to time.

"I suppose you know why I wanted to talk to you," Gillette said.

Megan met his glance and nodded. "I have a good idea."

"You've been doing fine work on each of your four major cases," Gillette continued, "but they've all been set for trial, and it's not going to be humanly possible for you to play a major role in all of them, so the time has come for some staff reassignments."

Just as Megan was going to encourage Gillette to cut to the bottom line, he did, and she wasn't prepared for it.

"The partners have decided to give you full control of the AIDS case."

Oh, shit! Megan thought. Aware that Gillette was looking at her intently, trying to gauge her reaction, she struggled to keep her expression from revealing that she felt like she'd just been kicked in the stomach.

"I know how hard you've worked on the plane crash," Gillette continued, "but Gene Stutzberger has an engineering background and it just makes more sense to let him take that one over. You can spend some time bringing him up to speed. I'd like you to stay involved in the prisoner suit, as time permits. The partners thought the discrimination case would be a good thing for Rita Montenero to sink her teeth into. She needs more trial experience. I'd appreciate it if you'd fill her in on the details and give her some guidance on what needs to be done next."

Megan nodded again, still wishing they could go back and start the conversation over. How could you do this to me? her mind was screaming.

"So, let's talk about the AIDS case," Gillette prattled on happily. "I know that Ron Johnson has been helping you with discovery, and we want him to second-chair the trial if that's okay with you." Johnson had joined the firm one year after Megan.

Megan's mouth felt parched, and she quickly ran her tongue over her lips to moisten them. She swallowed hard and hoped her voice wouldn't crack. "That's fine," she replied quietly, trying to sound upbeat. "Ron has been doing great work." What did I do to deserve this? she wondered. I'm a good person. I give to the United Way. I never park my car in handicapped spots.

"What's the status of the appeal?" Gillette asked.

The doctor who had transmitted the AIDS virus had died, and his estate was insolvent. The court had ruled that the doctor's personal malpractice insurance policy did not cover the plaintiffs' injuries because the doctor had intentionally continued to perform surgery when he knew he had AIDS. Assuming the appeals court upheld the ruling, in order for the plaintiffs to recover any money, they would have to convince a jury that the hospital was at fault because it had reason to know the doctor was ill and should have required him to submit to AIDS testing or lose his surgical privileges.

"The briefs have been filed with the Seventh Circuit. We haven't been notified of an oral argument date yet." Maybe I'm dreaming, Megan thought. Or maybe this was all an elaborate practical joke and any minute the other partners would all jump out from behind the drapes and yell "April Fool." She glanced over at the windows. The drapes were not moving.

"How are the plaintiffs doing? Is there still only one who has full-blown AIDS?"

"Yes," Megan replied. "Jeff Young. And he's failing. They've started some experimental drug therapy, but it doesn't look good. So far the other three still just test HIV-positive, but they're all on AZT, and they all get retested every three months." Maybe this was some kind of psychological test, and if she didn't run out of the room screaming, she'd automatically be made a partner.

Gillette made some notes on a legal pad. "You have a December first trial date?"

Megan nodded. "It's a bifurcated trial. That's when the liability phase starts."

"How close are you to completing discovery?"

Megan shifted slightly in her chair and cleared her throat. "As you know, it's been difficult to find qualified medical experts who are willing to stick their neck out and say the hospital should've suspected the doctor had AIDS and ordered him to be tested. Our strongest candidate so far is Dr. Leibowitz from the National Institutes of Health. He's given us some favorable preliminary reports, but he's been lecturing in Europe for the past two months and we haven't been able to schedule his deposition yet." Maybe she was on *Candid Camera,* or maybe someone was videotaping the conversation to submit to one of those other TV shows. She casually looked around. She didn't see any cameras.

"Has the hospital turned over all the medical files on their other doctors?" Megan had argued that she was entitled to see how the hospital had handled previous cases where a staff doctor suffered from another contagious disease. The hospital had refused to produce the records, saying they were irrelevant since none of their other doctors had AIDS.

"We're still fighting over that," Megan said. "We have a hearing scheduled for the day after tomorrow. It's in front of Magistrate Gordon, and you know how spineless he is, so I don't have much hope that he'll give us any relief. Frank Parks hasn't budged an inch from his position, so I'm sure we'll have to ask the judge to resolve it."

In spite of Megan's best efforts to remain calm, Parks's name had come out in a hiss, and the lapse wasn't lost on Gillette. "You don't like Parks, do you?" he asked with some amusement. "You know he *is* a top-notch lawyer."

"I'm sure he is," Megan said, her voice rising in timbre. She could feel herself getting red in the face. "But that man must have ice water running through his veins. Do you know he spent half an hour asking Edna Randolph, a sixty-five-year-old widow, detailed questions about her sex life? Now, I realize it's his job to try to show that the plaintiffs got infected with HIV some other way than from the surgery, but that kind of witness badgering is uncalled for. After about ten minutes, I asked for a recess of the deposition, and told Edna I was going to object to his continued line of questioning and instruct her not to answer. She's a feisty old lady and she said, 'I have nothing to hide. I'll answer any questions that bastard wants to ask me.' So I let him go ahead, and Edna told him in no uncertain terms that she had never had sex with anyone but her husband and he has been dead for twelve years." Megan paused a moment and brushed a strand of hair back from her face. "Every single aspect of the case has gone like that. I have never encountered an attorney as uncooperative as Frank Parks."

"You can handle him," Gillette assured her jovially. "Don't let him get you worked up. That's just part of his strategy. He wants to get your focus off the case. You can't let your personal feelings for opposing counsel interfere with your representations of your clients."

Megan clenched her jaw. Christ, Michael, don't patronize me, she thought. That sounded like a speech she'd heard as a wide-eyed, first-year law student. In theory, she agreed completely that personal feelings should have no bearing on professional judgment. In practice, it just wasn't possible, particularly when you were dealing with an arrogant dickhead like Parks.

"Stay focused on your goal and try to ignore the fact that Frank Parks is an SOB," Gillette added.

Megan gave a short laugh. "That's a whole lot easier said than done, but I'll try."

"I know you will. And Judge Edwards will be a real asset in helping keep Parks in line. He won't be able to pull any fast ones with Edwards hearing the case."

Gillette stood up, and Megan did the same. As he walked her to the door of his office, Gillette patted her on the arm. "You've been doing outstanding work for us, Meg. I have every confidence in you. Oh, there's just one more thing." Megan paused with her hand on the door knob. What else can you possibly do to screw up my life? she wondered.

"As you are well aware, this case has gotten a lot of national press," Gillette continued. "In fact, we just got word that the *New York Times* is planning to run a bit on it next month. You know that the firm likes favorable publicity. A high-profile trial is never bad for business, particularly if we win it."

"You're saying you'd prefer the case go to trial and not settle," Megan put in.

"Never turn down a lucrative settlement," Gillette said hastily. "But of course we would prefer a trial to a mediocre one."

"You don't need to worry about that, Mike," Megan said wryly. "I won't have the opportunity to settle because Frank Parks will never offer us a dime. I'll have to take it to trial."

As she started to open the door, Gillette reminded her, "Just remember first-year torts. Concentrate on what you have to prove—"

"Yes, I know," Megan interrupted. "We have to show that an act or omission on the part of the hospital caused the plaintiffs harm." Maybe she could mark Parks as Exhibit A. Any client who hired him for a lawyer must be guilty of something. She opened the door, stepped quickly out of Gillette's office, and closed the door behind her.

CHAPTER 2

As Frank Parks leaned back in his chair, his gaze focused on the Waterford vase full of fresh flowers sitting on the corner of his desk. His girlfriend thought his office could use just a hint of femininity and saw to it that a bouquet was delivered every Monday. Concentrating on the colorful mix of orchids, daisies, and roses sometimes helped keep Parks from completely losing his temper when dealing with difficult callers. Right now, though, he was at the end of his rope. He tapped the tip of his gold-and-black Mont Blanc pen impatiently on the yellow legal pad in front of him, as if to punctuate what he had been trying to tell the attorney on the other end of the phone for the last two minutes.

"I've told you, the answer is no," Parks said firmly in his deep, resonant voice. "I will not agree to an extension of time. If you had asked me a month ago, when we first served the document production request, I might have been willing to give you a few extra days. But since we didn't hear from you, we assumed you would be able to get us all of the documents by the date we requested, and we've already scheduled a time for our expert witnesses to go over them. Even if you don't produce any documents, the experts are still going to charge us for that time."

Parks rolled his eyes as he listened to the other lawyer make one last plea, then he threw the pen down on the large teakwood desk and switched the phone to his other ear. "Look," he said, cutting off the man's entreaties, "you're either going to have to come up with the documents by the day after tomorrow, or try to persuade the judge that you have good cause for being late. And I'll warn you right now, if you try that route I intend to ask the court to order your client to pay all costs related to the delay. That includes the experts' hourly rate of two hundred dollars and my hourly rate of three hundred dollars for the time we've already spent on the case in anticipation of getting your documents this week. Am I making myself clear?"

Parks moved the receiver slightly away from his ear to muffle the other lawyer's angry protests. He swiveled his deep, red leather chair around so that he could look out the bank of windows of his office. The view east from the eighty-first floor of the Hancock Building was magnificent. Lake Michigan sparkled in the morning sun, and rush hour traffic on Lake Shore Drive was beginning to diminish.

When the phone line became silent again, Parks said cordially, "I'll look forward to hearing from you tomorrow then. Good-bye." He turned his chair back to its proper position, replaced the receiver with a flourish, and smiled. The legal practice had gotten so sloppy. Everyone seemed to take it for granted that extensions of time would be automatically doled out. Parks played by the book and granted few favors. Of course that meant his colleagues cut him little slack, but that suited him just fine. He could handle whatever they dished out.

Parks brushed a small piece of lint off the right pants leg of his navy-blue Armani suit. He was tall and lean, with the kind of body that was made for expensive clothes. His dark straight hair showed no trace of gray as yet. He had strong, chiseled features, and his dark brown eyes were piercing. Most women declared him "handsome," and most men grudgingly admitted he was "not bad looking."

At forty-two years of age, Frank Parks was already at the top of his profession. He was one of seventy partners at Hagenkord & Phillips, a two-hundred lawyer, blue-chip Chicago firm whose roots predated the 1871 Fire. The firm specialized in business and defense work, and its strong base of conservative clients

included most of Chicago's major financial institutions. No sooner had Parks turned his attention back to
the file on his desk, than his direct line rang again.
"Frank Parks," he answered, picking it up after one
ring. The caller was the president of one of Parks's
most lucrative corporate clients.

"Harry, it's good to hear from you," Parks said
warmly. "How have you been?"

After a minute of small talk, the caller cut to the
crux of his problem: his company had just been informed that the Justice Department was investigating it
for price fixing.

"They haven't filed any charges?" Parks asked, rapidly jotting down some notes on his legal pad.
"They're just sniffing around? Good. The key here is
to be as cooperative as possible, show them you have
absolutely nothing to hide." He quickly flipped
through the black Filofax on his desk. "How about if
I meet with you tomorrow at ... oh, let's say two
o'clock? I'll be bringing along a young partner and
two associates and a paralegal who will need to go
through all your pricing records. Let's see ... today's
Wednesday. If the team works through the weekend,
we should be ready to meet with the people from Justice by early next week."

The caller expressed his gratitude for the prompt service. "No problem, Harry. We'll see you tomorrow."

Parks entered the appointment in the Filofax and in
another, larger desk calendar. He picked up his phone
and punched in one of his office's extensions.

"Joe Callaghan," a voice on the other end answered.
Callaghan was the young partner Parks had referred to.

"Joe, Frank Parks. I just got a call from Harry
Oscarson at Baseline Technologies. Justice is making
noises about filing price-fixing charges. I told him I'd
have a team out there at two o'clock tomorrow. Are
you available?"

When Frank Parks summoned an underling to a
meeting, availability was not an issue. "Yeah, no problem," Callaghan replied.

"Good," Parks said. "Can you line up Jones and

Detweiler and a paralegal to go along? I'll meet you
out there. I have a five o'clock meeting back here that
I can't get out of, so I'll introduce you to the client, sit
in on the preliminaries and then head back." Callaghan
responded he would comply with the request. "Great.
See you tomorrow."

Parks punched the reset button on the phone and
buzzed his secretary. "Lucille, I just set up an emergency meeting at Baseline Technologies for two
o'clock tomorrow. You'll have to cancel my three
o'clock meeting at the Harris Bank. See if you can re-
schedule for Monday."

His secretary said she would take care of it and
added, "Colin Williams is here for his ten-thirty appointment, Mr. Parks."

"Fine. Send him in."

Williams, a short, bespectacled, second-year student
at University of Chicago Law School and one of
Hagenkord & Phillips' thirty law clerks, opened the
door and stepped inside. He had received a number of
assignments from Parks in the six months he'd worked
for the firm, but their meetings had always taken place
in one of the firm's workrooms. This was the first time
he'd been summoned to a partner's inner sanctum. As
he looked around the spacious office, which resembled
an English lord's library, with rich walnut paneling and
overstuffed furniture, the young man's nervousness
was apparent. He hesitated near the doorway, legal pad
in hand, waiting for direction from Parks.

"Come in, Williams," Parks said gruffly. "Have a
seat."

The young man closed the door behind him, quickly
moved to one of the red damask chairs in front of
Parks's desk and sat down. He crossed his legs and un-
crossed them again, then fidgeted with the corner of
his legal pad.

While Williams looked on nervously, Parks sipped
cold coffee from a cup in front of him, then took his
time digging through a stack of documents on the corner of his desk. When he found the one he was looking

for, he threw it down in front of him. "I went over the draft of the brief you did in the CTA case," he said.

Williams gulped, afraid of what would come next.

Parks flipped leisurely through the document. "On page fourteen, you cited a case called *U.S.* v. *Berman*. Do you remember that?" As he spoke, Parks picked up a red pen and circled the reference to the *Berman* case.

Williams nodded.

"According to your discussion, *Berman* was a very strong case for us."

Williams nodded again.

"Well, there's just one little problem." Williams tensed as Parks continued. "The Seventh Circuit overruled *Berman* three weeks ago." Parks paused a moment to let Williams fully digest the import of that statement. "In light of that development, it probably wouldn't be too wise for us to cite the case. What do you think?" As he waited for Williams's response, Parks drew a large red "X" through the offending paragraphs.

A red flush crept over Williams's face. "I'm sorry, Mr. Parks," he stammered. His fists were clenched and his nails dug into his palms. "I must have missed it."

"I'm painfully aware of the fact that you must have missed it," Parks said coldly. "What I want to know is *why* you missed it. You're just damn lucky that I was up-to-date reading my advance sheets and that I remembered seeing the Seventh Circuit's decision. It would have been very embarrassing if we'd filed the brief with that reference in it."

Parks set the red pen down on the desk and leaned back in his chair. "This brief is due the day after tomorrow. I want you to go back to the library, hit the books, find some new authority along the lines of *Berman* and rewrite this section. I want a draft of your revision on my desk by six o'clock tomorrow night."

Parks tossed the draft of the brief across the desk to Williams, who clumsily caught it. "I hope this has taught you a lesson. Making sure your authority hasn't been overruled is the most important part of brief writing. It's better to file no brief at all than to file one that contains inaccurate cites."

"Yes, Mr. Parks. It won't happen again," Williams said contritely.

"I sincerely hope not," Parks said sternly. "Because the next time you might not be fortunate enough to have someone catch your error before it costs your client dearly." He pushed his chair away from his desk and stood up. Williams did the same. "Now get to work on those revisions."

"Yes, sir," Williams said, breathing a sigh of relief that Parks hadn't fired him on the spot. "I'll have the new draft to you by tomorrow noon. I promise." He started to edge toward the door.

Just as Williams was about to make his escape, Parks halted his retreat. "Oh, Williams, one more thing."

Williams gulped and turned around, fearing the worst.

"I thought the rest of the brief was quite well done."

Williams swallowed hard again, trying to dislodge the lump from his throat. "Thank you, sir." He turned again and fled before Parks had a chance to say another word.

When she left Gillette's office, Megan's head was throbbing. Assigning her the AIDS case was absolutely unbelievable. How could they do this to her? On the way back to her own office, she stopped in to see Rita Montenero, to let her know about her new assignment.

Rita looked up from the stack of law books on her desk as Megan stepped inside. Rita, a tall Hispanic woman with short, curly black hair and large dark eyes, was a third-year associate. The women had become good friends, and Rita considered Megan to be somewhat of a mentor.

"Hi," Rita said brightly. She'd known that Megan was going to be meeting with Gillette. "I want to hear all about it. How did it go?"

Megan slumped into a chair. "Well, I've got some good news and some bad news. The good news is that you're taking over my place on the discrimination case. If you play your cards right, they might even let you try it."

"That's great," Rita said exuberantly. "What's the bad news?"

"The bad news is that I have to take over the AIDS case." She put her hands over her eyes and leaned her head back.

"Jeez, Meg, I'm sorry," Rita said. "I know how hard you worked on the plane crash. I don't know what they could've been thinking."

Megan put her hands down and sat up straight. "Well I sure as hell don't know either." She sighed. "Mark my words. Either Frank Parks will drive me into a mental institution or I'll be forced to kill him, in which case you might get some criminal law experience by having to defend me."

Rita laughed. "Everybody in Chicago knows how difficult Parks is. We could get you off on mitigating circumstances. Say, I just heard something really juicy." Rita was well known as the firm's gossip maven. She had an uncanny knack for picking up all tidbits worth knowing about firm members. "Guess which partner was seen at a very cozy luncheon with an unknown attractive woman at the Chestnut Street Grill?"

There was no response from Megan.

"Give up? Reggie Stroheim! Can you imagine that? Mr. Happily Married Family Man himself. Of course, there may be a perfectly innocent explanation," Rita gleefully rattled on, "like maybe it was his long-lost cousin or something." Seeing that Megan's mood wasn't brightening, Rita said seriously, "You're *really* unhappy about this, aren't you?"

Megan shrugged. "It's my own damn fault for getting my hopes up so much that they'd give me the other case."

"I'm sure once you get used to the idea, it'll be fine," Rita said reassuringly.

"Yeah," Megan said dejectedly. "They say you get used to hanging, too." She got up from the chair. "I guess I'd better go give Ron Johnson the good news that from now on it's just him and me against the big guns. He's really going to be crowing. He bet me five bucks that I'd get the AIDS case." She headed toward the door. "Let's talk about the discrimination case in a day or two, after I get myself organized," she said over her shoulder. "Maybe by then they will have come to their senses and realized they meant to assign the case to somebody else."

"I wouldn't hold my breath on that one," Rita called after her.

"Don't worry, I'm not," Megan muttered.

Megan slowly walked back to her office. Partners were very clever people, she thought, gritting her teeth. She was confident she had the legal ability to handle the case. The problem was going to be trying to keep her temper in check, and that was a much taller order.

She thought of her luncheon date with Paul. She sure wasn't in the mood for celebrating. Maybe she'd call him and cancel. He'd understand. On second thought, a bottle of champagne might take the edge off her depression. Of course a few belts of good scotch would work even better. She checked her watch. Maybe she'd call Paul and ask if he could get away early and if he'd mind skipping lunch and just meeting her at a bar. After all, it'd be a shame to waste good food when what she really wanted was to get bombed.

Parks had just finished making several phone calls and dictating a memo to an associate asking her to do some research when his intercom buzzed. He glanced at his watch. It was five-fifteen. "Yes," he said curtly as he picked up the phone. As he waited for the caller to respond, he quickly filled out a time slip detailing the work he'd just completed so that the appropriate client could be billed for it.

"Ms. Winters is here," his secretary announced.

Parks's expression immediately softened. "Send her in," he said. Hanging up the phone, he stood up and started toward the door, straightening his red paisley tie as he went.

The door opened and Madeline Winters, Parks's girlfriend for the past two years, walked in exuding glamour, smoldering sensuality, and expensive perfume. Madeline, an executive with one of the city's top ad agencies, was in her mid-thirties, tall with long blond hair and a screen actress's looks. The skirt of her black wool-gabardine suit stopped several inches above her knees, revealing what seemed to be an endless expanse of long, shapely leg. Her black high heels enhanced the illusion even further. The top two buttons of her white silk shirt were open, showing just a hint of her bountiful cleavage. A black, quilted Chanel bag, a Christmas present from Parks, was casually draped over one shoulder. In the other hand she carried a black Mark Cross briefcase.

They met in the center of the office and Madeline kissed Parks on the cheek. "Hi," she said, in a low sexy voice, "I had an appointment in the building, so I thought I'd stop in."

"I'm glad you did," Parks replied, putting an arm around her shoulder and nuzzling her hair. "Mmm, you smell wonderful."

"Aren't you sweet?" she said coyly.

They moved over to the red-and-green plaid damask couch in one corner of the office and sat down. On the wall behind them were a series of antique English hunting prints in lavish gilt frames. Madeline crossed her legs, revealing more smooth skin.

"Who was your meeting with?" Parks asked, lightly stroking her left hand.

"Tri-State Travel," Madeline replied, casually placing her right hand on Parks's knee. "They called us in January and said they were unhappy with their present agency and wanted us to work up some proposals. This is the third meeting I've had with them, and I'm beginning to think their old agency will be glad to see them go." Her hand seductively inched higher. Parks stiffened with pleasure. Even after two years together, Madeline's touch was still enough to make him as horny as a teenager.

"They're very opinionated but have dreadful taste,"

Madeline continued. "I left off yet another set of proposals today. If they reject those, I'm going to wash my hands of them and turn them over to someone else in the office. They *are* the largest travel agency in the midwest, though," she admitted, removing her hand from his thigh and toying with one of the gold chains around her neck. "It would mean a nice bonus for me if I could sign them."

"I'm sure you'll win them over. I know how very persuasive you can be," Parks said, putting his arm around her shoulders and giving her a slight wink.

Madeline smiled and fidgeted with one of her gold Paloma Picasso "X" earrings. "Well, I suppose I should go back to the office for a bit. I have some paperwork I'd like to finish. What time shall I meet you at Ambria?" she asked, referring to a four-star restaurant in nearby Lincoln Park.

"I made a reservation for seven-thirty," Parks replied. "I have some things to finish up, too."

They got up from the couch simultaneously and walked to the door. Parks pulled her close and kissed her on the lips. Madeline pressed her breasts and pelvis against him. He shuddered as he felt her tongue slip into his mouth. "See you later, gorgeous," he said hoarsely.

" 'Bye," she said, flashing another big smile. She took her time walking out, fully aware of the effect she had on him.

After she had left, Parks returned to his desk, picked up the phone and punched a number programmed into his speed-dial system. He cleared his throat as it began to ring. "Hello, Mrs. Gurney," he said when the call was picked up. "Are either Kate or Jack home?"

Netty Gurney, a kindly woman in her early sixties, had been Parks's live-in housekeeper and nanny since his divorce eight years earlier. "Good afternoon, Mr. Parks," Mrs. Gurney replied. "Kate phoned me after school to say she's at a friend's house, but Jack is here. Would you like to speak to him?"

"Yes, I would. I just wanted to remind them that I

have dinner plans and probably won't be home until late."

"I mentioned it to them this morning," Mrs. Gurney said. "Just a moment while I call Jack."

While Parks waited for his son to come to the phone, he looked at the picture of the children he kept on his desk. It had been taken at Christmas time and showed the two of them standing next to the twelve-foot Christmas tree in the foyer of their home. Kate, a tall, well-developed girl of thirteen with long, wavy auburn hair and large, expressive brown eyes, was looking solemnly at the camera. Jack, a sturdy easygoing boy of nine with curly, sandy-colored hair and blue eyes, was sporting his ubiquitous half grin and slightly mischievous expression.

"Hi, Dad!" a cheerful voice exclaimed.

"Hi, Jack," his father answered. "How was school today?"

"Okay," the boy answered easily. Both children were enrolled in private schools. While Kate was hardworking and scholarly, Jack's interests ran more toward sports and Nintendo. "We got to dissect a frog in science class."

"Sounds fascinating." Parks laughed. "I just wanted to let you know that I won't be home for dinner tonight. I'm meeting Madeline."

"I know. You told us that yesterday," Jack said, a bit forlornly. Then he added, "Mrs. Gurney is making lasagna for supper."

"I'm sorry I'm going to miss it," Parks said. "Her lasagna is one of my favorites."

"Yeah. Mine too," Jack agreed. "Hey, Dad, is it okay if I play in the garage tonight?" The boy had reached the age where he was fascinated with cars. Parks suspected he'd love to disassemble one of the family's vehicles if he got the chance.

"I'd rather you didn't, son," Parks replied. "I don't want you getting into some grease and then tracking it all over the house. You know how much Mrs. Gurney hates that." There was a disappointed silence on the other end of the line. "I've got an idea, though," Parks continued. "Maybe you can help me change the oil in the Corvette tomorrow night. How's that?" Parks had a mint-condition, black 1957 Corvette convertible that he drove in the summer months. It was almost May first, and time to get the car ready for its first outing of the season.

"All right!" the boy exclaimed. "You promise?"

"Promise," Parks assured him. "I'll see you tomorrow. Be sure to do all your homework."

"I will," Jack replied without enthusiasm.

"Ask your sister for help with your math if you run into problems."

"Okay."

"Good-bye, son."

"Bye, Dad."

Parks replaced the receiver, stretched his arms back to loosen up the tightness in his shoulders and turned his attention to another file. He'd just gotten in a new medical malpractice case and hoped to finish reviewing it before his dinner with Madeline. The thought of her brought a smile to his lips. She looked especially luscious today. He couldn't wait to get her out of those clothes. Maybe they should skip dinner. He'd rather feast on her instead. He knew from past experience that she was completely edible. Down, boy, he admonished himself. There'd be plenty of time to play later. Unfortunately, he now had work to do.

CHAPTER 3

Lieutenant Mike O'Riley swung his right leg over his left and flexed his right ankle up and down, noticing with great satisfaction the high polish on his black leather shoes. It had taken him an hour of strenuous buffing to achieve that degree of luster. He sat back slightly in the tan upholstered chair, taking pains not to wrinkle his best dress uniform and lay waste to his wife's hour-long ironing effort. Long accustomed to working in casual clothes, O'Riley was all spit and polish this morning. Well, why not? It wasn't every day that he was summoned to City Hall for a meeting with the mayor.

A phone on a nearby desk rang. "Yes?" A pleasant looking young woman answered expectantly. "Yes, sir. Right away." She replaced the phone's receiver and looked up. "Lieutenant O'Riley, Mayor Daley will see you now."

O'Riley took a deep breath and stood up. The young woman got up from her desk, crossed the anteroom to the door of the mayor's office, and opened it. O'Riley strode briskly inside, and the woman quietly closed the door behind him.

Mayor Richard M. Daley, a stocky, broad-faced man in his late forties, got up from his chair and came around his large desk as O'Riley entered. "Good morning, Your Honor," O'Riley said cordially.

"Good morning, Lieutenant," the mayor replied, extending his hand. After a formal handshake, he reached out and embraced O'Riley warmly. "It's good to see you, Mike. It's been too long."

"That it has, Richie," O'Riley replied, clapping the

mayor on the back. "But I forgive you. I know how busy you are these days."

"A man should never be so busy that he loses touch with his friends," the mayor replied. He gestured to a chair next to his desk. "Here, come sit down."

O'Riley sat down, and the mayor likewise returned to his chair. He was dressed in a navy-blue suit, light blue shirt, and blue silk tie with yellow flecks. "You're looking good, Mike," he said with a broad smile.

"So are you," O'Riley replied.

The mayor ran his hand through his thinning brown hair. "Ah, well, a little less hair, a little more gut." He patted his stomach. "What can I say? I take after my dad."

"So you like to eat and drink. Nothing wrong with that."

"I guess not," the mayor chuckled. "Being alive and fat still beats the hell out of the alternative. How's Anne?"

"She's fine. She sends her love. She's been doing some volunteer work at a nursing home a couple days a week."

"Really? How'd she get interested in that?"

"Her mother was in that home for a year before she died, and Anne used to visit her a lot. She soon realized that a lot of the residents never had any company and died more from loneliness than from anything physically wrong with them. So one day after her mom passed on, Anne decided she wanted to try to make those old folks feel that whatever time they have left is worth living. They just love her."

"I'm sure they do," the mayor said warmly. "I know I always have. And how are your kids?"

"They're fine, too," O'Riley said, settling comfortably into his chair. "Colleen just had her third son, and Bill finally got his master's degree in business last year. He got a good job at a brokerage firm out in Boston. We were happy for him, but of course we miss him and Lorraine. Mike, Jr., is still teaching tenth grade history, and Ruth's boy started school this year, so she went back to work part-time at the hospital."

"Such a nice family," the mayor said, leaning back in his chair and reminiscing. "You know, I'll never forget how your uncle Marty gave me my first ride in a squad car. I was seven years old, and I thought I'd died and gone to heaven. He even let me turn on the siren."

"He was quite a guy," O'Riley agreed. "He was the one who got me interested in police work." He shifted slightly in his chair. "It's hard to believe he's already been gone ten years. I still miss him."

Mayor Daley nodded. "So do I. He was a good friend. The O'Rileys have all been good friends."

"So have the Daleys," O'Riley responded. "I think your father literally saved my dad's life when he appointed him assistant streets commissioner." The present occupant of Chicago's highest elected office was the son of longtime mayor Richard J. Daley. "Dad had just lost his job and was so depressed. He didn't know how he was going to provide for Mom and the younger kids. Years later, Mom told me that she was afraid he was going to jump in the river because he did have a small insurance policy. I'll never forget the look on his face when your dad called and told him about the appointment. He was just beside himself. He didn't come down to earth for days."

Mayor Daley smiled. "Dad told me many times that Bill was the best man for the job." He straightened some papers on his desk. "So, how are things going at work? Have you had any breaks in the Collins murder?"

O'Riley crossed his legs and shook his head ruefully. "No, not yet. We've been canvassing the area, conducting door-to-door interviews, but we haven't come up with anything except for that one witness."

The mayor nodded. "I've read the police and autopsy reports, but I'd like your opinion on a couple points. Do you think the guy who killed Mary Collins also killed those three other women?"

"I'm almost certain of it. The women looked so much alike it's scary, and the chest wounds are all identical: one to the heart and another to the left lung.

The medical examiner says it looks like the same knife was used in all cases."

The mayor nodded. "Do you believe a cop is responsible?"

O'Riley shrugged. "I don't know. The witness thinks that's what he saw, but it was dark, he'd been drinking, and I really doubt that he was paying much attention. It also turns out that he'd had a prior couple run-ins with the law, so who knows, maybe he sees this as a way to get even. On the other hand, at this point we don't have any other leads, so we can't rule anybody out. I sure as hell hope it isn't a cop, but yeah, it's possible."

The mayor shuffled through some papers on his desk. "Why would the guy target women who all look the same?"

O'Riley scratched his chin. "The department's shrink theorizes that he's using the victims as surrogates for someone who hurt him deeply."

"What do you make of the identical heart and lung wounds?"

O'Riley shrugged. "I asked Dr. Packard if he thought the killer might have some special medical knowledge because, although there were other superficial wounds, the killer always struck in two places that would assure death. Dr. Packard said he wouldn't go that far, but that it did look like the guy might have a better than average grasp of anatomy."

"Such as?" the mayor prompted.

"Well—" O'Riley said reluctantly, "cops have all had some EMT training. That would probably be enough background to get the job done."

The mayor nodded. "So we're back to that. Any thoughts on who it might be, if it's not a cop?"

"It's hard to say. We're trying to find out if there was any connection between any of the victims. So far it doesn't look like it. We've checked with the FBI and the National Crime Information Center, and they didn't have any unsolved murders that match our profile. We're contacting corrections departments throughout the Midwest for names of any known sex offenders who were recently released from prison, but that kind of thing is like looking for a needle in a haystack."

"Because Julie Santini was a city employee and so is Mary Collins's father, I've been thinking of offering a five-thousand-dollar reward to anyone who comes forward with information leading to the killer's arrest. Do you think that'd help bring witnesses out of the woodwork?"

O'Riley pursed his lips. "It sure can't hurt. People are motivated by money, after all."

The mayor nodded. "Good. I'll make the announcement later today." He straightened up in his chair. "I understand you're scheduled to retire soon."

"That's right," O'Riley said. "Eleven more working days to go. Eighty-eight more hours. Not that I'm counting," he added with a laugh.

The mayor was now obviously getting to the reason for the visit. O'Riley had wondered what it was all about. True, their families had known each other for decades, but if the mayor merely wanted to wish an old friend well in his retirement, he could've called the house or sent a case of beer. Although he hadn't confided it, even to his wife, O'Riley was secretly hoping that the mayor would announce that he was going to reward O'Riley with some sort of distinguished service award. That would be quite an honor. But hell, a man should get some recognition for putting his life on the line every day for thirty years.

The mayor gave a slight smile. "Nobody I know deserves a long, peaceful retirement more than you do, Mike," he said. "You've been a model cop all these years."

O'Riley shrugged, but smiled broadly at the praise. Maybe there'd even be a cash stipend to go along with the award.

"But before you go, I have a favor to ask of you," the mayor went on.

O'Riley stopped smiling. "What's that?"

"I'd like you to delay your retirement and head the search for the killer."

O'Riley felt like he'd been jolted with a cattle prod.

He bolted upright in his chair. "No," he said at once, shaking his head firmly. "That's the last thing on earth I want to do."

The mayor leaned forward. "Please hear me out, Mike. I know what I'm asking. And I know how much you've looked forward to retirement. But I also know that you're the right man for the job."

O'Riley shook his head again. "I'm afraid you're sadly mistaken on that score."

"How can you say that?" the mayor asked. "You've had experience hunting serial killers. You worked on the Gacy case." John Wayne Gacy had brutally slain two dozen young men in the Chicago area in the 1970's.

"Yeah, I worked on it along with dozens of other cops," O'Riley protested. "I wasn't in charge of anything."

"You found a key witness who saw Gacy with two of the dead boys," the mayor countered. "You're a born leader, and I know how much the men respect you."

"No," O'Riley said forcefully. "Absolutely not. No way in hell I want anything to do with the case."

"Give me one good reason."

O'Riley snorted. "One good reason? I'll give you a bunch of reasons. For starters, I'm old and I'm tired. The kind of guy you need to catch this maniac needs to have unlimited energy and, more important, he needs to be hungry. He needs to see this case as a stepping-stone in his career. He needs a reason to make this a personal vendetta." O'Riley balled his right hand into a fist and punched his left palm. "Goddamn it, I don't have any of those things anymore."

"Sure you do. You're in top form."

"The hell I am!" O'Riley retorted, his eyes flashing. "I'm fifty-eight-years old. I've paid my dues. I want out. I'm sorry, Richie, but you'll just have to find somebody else."

The mayor slowly ran his index finger back and forth on the surface of his desk. "The autopsy report indicated that Mary Collins was probably still alive and maybe still conscious when she was sodomized with a blunt object."

O'Riley swallowed hard and averted his eyes. "Yes."

"Have you talked to her parents?"

"Yes." O'Riley sighed deeply. "I was the one that had to break the news to them."

Memories came flooding back. It had struck O'Riley at the time of his visit how much the Collins' household resembled his own. A modest, well-kept house. A living room full of well-worn furniture and family photos.

It had been late afternoon when police had identified Mary's body. Her parents had reported her missing at nine that morning. They'd realized she hadn't come home the night before, but she sometimes spent the night with a girlfriend. She was eighteen, six weeks away from high school graduation, and they trusted her completely. They hadn't been worried until the girlfriend had called Mary's mom and asked if Mary was sick because she hadn't shown up for school. Even when parents are expecting the worst, it was still hard to find the words to tell them their child was dead. Joe and Margaret Collins had handled it better than most.

"Mary was so pretty, so full of promise," the mayor put in. "It's such a tragedy when a young person is cut down like that."

O'Riley nodded.

"I've talked to her parents, too," the mayor went on. "And to Julie Santini's parents. They're all coping pretty well, considering."

"I'm glad to hear that," O'Riley said sincerely.

"But they want answers," the mayor went on, "and I don't have any to give them. They want the lunatic who did this caught and punished. They want to spare other families from going through the same hell they have."

"We all want that," O'Riley said. "I'm just not the right man to carry it out."

The Mayor ignored the last remark and continued. "I've had dozens of calls and letters from people beg-ging me to do something. They're scared, Mike. Even though it hasn't been officially announced to the press, people have heard rumors that we've got a psycho on the loose and that it might be a policeman, and now they don't know who to trust. A situation like this makes everyone feel so damned helpless." He slammed his fist down on the desk. "But you know what? The more I thought about it, the more I became convinced that I *could* do something. I could handpick the best man to head this investigation, a man whom I'd trust with my life, and with my family's life. And that man is you, Mike."

"Richie, you know I love you like a brother, and I'd do anything for you, but please. I beg you, don't ask me *this*," O'Riley implored.

"I know how you work, Mike, how you put your heart and soul into a case. That's what we need here." The mayor leaned across his desk. "I know how much you've been looking forward to getting out, but can't you just hang in there for one last case? Maybe it can be wrapped up in a few weeks."

"A few weeks!" O'Riley snorted. "Look how long it took to find Gacy. They hunted for the Hillside Strangler for years. They never found Jack the Ripper. Christ, the chances are this case will be a life sentence for the poor chump that heads it. I want to retire before I'm in a wheelchair or tripping over my beard."

"If you agree to take this on, you'd have free rein to handle it any way you see fit," the mayor persisted. "You can pick the team you want to work with you. Anything you need, manpower or equipment-wise, just ask and it's yours. I'll personally authorize any expenditure. You won't have to worry about central accounting jacking you around."

"The only thing I want from central accounting is my retirement check," O'Riley retorted.

"Come on, Mike, I know every cop has a secret dream to head an investigation like this. Your name will go down in Chicago police history."

"As what? The stupid SOB that tried to find a killer and failed?"

"Come on, Mike ... please."

O'Riley closed his eyes, as if meditating, then opened them again. "I want to get one thing straight here. Are you ordering me to take this assignment?"

Daley slowly shook his head. "No. You can turn it down, walk out of here, and never look back. No one knows I'm talking to you about it, not even the superintendent. I did tell him I had someone in mind for the job and that I'd be speaking to that person today, but I didn't give him your name." The mayor's eyes met O'Riley's. "No, Mike, I'm not ordering you to do this as your mayor. I'm asking you as your friend. . . . Please."

O'Riley tipped his head back and stared at the ceiling. "My grandson Billy, Colleen's oldest boy, is looking forward to having me take him fishing this summer."

"You'll probably have this all taken care of by then," the mayor said eagerly.

"Shit!" O'Riley snorted. "Knock off the blarney, Richie. We're both old enough to know better. The next thing I know, you'll be telling me you still believe in Santa Claus."

"Well, then, how's this for a proposition?" the mayor asked. "If you agree to take the case, when it's over I'll see to it that you get a new dinghy as a retirement bonus."

"Offering bribes now, are you? Your old man must be turning over in his grave."

"Are you saying you'll do it?" the mayor pressed.

"Anne has been looking forward to my retirement even more than I have," O'Riley said slowly. "And I don't know if she'll be able to forgive me if I say 'yes.' " He paused a moment. "But I know for certain she won't if I say 'no.' All right, Richie, you win," he said, extending his hand. "But I want you to shake on the side deal about the new boat."

The mayor clasped O'Riley's big hand in both of his and pumped it vigorously. "Thank you, Mike. You aren't going to regret this."

"What the hell are you talking about?" O'Riley snorted again. "I already do."

"Just remember, Mike," the mayor said in a low voice, "the next victim could be my daughter. Or it could be yours."

CHAPTER 4

"Call the next case," Federal Magistrate Gordon instructed the court clerk. The magistrate, a rather distinguished-looking man of sixty, was seated behind the bench in one of the courtrooms in the federal center. In his black robe, he was indistinguishable from the judges who normally occupied that chair. The fact that the uninformed often mistook him for a judge pleased Magistrate Gordon immensely.

In truth, magistrates were merely the judges' flunkies. They handled routine matters such as pretrial conferences, tried to talk parties into settling cases, and sometimes made decisions in uncomplicated evidentiary squabbles. Magistrate Gordon had three years to go on his second fifteen-year term. He had been appointed to his position at a time when the old Chicago patronage system was at its height, and most lawyers thought little of his ability. That did not bother Magistrate Gordon, who was waiting for retirement, and in the meantime happily collecting his $100,000 salary and doing as little as possible to earn it.

"Case number 91-001423, *Young, et al.* vs. *Chicago Memorial Hospital,*" the heavyset middle-aged female clerk read the names off the docket sheet in front of her in a monotone. It was late afternoon, and she was counting down the minutes until she could escape her boring job and catch an express bus back to her home in the western suburbs.

Magistrate Gordon looked out at the courtroom over the top of his tortoiseshell reading glasses as the attorneys for the parties took their place at the counsel table. When they were in position, the magistrate said, "May I have the appearances, please?"

Megan got to her feet. She had had two days to get used to the fact that she was going to be stuck with the AIDS case until the bitter end, and while she now accepted that reality, she was still far from pleased with it. "Megan Lansdorf and Ronald Johnson of Barrett, Gillette & Stroheim appearing on behalf of the plaintiffs."

Megan sat down again and tucked the skirt of her light gray, double-breasted suit under her. In the next chair, Ron Johnson, an athletic-looking man in his late twenties, with blond hair that he wore a bit too long, smiled at her. Megan smiled back.

Ron was one of Megan's favorite people at the firm and, unlike her, he was enjoying his assignment to the case. Ron was a good lawyer, and as big city attorneys went, he was also something of a bohemian. He sometimes wore a diamond stud in his left earlobe and loved outrageously patterned neckties. Today he was sporting one in shades of blue with a red bull's-eye in the center. Ron was also the firm's lothario. Megan had long since given up trying to keep track of his parade of girlfriends. She had chided him, saying that the reason he wanted to work on the AIDS case was that he hoped he'd be able to learn some new safe-sex techniques.

Ron's passion, besides women and the law, was classic rock music. He had an endearing way of bursting into song in the middle of a conversation. When Megan had informed him that she'd been assigned the case, he'd serenaded her with "You Can't Always Get What You Want." Megan had told him that while he was no Mick Jagger, he did have nicer lips.

"Appearances for the defendant," the magistrate went on.

Parks stretched and leisurely stood up. "Frank Parks on behalf of the defendant," he said.

Megan glanced over at Parks. He was wearing a navy pinstripe suit. With his dark hair and almost swarthy complexion, he looked like Mafia. Maybe

someone named Guido would burst into the courtroom
and rub him out in a blaze of machine gunfire, she fan-
tasized wildly. Then she'd be more than happy to continue working on the case *pro bono*.

Megan looked down at the notes she'd scribbled on
a legal pad, outlining the points she wanted to make.
Local court rules required that disputes concerning pretrial discovery be heard by a magistrate, ostensibly to
free the judges' time up for more important matters.
Megan suspected that the real reason was to make sure
the magistrates had something to do. Most of them
were afraid to make any real rulings and simply chas-
tised both sides to try to resolve their differences. That
was especially true for Gordon. Megan had wanted to
bet Ron five dollars that the magistrate would somehow manage to sidestep making a decision, but Ron
had declined, saying that while he might be a compul-
sive gambler and a womanizer, his mama hadn't raised
no fool.

The magistrate glanced at the file that the clerk had
placed in front of him. He rubbed the back of his bald
head with the heel of his left hand. "I see we have a
motion to compel the production of some documents,"
he said, addressing Megan. "Would counsel for the
plaintiffs please give the court a brief summary of
what is in dispute."

"Certainly, Your Honor," Megan said politely, getting to her feet once again, all the while thinking to
herself, You dumb jerk. It's all laid out in our motion,
if you'd bothered to take two minutes out of your busy
schedule to read it.

Referring to her notes, Megan explained that the
case involved a doctor who had infected four patients
with the AIDS virus; that although this was the first
time a staff doctor had come down with AIDS, she assumed that over the years there must have been times
when doctors had suffered from other communicable
diseases, and the plaintiffs were entitled to know how
the hospital had handled those cases. She introduced as
exhibits the written demands for the files she had
served on Parks, and she informed the magistrate that

so far Parks had not only been unwilling to produce any of the files, he had also refused to give a concise reason for the refusal, merely claiming the request was vague.

"In short, Your Honor, while we dislike bothering the court with these matters, we believe we have shown that this information is relevant, and that we have made diligent efforts to obtain it. We also believe it is clear that the defendant is not going to produce the files voluntarily. Therefore, we request that the court enter an order requiring the defendant to turn over the records requested within a reasonable time. Thank you." As she sat down again, she turned to Ron. He nodded his approval at her presentation.

The magistrate peered out over his glasses at Parks. "Mr. Parks, do you have a response?"

"Yes, Your Honor, I do," Parks said as he stood up. He was even less impressed with Magistrate Gordon's legal acumen than Megan, but today, being on the defensive end of the motion, he felt confident that Gordon would do the right thing by his client.

Although Parks was a stickler about following to the letter the rules of civil procedure, he believed it was acceptable—no, even required—to occasionally ignore a rule's spirit when it suited his client. In theory he agreed with Megan that the hospital's handling of other sick doctors was probably relevant here, because it might establish the hospital's policy on such matters, if there was such a thing. However, Parks also believed that the document production request Megan had served was vague and overly broad, so he had refused to comply with it. He realized that Judge Edwards would undoubtedly require him to produce *some* documents, but he was going to hold off until the judge made a ruling. Delay was almost certain to benefit his client.

Megan watched Parks closely as he made his remarks. Although he spoke extemporaneously, he seemed to have complete recall of all pertinent dates and the contents of various correspondence that had passed between himself and Megan. He explained that

Chicago Memorial was the largest hospital in the city, with seven hundred doctors on staff. He said the plaintiffs had been very vague about just what records they were looking for, and he construed their request to mean they wanted to see files of all physicians who had been on staff at any time during the last twenty years. That would mean going through thousands of files. A great number of those records were now on microfilm, assuming they could be found at all, and it would probably take a thousand hours to look through them.

As Megan listened to Parks's reply, she lightly tapped the toe of her black leather pump on the floor under the counsel table. Parks was an excellent speaker, she thought grudgingly. His delivery was very smooth, and he sounded so sincere. Too bad his whole argument was a crock of shit.

"So as you can see, Your Honor," Parks concluded, "the plaintiffs' request is so vague and broadly phrased that it would be unduly burdensome for my client to even attempt to respond to it."

"Hmmm," Magistrate Gordon mumbled as he made some notes on a legal pad. "Ms. Lansdorf, would it be possible for you to modify your request in some manner, to possibly pare it down to a level where the defendant could more easily respond?"

Megan cleared her throat and stood up again. "Your Honor, this is the first I have been informed that the files are on microfilm or that their whereabouts are unknown. We have asked the defendant, repeatedly, to tell us where the files are, how many of them there are, and how long it might take to go through them. Until today Mr. Parks has refused to answer those simple questions."

As she spoke, Megan could feel her voice getting louder. She knew she was getting off the subject, but she also sensed where the magistrate was headed and she wanted the satisfaction of having her say before he got there. "The truth is, Your Honor, I doubt very much that Mr. Parks would agree to turn over even one file—"

"Ms. Lansdorf," the magistrate interrupted, "you haven't answered my question. Would you be willing to modify your request?"

Megan took a deep breath. "Your Honor, we have already offered to do that, and it has gotten us nowhere. If you will refer to Exhibits five through eight. . . ."

The magistrate held up his hand. He was clearly not interested in looking at exhibits. "It appears to me that your motion is premature, Ms. Lansdorf," he said in his best judicial tone. "I suggest that you reformulate your request and ask only for those files you absolutely need. If I am reading Mr. Parks correctly, I believe you will get those files." The magistrate spoke slowly and enunciated each syllable as though he were talking to someone unfamiliar with the English language. "If, after you have revised your request, you still find you're having problems reaching an amicable resolution of this matter, then I suggest you call Judge Edwards's clerk and schedule a motion time with him." He slammed the file shut and turned to the clerk. "Next case."

Megan made a low growling sound as she slipped her file into her brown leather briefcase. She turned to Ron and frowned deeply. He nodded in agreement. They silently walked out of the courtroom. "Can you believe that?" Megan spouted off as soon as the door closed behind them. "What a supreme waste of time this was!"

"No kidding," Ron said, shifting his own briefcase to his other hand. "Why do you think I didn't want to bet with you?" He looked down at Megan and chuckled.

"Stop laughing! It's not funny," Megan grumbled. "Worthless SOB. He should've been retired years ago."

"Personally, I'm glad he didn't waste any more time on it," Ron said, looking at his watch, a luminous dial with a fish's face in the center. "I'm meeting Verna for drinks at five-thirty."

"What happened to Betsy?" Megan asked.

"She's history," Ron replied.

Meg shook her head. "I certainly hope you're planning to will your little black book to the *Guinness Book of Records*." Ron laughed.

As they started to walk down the hall toward the elevator, Parks caught up to them. "Tough break," he said to Megan in a sincere tone. Then he stepped back, anticipating her reaction.

There was a fire in Megan's eyes as she looked up at Parks's smiling face, and she fought to suppress the urge to kick him in the shins. "Say, Ron, why don't we stop by Judge Edwards's office right now and schedule a time for a hearing," she said tersely, "since I think we all realize that Mr. Parks is never going to produce any files, no matter how many times I reframe my request."

"I don't think that would be wise," Parks said genially. "The magistrate specifically said that you were to redraft your request and that I was to have a reasonable time to respond. I'd hate to have to tell Judge Edwards that you disobeyed the magistrate's instructions. The judge would have no choice but to dismiss your motion as premature and award me substantial costs." He smiled again. "Besides, how do you know I won't turn over everything you ask for this time, that is, of course, assuming you ask for it properly?"

"Because I know you," Megan snapped back, "and you don't have a cooperative bone in your body."

Parks glanced down at his expensive gold watch. "I'm late for a meeting. Gotta run," he said. "I'll look forward to getting that new request," he called over his shoulder as he sprinted down the hall and disappeared.

"Ughhhh!" Megan stomped her foot on the floor. "I hate that man!"

"That's obvious," Ron said, trying not to laugh at her.

"I don't know why he affects me this way," Megan said as they continued their walk toward the elevators.

"I don't either," Ron replied. "I really don't think he's all that bad."

"Oh, great!" Megan snapped. "Now you're on his side."

"I'm not on his side," Ron protested. "I just think you overreact a bit."

"I know I do," Megan conceded. "Every time I have to deal with him, I give myself a little pep talk so I won't let him get me riled up. And every time it ends up like this."

"You're going to get a lot more practice in handling him before the case is over," Ron said. "By the end of the trial, you'll be a real pro."

They had reached the elevators, and Megan pushed the DOWN button. "I know," she said dejectedly. "What a depressing thought. Hey, do you suppose I could put that on my resumé next year when I'm looking for a new job? 'Has great facility in handling difficult people, *i.e.* Frank Parks?' "

The DOWN arrow on the elevator lit up, and the door opened. "I doubt it," Ron replied. "But it might come in handy if you ever have kids or in-laws who are psychopaths."

CHAPTER 5

Megan sat with her feet tucked under her on the camel-colored, down-filled sofa, a yellow legal pad balanced on her lap. She leaned over and plucked another handful of tortilla chips out of the bag on the floor next to her. As she mechanically shoveled the chips into her mouth with her left hand, she made some further notations on the legal pad with her right.

"Is that your idea of supper?" chided her fiancé, Dr. Paul Finley, who was seated next to her. "Were you absent from school the day they talked about the four basic food groups?"

"No," Megan shook her head, her mouth full of chips. She was still smarting from the magistrate's ruling that afternoon, and junk food could be so comforting. "I grabbed a chocolate éclair and a carton of milk from Let Them Eat Cake on the way over here, so that takes care of carbohydrates and dairy products. I had orange juice this morning and a taco salad for lunch, so I'd say my diet is perfectly balanced." She wiped her hands off on her well-worn blue jeans, being careful not to get salt on her new white sweatshirt emblazoned with a red BLOOMIES CHICAGO logo. "You're not really concerned about my eating habits anyway," she teased. "You're just jealous that I can eat a lot without gaining weight. Say, you don't have any picante sauce, do you? These chips are a little bland."

Paul laughed. "No, don't you remember? You finished the last of it Sunday night."

"Oh, yeah, that's right. I'll have to remember to pick up another jar."

Paul lightly tickled the bottom of one of her bare

feet. She kicked him in the thigh in response. Paul was thirty-five-years old, but like Megan, he looked younger. He had wavy brown hair, big brown eyes, and ears that were just a bit oversized. He was tall and lean and unmercifully put himself through a five-mile run every morning regardless of the weather. In his L.L. Bean khaki pants, plaid, button-down shirt, and brown cardigan, he still looked like the prep-school graduate he'd once been.

They were seated in the living room of Paul's co-op apartment on the thirty-eighth floor of a glass-and-steel high rise on Lake Shore Drive, within walking distance of Northwestern Memorial Hospital, where Paul was on staff. He had lived in the apartment five years. He was an avid collector of arts and crafts and art nouveau, and the place abounded in muted earth tones, handprinted Bradbury & Bradbury wallpaper, mission oak, and leaded glass. On the living room walls were four Toulouse-Lautrec posters, which Paul had purchased in a Left Bank gallery in Paris.

Paul and Megan had met at a New Year's Eve party given by mutual friends two years before. Both had come alone. Megan was just coming off a relationship with a lawyer who had recently moved back to San Francisco to join his family's firm. The relationship had lacked true fire and passion and when the man had left town, Megan had been more downcast over the loss of a good friend than weepy about being deserted by a lover.

When Paul first set eyes on her at the party, she was in the midst of a rather heated discussion with another man. She had been minding her own business, standing at the buffet table helping herself to smoked salmon, crab dip, and rye rounds when the man, who had obviously started partying early in the day, had made a derogatory comment to no one in particular about lawyers. "What do you mean by that?" Megan had challenged him.

"Bunch of damn parasites, that's all they are," the man had grumbled.

"Is that right?" Megan had said, bristling. "Well, it

just so happens that I'm a lawyer, and I find stupid remarks like that highly offensive, so I suggest that you check out who your audience is before you start spouting off."

The man's face had reddened in anger, and he had pointed his finger at Megan. "You're a lawyer, huh?" he'd snarled. "You here with somebody? No? It figures. You're probably a dyke, too."

Megan had been about to throw her drink in his face when Paul had walked up and intervened. He'd taken her by the arm and steered her away from the table. "There you are," he'd said brightly. "I've been looking for you all over."

Megan had been incensed. "Let go of me!" she'd hissed as Paul had led her across the room. "I don't even know you."

When they were well out of earshot of the drunk, Paul had grinned and said, "I know that, but I've been wanting to meet you all night."

"Who asked you to fight my battles for me?" she'd said, tossing her hair back defiantly, her face flushed. "I am perfectly capable of taking care of myself."

"I don't doubt that for a minute," Paul had replied easily, "but you seem much too nice to be wasting New Year's Eve fighting with that asshole when you could be having a nice conversation with me instead." He'd raised his glass and winked at her.

Megan had laughed in spite of her anger, and they'd spent the rest of the evening talking. She found Paul endearing because he was handsome, fun, and most important, not the least bit threatened by Megan's career. They'd gotten engaged last New Year's Eve, on the second anniversary of their meeting.

"Would you like something to wash those chips down with?" Paul asked.

"Yeah, a glass of water would be good."

"Mineral water?"

Megan made a face. "You know I don't like that stuff. No, good old tap water."

Paul grimaced. Megan was probably the only person in Chicago who thought the tap water was fit to drink.

"Whatever you say," he replied cheerfully. He got up and walked to the kitchen. As he opened a cupboard and took out a glass, he said, "I heard that Dean & DeLuca are thinking of opening a store on Oak Street. Wouldn't it be great to have a nice selection of fresh food within walking distance?"

"Umm-hmm," Megan replied, crunching another mouthful of chips.

"I saw Hal Timkin at the health club at noon," Paul said, moving over to the refrigerator.

"The guy from the medical examiner's office?"

"Right. He says the word is the wacko who killed the Collins girl might be a cop." Paul plopped several ice cubes into the glass.

"Really?" Megan asked with surprise.

Paul filled the glass with water and returned to the living room. "Yeah. That gives you a nice, safe feeling, doesn't it?"

Megan took several big swallows of water. "Is Hal sure about that?"

"Well that's what he heard."

"Is he supposed to be running around telling people about it?"

Paul shrugged. "As far as I know, I'm the only one he told. Say, Hal's getting a new car and wants to sell his two-year-old Lexus. It's mint. Only twenty thousand miles. I said I'd mention it to you."

"What for?" Megan asked, taking another drink. "There's nothing wrong with my car."

"Nothing a new body wouldn't cure," Paul murmured.

Megan wrinkled her nose. "So it's got a couple rust spots. At least I don't need to worry that somebody's going to steal it." The previous winter two teenagers had taken Paul's BMW for a joyride and inflicted five thousand dollars damage.

"Okay," Paul said, conceding. "I just wanted to give you first crack at it. What are you working on so intently?"

Megan had drained the glass and set it on the floor. "A memo to Gene Stutzberger giving him my brilliant thoughts on what he should do next in the airplane crash case. If I can't work on the case myself, maybe at least I can get some vicarious enjoyment out of it." She unconsciously rubbed the base of her pen over the beauty mark next to her lip as she read over what she had just written.

"Are you still fuming over not being assigned that case? If you ask me, it was a blessing."

"Well, nobody asked you," Megan retorted, reaching over and tousling Paul's hair.

"It's not like you have to work on the AIDS case exclusively. They didn't take your other files away, did they?"

"No, but it *is* going to be my most important case for the rest of the year," Megan replied.

"It just seems like you're overreacting," Paul insisted.

"I know there's nothing I can do about the assignment," Megan said, "but yeah, I'm still kind of bummed out. I worked so damn hard on the plane crash. . . ." Her voice trailed off. "And my encounter with Parks this afternoon wasn't exactly a morale booster."

"But Meg, think of the stimulating dinner conversations we'll be able to have with you working on the AIDS case. You can talk shop, and I'll finally understand what the hell you're talking about. After all, I don't know a damn thing about airplane design, but health-care issues are right up my alley. Just think, this could open up a whole new facet in our relationship."

Megan stuck out her tongue. Bits of chips still clung to it. "That's gross!" Paul teased. Megan socked him in the arm.

"I'm glad someone's happy about the assignment," she said. She unfolded her legs and sat up straight. "Okay, Mr. Expert, tell me this: Why haven't I heard from the great Dr. Leibowitz in almost a month? The last time I talked to him, he said he'd have his preliminary report off to me in a week. I was putting off getting ahold of him, figuring somebody else would be taking over the case. But now I'm beginning to wonder if maybe he's fallen off a glacier. That'd be just my luck. I finally find an expert with impeccable credentials who agrees with our position and he drops out of sight."

"Maybe he just needs a little gentle prodding. Why don't you call him in Munich and tell him you need his report right away," Paul suggested. "He probably got busy with other commitments, and he might not realize your time constraints."

"Yeah, I suppose that's not a bad idea. I've got to get him pinned down, and I also need to schedule his deposition as soon as he gets back to the States."

"I think he'll come through for you," Paul predicted confidently. Paul was the one who had found Dr. Leibowitz's name in a medical journal and had suggested Megan contact him.

"I hope so. I'd sure hate to have to start hunting for a new expert witness at this stage of the game." She stroked Paul's hand. "I can't wait to see Leibowitz in person. He's got a great accent. He sounds like he belongs in an old war movie. Or maybe in an episode of *Hogan's Heroes*. 'Ya, Miz Lanzdorf, I tink I can help yoo out. Vat simptims did der doctor haf?' "

Paul laughed. "That's good. Have you ever thought of going on the stage?" Megan socked him in the arm again. "Ow!" he yelped. "Has Parks named an expert yet?"

Megan nodded. "Yeah, Dr. Jay Gillian from Johns Hopkins. Ever heard of him?"

Paul shook his head. "No, but I'll do some checking for you." He put his arm around her shoulder. "So you lost your temper with Parks again today, huh?"

Megan tapped her pen on the legal pad. "I swear somebody must put something in my food to make me react to him the way I do." She brushed her hair off her face. "I'm embarrassed that I can't seem to keep my cool when that man is around."

"You've dealt with lots of other difficult people. What makes him different?"

Megan thought for a moment. "I don't know. I think part of it is that most people find him so charming. He *is* very smooth, and when we're in court, he's on his best behavior. But when it's just him and me or when he's questioning my witnesses, he's the biggest jerk in the world."

"You're gonna prevail in the end. Didn't your father ever tell you patience is a virtue?" Paul teased.

"My father is like a walking *Bartlett's Quotations*," Megan replied, throwing back her head. "Let's see, what did he have to say about patience? Oh, yeah, 'Beware of the fury of a patient man.' That's John Dryden. 'Learn to labor and to wait.' That's Longfellow."

"You must have had an unusual childhood."

"I did," Megan murmured. "Why do you suppose I turned out this way?"

"Well, don't worry too much about Parks. You'll have plenty of time—" Paul began.

"*Please* don't remind me," Megan cut him off. She made a few more notes on her legal pad and then set it down on the floor. "Well, enough about my problems. How was your day, dear?"

Paul's specialty was reconstructive surgery of accident victims and the repair of disfiguring birth defects. "Actually, my day was outstanding. Remember that woman who was thrown through the windshield of her car about six months ago and had her face sliced to ribbons?"

Megan nodded.

"Well, I had a follow-up visit with her today," he continued, his brown eyes shining, "and you should see her. She's got only a couple of small scars. It's amazing, if I do say so myself. I've got photographs documenting every stage of her progress, and I think I just may write the case up for one of the medical journals."

"That's great!" Megan said enthusiastically. "She doesn't know how lucky she was that you were on call the night she was brought in. She could've just as easily got stuck with some old geezer who should've retired ten years ago and has a severe case of the d.t.'s."

"Now, Megan, I won't have you disparaging my profession," Paul said, affecting a hurt tone.

"Why not?" she retorted. "You're constantly disparaging mine."

"That's different," he said. "Medicine is still considered a noble pursuit. Nobody in their right mind trusts lawyers these days. Say, I heard a new lawyer joke today. What do you call five hundred lawyers at the bottom of the ocean?"

"I don't think I want to know," Megan said.

"A good start!" Paul said, laughing heartily. "Just kidding," he added, holding his hands over his face as Megan hurled a pillow at him.

Megan stretched her arms over her head. "Don't mess with me. I'm not in the best mood, in case you hadn't noticed."

The oak clock on the mantel melodiously struck ten. "Just how bad a mood are you in?" Paul asked.

"That depends," Megan said, nuzzling her head against his shoulder. "What did you have in mind?"

"Are you going to spend the night?" Paul asked, rubbing her thigh.

"I can't," she replied. "I didn't bring along anything to wear tomorrow, and I didn't put out extra food for the cat."

"Get him a bag of chips and some picante sauce," Paul suggested. "It might help his disposition."

Megan laughed. She was still working on getting Paul and the cat to like each other. "He's finicky," she said, shoving her hair behind her ears. "He only eats 9 Lives." She leaned over and stuffed her legal pad into a red canvas Neiman-Marcus bag, which also contained the gray suit and silk blouse she'd worn to work that day.

"I still don't understand why you don't just move in here," Paul said. "We're together almost every night anyhow, and it seems silly for you to be paying rent."

"We've been through all this," Megan said wearily. "I won't move in for two reasons. Reason number one: Until partnership decisions are made next year, I need my independence and my own space."

"But . . ." Paul interrupted.

"Let me finish," Megan said firmly. "We can make

jokes now about me handling the AIDS case, but believe me, the fun is just beginning. I'm probably going to be climbing the walls before this thing is over, and as much as I love you, it's very comforting for me to know that I have my own walls to climb and that I can resort to primal scream therapy or whatever else it takes to keep myself sane without having to worry about upsetting you or your extremely upscale neighbors."

"You worry too much about this partnership thing," Paul said, continuing to stroke her leg. "You're a perfect fit for that firm, and everybody there knows it."

"Partnership still has to be earned," Megan said. "There's no guarantee I'm going to get it."

"Be realistic. When was the last time they asked an associate to leave?"

"About six years ago," Megan admitted. "But three other people left in the last four years because, after getting assigned their test case, they realized they didn't have what it takes to be a partner."

"That's not going to happen to you. You've handled other cases on your own."

"Yes, but they weren't this high-profile. We're going to be making new law here, and I'm scared I'm going to screw something up. What if I go totally nuts and throw something at Parks in the middle of the trial?"

"That's all the more reason you should move in with me," Paul persisted. "I could exert a calming influence."

Megan shook her head and smiled sweetly. "That leads me to reason number two. You know I won't move in here because you lived here with Sylvia. Spending the night here is one thing, but I know if I actually lived here, I'd always feel her ghost lurking about." Sylvia was a former girlfriend with whom Paul had briefly shared the apartment four years earlier. One weekend when Paul was on call, she had packed up abruptly and moved in with another man.

"We could have an exorcism," Paul suggested hopefully.

Megan made a face. "That wouldn't help. That's

why when we get married, I want us to get a brand-new place where we can start our life together."

"Well, I'm certainly not moving into your apartment," Paul said with a grimace. "My first requirement for living quarters is that it have covered, off-the-street parking."

For the past five years, Megan had rented the first floor of a town house in Lincoln Park. She and her fellow renters competed with each other for parking places on the street in front of the building. "Where's your sense of adventure?" Megan chided. "You haven't lived until you've arrived home with six bags of groceries and ended up having to park three blocks away. Then there's the thrill of rushing out of the house in the morning and forgetting where you left the car the night before." She laughed. "No, of course I don't expect you to move in there. Like I said, I'm looking forward to us getting our own place." She leaned over and kissed him lightly on the lips.

"Hmmm, that's nice," he said, putting his arm around her. "But, you know, I wish you didn't live on the ground floor. You'd be safer if you were upstairs. I really wish you'd think about moving, especially if there's someone running around slicing up women."

"You worry too much," Megan protested. "The area is perfectly safe. We're part of Neighborhood Watch. No one's going to get me. Besides, there's no elevator and it's much handier not having to schlep packages up four flights of stairs." She kissed him again.

"I just don't want anything to happen to you," he said seriously.

"It's very sweet of you to worry about me, but nothing is going to happen. I'm a big girl, and I can take care of myself."

"Okay," he said grudgingly.

"Okay," she said, kissing him once more.

"Not to change the subject," Paul said, running his hand up her leg, "but you never answered my question about how bad a mood you were in." He slid his hand under her sweatshirt and cupped one of her breasts.

"Why do you want to know?" Megan asked, arching herself against him.

"Because I was thinking of ravishing you unmercifully before you leave."

"Is that your idea of an invitation for safe sex?" she asked playfully.

"Any kind of sex you want is fine with me," he answered.

She put her arms around his neck. "I think we can probably come to some kind of agreement."

"I was kind of hoping you'd say that," he said. In a swift motion, he slipped one arm under her legs and the other across her back and lifted her onto his lap. Then he stood up and started carrying her toward the bedroom.

"How romantic! Just like in the movies," she giggled, leaning her head against his neck.

"That's right, sweetheart," he said in his best Humphrey Bogart voice. "Better hang on. The show is about to start."

CHAPTER 6

"Mike, why don't you go up to bed? You're going to get a stiff neck if you sleep there. Mike? Can you hear me? Mike?"

As his wife's voice wafted into his unconscious, O'Riley's head jolted up off the worn La-Z-Boy recliner, and his eyes flew open. His left hand was clasped around a bottle of beer that he'd clamped between his legs to avoid spills. His other hand rested on the arm of the chair on top of a file containing the results of Mary Collins's postmortem.

O'Riley blinked hard and his wife's face came into focus. She was sitting in a brown-tweed rocking chair about six feet away, reading a women's magazine. Behind her was the living room fireplace in their modest residence on Chicago's near northwest side that the O'Rileys had called home for the past twenty years.

"I wasn't sleeping," O'Riley said. He shifted the position of his feet on the chair's raised footrest and rubbed his stiff right thigh through his blue jeans.

"You could've fooled me," Anne O'Riley answered with a slight smile. At fifty-five, she was still an attractive woman. She'd put on a little weight over the years, mostly around the hips, but her skin was soft and unwrinkled, except for some laugh lines around her blue-green eyes, and her reddish-brown hair was just beginning to gray around the temples. She considered it unfeminine to wear slacks and was dressed in a brown-and-gold plaid cotton skirt and gold pullover sweater.

"I was just doing some deep pondering," O'Riley replied. He lifted the bottle of beer to his lips and took a big swallow. "This is one hell of a case. There's a lot to think about."

"You're going to have heartburn tomorrow if you drink too much of that stuff," his wife chided gently.

"Nay," O'Riley said. "I just need something to numb my senses a little while I read the autopsy report." He took another swallow.

"I'm sure it's rough," Anne commiserated.

"The worst," O'Riley said. He glanced at the fireplace mantel, which was brimming with family photos, starting with their wedding picture of thirty-five years ago, continuing through the births, high school graduations, and marriages of their four children, and culminating in the births of their four grandsons. His gaze focused on a recent school photo of his oldest grandson, Billy. Although O'Riley adamantly denied any favoritism, he had to admit that the boy was his special pal.

He sighed and looked over at his wife. "Tell me the truth. Are you very disappointed that I delayed my retirement?"

Anne's eyes met his. "Of course not," she answered at once. "You couldn't turn the mayor down. This is an important assignment, and your involvement could make all the difference."

O'Riley grunted. "Well, I guess the overtime pay will come in handy anyhow. Maybe we'll finally be able to afford to add a deck onto the house."

He returned the bottle to its position between his legs and, reaching into his shirt pocket, pulled out a pack of Camels and a disposable lighter. He deftly took a cigarette from the pack and lit it, setting the pack next to a half-full ashtray on the floor next to him. He took a drag of the cigarette and flipped through the pages of the autopsy report, exhaling through his nose. Dr. Packard's narration stared up at him. Impersonal words. Hard to connect them with the vivacious teenager the corpse had so recently been.

Name of deceased: Mary Margaret Collins, 18-year-old Caucasian female. Estimated time of death: 2200 hours. The immediate cause of death was hemorrhaging as a result of a stab wound to the heart. Five other stab wounds were also noted, including one that pierced the victim's left lung. The wounds appear to have been inflicted by a knife with a blade approximately seven and three-quarter inches long and one inch wide. Full-thickness rectal tears were noted. There was stool throughout the abdomen. Hemorrhaging was noted in the uterus, vagina and ovaries as a result of stab wounds to those organs. There was no sign of recent sexual intercourse, and no seminal fluid was detected.

O'Riley closed his eyes. He hated autopsies. He hadn't attended this one because he hadn't known he'd be handling the case. But if there were more murders, he'd be expected to attend the postmortems. Think positive, he admonished himself. Maybe they'd be able to catch the guy before he killed again. Or maybe there just wouldn't be any more slayings. He snorted quietly. Fat chance of that.

"Greg Jablonski must be thrilled that you chose him to be your second in command," Anne said, turning the pages of her magazine.

"Umm-hmm," O'Riley mumbled assent. Mechanically, he puffed on the cigarette, reaching down from time to time to tap the ashes into the ashtray.

"I was a little surprised that you picked him," Anne went on. "I mean as many times as I've heard you call him a prima donna."

O'Riley pressed his head deeper into the chair's headrest, recalling the conversation in which he'd offered Jablonski the assignment. "My goal is to wrap this miserable case up and retire as soon as possible," he'd said. "Now the way I see it, we can accomplish that in one of two ways. We can bring this mess to a quick conclusion by making an arrest, or we can fuck things up so miserably that the mayor will be forced to rethink his decision and replace me with somebody more competent. While I'd obviously prefer that we try for the first scenario, if this thing drags on too damn long, I may be willing to settle for the latter."

Jablonski had laughed and said something reassuring like, "Don't sweat it, Mike. We'll catch him."

O'Riley had replied, "That's what I like most about you, Jablonski, your unbridled enthusiasm and bravado. Just try to maintain that mind-set till we catch that bastard, okay?"

O'Riley knew his biggest problem was going to be getting Jablonski to keep an open mind. The kid was awfully quick to jump to conclusions. He clearly wanted to believe that the perpetrator was a cop.

"You really think so?" O'Riley pressed.

"Yeah."

"On the strength of a statement made by a guy that was half drunk and has a prior record."

"I interviewed him. He seems clear on what he saw," Jablonski said.

"I interviewed him, too," O'Riley retorted, "and I sure as hell wouldn't bet the farm that his statement is gonna turn out to be worth much." After he'd agreed to head the investigation, O'Riley had arranged for a second interview with their prize witness, a retired factory worker in his early sixties. The guy was paunchy, red-faced, and had a blowsy look about him that spoke of years of heavy drinking.

He'd admitted to Jablonski that he'd had three or four beers before walking his dog the night of the Collins murder. O'Riley didn't think he looked like a guy who could stop at three or four and sure enough, when pressed he'd said it could've been six. He still insisted that he'd seen a tall, dark-haired policeman running from the direction of St. Michael's. His drinking plus his criminal record, a couple disorderly conducts and one arrest for public drunkenness, in O'Riley's opinion added up to a witness of very questionable credibility.

"It's as good a premise as any to start from," Jablonski continued. "Think about it: Who has better opportunities to commit crimes than a cop?" O'Riley raised his eyebrows. "Come on, Mike," the young man pressed. "A cop in uniform can turn up anyplace in the city, day or night, and look like he's got a legitimate reason for being there. Most people still trust cops. It wouldn't be too hard for a guy in uniform to lure a young woman into a dark alley by telling her there's been an accident and he needs her help."

O'Riley frowned. "It's gonna take a lot more than that to convince me."

"Besides, our man is careful and knowledgeable about the investigative process," Jablonski added.

"And just how the hell did you come to that conclusion?" O'Riley asked.

"The jobs were clean. No prints, no sign of skin under the victim's nails, and most interesting of all, in the Collins case, the manner of the sexual assault. No sign of semen."

"So?"

"Don't you see—he wanted to assault her but didn't want to leave any clues. I think our guy is smart enough to know that semen is a calling card, like blood. It can be typed and used to trace him."

O'Riley snorted. "Did it ever occur to you that maybe the guy just can't get it up?"

Jablonski waved his hand. "Come on, Mike. Let's face it. We're dealing with a very smart killer here."

"I agree with you on that," O'Riley said, "but that still doesn't mean it's a cop. Anybody that reads detective novels knows about the latest in crime-solving techniques."

Jablonski smiled. "You know what your problem is, Mike? You're from the old school that thinks cops are sacred cows. You don't want to admit that one of your own kind could be capable of such heinous acts."

"You're full of shit, Jablonski," O'Riley retorted. "All I care about is catching the bastard. I don't care if it turns out to be a cop or the archbishop of Chicago or the mayor's crippled uncle. But let me give you some advice." He pointed his right index finger at Jablonski's chest. "I know you pride yourself on your theories and your gut reactions, but I've been around a long time and let me tell you, you can do yourself and the investigation a lot of harm by prejudging things.

You gotta keep an open mind. You gotta operate on facts. I know you're not always big on listening to your elders, but take it from me, kid, you count too much on theories and hunches and you're likely to end up with your ass in a sling."

"What about the precision placement of the wounds?" Jablonski shot back. "You admitted that could be the mark of somebody with EMT training."

"Maybe the guy carries a ruler and measures off where to stab them," O'Riley said, refusing to concede a point. "And while we're on the subject of wound placement, I've got a feeling that could turn out to be key in solving this thing, so that's one area of discussion that I want kept strictly under wraps. And that's an order. I know you sometimes like to impress civilians with your great knowledge, but if I hear you've leaked so much as a pinprick of information, you're history in this department. Got it?"

"Hey, give me a little credit, will you?" Jablonski said indignantly.

O'Riley gave the younger man some personal advice as well. "I hear your wife's pregnant." Carol Jablonski was a secretary in the city clerk's office.

"Yeah, she's due in September."

"This your first?"

Jablonski nodded. "We're both really excited."

"I know you're used to putting in long hours, but this investigation is going to be more demanding than anything you've ever worked on. That might not set too well with the little lady."

Jablonski smiled. "Carol is very supportive of my career. And with the baby coming, the overtime pay will come in handy."

"Yeah, well maybe she's been supportive in the past," O'Riley said, "but this case is different and women change when they're pregnant. Their hormones get all screwed up and all of a sudden they start worrying all the time that you're going to get shot and the baby will be left without a father and all kinds of shit like that. I just want you to realize what you're going to be in for."

Jablonski smiled again. "Thanks for the caution, but I guarantee I'll get no flack from Carol."

"Don't say I didn't warn you," O'Riley said.

"Aren't you afraid it's going to be hard to keep Jablonski in line?" Anne continued, bringing Mike back to the present.

O'Riley opened his eyes and stubbed out the cigarette. "Nah, I can handle him. He's a good organizer, so the first assignment I gave him is to assemble a team of experts. You know, a doctor, a social worker, a shrink, a psychic, anybody who might be able to contribute some theory about what kind of guy we're looking for. I never did have the stomach to kow-tow to people like that. Jablonski's a college graduate and fancies himself as being upwardly mobile, so that stuff's right up his alley." He took another sip of beer. "I gave him strict orders not to talk to the press or make any tactical decisions without my say-so. He's smart enough to know that a bad recommendation from me could deep-six his chance of a promotion, so I don't think he'll give me much trouble."

"This could be a big stepping-stone in Greg's career," Anne said. "He must be very grateful to you for giving him the chance to work on something this important. After all, you had your pick of anyone in the department."

"I figured one senior citizen on the case was enough," O'Riley said, sipping his beer. "I wanted some fresh blood, somebody who knew that doing a good job here could help him climb the ladder in the department."

"And he'll benefit so much from your experience," Anne said. "You'll be able to give him so much advice."

"I already have," O'Riley said. "The problem is, I don't think he takes too kindly to it." He lit up another Camel.

"What are you going to do next?" Anne asked.

O'Riley stretched and yawned. "We're interviewing people who knew the victims, and we're still doing door-to-door canvassing in the areas where each of the

bodies were found. That's probably a lost cause as far
as the earlier murders go, but you never know. We
might luck out and find somebody who's been out of
town or in a coma who might be able to tell us something."

"Are you going to have to do a lot of leg work yourself?" Anne asked.

"Oh, not too much I don't think," he said. "That's
one of the advantages of being in charge of this delightful operation—I can pretty much pick and choose
my own assignment. At least at first, I guess I'll probably spend most of my time in the office, overseeing
things."

They both knew he was lying. An investigation like
this necessarily entailed a lot of time in the field for
everyone, from the senior investigating officer on
down. But in the past couple of years Anne had started
to worry that her husband was going to have a heart attack out on the street or some damn thing, so he routinely kept the details of his job from her. She was
much too bright not to realize what was happening, but
the half truths seemed to make her feel better, so she
never let on.

Anne nodded, then put down her magazine and
stood up. "Do you want a sandwich or some ice
cream?" she asked.

He shook his head. "Nah, I'm not hungry," he said.
He put out the cigarette, drained the rest of his beer,
and shoved Mary Collins's postmortem report back in
the manila folder. "I'm tired. Maybe I'll go to bed."
With his left hand, he reached down and pulled on the
brown wooden lever that returned the recliner to its
normal upright position.

Anne walked over and stood behind him. She put
her hands on either side of his neck and kneaded it.
"That feels nice," he murmured.

"I know you're worried about this case," she said
quietly, "but you're going to do a great job."

O'Riley stiffened slightly, then reached up and took
her hands in his. "I'm not worried, Annie," he said un-

convincingly. He pulled her around the chair and onto his lap.

She reached up and rubbed the back of her hand against his cheek. "It'll be all right, you'll see."

O'Riley shook his head. "I should've stuck to my guns and told the mayor to find somebody else. We'd all be better off."

It was Anne's turn to shake her head. "I don't believe that for a minute, and in your heart, I know you don't either."

He heaved a great sigh and put his arms around her. "There's too much riding on this one. People are expecting the impossible. What if we never find the killer? I don't want to have to retire in disgrace."

"You have a distinguished record," Anne reminded him. "And whatever happens with this case isn't going to change that."

"How can you be sure?" he asked, searching her face. "How do you know I'll have what it takes to see this through?"

Anne smiled serenely. "Because I know you," she said. "But since you look as though you could use a little extra help, I'll say some special prayers for you tomorrow morning at mass."

O'Riley hugged her tightly. "With help like that, how can I miss?" He leaned his head against her. "Now I'm gonna go to bed. I'm beat."

As he slowly climbed the stairs, holding on to the bannister, O'Riley wished to God he had Anne's optimism, but he was afraid it was going to take a miracle to crack this one. Reaching the top of the steps, he shuffled into their bedroom and turned on the light.

As he sat down on the edge of the bed and began to unlace his tennis shoes, he wondered why he'd agreed to take the case. To prove his loyalty to the mayor? To show that even though he was nearly sixty-years old, he wasn't all washed up, that he still had what it took to make it in a world of men thirty years his junior? Or did he really believe he was capable of catching this bastard?

He snorted. There was probably a grain of truth in

all those reasons. But he knew his first impulse had been the right one. He should've turned the damn case down. Because he had a growing hunch that no matter how it turned out, nothing good was ever going to come of this sucker.

With a deep sigh he yanked off his socks. "No, Annie, my love," he muttered to himself, "I'm not worried. I'm scared to death."

Lift the scrapbook from its sacred place on the shelf. Carry it to the table. There was yet another clipping about pretty Mary Collins in today's paper. You must add it to the book at once. You scrupulously combed each morning's edition. You wouldn't want to miss any mention of Mary. It wouldn't do to have an incomplete record.

Carefully apply rubber cement to the back edges of the clipping and gently pat it into position on the page. There. Lovely.

Mary had looked so lovely as she'd walked down the sidewalk away from St. Michael's, her ponytail bouncing jauntily on her shoulders. And the verse you'd chosen was so appropriate. Mary was indeed graceful and swanlike in life, and even more so in death. There had been virtually no struggle. As you'd held her, she simply faded away, like the final chord of music that ends a beautiful song.

CHAPTER 7

Frank Parks looked up from his antique oak rolltop desk, gazed out the window of the study at his home in the Chicago landmark district of Kenwood, and nodded in approval at the beauty of the sunset and the condition of the spacious backyard. June was such a gorgeous time of year in the midwest. Parks employed a gardener, a rosy-cheeked old gent who used to own a greenhouse, to come in two days a week, and the fellow did outstanding work. The lawn was green and lush, thanks to Mr. Krebbs's special fertilizers and the underground sprinkler system.

At the back of the property was a formal English border abounding in majestic delphiniums, naturalized lilies, and phlox. To one side was a rose garden that contained dozens of varieties of the exquisitely scented flowers. Finally, near the three-car garage, was a small vegetable garden tended by Mrs. Gurney that yielded tomatoes, lettuce, potatoes, and beans, along with fresh basil, sage, chives, parsley, and thyme.

Parks's English-style mansion had been built in 1910 by a Chicago lumber baron. The first floor featured a two-story foyer with an open staircase sweeping dramatically to the upper levels, a thirty-by-forty-foot living room, a dining room with a huge antique Waterford chandelier, a music room that held a Steinway studio grand, a library that contained Parks's extensive rare book collection, the study, and a recently remodeled gourmet kitchen with two large work islands, and an industrial-size Gaggenau range.

The second floor contained bedrooms for Parks and the children, and a suite of rooms for Mrs. Gurney. The third floor, which had originally been a ballroom, was now used for storage and a play area for the kids. In the lower level was a richly panelled great room with a fireplace and bar, and a well-stocked wine cellar. Parks had an eye for decorating, and the home was furnished with a combination of fine antiques and contemporary pieces.

At the time Frank purchased the house, he had just made partner at Hagenkord and had also just inherited a sizable sum of money from his grandfather, the former president of a Chicago brokerage firm, so he felt he could be a little frivolous and buy more house than a conservative young man in his early thirties really needed. The Parks family had moved to Kenwood at the insistence of Frank's ex-wife, Caroline, a former debutante whose family had founded one of Chicago's premier department stores. Frank would have preferred living on the North Shore where the kids could wander safely along tree-lined streets. But Caroline, an avid preservationist, had fallen in love with the house several miles south of the Loop and had been almost manic in her quest to own it, even though once you crossed Drexel Avenue several blocks to the west, you were in the ghetto, where racial tensions ran high.

Caroline had been pregnant with Jack at the time, and Frank had acquiesced, thinking it might bolster their already flagging marriage. Once they'd moved in, Frank had become smitten with the house, too. It afforded easy access to the downtown, and after some rather extensive remodeling, Frank knew it rivaled anything the North Shore had to offer. Unfortunately, it hadn't been enough to save their marriage, and when Jack was five months old, Caroline had run off to the West Coast with a graphic artist.

Caroline had welcomed the divorce, which was granted to Frank on the grounds of her adultery, and had agreed to alimony payments for five years, by which time she was supposed to have become self-supporting. The relationship with the graphic artist had failed, too, and the last Frank had heard, she was living in L.A. with a commodities broker. For the first year or so, she had seen the kids every few months, but the situation caused Kate so much stress that a child psychologist had advised them that it would be better if Caroline discontinued all contact. For a while she had sent the children cards and small gifts on their birthdays and at Christmas, but in the last few years she hadn't been heard from at all.

While Jack was too young to have any memory of his mother, Kate had been deeply attached to Caroline and had been devastated by her departure, crying herself to sleep every night for the better part of a year. As he watched the sun begin to slip below the horizon, Parks could hear strains of Chopin coming from the music room. At thirteen, Kate was nearly a concert-level pianist and studied with a professor at the nearby University of Chicago. She was beautiful, talented, and high-strung, and sometimes her resemblance to her mother—both physical and emotional—made Frank a bit uneasy.

Frank leaned back in his butter-colored leather chair. He was wearing white shorts and a blue T-shirt, and he felt something tickle his bare legs. He looked down and saw the family's white Persian cat, Marc Antony, rubbing against him. He reached down and stroked the cat's head and was rewarded with a loud purring sound. Marc was Jack's cat and had the boy's sunny disposition. His companion, Cleopatra, a gray Persian, was Kate's pet and was as moody as her mistress. Apparently deciding that he'd had enough attention, Marc ambled across the room and jumped up on a table that held an IBM PC. He curled up on a stack of papers next to the computer and promptly fell asleep.

Frank turned his attention back to the file on his desk. He was preparing for the deposition of one of his key witnesses in the AIDS case. Dr. Theodore Lenz was the administrator of Chicago Memorial Hospital, and was responsible for setting policy for handling sick doctors. The results of the staff doctors' annual medical exams passed through Lenz's office, and Lenz had known that Dr. Dan Morris, the surgeon from whom the four patients had contracted the AIDS virus, had

suffered from oral thrush, swollen glands, and a skin
rash at the time of his exam four years ago. Lenz had
also known Dr. Morris personally, and knew he'd been
looking under the weather for some time, but no one
had followed up on the cause for his malaise. However, there was no proof anyone at the hospital, other
than Dr. Morris himself, knew that he had AIDS until
six weeks later when he became too ill to work.

Dr. Lenz had the potential to be an outstanding witness. In his mid-fifties, with a B.A. in classics from
Yale, he was a graduate of Stanford medical school and
had held his present position for eight years, prior to
which he'd had a distinguished practice in orthopedic
surgery. The doctor was a riveting, articulate speaker
who was used to being able to persuade people to see
things his way—a characteristic which made him and
Frank kindred spirits. Unfortunately, Frank was afraid
that Lenz's personal involvement in the case might
have clouded his judgment.

Several days earlier, the two men had had a discussion that had unexpectedly turned into a heated argument. Frank had stopped by Lenz's office to drop off a
copy of the preliminary report prepared by Dr.
Leibowitz, the plaintiffs' expert. To Frank's surprise,
not only did Leibowitz think the hospital was at fault
for failing to see that Dr. Morris was suffering from
some vague undetermined illness; he actually believed
someone should have suspected AIDS.

"To a jury that testimony is going to come across
like a smoking gun," Frank had told Lenz candidly.
"I've really got to hand it to Megan Lansdorf for finding a witness like Leibowitz. I may have underesti-
mated her at first, but she obviously knows what she's
doing."

Tall and lean, with piercing dark eyes and a slightly
oversized nose, Dr. Lenz radiated the confident air of a
busy CEO. He had scarcely looked up from typing
notes into a laptop computer as Frank spoke. "We have
our own expert who'll say Leibowitz is full of shit, so
what's the big deal?" he'd asked, dismissing Frank's
concern with a wave of his hand.

Frank responded with a wry smile. "I wish it were that simple."

Lenz stopped typing and frowned. "Cut to the chase here, counselor. Just what the hell are you trying to tell me?"

Frank looked his client in the eye and said, "I think the hospital should give serious thought to trying to settle the case before we go any further. I've often found plaintiffs to be willing to take a modest settlement early on, before they've become emotionally involved in the lawsuit. I was thinking—"

"Never!" Lenz boomed, slamming his fist down on his desk with such force that the laptop computer had jumped. "I will never authorize paying those people a dime!" His face turned crimson with rage as he continued. "What the hell are you trying to do, sell us down the river? In case you've forgotten, the hospital is paying the bills here and that means we get to call the shots. And I say 'no settlement!' "

Frank was unaccustomed to being dressed down by clients, and his anger, too, had boiled over. "Nobody tells me how to run my cases!" he shouted back, pointing his finger accusingly at Lenz. "If you can't play by my rules, you can find yourself another lawyer!"

This exchange was followed by an uneasy pause as both men caught their breath. Lenz broke the silence first. "Sorry," he said, running a hand through his hair. "I guess I got a little carried away. It's just that my reputation is on the line here. The plaintiffs are painting me as the bad guy, and the way I see it, paying them money would be an admission of guilt. But damn it, I did nothing wrong, and they don't deserve any money."

"I'm sorry, too," Frank said. "And I understand your position. But as your attorney, I have to make sure you're aware of the risk involved in going forward. If we lose this thing, the hospital could be looking at a multimillion dollar verdict."

Lenz nodded. "It's a risk we're willing to take. You do whatever you have to in order to counter Ms.

Lansdorf's tactics. But there will be no settlement, now or ever."

Although Frank was relieved he hadn't been fired, the encounter had left him feeling a bit uneasy about both the case and his client.

Frank flipped through the personnel manual that detailed the hospital's requirement that all staff members submit to an annual physical consisting of a check of vital signs, a chest X ray, and some routine blood work. The lab doctor who had performed the tests on Dr. Morris had quizzed him about his symptoms, and Dr. Morris had replied that he was suffering some side effects from having wisdom teeth removed, but that it was nothing to worry about.

Frank picked up his Parker pen and jotted some notes down on a legal pad. Actually, he was glad the hospital didn't want to settle. He did a lot of medical malpractice work, and this AIDS case was a particularly interesting one. While Frank certainly sympathized with the plaintiffs, the legal profession was no place for rampant emotionalism. Intelligence, clear-headedness, logic, and a bit of cunning were the tools a good lawyer needed.

Frank's older brother had followed their father into the family brokerage firm. Although his dad had never put any overt pressure on Frank, it had been pretty much taken for granted that he, too, would join the business. Frank had rebelled in his freshman year of college when, as an English major, he had discovered how much he loved the language. Manipulating words, making them convey a precise thought, harnessing their persuasive power, all of these things had delighted the young man. He knew he would never be satisfied sitting behind a desk reviewing corporate annual reports or counseling doddering, blue-haired dowagers on the pros and cons of AAA bonds.

A sophomore class in government and the law had clinched Frank's career choice. The legal profession was a perfect blend of creative writing, oratory, and psychological warfare. He had never regretted his decision. If his dad and grandfather were disappointed that brokerage hadn't been in his blood, they had never let on. And his family's ties to major midwest businesses had brought Frank hundreds of thousands of dollars in legal referrals.

Frank turned his attention back to his file. His primary line of defense in the AIDS case was going to be that Dr. Morris was the bad guy, and he had deceived the hospital just as much as he had deceived his patients. Wanting desperately to keep working as long as possible, Dr. Morris had hoped that if he wore a mask and gloves while operating he could avoid contaminating his patients. Unfortunately, in his last weeks on the job he'd grown sloppy. He admitted that when operating on Jeff Young the scalpel had slipped and he had cut through his glove into his finger, causing his blood to mingle with Jeff's. The other three plaintiffs' surgeries had been performed within a few days after Jeff's, and Dr. Morris conceded that by this point his mental state was fragile and he had been less than scrupulous about sterilizing his instruments. Frank intended to harp on Dr. Morris's culpability over and over until, hopefully, it would be indelibly etched in the jurors' minds.

As he jotted down a few more notes, Frank flipped through the portion of the correspondence file he'd brought home with him. He saw a letter with Megan's signature and smiled as he skimmed it. She had dutifully followed the magistrate's instructions to redraft her request for access to other instances where staff doctors had suffered from communicable diseases. Her righteous indignation at Frank's continued refusal to produce the documents virtually leapt off the page: "We simply cannot understand your continued refusal to produce these files. If you persist in your refusal to turn them over voluntarily, we will have no alternative but to schedule a motion hearing with Judge Edwards. We would, of course, prefer to be able to reach an amicable resolution of this matter without the need for burdening the court's already overloaded calendar."

Poor Megan. It should have been obvious to her by now that Frank was not going to turn over any files voluntarily. Why was she waiting to ask the judge for relief? He smiled again. He remembered—although somewhat vaguely now—what it was like to be an associate who had been put in charge of a case, having to deal with an obstreperous opposing counsel. Not that Frank saw himself that way, of course. He preferred to think of his hard-nosed attitude as merely setting a good example for young attorneys to follow.

Frank was very impressed with Megan's performance on the case. She'd presented a fine argument in front of the magistrate, and finding Dr. Leibowitz had been a stroke of genius. She had a temper, and Frank exploited that weakness every chance he got, but she was capable and would probably be quite a good lawyer one day, assuming she learned not to take every adverse ruling personally. She was an attractive little thing, too, Frank thought with a smile. Not a stunner like Madeline, but pretty and fresh. With a look his grandmother might have referred to as "wholesome." And her firm must have confidence in her, since it looked like they were going to let her try the case. Frank had been a bit surprised at that. He would never let even a senior associate handle an important case alone. But then Barrett, Gillette was known for taking risks and generally being avant garde. They topped the list of Chicago firms for having the highest percentage of minority and women partners. As a result, some lawyers facetiously referred to them as "the Rainbow Coalition." All joking aside, Frank considered them fine lawyers, even though their politics and client base were quite different from his.

Frank's concentration was suddenly broken by some very discordant sounds coming from the music room.

"Get away from me! Can't you see I'm trying to practice?" Kate's voice was shrill.

"I'm not bothering you," Jack replied easily.

"You are too bothering me! Now get out!"

"This is my house, too," Jack retorted. "Maybe I don't want to get out."

"Get out now!" Kate screamed.

Frank heard rapid footsteps on the marble floor in

the hall, coming from the direction of the kitchen. The row must have reached Mrs. Gurney's ears.

"What's the matter here?" Parks heard her ask in her soothing voice.

"He's bothering me *again*," Kate said in a disgusted tone. "I've told him not to come in here while I'm practicing."

"I gotta be somewhere," Jack said reasonably.

"Yeah, well it doesn't have to be here," Kate shot back. "You've got the whole rest of the house to play in."

Mrs. Gurney sighed. She was well used to their spats. "Jack, why don't you come help me in the kitchen. I was just going to make some lemonade."

"I don't want lemonade," Jack said stubbornly. "I want to stay here."

"You can't stay here!" Kate yelled. "How can I practice? I'm never going to be able to learn this piece if you don't quit bothering me."

It was obvious this fight was beyond Mrs. Gurney's powers of mediation, so Frank slipped his bare feet into his brown Cole-Haan loafers, pushed back his chair, got up, and began walking toward the music room. As he reached the door, Jack was jumping up and down and taunting his sister. "Only sissies play the piano anyway. Sissy!"

"You are so childish," Kate hissed back. "You're nothing but a big baby!"

"All right, that's enough out of both of you," Frank said as he walked into the room. "What's the matter with you guys, is the heat getting to you?"

Jack was standing on the rose-and-blue oriental rug in the middle of the oak-and-mahogany parquet floor. His freckled face had gotten very red. "She's always picking on me," he complained, rubbing a bare foot on the rug.

Kate, who was still seated at the piano bench, gave her long hair a toss. "He's *so* childish," she repeated. "He knows I need to practice, and he won't leave me alone."

Mrs. Gurney, a plumpish woman with a kind face,

smiled at Parks, confident that he would be able to bring the situation under control, and walked back to the kitchen.

Parks walked over and put his hand on Jack's shoulder. "Why don't we give your sister some peace and quiet—" he began.

"No! I want to play in here," Jack interrupted.

"Well, okay," Parks went on, "suit yourself. I was going to ask if you'd like to help me out in the garage, but if you're too busy, I guess I'll have to take care of it."

At the word "garage," Jack reconsidered. A foray to the garage had to have something to do with cars. And cars were his passion. "Well, I guess I *could* help you," he said, trying not to appear too eager.

Frank smiled. "Good. Put your shoes on and let's go."

Several minutes later, Jack skipped happily ahead of his father down the brick driveway. Frank unlocked the side door to the garage and flipped on the overhead light, revealing the blue Mercedes 500 SL that he drove to work, a brown Range Rover that Mrs. Gurney used to chauffeur the children around, and the 1957 Corvette.

"What are we going to do tonight, Dad?" Jack asked.

"Oh, I thought maybe we'd take the 'Vette for a little spin. The last time I had it out there seemed to be some engine noise, and I thought we should check it out."

"Good idea," Jack said, trying to mask his excitement.

Within minutes they were heading east on 47th Street. "How does it sound, Sport?" Frank asked, shifting into fourth. "Do you hear anything?"

Jack listened intently, then shook his head. "It sounds okay *so far*," he said. "But we'd better drive it a while just to make sure."

Frank smiled. He knew—and so did Jack—that the 'Vette ran better than when it was brand new, but cruising around Chicago in a vintage car on a warm summer night with the wind in their hair was one of the best forms of father-son bonding there was. He turned south onto Lake Shore Drive and floored it.

CHAPTER 8

Megan was running late. She pulled her car, a slightly rusted five-year-old Buick, into her parking space on the fifth level of a ramp a block west of her building, turned off the ignition, and threw her keys into her tan leather shoulder bag. Quickly sliding out of the car, she reached over the backseat to retrieve her briefcase and red-and-yellow canvas carryall. With all of her baggage firmly in tow, she pushed down the lock, slammed the door shut, and jogged toward the elevator.

As she punched the DOWN button, she glanced at her watch. Damn. It was eight-thirty-five. She had scheduled a meeting with the plaintiffs in the AIDS case for eight-thirty. Ron Johnson had been called out of town on an emergency, and the clients were no doubt waiting. The day was not getting off to a good start.

To begin with, she must've forgotten to switch her clock radio to the "wake" position the night before, and she'd overslept. Then, when she had been almost ready to leave the house, her cat had jumped up on the table and knocked a cup of coffee into her lap. That had meant time-out for a quick change of clothes. To top things off, traffic had been horrendous, and an accident at Wells and Division had brought her to a complete halt for a full five minutes.

Stepping into the elevator, she reflected that a psychiatrist would probably charge her big money to tell her that subconsciously she had somehow brought about all of these events in order to delay having to work on a case that she found distasteful. "What the hell did shrinks know anyway?" she grumbled to herself.

It was already over eighty degrees, and the fetid air in the parking ramp elevator made her stomach roll. She wished there was time to stop at a deli to pick up a chocolate donught and an iced coffee. She promised to treat herself to a snack after she finished her meeting. The instant the doors opened on the ground floor, Megan raced out of the ramp and sprinted across the street where she entered the rear of her building through revolving doors.

The twelve-story Beaux Arts building had been slated for demolition in the late 1970's but had been saved by a Japanese developer who evicted all of the former tenants and closed it for a year for extensive remodeling. The lobby now featured an atrium which extended up through the entire twelve floors. Passengers were conveyed to their destinations by two glass elevators. The first floor was given over to retail shops and restaurants, while the remaining floors contained high-priced office space.

Barrett, Gillette had moved into the top floor the year the building reopened. The firm had now grown to the point where it was ready to exercise its option to take over part of the floor below.

When the glass elevator stopped on twelve, Megan got out and bypassed the heavy cherry-wood door where the firm's name was emblazoned in large gold letters, entering instead through an unmarked door that led to a back hallway. As she headed toward her office, she passed the exhibit room, a sort of "show-and-tell" area which contained all sorts of products and devices that were currently the subject of lawsuits being handled by the firm. Sometimes when she needed a break, Megan would wander down there and take a look at the newest additions. As she hurried by, she could hear the sound of hammering. One of the firm's clients was a woman who had fallen down a flight of stairs at a hotel. The partner in charge of the case was having a duplicate stairway constructed for use as a trial exhibit.

Megan nodded to several associates as she passed them in the hallway. Reaching her office, she rushed past her secretary and deposited her bags on her desk.

"Don't say it. I know I'm late," she said, sitting down and quickly exchanging her well-worn, high-top Reeboks and white socks for white snakeskin pumps, which she fished out of the canvas bag. "Is everyone here?"

Her secretary, Karen, an attractive blond woman about Megan's age with a ready smile, nodded. "I made everyone comfortable in conference room two and served coffee all round. No need to hurry. They're having a great time without you."

"I'm glad someone's enjoying themselves," Megan said. Her office was small, although it did have a window—albeit with a view of the parking ramp—and it was littered with files and law books. Her law school diploma, and certificates of bar admission shared wall space with several antique *Spy* prints showing English barristers in their robes and wigs. Her desk held two photos—one of her and Paul taken the previous summer on the island of Crete, and one of her black cat, Andy, playing with his favorite toy, a pink bunny.

Megan tossed her purse in her bottom desk drawer, then stood up and tried to smooth the wrinkles out of her white, low-waisted, linen dress. She hated feeling rumpled this early in the day, but there'd been no time to iron. Oh, well. It was fashionable for linen to look wrinkled, wasn't it? She opened her top desk drawer and pulled out a mirror and a brush. Running the brush quickly through her thick hair, she made a face into the mirror before throwing brush and mirror back in the drawer. She glanced at her watch again. Eight-forty-three. Not bad.

"You know where to find me," she said to Karen over her shoulder as she headed down the hall, clutching a legal pad and pen to her chest.

Megan paused for a moment as she reached the conference room door. She could hear animated chatter coming from inside. She took a deep breath and pushed the door open. The four plaintiffs, along with two spouses, were seated in plush, rose-velvet chairs placed around the large oval table.

"Good morning, everyone. Sorry I'm late," Megan

said, taking her place at the head of the table. She was greeted with a chorus of warm "hello's." As she poured herself a cup of coffee from the silver service in the center of the table, she glanced around her.

Jeff Young, a forty-year-old computer programmer, had become infected during surgery to correct an intestinal blockage. He was the only plaintiff to have developed full-blown AIDS. Megan hadn't seen him in two months, and she was shocked at his rapid decline. He was very thin and his complexion was sallow. A lot of his brown hair had fallen out, and he seemed to be breathing with difficulty. Jeff was a devoted husband and father, who was determined to make the most of whatever time he had left. His wife, Sara, was also showing the stress of Jeff's illness. There were circles under her eyes, and her blond hair had lost its luster.

Claudia Hartley, a thirty-year-old secretary, had been infected during an appendectomy. She had passed on the HIV virus to her first child, who had been born a year after her surgery. The baby had lived only six months. Claudia had undergone a tubal ligation to prevent a repeat of that tragedy, but her husband had been unable to cope with the strain her condition put on their relationship, and he had left her. Claudia was pretty but looked streetwise, with long, frizzy brown hair, heavily made-up eyes, and a skirt that was too short. She was thin and nervous, and from the looks of the ashtray in front of her, had already smoked the better part of a pack of cigarettes that morning.

Sam Gardner, a fifty-one-year-old maintenance worker, had been infected during surgery to remove a noncancerous stomach tumor. A robust-looking black man, Sam was soft-spoken and easygoing. His wife, Monique, a tall, striking Jamaican woman, sat next to him.

Edna Randolph, the widow, had been infected during gall bladder surgery. She was a pistol, with wiry white hair, sharp blue eyes, and a tongue to match. Megan especially liked Edna because she reminded her a lot of her grandmother.

When Dr. Morris gave the hospital notice why he

was unable to continue working, Chicago Memorial had written letters to all of the doctor's known patients, urging them to come in for AIDS testing at the hospital's expense. The hospital contended that this was all it was required to do, and it denied any responsibility for causing the plaintiffs to become HIV infected.

"I asked you to come in today so I could bring you up to date on what's been happening, and to let you know what you can expect between now and the trial," Megan said, sipping her coffee. The six people around the table listened intently.

"I have some good news to share with you," she went on, tapping her pen lightly on the legal pad, "Dr. Herman Leibowitz from the National Institutes of Health has agreed to act as our expert witness. He has prepared a report saying the hospital should have realized there was something wrong with Dr. Morris and should have ordered him to submit to more tests. Dr. Leibowitz is very highly regarded in the medical community, and I know the jury will be very impressed with him. He's going to be in Chicago on other business early next week, so we'll be taking his deposition next Tuesday, right after the deposition of Dr. Lenz, the hospital's administrator. If any of you are interested, you're welcome to sit in on either or both of those depositions.

"Oral argument should be scheduled soon in the appeal of the court's order dismissing Dr. Morris's insurance company from the lawsuit." Megan looked at the notes she'd made on her legal pad. "As you know, the liability phase of the trial is set for December first. Before then, it's possible that the hospital's lawyer may want to take an updated deposition from each of you to find out if there's been any change in your condition." She looked up and poured herself another cup of coffee. "Do any of you have any questions?"

Jeff Young and his wife exchanged anxious looks. Then Jeff cleared his throat. "Sara and I have a question," he said quietly. "We were wondering what will happen if I don't last until the trial. We're worried that it could postpone things for everyone else."

Just looking at his emaciated form, Megan, too, wondered if Jeff would be alive in five and a half months, but she said encouragingly, "Of course you'll make it, Jeff. Your doctor says you're doing very nicely with your new drug therapy."

"But what if I don't make it?" Jeff pressed.

Megan answered honestly. "The trial will still go on. Sara is already a named plaintiff in her own right, and if something were to happen to you, we would immediately have her appointed personal representative of your estate, which means she would have the right to continue your part of the lawsuit on your behalf. Your deposition is on videotape, and that would be played to the jury so they'd have a chance to see you and hear you tell your own story. So I don't want you to worry about that. Just concentrate on hanging in there."

"Yeah," Edna Randolph said, reaching across the table and squeezing Jeff's hand, "don't give up on us. We all need to stick together so we can beat those bastards."

Jeff managed a wan smile. "I'm doing everything I can think of to fight it," he said in a weak voice. "I go to AIDS support groups. I've been reading Norman Cousins's books and listening to inspirational tapes. But I gotta tell you," he said, shaking his head, "it's been tough." He put his arm around Sara. "On all of us."

"We're very proud of you," Megan said softly. Sara Young's eyes were moist.

"I have a question," Sam Gardner said. "It's something we were all talking about before you got here." He folded his hands in front of him on the table. "I know lawyers don't like to talk about odds, but what do you think our chances are of winning this thing?"

Megan chose her words carefully. This was a question plaintiffs often asked. She wanted to give them encouragement without raising unreasonable expectations. "You're absolutely right that lawyers don't like to give odds, Sam, because, frankly, no one can ever predict what a jury is going to do. But I truly believe, from the bottom of my heart, that we can win this. This firm is very selective about the cases it takes. If we didn't think we could win, we would never have started the lawsuit."

"But there's been so many articles in the papers lately saying that doctors shouldn't have to be tested for AIDS," Claudia put in, as she lit another cigarette. "If that's what most people think, why will the people on our jury think differently?"

Megan leaned forward. "I'm glad you brought that up. It's real important to keep in mind what the articles in the paper are referring to. What they're saying is that most doctors don't think there should be across-the-board, mandatory AIDS testing as a requirement for keeping their medical licenses. That's not what this case is about. We're not saying the hospital should have tested Dr. Morris just to be testing him. But the hospital does require its doctors to go through some routine tests every year, and the results of Dr. Morris's tests showed there was something wrong with him. What we need to convince the jury is that the hospital should have required Dr. Morris to take some more tests to find out exactly what was the matter because if they had done that, they would have discovered he had AIDS and could have stopped him from operating on the four of you. Do you see the difference between our theory and what the papers are talking about?"

"I think so," Claudia said, exhaling smoke through her nose. "We're saying the hospital knew Dr. Morris was sick, and it screwed up by not testing him to find out what he had."

"Right," Megan said. "He might have had hepatitis, which is also very contagious and can be fatal if it's transmitted to patients. The bottom line is they saw he wasn't well and didn't bother to find out why."

"Greedy sons of bitches," Edna said. "They proba-bly didn't want one of their surgeons to have to take any time off for being sick because they would've lost money if he couldn't operate."

Megan had to fight to suppress a smile. Edna was

certainly refreshing. Megan hoped she would have half
as much spunk when she was a senior citizen.

"I get it," Sam said. "So you really think we have a
good chance of winning?"

Megan nodded. "I really do."

"Then why doesn't the hospital want to settle the
case?" Claudia asked. "They should be able to see they
were in the wrong."

"It's not going to be quite that easy," Megan cautioned. "The hospital is entitled to have a jury decide
whether they were at fault or not. Besides that, I think
the hospital is under a lot of pressure not to settle."

"From who?" Jeff asked.

"From other hospitals around the country. This case
is unique. You may not realize it, but you are all celeb-
rities. This is the first time a hospital is being blamed
for not discovering that one of their doctors had
AIDS." Megan paused and took a sip of coffee.

"Sadly enough," she continued, "the number of doctors infected with the AIDS virus keeps growing, so
it's very possible that this situation may arise again. If
it does, this case will be what's called a precedent.
That means other courts are likely to go along with
whatever the result was in your case. Obviously, other
hospitals are hoping you'll lose. So there's a lot at
stake here, and I guess Chicago Memorial would rather
roll the dice than voluntarily pay you a settlement."

"Could you explain again how your firm gets paid?"
Sam asked.

"Sure," Megan answered. "We only get paid if we
recover some money for you. If we settle before trial,
we take one quarter of the settlement. If we go through
the trial, we'll get one third."

"But the hospital has to pay its lawyer win or lose,
doesn't it?" Claudia asked.

"Yes, it does," Megan replied. "And I'd be willing
to bet Mr. Parks's hourly rate is around three hundred
dollars."

"That bastard makes three hundred dollars an hour!"
Edna exploded. "My lord, there is something very wrong
with our legal system if he makes that kind of money."

Megan smiled. "I'm afraid that's a pretty typical rate for a partner in a large firm."

"How can anyone afford a lawyer if that's what it costs?" Monique asked.

"Unfortunately, a lot of people can't," Megan said.

"I can't believe he makes that much." Edna was still sputtering. "I didn't like him one little bit, and let me tell you something else right now." She wagged her index finger at Megan as if scolding a naughty child. "The next time he starts asking me questions that are none of his damn business, I'm not gonna be so polite as I was the last time. No siree." She set her jaw. "In fact, I might just tell him what I think of him."

"We'll talk about the kinds of questions you might be asked at trial later on," Megan said. "But you don't need to worry, because if you're asked a question that I don't think is proper, I'll object and we'll get a ruling on it from the judge. Okay. Any other questions?"

Everyone shook their head "no."

"All right, then. I'll keep you posted on what's happening." She paused a moment and looked around the table, making eye contact with each one. "And if you get home and think of something you forgot to ask or if you don't understand something you read in the paper or if you just want to talk, please call me. That's what I'm here for. And be sure to keep taking your AZT and keep going in for your follow-up HIV testing. That's really important. And if there's any change at all in your condition, let me know right away."

After the plaintiffs had all filed out of the conference room, Megan leaned against the wall for a moment, deep in thought. She was gratified by the confidence her clients had expressed in her, but she was scared, too. What if she lost the damn case? She gritted her teeth. No, she just couldn't let that happen. In spite of the fact that she knew Frank Parks was going to be a thorn in her side every step of the way—no, because of it—she was going to pull out all the stops and win this thing. She owed that much to her clients. And she owed it to herself, too.

CHAPTER 9

Mike O'Riley was seated at his beat-up wooden desk in the small cubicle that served as his office. The area was only about seven by nine feet, so there was no wasted space. The back wall was at the rear of the area headquarter's building and boasted a small window with a view of an alley. The remaining three walls consisted of hard plastic partitions. The floor was covered with worn gray linoleum. Besides O'Riley's desk and ancient swivel chair upholstered in ripped, gold naugahyde, the space held a green vinyl chair for visitors, four file cabinets, and a dozen cardboard boxes of assorted sizes which held the files' overflow. Although the building had central air conditioning, Chicago was in the midst of an early summer heat wave and the system wasn't able to keep pace. A rusted fan positioned on top of two boxes whirred away, circulating the air around O'Riley's head. It also helped disperse the haze of cigarette smoke that hung over the office like a mushroom cloud.

O'Riley's desk was piled a foot high with paperwork on the murders. It had been five weeks since he had been put in charge of the case, and there had been no progress to speak of.

The door-to-door canvassing had yielded no results. O'Riley had established a toll-free hotline where people could call in leads. While he received a couple dozen calls a day, most wanted to know what they had to do to cash in on the mayor's five-thousand-dollar reward. He'd been in contact with police departments all over the Midwest, as well as the FBI, to see if there had been similar killings elsewhere. The fact that there hadn't, indicated that the slasher was probably a local.

O'Riley lit up a cigarette. Since he'd been working on the case, he'd gone from smoking one pack a day to damn near two. He inhaled deeply and immediately began to cough. Christ! He knew it wasn't good for him, and he'd been threatening to quit for years, but it helped him concentrate.

He flipped open a file that contained statements from six people who claimed to be responsible for Mary Collins's murder. Whether the poor bastards really believed they did it or were just hungering for their fifteen minutes of fame, it was inevitable that their kind would come out of the woodwork in almost every homicide. Oftentimes these nut cases provided some sorely needed comic relief. O'Riley snorted as he paged through the file.

A thirty-five-year-old, long-haired, bearded man had showed up barefoot, dressed in rags, and smelling like he hadn't been anywhere near soap or water for the better part of a year, claiming that he was the reincarnation of Christ and that he had killed Mary Collins as part of some New Age sacrificial rite.

A forty-year-old man, who looked and dressed like a stockbroker, said that the spirit of Charles Manson had taken over his body and committed the murder.

A sixty-year-old woman claimed that she had discovered Mary Collins in bed with her husband and killed her in a fit of passion.

O'Riley's favorite was a serious-looking young man in his twenties who swore that he and Mary Collins had been abducted by space aliens wearing tin foil on their heads, and that Mary had died when the alien leader tried to mate with her.

In a homicide investigation all leads were assiduously followed up, so all these bozos got the chance to give their spiel and, in return, received the department's heartfelt thanks—and in the longhair's case, the address of the nearest homeless shelter—before being sent on their demented way.

Jesus! There were sure a lot of weirdos around these

days. O'Riley puffed on his cigarette. He wondered what his uncle Marty would think of the current state of police work. When Marty had talked Mike into joining the department back in the early 1960's, life was still pretty simple. There were no teenagers killing each other over clothing, no kids selling crack in grade schools, no religious zealots bombing abortion clinics in an effort to save unborn babies, no marches for gay and lesbian rights. He was thankful Marty had checked out when he did. If he weren't already dead, the unrest in the world today would probably kill him.

O'Riley flicked a speck of ash off his navy cotton pants, put out his cigarette, tossed the nut case folder aside, and picked up another file that contained reports of interviews with the victims' acquaintances. Other than their appearance, the four young women seemed to have nothing in common.

Mary Collins had been an eighteen-year-old senior at a public high school. An honor student, she had won a music scholarship to a local community college. She was active on the school newspaper and on the girls' volleyball team. Everyone seemed to like her. Her teachers described her as "bright, vivacious, a real sweetheart." Her friends said she was "warm and caring." She'd had a steady boyfriend named Tom Porchensky, who was the school's leading quarterback. He'd been in Minneapolis at his grandmother's funeral the night of the murder. The poor kid had come absolutely unhinged while O'Riley was questioning him. He seemed to think Mary would still be alive if he hadn't gone out of town because he'd often drive her to her evening engagements and either wait for her or pick her up. With him gone, she'd had to walk.

Mary had been an assistant youth choir director at St. Michael's. She had arrived at choir practice at six-thirty the night of the murder. She lived about a mile from the church and had walked there alone. Practice had broken up before eight-thirty and all the youngsters in the group, along with the senior choir director and organist, reported seeing her walk down the steps of the church and head toward home. She had not mentioned that she was planning to meet someone or stop anywhere on the way. There were a number of convenience stores, gas stations, and small restaurants in the area, but no one working that night admitted to seeing her. Dr. Packard estimated the time of death at around ten. Where had she been during those ninety minutes? Had she been in the killer's clutches all that time? O'Riley fervently hoped not.

Julie Santini had been a twenty-four-year-old, second-grade teacher. Her body had been found in an alley about a block from her South Side apartment. Her roommate had spent the night with a boyfriend, so no one knew Julie was missing until she failed to show up for work the next day. Like Mary Collins, Julie was a Catholic. Could there be a connection there? O'Riley wondered, rubbing the bridge of his nose. It was doubtful, since the two women's parishes were miles apart, but he made a note to check it out just the same.

Cheryl Lucas, the girl murdered on Valentine's Day, had been a twenty-eight-year-old veterinarian. She had left the town house she'd shared with her fiancé in the early evening hours to attend a modern dance class. Other class members reported that she'd seemed in great spirits and had given no indication that she had plans other than driving straight home. Street cleaners had found her body the next morning.

They knew nothing at all about the Jane Doe. The fact that no one had come forward to claim her probably meant that she had been a runaway from another part of the country. Perhaps she'd come to Chicago in search of a better life. Whatever her past might have been, her dreams of a better future had died with her.

O'Riley lit up another cigarette and turned to the next folder, which held preliminary reports from the forensic psychiatrist and clinical psychologist that Jablonski had retained to work on the case. They both agreed that the perpetrator was a "sociopath with violent tendencies." No shit, Sherlock, O'Riley thought. You didn't need a fancy degree to figure that out. And to think the city was probably being billed two hundred bucks an hour for those pearls of wisdom. No wonder taxes were so damn high, he thought as he continued reading.

The psychologist, Dr. Elizabeth Monson, was cautious in making predictions about the killer's personality. She speculated that the man was a white male in his forties who lived alone and possibly tortured animals for fun. She also suggested the killer was from the middle class and had probably suffered a severe rejection or injury at the hands of a woman who looked like the victims.

The psychiatrist, Dr. Stanley Sheridan, specialized in sex deviants and offered a more in-depth profile. He opined that the killer was a middle-aged male of above-average intelligence, that he was employed, and that he was neat, possibly even meticulous. He probably enjoyed reading accounts of the murders and possibly saved the articles to help him relive the women's deaths.

O'Riley shook his head. These theories might sound great to laymen, but in his opinion, when it came right down to trying to solve a case, you might as well consult a Ouija board.

As O'Riley threw that folder down and picked up a file containing photos of all four victims, he felt a stab of indigestion. He looked at his trusty Timex watch. It was three o'clock. Imagine that. He'd been having so much fun that he'd worked straight through lunch. He pulled open a desk drawer and rummaged around until he found a jar of Tums, the colored ones that were supposed to be assorted flavors. He pried the lid off the jar and popped three in his mouth and chewed them up. Flavored, hell! They still tasted like chalk. They did help to settle his stomach though. He replaced the lid. The label promised that "Each tablet provides 20% of the adult U.S. RDA for calcium." Great. He'd probably wind up with lung cancer from all the smoking, but maybe working on this miserable case would help build up his bone mass.

O'Riley spread the photos of the four women out in front of him. They had all been tall and thin and, most significantly, all had red hair that cascaded halfway down their backs. They were all attractive, girls who would have stood out in a crowd. Could one of the four possibly be the woman who had triggered the killer's murderous impulses? O'Riley doubted it. Then the question became—who was that elusive woman? For if there was some way they could find her, they'd also find the killer.

O'Riley slipped the photos back into their file and turned to the autopsy reports. Using a black, medium-point Bic pen, he divided a piece of white paper into sections, labeling each one with the name of a victim. As he compared the reports, he began to fill in details, hoping some heretofore undetected similarity would jump out at him.

As he continued to pore over the reports, his concentration was broken by a squeaking noise. The flimsy door to his office swung open, and in came Greg Jablonski, pushing an old, wheeled, typewriter cart that held a computer monitor, hard drive, and keyboard. "What the hell is this?" O'Riley asked, frowning. He threw down his pen.

Jablonski was smiling broadly. "Where's an outlet?" he asked, looking around the office. "Oh, here we go," he said, spying the outlet on the back wall under the window, where the fan was plugged in. He pushed the cart over in front of one of the file cabinets and deftly reached down and pulled out the fan's plug and inserted the computer's plug in its place. The fan sputtered to a halt. Jablonski sniffed the air and waved his right hand in front of his face. "Pee-yew," he said. "You know you really ought to try to stop smoking. The smell in here is obnoxious."

"Mind your own damn business. What the hell do you think you're doing?" O'Riley said, getting up from his desk. "Who told you to bring that thing in here? Turn my fan back on. It helps clear the air."

"It doesn't clear the air. It just blows the smoke around," Jablonski said as he flipped the main switch on the computer. The hard drive started humming. "Wait till you see this," he said happily. "I've set up a database, and Marge Petronek helped me load all the

information we've got on the murders so far. This is
gonna be great." He rubbed his hands together in anticipation.

The computer had finished loading DOS, and
Jablonski quickly typed in the command to retrieve the
database. "Just take a look at this," he said. "You're
gonna love it."

O'Riley waved his hand. "That's real nice,
Jablonski," he said, sitting down again. "I'm sure
you'll have a lot of fun playing with it. But I'm kinda
busy now, so why don't you take that thing back to
your office and you can show it to me some other time.
And turn my fan back on as you leave."

"You don't understand, Mike," Jablonski said, pulling the green vinyl chair over to the cart and sitting
down in front of the computer. "I already have one just
like it in my office. This is your computer. See, I typed
out some instructions to help you learn how to use it."
He reached into his pocket and pulled out a couple of
folded sheets of paper and set them down next to the
keyboard.

"Mine?" O'Riley looked at the machine as though a
flying saucer had set down. "I don't want the goddamn
thing," he spat out. "Get it out of here."

"Just wait till you see what it can do," Jablonski
said. "It's amazing. Come here and I'll show you how
it's set up."

"I don't care how it's set up. I just want you to take
it away. Who told you to order this anyhow?"

"You did. You signed the purchase order."

"Well, if I'd known you were ordering it for me, I
never would have signed it," O'Riley sputtered. "I figured it was something for you."

"I ordered five of them," Jablonski explained. "To
make sure everyone on the team has easy access to
one."

"I don't know anything about computers," O'Riley
said, ignoring Jablonski's obvious enthusiasm. "I don't
want to know anything about computers. If I need to
type something, I use my trusty Smith Corona." He
patted the old typewriter, now buried under stacks of

paper. "If I need some information that you can only get off of a computer, I ask somebody to get it for me. I don't know what this thing cost, but I'm sure you can send it back and get a refund. Now scram. I got work to do." He waved his hands as though he hoped the machine would magically disappear in a puff of smoke.

"Okay, Mike, okay," Jablonski said easily, attempting to make peace. "I just thought I could save us some work, that's all. You know, the quicker we catch the guy, the quicker you can start fishing full-time and I can maybe move into your office." Jablonski grinned impishly. "I didn't mean to imply you weren't doing your job."

O'Riley took a deep breath in an attempt to rein in his anger. "I'm sorry, kid. This case is driving me nuts, and the goddamn heat has me a little under the weather. I don't doubt that this stuff may be all well and good," he grudgingly admitted, "but if you have all those other machines, why do we need this one? And why does it need to be parked in here?"

"I've told you," Jablonski said, refusing to concede defeat, "this one is *yours*. Once you get the hang of how it works, I promise you're gonna be using it all the time. It's so much quicker than digging through a stack of files trying to find one little piece of information. I'll just give you a few lessons—"

"The hell you will!" O'Riley's temper flared again, and he brought his fist down on the desk. "Read my lips, Jablonski. I don't want to learn how to use that thing." He wrinkled his nose in disgust. "This newfangled shit is one of the reasons I want to retire. Everybody's in such a hurry. They can't wait five minutes to look through a file. They want to punch a few buttons and have some machine spit out an answer in five seconds. Well, you better watch out or one of these days machines are going to take over your job, too, just like in those *Terminator* movies. Then you won't think all this technology's so smart," he said smugly, folding his arms across his chest.

Jablonski fought back the impulse to laugh. "Okay,

Mike, I hear you," he said. "We'll save the lessons for later." He logged out of the database and turned off the monitor.

As Jablonski turned to go, O'Riley hollered, "Hey, I thought I told you to take that thing with you."

Jablonski paused in the doorway. "I don't have anyplace else to put it, so why don't we just leave it here for now. Maybe one of the other people on the team will want to come get it later."

As Jablonski beat a hasty retreat, O'Riley hollered after him, "What about my fan?"

O'Riley got up, savagely yanked the computer's plug out of the socket and returned the fan's plug to its rightful spot. As he returned to his desk and felt the air begin to circulate again, he stared at the foreign object on the cart and emitted a low growl. Jesus Christ! A man wasn't even safe in his own office. What the hell was the world coming to? His stomach churned in response. He jerked his desk drawer open with a violent motion and retrieved the jar of Tums. He popped three more into his mouth and ground them into tiny pieces. Then he slammed the drawer shut, lit a cigarette, and turned his attention back to the autopsy reports.

Turn the pages of the scrapbook. The clippings about Mary Collins take up six pages, more than any of the other victims. The press had just loved Mary. She was their little sweetheart.

How lovely Mary had looked in the photo all the papers had used. It must have been her high-school graduation picture. Yes, Mary was stunning. But then all of the girls had been beautiful. They'd all looked pretty, even after they were dead. That was unusual. Yes, indeed. It wasn't very often you'd see a dead body that you could call attractive.

And what gorgeous long red hair they'd all had. She had had hair just like that. That beautiful woman who had destroyed your life, your very reason for being. Well, not exactly yours. That other pathetic individual with whom you were forced to share your existence. He was weak and passive. He had allowed himself to be victimized. Lucky for him you were here to look out for him.

Looking at the pictures and clippings about all the girls gives you great comfort. It makes you feel at peace with yourself. You feel calmer than you have felt in a very long time. In fact, just today you had pondered whether before too much longer you might finally be able to put the past behind you and draw the curtain down on that horrible episode in your life.

Not just yet, of course. There is still work to be done. But before too much longer the end to your quest will be in sight.

CHAPTER 10

"Dr. Lenz, am I correct that one of your duties as Chicago Memorial's administrator is to review the results of the yearly medical exams performed on staff members?" Megan asked.

The doctor looked at her coolly. "Yes."

"Would you please explain what you look for when you review those results?"

The doctor shifted in his chair. His deposition—the recording of his testimony in advance of trial—was being conducted in one of Hagenkord & Phillips's smaller conference rooms. The area had recently been redecorated at Frank's suggestion, and in his opinion it was one of the most attractive rooms in the office. The windows on the back wall, which overlooked Michigan Avenue, were framed in powder blue damask drapes. The walls were covered in blue-and-cream striped paper. The rollered chairs surrounding the oval walnut table were upholstered in multishaded blue velvet. Cream-colored art deco sconces hanging on the walls provided soft lighting.

Megan and Ron Johnson sat on one side of the table, with Dr. Lenz and Frank on the other. Claudia Hartley had taken Megan up on her invitation to attend the proceeding and was seated beside Ron. Next to Frank was Colin Williams, the young law clerk from Frank's office. Frank had suggested the young man sit in to gain some practical experience on how cases were prepared for trial. A court reporter sat at one end, taking down everything that was said in mechanical shorthand. The strange-looking symbols would later be transcribed to provide a full record of the proceeding, which could be referred to at trial.

Looking cool and dapper in his well-tailored gray suit, Dr. Lenz fielded Megan's questions with a combination of self-confidence, and incredulity that anyone would question his judgment. His responses gave away nothing, and Megan had been forced to work hard for each nugget of information. Lenz was going to be a good witness for the hospital, Megan thought grudgingly. And now that she'd met him, she could definitely understand the hospital's choice of attorneys. The doctor was every bit as big a jerk as his counsel. Lenz and Frank Parks, what a pair.

Parks had been unusually docile so far, making only a few minor objections. Although he had a legal pad and his Mont Blanc pen in front of him, he had not written down so much as one notation. For the most part he sat staring out the windows, seemingly disinterested in the proceedings. Of course, Megan knew from experience that when you had an ace witness, the best strategy was to just sit back and let him impress the hell out of the other side with as few interruptions as possible. As she waited for Lenz's response, Megan unbuttoned the jacket of her blue, raw-silk suit and casually glanced over at Frank. He was wearing a navy suit with a rather bright pink shirt and a bold fuchsia tie. Most men would look silly in those colors, but Parks didn't. He was rather nice looking, she admitted to herself reluctantly.

Dr. Lenz poured himself a glass of ice water from a crystal pitcher, which sat atop a tray in the middle of the table, before answering Megan's question. "Generally speaking, I skim through the results to see if there are any glaring medical problems," he said in his resonant baritone.

"Can you give me an example?" Megan prompted.

The doctor rolled his eyes toward the ceiling. "Yes. High blood pressure."

"And what do you do if the report reveals this problem?"

"I check back with the lab doctor who performed the tests to see if a follow-up has been conducted."

"Then what happens?"

"In most cases the lab doctor will inform me that the staff member has been retested and the blood pressure reading was found to be within normal limits."

"And what if it's still not normal?" Megan asked.

Dr. Lenz shrugged. "Then there are several possibilities."

Megan bristled. "Why don't you give me one."

The doctor looked back at the ceiling. "In most cases where the retest continues to indicate a problem, medication to lower blood pressure will have been prescribed."

"Dr. Lenz, do you recall reviewing the results of Dr. Dan Morris's medical tests four years ago?"

The doctor gave a small chortle and his lower lip curled down sardonically, conveying to Megan in no uncertain terms that he thought her question was inane. "If I didn't remember it, I wouldn't be here, would I?"

I wish I wasn't here, Megan thought to herself. God, what an ass this guy was! Looking up, she caught Claudia Hartley's eye. The young woman's eyes were wide, as though she couldn't quite believe what she was hearing. Welcome to the wonderful world of litigation, Megan thought to herself. She motioned to Ron Johnson. As he reached into a red expandable folder in front of him, Megan smiled to herself at the sight of his black necktie with red and white letters of the alphabet exploding all over it. She could always count on Ron to keep her work from getting dull. He pulled several sheets of paper from the folder and handed them to her. She, in turn, passed them across the table.

"Dr. Lenz, this is a copy of Exhibit 261, which was marked at an earlier deposition. Do you recognize it?"

Dr. Lenz carefully scrutinized the exhibit. Frank gave it a passing glance. "Yes," Dr. Lenz answered, "this is a copy of the medical results on Dr. Morris for the year in question."

"Doctor, when that report first came across your desk, what did you notice about it?"

"Objection," Frank put in. "The question assumes he noticed something."

Megan smiled sweetly. "What, *if anything*, did you notice about the report?" Megan qualified the inquiry. The law was full of magic words without which Pandora's box couldn't be opened.

"I don't recall noticing anything in particular."

"Nothing at all?" Megan asked with surprise.

The doctor glared at her. "Is there something specific you think I should have seen?"

"Yes," Megan replied testily. "How about the comments on page two, beginning with the line 'the examiner noted that Dr. Morris was suffering from a low-grade fever and oral thrush and that his lymph glands were noticeably enlarged'?"

The doctor flipped to the appropriate place. "Oh, that. Yes, I did see that notation."

"And what, *if anything*, did you think when you read that?"

Dr. Lenz's dark eyes bored into Megan's face. "Nothing, because, as you can see from the next lines, Dr. Morris explained that he had recently had wisdom teeth extracted and had suffered some side effects, but had just finished a course of antibiotics."

"And that explanation seemed satisfactory?"

"Yes."

"It turned out to be a lie, though, didn't it?" Megan asked, staring back at him.

"Objection," Frank said. "Argumentative. You can answer if you're able to," he added, as the doctor looked to him for instruction. Colin Williams grinned as his mentor scored another point.

The doctor's brow furrowed ever so slightly. "Yes, Ms. Lansdorf," he said, putting unnecessary emphasis on her name, "Dr. Morris's explanation turned out to be false, but that's all hindsight. At the time, there was no reason to doubt him."

Megan leisurely poured herself a glass of water and took a sip. She would've dearly loved to throw the entire pitcher at the good doctor and his counsel. "Did you know Dr. Morris personally?"

"Yes, informally. I am acquainted with most of the staff doctors, at least by sight."

"How often would you see him?"

"Oh, maybe once a month."

"In the last year he was on staff, did you notice any change in Dr. Morris's appearance?"

Dr. Lenz considered a moment. "Not really."

"You didn't notice that he'd lost thirty-five pounds?"

"I usually just saw him in passing. Often he'd be wearing a lab coat, which makes it difficult to estimate someone's weight. I guess he might've looked a little thinner."

"Did you notice anything else about his appearance?"

"Really, Ms. Lansdorf," Lenz said with a smirk, "I have a hospital to run. I can't waste my time scrutinizing our doctors' hairstyles or wardrobes."

"I'm not interested in Dr. Morris's hairstyle or wardrobe," Megan said hotly. "What I'd like to know is whether you are so busy that you don't notice when one of your employees looks ill. Isn't it true, that at the time of his examination, Dr. Morris looked pale, drawn, and haggard?"

Dr. Lenz gave a short laugh. "Most of our doctors are overworked, Ms. Lansdorf. The description you just gave would probably fit at least fifty percent of them at any given time, including me."

"Are you saying you thought Dr. Morris looked healthy?"

"No," the doctor shot back. "I'm saying that from my very limited observations, his appearance gave me no reason to suspect there was anything seriously wrong with him."

Megan took another sip of water. "Doctor, what if Dr. Morris's temperature had been one or two degrees higher at the time of his exam? Then would you have thought there was a reason for concern about his health?"

"Objection," Frank said. "This line of questioning is purely speculative." He nodded to Dr. Lenz. "If you are able to formulate an answer, Doctor, you may do so."

The doctor rolled his eyes toward the ceiling. "I couldn't possibly answer that question without more information," he replied in a condescending tone.

Megan took a deep breath to suppress her irritation and switched gears. "Dr. Lenz, in the time you've been the administrator of Chicago Memorial, have any doctors ever been suspended from practice for health reasons?"

"Objection," Frank interrupted. "As you already know, counsel, Dr. Morris was the first doctor in the history of Chicago Memorial to be diagnosed with AIDS."

"I'm not talking about AIDS cases," Megan said, glaring at Frank. "My question is directed to doctors who were suspended for any health reason."

"In that case," Frank said, "I object to this entire line of questioning. It is vague, overly broad, and beyond the scope of appropriate inquiry, given the issues in this case, and I instruct Dr. Lenz not to answer."

Dr. Lenz smiled serenely.

Megan clenched her teeth and fought to keep her voice calm. "Counsel, as you are well aware, it is our position that Chicago Memorial's handling of staff doctors with health problems other than AIDS that might impact upon their ability to provide safe, quality medical care is extremely relevant." The court reporter had stopped taking notes, and Megan snapped at her. "I want all this on the record." The woman immediately obliged, her fingers flying over the keys of the steno machine.

"As you also know," Megan continued, her voice rising, "we have made repeated requests, in various forms, for access to the hospital's medical files on its personnel. So far we have not received even one file. I am renewing those requests, and I'd like your final answer, now and on the record: Are you going to produce any records?"

"Ms. Lansdorf," Frank said smoothly, "as we have informed you, we believe your requests are irrelevant, vague and so overbroad as to make compliance virtually impossible." Dr. Lenz sat impassively throughout the exchange, smiling at Megan like a cheshire cat, while Colin Williams gazed wide-eyed at Frank, hanging on his every word.

"Is that your final word on the subject?" Megan snapped.

"It is, unless you would care to redraft your requests."

Megan tossed her hair back and said heatedly, "In that case, I suggest that we take a short recess right now and place a call to Judge Edwards's clerk to schedule a time for a hearing when he can rule on this matter once and for all."

"Good idea," Frank said easily.

Ten minutes later they had scheduled a hearing date with the judge in three weeks' time, and Megan and Ron Johnson were temporarily left alone in the conference room.

"As usually happens in this case, things went straight to hell," Megan said, pacing back and forth in front of the windows. "You missed your chance, Ron. You should've accepted my offer to question Lenz. Maybe you could've gotten farther with him."

A lawyer second-chairing a trial was a lot like an understudy in a play. He had to have the star's role down pat and be ready to go on at a moment's notice, but his chances of actually making use of all his hard work were minuscule. Megan had heard of partners who never let their second-chair open his or her mouth. She tried to give Ron his fair share of meaningful work and not just relegate him to the role of note taker. He had declined her offer to take this deposition, saying that since Lenz was a key witness, Megan should do the honors.

"You're doing just fine," Ron said, pouring himself a glass of water. "Unfortunately Lenz knows just exactly how much to reveal and how to reveal it. Either he's had a lot of coaching or the guy's just naturally a smooth operator."

"I think the bastard was lying through his teeth,"

Megan said, continuing to pace. "Other staff members said Morris already looked like death warmed-over by the time he was examined. Lenz couldn't possibly have thought he was the picture of health." She fought to calm herself. She had to learn to control her temper. Both Lenz and Frank certainly knew how to push her buttons. They were probably having a good laugh at her expense right now.

"You know, for a minute there I had this crazy feeling you might be able to get Parks to make some concessions about the medical records," Ron said, sipping his water, "but I see now that was wishful thinking."

"That man is impossible," Megan sputtered. "He must know he's going to have to turn over at least *some* records eventually. Why doesn't he just get it over with?"

"And miss a chance to put on a show in front of his client?" Ron reminded her. "No way."

Megan stopped pacing. "I should have scheduled that hearing long ago. The hospital must have something to hide or they would have turned over those files by now." She pushed her hair out of her face and said defiantly, "Well, whatever they're holding back, they won't be able to hide it much longer."

"That's right. 'Got nowhere to run to, baby,' " Ron crooned. "Once we see the judge, we'll get some answers."

Frank's secretary set a bone-china cup and saucer filled with coffee on an edge of his desk in front of Dr. Lenz, then briskly walked out, quietly closing the door behind her. Frank shuffled through the phone messages that had come in while the deposition had been going on.

The doctor took a sip of coffee. "In a perverse sort of way, lawsuits are fun, aren't they?" he asked in a lilting voice.

"I'm afraid most of my clients don't share your enthusiasm," Frank replied.

The doctor leaned back in his chair. "I must say I rather enjoy adversarial situations. Maybe I missed my calling." He chuckled. "That woman's quite a pistol. For a minute there, I thought she was going to scratch our eyes out."

Frank laughed. "She's just doing her job."

"She's rather attractive, isn't she?"

"Hmmm?" Frank said absentmindedly, scribbling a note to Lucille to return two of his calls. "Oh, yes, I guess so."

"I know it's terribly chauvinistic of me, but for some reason I still expect female attorneys to have that androgynous look."

"They come in all varieties," Frank replied.

Dr. Lenz set down his cup and picked up the photo of Jack and Kate from Frank's desk and studied it a moment. "Are these your children?"

Frank nodded.

"They're charming." The doctor replaced the photo.

"Thank you," Frank said, finishing his note. "Do you have children?"

The doctor shook his head sadly, and his shoulders slumped. "My wife and twin sons were killed in a car accident six years ago."

"I'm sorry to hear that," Frank said.

The doctor sighed and briefly squeezed his eyes tightly shut. When he opened them again, they were moist. "It was a senseless tragedy," he said, his voice quivering a bit. "Completely senseless. A drunk driver hit them. Three brilliant careers were ruined. My wife was a college professor, and my sons were both in medical school." He picked up his cup and took another sip of coffee. "But that's ancient history, isn't it?" he said, clearing his throat. "Now, getting back to the matter at hand, I have a question for you," he said. "Why have you been fighting so hard to keep them from looking at our old medical files? I know I told you I didn't want to divulge any information unnecessarily, but I don't think there's anything there that will particularly hurt us or help them."

"Neither do I," Frank said, smiling mischievously. "But let me tell you how I see it." He pushed his chair back from his desk and casually crossed his left leg over his right. "If their initial request had been framed narrowly enough, I would have had to comply with it. Judges don't like lawyers who are unreasonable. But I honestly think the requests have been both broad and vague, so I decided to take a hard line and not turn over anything until we have to. In the meantime, the other side is sure we're dragging our feet for a reason, and when they do get access to some files, they're going to waste hours tearing them apart. They still won't find anything, but every hour they spend spinning their wheels is one less hour they'll have to spend on research that might hurt us."

Dr. Lenz spent a moment digesting this response, then smiled broadly. "I like that. Very clever. Very clever, indeed."

"I thought so, too," Frank said.

"So, give me your honest opinion," Dr. Lenz said. "Are we going to win this thing?"

"It's too early in the game to make any predictions," Frank cautioned. "As you know, the big test is going to come tomorrow when Leibowitz testifies. But I will say this: You're a dynamite witness and right now it looks like we've got them on the run." Lenz smiled in acknowledgment of the praise.

"I need to make a couple of phone calls," Frank said. "Why don't you head back to the conference room. I'll join you shortly and then you can dazzle 'em some more."

Megan decided to make a quick trip to the ladies' room before the deposition resumed. As she approached the alcove that housed the restrooms, she heard Dr. Lenz's voice.

"So, are you happy with the representation you've been getting from Ms. Lansdorf?"

Though Megan's ears pricked up, she couldn't make out the muffled reply.

"Is this your first experience in suing someone?"

Again the response was too soft for Megan to pick up.

"How did you happen to choose her law firm? Did

you know when you hired them that a woman would be representing you?"

By this point, Megan realized what was happening and sprinted down the hallway and around the corner, where she discovered Claudia Hartley standing outside the door to the ladies' room, her back pressed against the wall. Lenz was looming over her. When she saw Megan, the look of extreme discomfort on Claudia's face turned to one of relief.

"What the hell do you think you're doing?" Megan shouted at Lenz as she positioned herself between him and Claudia. "You have no right to badger my client or ask her personal questions!"

"I was just making conversation," the doctor replied innocently, but his eyes were dark.

"If you're lonely, I suggest you go talk to your attorney," Megan shot back. "And I'd better not ever catch you intimidating my clients again, or I'm going to haul your ass in front of the judge!"

"There is no need for histrionics," Lenz said indignantly. "I assure you my intentions were perfectly innocent."

"Come on, Claudia," Megan said, putting her arm around the young woman's shoulders. "Let's go freshen up." Shooting Lenz a withering glance, Megan drew her client into the refuge of the ladies' room.

The day after Dr. Lenz's deposition, Dr. Herman Leibowitz's testimony was taken in a Barrett, Gillette conference room. Dr. Leibowitz, Chief of Staff of the National Institutes of Health's General Medical Sciences Division, and a member of its AIDS executive committee, was a gregarious, outspoken man of sixty-five who had opinions about virtually everything pertaining to medicine and ethics and loved nothing so much as sharing his views with others.

Dr. Lenz was speaking at a medical convention in Cleveland and was unable to attend the Leibowitz deposition. Frank was grateful for his client's absence since it would hopefully give Megan a chance to cool off. When Lenz's deposition had resumed the previous day, Megan had burst back into the conference room with blood in her eyes and had given Frank holy hell, accusing him of encouraging Lenz to harass Claudia. While Frank had disavowed any knowledge of the encounter, and Lenz had apologized and promised he would never again speak to the plaintiffs outside of Megan's presence, to Frank the incident was just one more indication that this case was not going to go smoothly.

And now, to his dismay, he had discovered that Dr. Leibowitz was even more impressive in person than he had sounded in his written report. The doctor had a first-rate background: Harvard medical school, residency at the Mayo Clinic, six years as a cancer researcher at Memorial Sloan Kettering in New York, before coming to NIH. A native of Dusseldorf whose parents had immigrated to the U.S. when he was twelve, the doctor still spoke with a pronounced accent, which Frank suspected he exaggerated for effect. His responses to Frank's questions, though, were quick, complete, and very persuasive. In short, the doctor was a class act, and the jury was going to love him. Frank dreaded having to give Dr. Lenz the bad news.

Frank had spent a good deal of time probing the doctor's attitude toward mandatory AIDS testing for all medical personnel. "Ya, Mr. Parks, I do believe that would be the most prudent course," the doctor had said without hesitation, running both hands through his shock of curly white hair.

"Even though the AMA and such prominent figures as former Surgeon General Koop have come out against it?" Frank probed.

Dr. Leibowitz shrugged. "What do I care about the AMA's views on dat subject?" the doctor said, throwing his hands in the air. "Ya, I am a member of the AMA, but their word is not the gospel. And Dr. Koop, sure, he is a smart man, but why should his opinion be any more important than anyone else's?" He surveyed Frank with his deep blue eyes.

"Why indeed?" Frank asked rhetorically. He looked across the table. Megan was looking extremely smug.

Before Frank was able to ask his next question, the doctor cut in, "Of course, Mr. Parks, in this case my belief about mandatory testing makes no difference."

"And why is that?" Frank asked.

"Because here der were many warning signs that should have put the hospital on notice that Dr. Morris was sick."

"What signs are you referring to, doctor?"

"Ach, the low-grade fever, the swollen glands, the oral thrush, the extreme weight loss. So many signs."

"All right," Frank said. "Assuming you had been in charge of performing Dr. Morris's annual physical exam and saw these signs, what would you have done?"

"Well, to begin with, I wouldn't haf believed that cock-and-bull story about the wisdom teeth."

"Why not?"

"Because according to Dr. Morris the tooth extraction took place two weeks beforehand and he vas supposedly finished taking antibiotics for the infection. If it was just a tooth problem to begin with, it would have cleared up by then. And if there is still signs of infection two weeks later, den dere is more serious problem. Any decent doctor would know that."

"So what would you have done if you had examined Dr. Morris?"

"I would have ordered more tests to find out what is the matter with him."

"What kinds of tests?"

"To begin with, complete blood workup, including AIDS test."

"Are you saying that from the symptoms Dr. Morris was displaying at the time of his examination, you would have specifically suspected AIDS?"

"Ya, dat's what I'm saying," the doctor said, nodding emphatically. "By the time Dr. Morris was examined, AIDS had been around for long enough dat all medical workers should have been familiar with the symptoms. Dr. Morris had enough symptoms that should have made a reasonable medical worker suspect that's vat he had."

"Excuse me," Megan cut in, "but it's now four o'clock, and Dr. Leibowitz has to catch a plane from Midway in an hour. I'm afraid we're going to have to call a halt to this session and resume the doctor's deposition next month in Bethesda."

"I'll look forward to it, Doctor," Frank said, clenching his jaw. In the meantime he'd have to try to find some way to poke holes in the doctor's theories. There was no doubt about it, this case was going to be one tough son of a bitch.

"Der pleshur will be mine, Mr. Parks," the doctor said cordially.

As Megan gathered up her legal pad and other materials, she smiled to herself with satisfaction at Dr. Leibowitz's performance. For the first time in two days, she felt the tension in her shoulders begin to ease. Things were definitely looking up. Maybe, just maybe, she might have a shot at winning this sucker yet.

CHAPTER 11

Frank's internal clock told him it was time to get up, so he opened his eyes, propped himself up on one elbow and carefully leaned over Madeline's sleeping body to look at the clock on her nightstand. The red digital readout showed it was twelve-thirty. He laid back down and stretched first one leg and then the other.

Madeline felt him stir and opened her eyes. "What time is it?" she asked.

"Twelve-thirty," he answered.

"Mmmm," Madeline sighed sleepily. "You don't have to go yet, do you?"

"I'm afraid so," Frank said. "I have an early hearing with Judge Edwards tomorrow in the AIDS case. I expect to lose the motion, but it probably wouldn't be good form if I fell asleep in the middle of the hearing."

Madeline lightly ran a hand over the sprinkling of hair on his chest. "Don't go," she murmured. "I'll make it worth your while to stay." The hand moved lower, and Frank groaned with pleasure as he felt her fingers close around him. Taking that sound for an assent, Madeline slid over and rolled on top of him. Frank wrapped his arms around her back and looked up at her. A small lamp was burning on the nearby dresser, and in the soft light she looked so beautiful.

Her long blond hair fell over her face. Frank reached up with one hand and smoothed it out of her eyes. Her lips were full and sensuous. Her face was still flushed from their earlier lovemaking. Madeline leaned down and kissed him, her tongue seeking his. Her mouth was like velvet. He'd never met a woman who could kiss the way she did.

He could feel her lush breasts against his chest. His hands roamed down her back, over her full hips, to her firm ass. She had a magnificent body, soft and curved yet taut, and she was a superb lover, sensuous and insatiable. She was the kind of woman whom teenage boys dreamed about, but few men were lucky enough to ever encounter. Frank still marveled at his good fortune in finding her at age forty. He sometimes teased her by saying that she was his lucky talisman for warding off old age. There was some truth in it. She made him feel like a kid, and he sure as hell had never had any more strenuous workouts than his sessions in bed with her.

They had met at a charitable soirée. Madeline, who had never been married, had come with someone from her ad agency. Frank had come alone. The attraction had been instantaneous, like a flare going off in the room. He could remember it as clearly as if it were yesterday.

Madeline wore a short, clinging, low-necked white dress which showed off her tan. A gold pendant dangled between her breasts. Frank watched it swaying back and forth all evening. It hypnotized him. He felt as though she had cast a spell over him. From the moment he saw her, he was unable to leave her side. He bought a round of drinks for Madeline and her companion. She flirted openly, putting her hand on Frank's arm, tossing back her gorgeous mane of hair, smiling up at him, running her tongue sensuously over her lips. He was wild with desire, and he knew she savored every minute of it.

Frank had asked her to dinner the following evening. They'd never left her apartment. He wasn't sure who had been the seducer and who had been the prey. Some of the evening's events were a bit hazy. He remembered sitting next to her on a cream-colored velvet sofa. She had been wearing a short blue skirt and a blue-and-cream silk blouse. It was summer, and her legs were bare and tan. He didn't know if he had put his hand on her leg or if she had placed it there, but he vividly recalled the hand snaking up under her skirt as if it had a mind of its own, and he remembered his surprise and delight at discovering she was wearing nothing underneath.

Some time later, when they were entwined in each other's arms in Madeline's bed, catching their breath, Frank tried to describe what he was feeling. For once in his life, words seemed to fail him, and he ended up telling her she felt like warm butter. Madeline laughed in her throaty voice and said no one had ever told her that before, but she'd take it as a compliment. And, she added, while they were on the subject of food, she knew some nice things you could do with champagne besides drinking it. The mere anticipation of things to come was enough to instantly make Frank hard again. It was the most sensuous night of his life.

Around three in the morning, when they were finally both exhausted, Madeline got up and made them scrambled eggs and toast. She was completely at ease with her body and didn't bother to put on any clothes. The sight of a gorgeous nude woman cooking for him nearly blew Frank's mind. Right from the start, he was hooked.

Frank had always had an active libido. In high school he'd been rather shy around girls and hadn't had the courage to ask his longtime girlfriend to have sex until the night of the senior prom, after they'd shared a pint of Five Star Brandy that Frank had managed to pilfer from his mother's kitchen. He had found the experience akin to communing with the gods. His girlfriend had been less enthusiastic, and they'd broken up before graduation.

He'd been popular in college and had gone out with lots of girls. One uninhibited free spirit, upon learning that his birthday was November fifteenth, had said, "Oh, you're a Scorpio. Well, that explains it then. No wonder you're a sex maniac." Although Frank had never thought of himself in quite that way, he'd secretly been pleased that someone else thought so.

Frank had started dating Caroline in law school. Her parents, like so many wealthy Chicagoans, were clients of the Parks' family brokerage firm. She was three years his junior, had just finished a degree in art history, and was working as an assistant curator at the Art Institute. The first time he'd met her it had struck him that she looked like a dancer—tall and thin and delicate, with long flowing hair and a graceful carriage.

They had married in Frank's second year at Hagenkord and had honeymooned in Europe. Their families had both been mightily pleased with the match. So was Frank. He thought she was an angel. He was never quite sure what Caroline thought of him. She never completely let down her guard. There always seemed to be a wall between them, even in their most intimate moments. While at first their physical relationship had been very good, Frank had always sensed that Caroline never derived the same pleasure from sex that he did.

She had seemed to be a bit more content for a time after Kate was born. Even though the baby was fussy, Caroline had been a patient, caring mother. But by the time Kate became a toddler, Caroline had begun to feel trapped and things had gone steadily downhill. They had both hoped that Jack's birth might bring them closer together, but unfortunately it had turned out to have the opposite effect. Frank had not spoken to Caroline in nearly eight years, but there were times—especially when he caught a glimpse of Kate in the right light—that he still missed her and wondered if there wasn't something more he could have done to make her stay.

Frank had had a succession of women in the years since the divorce, a few fairly long-term relationships intermingled with some one-night stands, but he'd never experienced the raw sexuality he'd found with Madeline. They met for dinner two or three nights a week and always ended the evening in bed at her apartment in a swank high rise a few blocks off Michigan Avenue.

Madeline was intelligent, well-educated, and self-sufficient. And she was so gorgeous she turned men's heads wherever they went. It was a rush just to be in her company. Utterly demanding in bed, she was otherwise completely nonpossessive. Unlike so many other women Frank had encountered, she seemed to have little interest in marriage, which suited him just fine. He wasn't accustomed to failing at any endeavor, and he wasn't particularly eager to find out if a second marriage would be more successful than his first.

While Madeline continued to kiss him, she moved one hand underneath her to monitor the state of Frank's erection. Upon confirming that he was extremely aroused, she parted her mouth from his, sat up, and straddled him. With one deft motion of her hips, he was inside her. He reached up and caressed her breasts. She had magnificent breasts. He'd never realized how much of a breast man he was till he'd met her. They were large enough that he could push them together and take both nipples in his mouth at once. What a feeling that was.

Madeline put her hands on his chest to steady herself. She began to move up and down, slowly at first, then harder and faster, until the queen-size brass bed was shaking. They were both rocking, joined together in a sort of frenzied dance. Frank put his hands on her hips so he could help control her movements, lifting her and then pulling her back down onto him with even greater intensity. Madeline's breaths were coming in low shallow gulps. He heard her moan with pleasure.

"Oh, yes . . . oh, Frank, I'm gonna come . . . oh . . . oh!" Frank's own orgasm was already perilously close, and he was pushed over the edge by her spasms. He raised his hips and simultaneously pulled her down, ramming himself into her. He felt himself come in a series of hot spurts.

Madeline remained on top of him for a minute while their pulse rates and breathing returned to normal levels. She leaned down and licked Frank's sweaty face. "Are you glad you stuck around for that?" she asked.

Frank reached up and rubbed her cheek. "Am I ever," he said. "You are fantastic."

"We're pretty good, aren't we?" she said in a hoarse whisper.

"We're the best," he said with feeling. "I never dreamed it could be like this."

Madeline disengaged herself and lay down on her back next to Frank and stroked his arm. "Would you do me a favor?" she asked in a sultry voice.

"What?"

"Stay here tonight."

Frank exhaled deeply. He reached over and took her hand, then looked into her eyes in the dim lamplight. "I can't."

"Why not?" Madeline asked, her voice taking on the tiniest bit of an edge.

"We've been through this," Frank said. "I want to be there when the kids get up in the morning."

"Refresh my memory. Why is that?" Madeline asked with mock patience.

"Because I want them to have a stable home life. It's important that they know I'm always there for them."

"That's admirable," Madeline said, "but what does that have to do with being able to spend the night with me? You spend nights away from home when you're traveling on business, and the kids haven't fallen apart."

"That's different," Frank said. "They know that traveling is part of my job. They accept that."

"That's my point. If you'd just explain it to them, I'm sure they'd understand that sometimes you want to spend more time with me."

Frank was at a loss to understand what she was getting at. "But they already know how much time we spend together."

"Then why can't you tell them you're out of town and spend the night here once in a while."

"I'm not going to lie to them," he protested.

"Oh, Frank, don't be such a prude! You're being positively Victorian."

Frank let go of her hand and sat up. "I have to go," he said. He retrieved his shorts from the chair where he'd tossed them.

Madeline sat up, too. She swung her legs over the side of the bed and pulled on a short white silk robe.

She stood up on the cream-and-salmon colored Oriental rug, and walking past her Stairmaster and Life Cycle, she went to the nightstand and turned on another soft light. Then she went to her dressing table and picked up a hairbrush. As she vigorously brushed out her hair, she crossed over to where Frank was dressing in silence.

"You know, Frank, sometimes I think you must be ashamed of me," she said, standing in front of him.

Frank searched her face. What had come over her? She had never talked like this before. "Of course I'm not ashamed of you," he said as he finished buttoning his shirt.

"Well it sure seems that way," Madeline shot back. "The only time you've spent the whole night here is when the kids were at camp. You hardly ever invite me to your house."

"That's not true," Frank protested. "You were at the house all day last Sunday." She had looked so sexy in a pink-and-white flowered dress. Frank had had a tough time keeping his hands off her.

"Yeah, but the kids were off playing with their friends, and you and I were cooped up inside with your housekeeper." A flush had risen to her cheeks. "I think it would do the kids good if you required them to spend some time with us so they could get to know me." Madeline put her hands on her hips. The white robe parted, exposing her breasts. "Jack and Kate are not babies anymore, Frank. I'm sure they have lots of friends whose parents are divorced, and I'd be willing to bet that it wouldn't shock them to learn that you and I sleep together. You can't shelter them forever. Maybe it's time for you to stop trying to make up for their mother running off and leaving them."

"I *am* the only parent they have," he countered. "And it is important that they know how much they mean to me."

"It just seems to me that you're cheating yourself out of a lot of good experiences by always catering to them."

Frank's expression darkened. He slipped into his

shoes. "I have to go," he said. He turned and started walking toward the door of the bedroom.

Madeline realized she'd gone too far. She threw the hairbrush down on the bed and ran over and grabbed Frank by the arm.

"I'm sorry," she said contritely. "I didn't mean it." She put her arms around his neck. He looked down at the expanse of velvety skin. "I just get frustrated because I'd like to be able to spend more time with you, that's all." She kissed him lightly on the lips and simultaneously took his right hand and pressed it to her breasts.

Frank looked into her eyes. He didn't know what had prompted her remarks, but he found the conversation very upsetting. Madeline had never pressed him for more than he felt he could give, nor had he pressed her. That was part of what made their relationship so wonderful. He reflected for a moment. Maybe she was right. He probably was overly protective of the kids. Maybe it wouldn't hurt to loosen up a little bit. He managed a small smile. "I know. I'd like that, too. We'll work on it. I promise." He kissed her. "But right now it's late, and I gotta go."

After he'd left, Madeline closed the door to the apartment behind him and snapped the deadbolt into place. She stood quietly for a moment, leaning against the door frame. That's right, Frank, she thought to herself. We are *definitely* going to work on it. She flipped off the light, and walked back to her bedroom.

CHAPTER 12

Megan yawned, leaned back in her chair and stretched. "Better wake up," Ron Johnson chided, tapping his pen lightly on her desk. "If you're too tired to handle the hearing, I suppose I could always postpone my flight."

Megan sat up straight, picked up her coffee cup, and took a big gulp. "I think I can manage," she said sweetly.

It was seven o'clock on a hot July morning. Megan and Ron had met in Megan's office at six-thirty to make sure everything was in order for the hearing with Judge Edwards regarding Chicago Memorial's refusal to turn over its staff's medical files. Ron had to catch a plane for depositions on the West Coast, so Megan would be going solo to the hearing.

"I think I have everything I need," Megan said, stuffing some exhibits into a brown expandable folder. She yawned again and ate the last bite of a blueberry muffin she'd picked up on her way in.

Rita Montenero appeared in the doorway, holding a mug of coffee. "What are you guys doing here at this hour?" she asked brightly.

"Motion hearing at eight," Megan replied, brushing muffin crumbs off the skirt of her jade linen suit. "Boy, you're dressed to the nines today. What's up?"

Rita stepped into the office and pirouetted, showing off her new, navy, raw-silk suit and white blouse. "Roger Barrett and I are meeting with clients on a new case," she said. "So I thought I'd better look presentable. What do you think?"

Ron whistled. "You look like poetry in motion, darlin'."

Rita smiled. "And how about my shoes?" She held up one foot so they could get a better look at her navy-and-white pumps.

"They're great," Megan said.

"They're Maud Frizon," Rita confided. "Only two hundred and fifty dollars on sale at Neiman-Marcus."

Ron gave the shoes closer scrutiny, then caught Rita's eye. She was frowning. "Did you want to say something?" she asked.

"Well, I did, but I think I just forgot what it was," Ron said. Both women laughed. "What's your new case about?" he asked.

Rita perched on a corner of Megan's desk. "Medical malpractice. An obstetrician didn't notice a fetus was in distress in time to do a C-section, and the baby has brain damage. He's a cute little guy. It's really sad."

"Who's the doctor?" Megan asked.

"Fromstein at St. Mary's Medical Group," Rita answered.

"Oh, good, it's not someone in Paul's clinic," Megan said with relief. "He gets a bit testy if we sue one of his colleagues."

"Yeah, a multimillion dollar verdict *could* tend to cut into their profits," Ron teased. "You might have to hold off a few months on buying that mansion in Lake Forest."

Megan stuck out her tongue at him. She stood up and slipped on her jacket, then sat down again, pulled open a desk drawer and took out a mirror and a tube of Tawny Beige lipstick. "Got any scoops for us today?" she asked Rita, as she carefully outlined her lips.

"Mmm, let me think," Rita said, slumping into a chair and picking up the morning *Tribune* from Megan's desk. "It's been pretty dead this week. Oh, I did hear Gene Stutzberger broke up with his girlfriend."

"That's too bad," Megan said, replacing the top on the tube of lipstick. "I liked Helen."

"Me, too," Ron chimed in. "She had the biggest breasts. Do you suppose they're real? I asked Gene once and he wouldn't tell me."

Both women gave him dirty looks. "How childish," Megan said in a derisive tone. "Is that all you care about?"

"Yeah," Rita said. "Women would never think of discussing their partner's penis size, would they, Meg?"

"Of course not. We're mature enough to know that the size of a person's physical attributes has nothing whatsoever to do with who they are. A person's mind is what really matters, right?"

"Right," Rita said, nodding emphatically. "By the way, Ron, Meg and I have been wondering . . . just how big is your dick?"

The two women broke into gales of laughter. "Maybe we should ask Verna." Megan chuckled.

"I'm not seeing Verna anymore," Ron said indignantly. "I've been dating Margery for over two weeks."

"Then I'll bet Verna would be delighted to tell us all about you," Megan said devilishly.

Ron stood up. "I can certainly tell when I'm not wanted. I'd better head out to the airport. Good luck at the hearing," he said to Megan, "and try not to leave any teeth marks in old Frank's leg." He turned to Rita. "You can be in charge of monitoring her behavior. If she's bad, make her write 'I *will* be nice to Mr. Parks' one hundred times when she gets back."

"Have a good trip," Megan said as Ron walked back to his own office, humming "Leaving on a Jet Plane."

"Oh, your hearing is on the AIDS case," Rita said, suddenly looking up from thumbing through the paper.

"Yup," Megan replied, stuffing several files into her brown Mark Cross briefcase. "What a way to start the day."

"Oh, God, another woman was murdered!" Rita exclaimed.

"Another stabbing?" Megan asked, pulling a hairbrush out of her drawer.

"No, her boyfriend shot her because he claimed she poisoned his dog. There's sure a lot of violence in this city. Why do we live here anyway?"

"I don't know. Maybe because we have better jobs here than we could get in Peoria."

"I s'pose so," Rita said, throwing down the paper in disgust. "But every time I read stories like that, I get more nervous."

"You can't let stuff like that get to you," Megan said as she brushed her hair, "or before you know it, you'll be afraid to leave your house."

"I don't know how you can be so blasé about your own safety after what happened to your car," Rita said incredulously.

Ten days earlier Megan had worked late and as she got off the parking ramp elevator around ten P.M., she had heard the unmistakable sound of glass breaking. Moments later she'd discovered that someone had completely shattered the back window of her car. Megan had been shaken to think that if she'd been a minute earlier, she might have come face-to-face with the culprit.

She had reported the incident to the parking ramp attendant, who in turn had called the police. An officer had responded to the scene, taken down the pertinent information, and told Megan candidly that the chances of catching the person who did it were practically nil. Megan had thanked him and driven home, shivering in spite of the heat. A couple stiff belts of scotch and a warm bath had done wonders to soothe her nerves. She'd gotten the window repaired the next day and had pretty much put the incident out of her mind.

"I've lived in the city almost ten years without any problems," she said to Rita philosophically. "I guess it was just my turn."

"Well, I wish you'd be a little more safety conscious," Rita urged.

"I am," Megan replied. "If I'm going to be working late, I move the car closer to the attendant's booth. Now can we change the subject? This discussion is getting depressing."

"Okay," Rita said, thinking a moment. "Hey, did I ever tell you what I heard about Frank Parks?"

"That he's a direct descendant of the Marquis de Sade?" Megan speculated.

"No, about his wife running off and leaving him for some bohemian."

"Well I knew he was divorced," Megan replied. "If his charming work personality carries over into his home life, it's no wonder the poor woman decided not to stick around."

"Yeah, but it was like one of those deals you see in the movies, where she didn't give any hint she was gonna split. It was during the daytime. She'd hired a baby-sitter for the two kids—I guess one was only a couple months old—and said she was meeting a friend for lunch, but she never came back."

"Really?" Megan said, dropping her brush back in her drawer. "She must've been pretty desperate to abandon the kids like that."

"Parks was supposedly devastated. He didn't hear from her for weeks, and then one day she called and said she was out on the West Coast."

"That's kinda weird," Megan admitted, "but apparently it didn't keep him out of circulation for too long. I've heard he's quite the ladies' man."

"He *is* nice looking," Rita said.

"I suppose so," Megan admitted grudgingly, "if you like that type."

Rita laughed. "Actually, Meg, I think he looks a lot like Paul. I can't believe you haven't noticed."

"He does *not!*" Megan sputtered. She stood up. "I have to go. I wouldn't want to be late. Parks would probably ask to have me held in contempt. Good luck with your new clients," she said, picking up her briefcase. "Are you still free for lunch?"

"Sure am," Rita said.

"Great. See you later." Megan walked out toward the reception area to tell one of the firm's messengers that she was ready to be driven to the federal center.

The messenger dropped Megan off in front of the building at twenty to eight, and she reached Judge Edwards's office five minutes later. The judge generally held motion hearings in his chambers rather than in the courtroom, thinking that an informal atmosphere was more conducive to establishing a good rapport between himself and the attorneys. That was definitely wishful thinking in this case, Megan thought as she walked into the office.

Megan informed the judge's secretary, a well-dressed, middle-aged woman, that she was there, then took a seat in one of the brown plush chairs placed next to a low glass-topped table that held the most recent issues of *Architectural Digest, Town and Country,* and *The New Yorker.* Just like a dentist's office, only classier, Megan mused.

She picked up the copy of *Architectural Digest* and quickly flipped through it. There was a layout on Michael and Diandra Douglas's Manhattan apartment. "We live quite simply," Diandra was quoted as saying. Sure, you do, Megan thought, looking at the glossy photos of rooms filled with priceless art work. The couch in their living room probably cost as much as the average American made in a year.

The door from the hall opened, and Frank stepped inside. He set the briefcase down and strode briskly over to the secretary's desk. "Good morning," he said brightly. "Frank Parks. I'm here for the eight o'clock motion hearing."

"Good morning, Mr. Parks," the secretary said, smiling up at him. "Please have a seat. The judge should be with you shortly."

"Thanks," Frank said, smiling back at her.

Megan watched the exchange with distaste. Parks conducted himself like a man who thought all women were hot for his body. He did dress well, she'd give him that. He was wearing a light brown, silk-and-flax suit that looked fashionably wrinkled and a brown-and-white-striped shirt. She recognized the cuff links peeking out from underneath his jacket. They were a Jean Schlumberger design for Tiffany's, eighteen-karat gold with inlaid brown enamel. Megan had admired them when searching for a Christmas gift for Paul but had been put off by the two-thousand-dollar price tag.

As Frank turned around and began to walk toward her, Megan noticed with a start that his gold-and-brown paisley tie was the mate to one she had given Paul last year for his birthday. Oh, my God, Megan thought, we have the same taste. Rita's words rushed back to her. "He looks a lot like Paul." Did he? She tried not to stare.

"And how are you this morning?" Frank asked, sitting down in the chair next to her. "Thinking of redecorating?" He motioned to her magazine.

A nasty retort sprang to her lips, but she suppressed it. Try to be nice, she admonished herself. "No, this stuff's too pedestrian for me," she said, closing the magazine and putting it back on the table.

"Are you here alone today?" Frank asked, looking around the office.

"Yeah, the buddy system is only in effect on Monday, Wednesday, and Friday," Megan replied. Frank laughed. Megan hesitated a moment. Should she try to butter him up? Why not? "That's a nice tie," she offered. "It's from Mark Shale, right?"

"Yes. Thank you," Frank answered. The compliment took him by surprise. Maybe she'd left her barbs back at the office. He fought back a yawn. He'd been awake a good part of the night thinking about his talk with Madeline.

"I bought my fiancé one just like it for Christmas," Megan added.

"Then I'd say we both have good taste," Frank said. "Your fiancé is a doctor, isn't he?"

Megan wondered how he'd come by that information. She nodded. "Yes, he's a surgeon."

"What does he think of you suing doctors for a living?"

Megan bristled. So much for her attempts to be nice to the jerk. "We really don't discuss it," Megan said somewhat haughtily. "He has his job to do, and I have mine."

The phone on the secretary's desk buzzed, and she picked it up. "Yes? All right, I'll send them in." She replaced the receiver. "You can go into the judge's office now," she said brightly.

Frank and Megan stood up simultaneously. "Thank you," Frank said to the secretary, giving her another smile as they passed through the door into the judge's chambers.

The judge, a tall blond man of forty-five, read off the case name and number for the record, noted that Frank and Megan were present, and that this was a motion to compel the production of documents. "I've already read your submissions," he said, "so there's no need to rehash them in detail. Why don't you just give me a brief overview of what's in dispute." He turned to Megan. "Ms. Lansdorf, you have the floor."

Grateful that she was dealing with someone who was well-prepared, Megan outlined the requests she had made for the hospital's records and Frank's refusal to turn them over. "We believe that the defendant has been guilty of dilatory conduct, Your Honor," she said in conclusion. "And in addition to an order requiring the hospital to turn over the documents, we also ask for an award of costs."

Judge Edwards thanked Megan for her remarks and motioned to Frank that he could respond. As always, he spoke without benefit of prepared notes. His presentation was concise and articulate. "In short, Your Honor," he said, "the hospital believed in good faith that the plaintiffs' requests were overly broad and vague, and that it would be unduly burdensome for them to even attempt to respond."

Judge Edwards pursed his lips. He glanced down at some notes he had made earlier when reviewing the file. "As you are well aware, Mr. Parks, all forms of discovery requests necessarily place some burden on the party required to respond. That is one of the unpleasantries parties agree to tolerate in order to garner some of the corresponding benefits under our legal system. Just because a request might be burdensome does not mean it doesn't have to be responded to."

Sounds good so far, Megan thought.

"In addition," the judge went on, "I disagree that the

plaintiffs' requests were overly broad or vague. I particularly think that the plaintiffs' amended requests, which asked for all files going back ten years, were quite clear. Therefore, I am ordering the hospital to make all such files available within the next two weeks. Mr. Parks has indicated that some of the files are in a warehouse and some are on microfilm. As you both know, the hospital merely has to give the plaintiffs access to the information, in whatever form it currently exists. The plaintiffs will have to look through the files *in situ,* and if they wish to copy any of them, it will be at their own expense."

Megan nodded. That was how it always worked.

"As to the plaintiffs' request for costs," the judge continued, "while I normally do not grant costs unless there has been a clear showing that the requesting party was prejudiced by the delay in gaining access to the documents, I think costs *are* warranted here. It seems to me that the documents should have been made available following the amended request. The hospital is, therefore, ordered to pay the plaintiffs' attorney two hundred and fifty dollars within five days. Ms. Lansdorf, you may draft an order for my signature."

"Thank you, Your Honor," Megan said. "I'll have an order sent over this afternoon." She had been hoping for a more substantial award of costs, but this was a victory nonetheless.

Frank leisurely slipped his file back into his briefcase. The outcome had been about what he'd expected. The award of costs was merely a small slap on the wrist, and the advantage he'd gained by being able to deny Megan access to the documents for several months had been well worth it.

The court reporter picked up her steno machine and left the room. "This is one of my more interesting cases," the judge said as Frank and Megan snapped their briefcases shut. "Any chance it might settle?"

"Don't look at me," Megan said, throwing up her hands in a gesture of futility. The judge turned to Frank.

Frank merely smiled. "The trial is almost five months off," he said. "A lot can happen between now and then."

"That's true enough," the judge agreed. "But keep in touch. If there's any chance you're going to settle it, try to do it before the first day of trial so we can notify the attorneys handling the alternate cases to be ready." He closed his file and set it aside.

"I enjoyed the editorial about the litigation explosion you had in the *Sun Times* last week," Frank said. "I thought you made some good points."

"Thank you," the judge replied. "Nice to see both of you. Good-bye."

As Frank and Megan headed down the hall, she asked, "When are we going to be able to start looking at the documents?"

"I'll let you know later in the week," Frank responded.

"Please do that," Megan said. "I'd hate to have to bring another motion for sanctions."

"I guess we all do what we have to," Frank said cryptically as he turned down a hallway and began walking away from her.

"We expect access to those documents one week from today," Megan called after him.

Frank turned. "Is that a threat?"

"Consider it a warning," Megan replied testily.

They stared at each other a moment, then Frank turned again and walked off.

Megan walked out of the building's main entrance and down the steps, feeling very pleased. She'd won the motion and, without totally losing her temper, she'd let Parks know where things stood. Good job, she commended herself. As she spotted the messenger's car across the street and motioned that she was coming over, her stomach growled. The hearing had gone so smoothly, maybe she had time to stop for an Egg McMuffin before going back to work.

CHAPTER 13

"Rita and I walked through Saks bridal department at noon today," Megan said. Having finally set a wedding date, she and Paul were discussing some of the myriad of details that went into planning the event.

Paul lightly stroked her arm. They were lying in Megan's four-poster bed. It was a hot and steamy July night, and even with the air conditioner running full bore, the air in the apartment was close. With his other hand, Paul fanned the thin sheet that covered them to generate a breeze. "You're going to be the most beautiful bride this city's ever seen," he murmured. "Did you see any dresses you liked?"

"Oh, yeah. There was a gorgeous Edwardian-style dress with a high neck and lots of lace, but it was a bit more than I wanted to spend." She snuggled her head against his shoulder.

"How much?"

"Eight thousand."

"Did you try it on?"

"No. Why should I waste my time trying on things I know I'm not going to buy?"

"Why don't you go back and try it on. And if it's what you really want, go ahead and splurge."

Megan raised her head off the pillow and looked down at him. "Don't be silly. I'm not going to spend eight grand on a dress that I'll wear once."

Paul pulled on her earlobe. "Sometimes, my dear, you can be very cheap. Why don't you loosen your purse strings just a smidgen?"

"I am *not* cheap!" she protested. "I am thrifty.

There's a big difference. Besides, I intend to put the money toward a really posh reception."

"Did you check out the menu at the Drake?" Paul asked.

"They're in the process of revising it. The updated one is supposed to be available in ten days or so. But I looked over their old one, and frankly, I wasn't that impressed. I think we can do better somewhere else. Unless you have a better idea, my first choice is still the Yacht Club. They have such great food."

"That's fine with me," Paul replied. "Are you going to ask Mike Gillette to make the reservation, since he's a member?"

"Yeah. He said there'd be no problem. I think we should have a choice of two entrées, filet mignon and a seafood dish, maybe *coquilles St. Jacques* or salmon steak. What do you think?" Megan threw one arm over Paul's chest.

"Wouldn't it be easier to just have one entrée that might appeal to everybody, like chicken cordon bleu or veal oscar?" Paul suggested.

"But some people really prefer steak," Megan said.

"Do you think so?"

"I do," Megan said stubbornly.

"Yeah, but I'm not sure most people share your taste."

"What's wrong with my taste?"

"It really doesn't matter to me," Paul said quickly. "You can handle the menu," he added, rubbing her back.

"In case you hadn't noticed, Dr. Finley," she teased, "we don't seem to be agreeing on much. What do you think? Maybe we should call the whole thing off."

Paul put his arms around her and pulled her close. "Oh, no. You're not getting off that easy. These are just a few minor details brought about by the fact that we're both a little pigheaded. But everything's going to work out great because I'm absolutely nuts about you, and I can't wait till we both live in one place and can stop this shuffling back and forth." As he began to kiss her deeply, Megan's fuzzy black cat, Andy, jumped on the bed, landing on Megan's feet. Paul disengaged himself from Megan's embrace and reached down and swatted at the animal. "Get off!" he snapped with irritation. With lightning speed, the cat took a swipe back at Paul with one paw and then jumped back on the floor. He sat down on the rug next to Megan's side of the bed.

Megan raised up on one elbow. "He's not hurting anything," she said.

"I've told you I don't want an animal in bed with us," Paul said firmly. "Especially one that hates me."

"He's never going to like you if you keep hitting him."

"I don't care. I know how fond you are of him, but he's just going to have to learn that when I'm around, he has to find other sleeping accommodations."

Megan lay down again. She had found Andy—then a small kitten—huddled on her front steps three years before. He behaved more like a dog, fetching his toys if Megan threw them and growling if he heard strange noises. Megan knew Paul didn't care for cats, but she had been adamant that, when they were married, Andy was going to be part of their household.

"So, would you like to go to some open houses on Sunday?" Paul asked, stroking her hand.

"I thought we were going to the Wagners' Bastille Day party on Sunday."

"We are, but that doesn't start till five o'clock. We'd have plenty of time to look at houses earlier in the day."

"Sure, if you want to," Megan said. "Where should we go?"

"How about Lake Forest?" Paul asked.

"Do you *really* want to live there?" Megan asked with surprise.

"What's wrong with living there?" Paul countered.

"Nothing. It's just that it's so expensive."

Paul laughed. "Sweetheart," he said patiently, "you and I have substantial incomes. We can afford a nice house. Besides that, I should make a tidy profit when I sell my co-op."

"In your dreams!" Megan retorted. "The market for co-ops is really soft. Look how long it took Ted and Linda to sell theirs."

"Yeah, but theirs was in an inferior building and had only one bedroom. I'm positive my place will sell in a flash."

"I hope you're right."

Paul could sense she still wasn't sold on his choice of venue, so he asked, "Do you have some other, more fundamental objection to Lake Forest?"

Megan hesitated, knowing her answer would sound lame. "Well ... it's so yuppie."

Paul chortled. "What's wrong with being yuppie? As they say, if the shoe fits ..."

"There's nothing wrong with it. I just don't necessarily want to move to Lake Forest just because four other doctors in your group happen to live there."

"Okay, okay," Paul said in a conciliatory tone. " 'Methinks the lady doth protest too much.' I promise I'm not trying to emulate other doctors in my group. I just think it's a quality place to live."

"All right," Megan said, giving in. "I'm not convinced that's where we should end up, but yes, let's plan on going through some houses on Sunday. Hey, you know how much I like to snoop around and look at other people's decorating." She squeezed his hand. "But right now I think we'd better try to get some sleep. It must be after midnight." She rolled onto her other side and tucked her left hand under her pillow. Paul curled up behind her, spoon fashion.

Megan had almost dozed off when she was jolted awake by the sound of Paul's beeper. "Oh, Christ, now what?" he grumbled. Megan reached over, turned on the light on the bedside table next to her, and handed him the phone. He quickly dialed his service. "This is Dr. Finley. What's up? ... Yeah ... Yeah ... Okay, I'm on my way." He handed the phone back to Megan, rolled over, and sat up on the edge of the bed.

"What is it?" Megan asked, sitting up.

"There was an accident on Wells. An eight-year-old

girl got her face all mangled up. They're prepping her for surgery." He got up and hurriedly began to dress.

Several minutes later, Megan, who had slipped on a pink cotton nightgown, kissed Paul good-bye at the top of the brick steps in front of her building. "Good luck," she said.

"Thanks. I'll call you in the morning."

Megan leaned against the black wrought-iron railing and watched him walk down the street and turn the corner toward his car. The humidity was stifling. Thick clouds obscured the half moon. She quickly turned and walked back inside, locking the door behind her.

She had not turned on any lights except the one in the bedroom. She carefully made her way across the living room floor. The apartment was furnished with an eclectic mixture of antiques and modern pieces. In the far corner was an old upright piano. Megan had played regularly in college and still played for relaxation occasionally, although she hadn't touched the keys in months. As she walked past, her knee bumped against several months' accumulation of magazines that she'd stacked on the bench, intending to read them someday when she had nothing else to do. The pile kept growing. The top few slid off, hitting the hardwood floor with a thud. Megan leaned over and scooped them up, then neatly straightened the stack.

Megan's bedroom was at the right rear of the apartment. One wall was covered with old family photos, some dating back to the 1880's when her great-great-grandfather had arrived from England. Megan stopped for a moment in front of her favorite picture, a studio portrait taken in the late 1920's, showing an attractive, auburn-haired young woman in flapper attire staring defiantly at the camera, almost daring observers to challenge her dress, her morals, or anything else about her.

Megan couldn't look at the photo of her grandmother without smiling. Eighteen-year-old Hallie Evans had shocked her midwestern family when she had departed for New York in 1925, armed with two hundred dollars cash and a fervent conviction that if she was going to be a writer, and she had decided at age twelve that she was, New York City was the only place in the world where her dream could be realized.

To everyone's surprise Hallie had landed a job as a proofreader at *Vanity Fair.* In her spare time, she wrote short stories and managed to get several of them published. Hallie led a charmed life, doing exactly what she'd always wanted to do in the most exciting city on earth, until the Depression hit. Markets for her short stories dried up, and in early 1930, *Vanity Fair* eliminated her job. Always pragmatic, Hallie reasoned that she'd given writing and New York her best shot and had no regrets.

At age twenty-two, she returned to the Midwest as the bride of an up-and-coming young banker, Joseph Lansdorf. An ardent Lucy Stoner, Hallie sent her family and her new in-laws into hysterics by keeping her maiden name. She never lost her feisty spirit, and spent the rest of her life working for liberal reforms such as public family-planning clinics and homes for unwed mothers. Megan's father was the youngest of Hallie's four sons. Megan was very close to her grandmother, and from the time she was a little girl, Hallie had tried to impress some of her pioneering spirit on the youngster.

"Don't ever let anyone tell you how to live your life, Megan," Hallie had said many times. "Only you can decide what's right for you, and once you've decided what that is, don't let anyone talk you out of it. If you don't set your own course, you'll regret it forever."

Hallie had remained active and alert well into her eighties. The last time Megan had visited her, she was in the hospital suffering from congestive heart failure. Megan was in college then, and had decided to go to law school. The old woman had nodded with approval at her decision.

"Good choice, Megan," she'd said, caressing Megan's arm with a wrinkled hand. "You'll make an outstanding lawyer. You can think on your feet and you're stubborn as a mule, just like me. I only wish I could stick around to see how well things turn out for you."

That was ten years ago, and Megan still missed her. As she continued to look at the photo, she could imagine what a spitfire Hallie must have been in her youth. Megan knew she looked a bit like her grandma—the same determined gaze in her eyes, the firm set of her mouth. When she was confused or had a tough decision to make, Megan would sometimes stop and speculate what Hallie would have done in her place. She hoped she'd done the old girl proud.

Giving the photo a last tender look, Megan switched off the light and got into bed. She had no more than gotten comfortable when Andy jumped up on the bed next to her, his pink bunny clamped firmly in his mouth. "Hi, there," she said. "Did you decide it was safe for you to come back?" The cat rubbed its head against Megan's cheek and deposited the bunny on her pillow. "You know, it's really too warm to have a furry animal lying next to me. Why don't you sleep over here?" she said, patting Paul's side of the bed. "Come on. There's nobody here to throw you out." She picked up the cat and set him down next to her, then laid his bunny beside him. He promptly curled up and went to sleep.

Although Megan was tired, the heat made her restless, and she lay there for a time unable to doze off. She slid over toward Paul's side of the bed. The sheets were cooler there. This feels nice, she thought, moving over a bit more. As she was about to drift off, she had a fleeting thought that maybe she wasn't all that unhappy that Paul had had to leave. She rather liked having the bed to herself on hot nights.

The idea caused her to start, and she dismissed it immediately. It's this damn heat, she thought crossly. That's all it is. She wished she could get away for the weekend and drive north a few hours, where the temperatures would be more moderate. Next summer, she promised herself, she'd somehow see to it that she and Paul had plenty of time to relax. She found that thought comforting and finally fell asleep, dreaming about cool sea breezes and sailboats skimming effortlessly over placid blue waters.

CHAPTER 14

Sweat was running down Mike O'Riley's face as he methodically pedaled his stationary bicycle. He glanced down at the odometer. Jesus Christ! The damn thing must be broken. He couldn't have done only two and a half miles. He was already winded, and his leg ached. He groaned and kept pedaling.

O'Riley normally worked out in the partially finished room in the basement, but the heat of the past few weeks had been so intense it had even permeated the lower level, so he'd hauled the bike up to his bedroom, in front of the window air conditioner. The contraption was a no-frills model he'd bought at Sears twelve years earlier. The speedometer had given out a couple years back and he'd never bothered to have it fixed. He didn't give a rat's ass how fast he was going. The important thing was to keep at it.

He'd already done five miles earlier in the day, but lately his leg had been bothering him a lot, so he thought maybe he'd better do more miles. His family doctor had told him years ago it would just be a matter of time before arthritis set in. That news had been a hell of a lot more palatable than the doom-and-gloom speech he'd gotten from another physician shortly after the shooting.

"You'll never regain full use of your leg, Officer O'Riley," the thin-lipped, beady-eyed little moron had said. "If I were you, I'd start thinking about a new career."

"Well, lucky for both of us you're *not* me," O'Riley had spat back from his hospital bed. "You obviously don't know who you're talking to," he'd added with eyes flashing. "I intend to be back on the job in six months." The doctor had given him a look that said maybe he should bring in a straitjacket and had walked out without responding. O'Riley had been back on the streets five and a half months later. From time to time he'd wondered what had ever happened to the doc. He hoped he'd died of hemorrhoids.

Anyway, O'Riley knew he was probably lucky his leg had kept functioning as long as it had, but goddamn it, maybe he could fend the arthritis off just a little while longer. What would be the point of retiring if he was going to be a cripple?

He gripped the handlebars tighter, threw back his head, and tried to divert his mind from the pain. The only problem was he didn't have anything pleasant to think about. The murder investigations had come to a standstill. It was now mid-July, nearly three months since Mary Collins's body had been found, and they had no suspects, no theories, and no clues, only stacks of notes from countless leads that had gone nowhere.

It was so damn frustrating. They'd gotten printouts from the Illinois Department of Corrections of recently released prisoners who'd been convicted of sexual assaults involving knife play and had interviewed a dozen of the most likely prospects. Unfortunately, the men all either had rock-solid alibis, or came across as so sincere that O'Riley knew in his gut that their pleas of innocence were truthful.

Several days ago he and Jablonski had had a face-to-face meeting with their psychiatric experts, and after an hour of listening to them spout their goofy theories, O'Riley had lost his cool. He'd slammed his fist down on the table and said, "Jesus Christ! The city is paying you people tens of thousands of dollars to be of some use on this case. When are you going to start earning your money?" Needless to say, that had brought the meeting to a rapid conclusion. Dr. Sheridan, the fancy-shmancy psychiatrist who was the team's lead shrink, had been so taken aback, he'd looked like he might shit his pants.

O'Riley had heard Jablonski apologizing for his outburst, saying he'd been under a lot of stress. That had only made O'Riley's blood boil even hotter, and after the group had disbanded he'd read Jablonski the riot act.

"Since when do you think you have a right to speak for me?" he demanded.

"I guess since you gave yourself the authority to embarrass the entire department with your lack of tact," Jablonski shot back.

"I'm sick to death of this goddamn case," O'Riley had snorted. "I just want it over with, and I thought I'd make it clear to that bunch of whores you hired just where I stand."

"You made something clear all right, but I don't think it was quite what you had in mind," Jablonski muttered as he walked away.

Two and three-quarter miles. Why the hell had he gone into police work anyway? O'Riley grunted. He knew the answer. After high school he'd worked in a succession of manual labor jobs—construction, bricklaying, road crews. He'd been good at it, and the money wasn't bad when there was work. But most of those jobs had been seasonal, and by the early 1960's he and Anne had two kids and Mike knew he'd better start thinking about the future, making sure he had a steady income, disability insurance, all the stuff that went along with being a responsible adult.

Uncle Marty had been urging him to try police work for years, and finally Mike had decided what the hell, he might as well give it a shot. He'd switched jobs before. He could always quit if it didn't pan out. He'd spent nine years as a patrolman and twenty-one in homicide. And now here he was, damn near sixty-years old, busting his ass trying to catch one last bad guy.

Three miles. O'Riley wiped his right arm over his sweaty forehead. It was bad enough that they hadn't made any progress in the case. He could live with that, though he sure as hell didn't like it. But the last week or so he'd had an uneasy feeling gnawing away at his guts. He'd downed two bottles of Maalox in the last four days.

There was going to be another murder. He could feel it. And it would be his fault, because he hadn't been smart enough to find the bastard in time to stop him from killing again.

Three and a half miles. That's why he'd been in an especially foul mood lately. Yesterday Jablonski had come into his office and asked him point-blank what was wrong. O'Riley had never been big on sharing his feelings with colleagues, and he sure as hell wasn't going to unburden himself on a know-it-all like Gregarious, particularly since he was always telling the younger man to deal only in cold, hard facts rather than hunches. So the question had gotten O'Riley's usual cheerful response.

"Nothing's wrong," he'd snapped.

"Are you still pissed about what happened at the meeting the other day?"

"Nah," O'Riley had waved his hand. "I just can't sleep worth a damn in this heat."

"You sure there's not something else bothering you?" Jablonski had pressed. "Look, maybe I was out of line, but the way I see it, we're not gonna accomplish anything by alienating our experts. We *are* all on the same side. We all want to catch the bastard so we can move onward and upward."

Onward and upward. That was Jablonski's creed. Some days O'Riley wasn't in the mood for the kid's frigging eternal optimism and all his speculations about what rank he'd hold in five years. Sure, Jablonski was working hard. He put in long days conducting interviews and dutifully entered every shred of information into his damn database at night. But all that talk of his impending promotion could get up a guy's nose.

"If you don't like how I'm handling my end of this case, just say so," Jablonski had added, "and I'm sure we can work things out."

"I told you there's nothing wrong," O'Riley had said. "Now get the hell out of here so I can do some work."

There was something wrong, though. O'Riley was

experiencing a feeling of déjà vu. About twelve years earlier he had been working on a case where a little girl had been molested and then killed. Six weeks had gone by with no leads when all of a sudden O'Riley had gotten a sick feeling that the killer was going to strike again.

He was right. Two more girls had been killed in the next week. The killer had gotten sloppy on the last one, and they'd caught him, but O'Riley had never gotten over the feeling that if he'd been more on the ball, those two kids would still be alive.

Three and three-quarter miles. God it was hot. His white T-shirt clung to his damp body. Jablonski had paused on his way out of O'Riley's office, and Mike had felt bad that he'd lost his temper and made an effort to patch things up by inquiring about Greg's wife.

"She's fine. We're starting Lamaze classes at the end of the month."

"You mean where they teach you those stupid breathing exercises and you have to pretend you're a football coach calling plays?"

Jablonski had smiled. "Yeah, something like that."

"You really want to watch the kid being born?"

"Yeah. Wouldn't you have liked to be there with Anne?"

"Hell, no," O'Riley had shot back, but privately he wasn't so sure. In his day they didn't let the fathers get past the admitting desk, and they knocked the mothers out cold. He remembered how worried he was every time that something would happen to Anne or the baby. Maybe it would've been easier if he could've stayed with her. But he really didn't think Anne would've wanted him there. She was pretty old-fashioned about stuff like that.

Four miles. The hell with it. He decided to quit before there was nothing left of him but a big puddle of sweat on the floor. He stopped pedaling. He took a couple of deep breaths, got off the bike, and stood directly in front of the air conditioner until he had cooled down. Then he went into the bathroom, pulled off the T-shirt, tossed it over the edge of the tub, and splashed

cool water on his face. He looked in the mirror. Christ!
He was sure getting to be a grizzled old bastard. He
could almost see his gray hair multiplying. He wiped
his face and torso with a towel, went back to the bedroom and slipped on a clean, dry shirt, then slowly
walked downstairs where Anne was standing in the living room, ironing.

"How the hell can you stand to iron when it's this
hot?" he asked, as he walked past her. He went to the
kitchen, opened the refrigerator and took out a cold
bottle of Budweiser. He'd already had a couple beers
before he started exercising, but he must've sweated
off three pounds and Jesus, was he ever dry.

"It doesn't bother me," Anne replied as he came
back into the living room and flopped down in the
La-Z-Boy. "Besides, you know how much I hate wrinkled clothes."

"They never should've stopped making that double-
knit stuff," Mike said, taking a big swallow of beer.
Christ, did that ever taste good. "It never wrinkled.
These new natural fibers always look like you slept in
'em."

"What do you know about natural fibers?" Anne
asked, amused.

"I hear the women in the department talking," he
said, taking another long swallow of beer. "I'm not totally ignorant about current fashion trends."

"I'm glad to hear that," she said.

"I know you always look nice," he said, finishing
the beer. He got up and went to the kitchen to get another.

"How's your leg?" she asked as she finished ironing
a red-and-white cotton skirt. She draped it over the
back of a chair and reached for a white blouse.

Mike settled back in his chair. "It still hurts, but I
just worked the hell out of it." He took another slug of
beer and then lit a cigarette.

"Maybe you've been overdoing the exercise," she
suggested, carefully smoothing out the right sleeve of
the blouse.

"Nah." Mike waved his hand. "Best thing for it. The

son of a bitch is gonna have to get limbered up whether it likes it or not."

Anne frowned at his language, but ignored the remark. "I talked to Colleen today," she said. "She said Billy can't stop raving about what a good time he had fishing with Grandpa on Sunday."

Mike brightened a bit. "Bless his heart. The poor little guy's been cheated out of a whole bunch of fishing trips."

"He understands. Colleen says he's told all his friends how you're going to catch the killer."

Mike snorted. "That's wonderful. How's he gonna explain it to them when some other poor girl turns up dead?" He drained the rest of his beer.

Anne had finished ironing the blouse and hung it on a hanger, then unplugged the iron and set it on a low table. She brushed her hair back off her forehead. "Is that what's bothering you?" she asked, walking over to his chair and standing next to him. "You think there's going to be another killing?"

"Yup." He was staring at the wall.

"And if there is, I suppose you're going to blame yourself?"

He looked up at her. "That's right. I never should've taken this case. I could've collected two months' pension checks by now. I'm not doin' myself or the city a damn bit of good." He stubbed out the cigarette and stood up, empty beer bottle in hand.

"Mike, please don't drink any more," Anne said, putting her hand on his arm. "That isn't going to solve anything."

Anne's father had died of alcoholism, and although O'Riley was a moderate drinker, she kept rather close tabs on his consumption. He knew she had his best interests at heart, but sometimes she made him feel like he was sixteen years old.

"Who said I was gonna drink some more?" he asked indignantly. He had been planning to go the kitchen for another beer, but in deference to her, he'd forgo it.

Anne's hand remained on his arm. "Because I know

you, and that's how you react sometimes when you're upset."

"Thank you very much for your concern," he said, pulling his arm free, "but for your information, I was going to take this bottle back to the kitchen and then go up to bed. Is that all right with you?"

"That sounds like a very good idea," Anne replied quietly.

"Good. 'Cuz that's what I'm gonna do."

Anne folded up the ironing board and carried it to a closet near the front entrance. She had her back to Mike as he came out of the kitchen and started up the stairs. "Good night," she said quietly.

" 'Night," he answered sullenly.

Anne closed the closet door, went back to the living room, and sat down in her rocking chair. She knew Mike had been under a tremendous amount of strain. She'd been praying that there would be a break in the case, but she knew God didn't always follow strict timetables when providing solutions to problems.

Anne had been living with Mike so long that his moods no longer bothered her much. But he'd been looking so tired lately, and she knew he hadn't been feeling well. A lot of men who were younger than Mike and under a lot less stress had heart attacks. Mike wasn't exactly a kid anymore, and he had been smoking pretty heavily. A feeling of panic suddenly gripped Anne. The thought of life without Mike was unbearable.

She took a deep breath. She had to stay calm. Mike always called her his anchor. She had to be steady for him. She got up and walked out to the kitchen. Opening the inside compartment of her purse, she took out her rosary. She walked back to her chair in the living room and sat down again. Just feeling the black beads in her fingers eased her mind. Saying the rosary always made her feel better. She would say the five "Joyful Mysteries" and then go up to bed. She closed her eyes and began. "In the name of the Father, and of the Son, and of the Holy Spirit. Amen."

O'Riley stripped down to his underwear and got into

bed. The sheets felt cool and soothing. Although his body was weary, his mind remained alert. Nobody could commit multiple murders without leaving any clues. There had to be something there that he was missing, but he'd be damned if he could put his finger on what it might be.

As he lay on his back in the darkness, O'Riley silently addressed the faceless killer. "Where are you, you bastard? I know you're out there. Who the hell are you? Answer me, Goddamn it! Answer me!" But of course there was no reply.

CHAPTER 15

The grand ballroom of the Ritz-Carlton Hotel was teeming with formally attired men and women who had each paid two hundred and fifty dollars to eat delicacies prepared by the city's best chefs, drink the finest wines, and help raise money for a new Ronald McDonald House where the families of critically ill children could stay while the kids underwent treatment at nearby hospitals. The fund-raiser was sponsored by the Seventh Circuit Bar Association, and the featured speaker was an associate justice of the U.S. Supreme Court.

The cocktail hour was in full swing. Waiters carrying trays of crystal flutes filled with Moët circulated through the crowd. For those who preferred other beverages, well-stocked bars were strategically placed throughout the room.

"Nice party . . . for a bunch of lawyers," Paul said, smiling down at Megan.

She smiled back and lightly kicked him in the ankle. "Behave yourself or I'll make you wait in the car."

Paul put his arm around her. "I'll try. Say," he leaned down and whispered, "is it true they're serving Big Macs and fries?"

"Another crack like that, and I'll show you I can kick higher," Meg warned.

"Okay, I get the message," Paul said, taking a step back.

Megan sipped her champagne. She was wearing a tea-length, dark green silk dress with a deep V neck and green snakeskin heels. A black snakeskin bag hung from her right shoulder. An emerald-and-diamond pendant adorned her neck, and matching earrings glittered in her ears. Paul was wearing a tuxedo, and to Megan's eye he looked particularly handsome when he was all dressed up. He'll look just like that on our wedding day, she thought proudly.

They made their way around the perimeter of the room, stopping now and then to say a few words to people they knew. They had already checked out their table assignment and found they were seated with Reggie Stroheim and his wife, and Hal and Margie Washburn, a husband-and-wife team who practiced at one of the city's large law firms.

"Hello, Megan. Paul, how are you?" Michael Gillette came up behind them and clapped Paul on the back. His wife, Wanda, who was wearing a one-shouldered, clinging white sheath, was at his side.

"Hi, Mike. Nice to see you," Paul said, shaking Gillette's hand. "Wanda, you look lovely, as always," he said, kissing her on the cheek.

"Thank you," Wanda smiled. "How are you, Megan? That's a beautiful dress."

"I'm fine, thanks," Megan replied. "You look smashing, too."

"I booked your wedding reception at the Yacht Club for next July seventh, as instructed." Gillette, who was also wearing a tux, sipped on his glass of Johnnie Walker Black. "I know Megan thought I'd forgotten to take care of it."

"I never said that," Megan protested.

"No, you just told me you'd appreciate a written confirmation from the club's social director. I can take a hint." Gillette laughed heartily.

"I see you've caught on to his ways, too," Wanda teased.

Megan laughed. "I just wanted to be sure they didn't give the room to someone else. This is the only wedding I ever plan to have, and I'd like things to go smoothly."

"I'm glad you decided to have the big doings there," Gillette went on. "They handled my brother's reception last spring, and they really do a bang-up job."

"You'll want to meet with Gloria Stanhope," Wanda said. "She handles all their decorating. She'll be able to give you some wonderful ideas."

Megan nodded. "Thanks for the tip. I'll give her a call real soon."

Gillette waved to someone across the room. "The Wilshires are here," he said to Wanda. "We'd better go say hello. Ted referred a rather large products case to me recently, and I'd like to thank him. We'll see you two later," he said to Paul and Megan as he moved away.

"If you need an extra hand in planning your reception, just holler," Wanda said. "I'd be happy to help."

"Thanks. I just might take you up on that," Megan replied.

As the Gillettes made their way across the room, Judge Edwards and his wife, a very slender, blond woman in her mid thirties, attired in a filmy blue, floor-length Ungaro gown, took their place next to Paul and Megan.

"Hello, Megan," the judge said cordially. "Have you met my wife, Julia?"

"I don't believe I have," Megan replied. "Nice to meet you, Mrs. Edwards," she said, shaking Julia's hand. She turned to Paul. "Judge Edwards, this is my fiancé, Paul Finley."

"Pleased to meet you, Judge. Mrs. Edwards," Paul said, shaking hands with both of them.

"I see you're on the program tonight," Megan said to the judge.

The judge ran a hand through his straight blond hair. "Yes, I have the honor of introducing the person who introduces the master of ceremonies, who introduces everyone else. A bit too much pomp and circumstance to suit me," he chuckled. "I've always thought the featured speaker should just get up and start speaking. After all, everyone already knows who he is."

Julia Edwards put a hand on his arm. Her pale hair was pulled back into a chignon. Large diamonds glittered at her neck and in her ears. "Now, Alex, you know you've always loved pageantry." She leaned closer to Megan and Paul and said confidentially, "When we were in London, he insisted on going to see the changing of the guard three times. He would have gone every day, but I finally put a stop to it. I think he secretly wishes that judges here got to wear those silly white wigs like they do in England."

"Julia, really!" the judge said, feigning shock. "Must you reveal all my innermost secrets?" Everyone laughed.

"I'm glad they have such a good turnout," Megan commented, looking around the room.

"So am I," Julia agreed. "It's such a good cause."

Megan and Paul had finished their champagne and deposited their glasses on a passing waiter's empty tray.

"I hope you're not discussing our mutual case," a deep voice behind them said. Megan turned slightly and saw Frank Parks walking toward them with a statuesque blonde in tow.

"I assure you there have been no *ex parte* communications," Judge Edwards said jovially. "Frank Parks, this is my wife, Julia."

"Hello," Frank said, shaking hands with the judge and his wife. "Judge, Mrs. Edwards, this is Madeline Winters," he said, taking hold of the blonde's elbow. "Madeline, this is Megan Lansdorf. You may have heard me mention her. She's the attorney representing the plaintiffs in the AIDS case."

As Megan and Madeline exchanged greetings, Megan critically sized up the woman. She was a knockout. There was no other way to describe her. She was wearing a knee-length, red, beaded dress that clung to her curvaceous figure as though she'd been sewn into it. The dress had a plunging neckline that revealed the tops of her large rounded breasts. She carried a small jewel-encrusted Judith Leiber bag. Her red satin heels perfectly matched the color of her dress.

Megan could feel Paul ogling the new arrival and remembered she hadn't yet introduced him. "Paul, this is Frank Parks," she said hastily. "Frank, my fiancé, Dr. Paul Finley." While Megan had not bothered mentioning Paul's title to the judge, she took special pains to emphasize it now.

Paul and Frank shook hands and exchanged greetings. Then Paul turned to Madeline and extended his hand. "It's very nice to meet you," he said, smiling at her. Madeline smiled back, showing off a mouth full of perfect white teeth.

Stop drooling, Megan silently ordered, glancing up at Paul and frowning slightly. As Paul finally relinquished his grip on Madeline's hand, she continued to look at him, batting her eyes and smiling. Then she nibbled on her lower lip. It was apparent she was used to having men make fools of themselves over her. The sad thing was that Paul was buying into her act. Men were such chumps, Megan thought with disgust.

As the judge and Frank fell into relaxed conversation, Megan surveyed the group with a detached eye. The three men were all tall and handsome in their formal wear. Judge Edwards, golden haired and muscular like a Greek statue; Paul, darker and leaner, with an athlete's body; and Frank, darker still, with a mysterious, brooding quality about him. Julia Edwards was regal and serene, like a young Grace Kelly. Madeline was hot and sultry, like a brainy Marilyn Monroe. And I look like somebody's kid sister, Megan thought, her mood suddenly darkening.

"I imagine I should start making my way toward the head table so I can go over my remarks," the judge said. "I'd hate to embarrass myself by mispronouncing someone's name. See you all later." He took his wife's arm and steered her toward the front of the room.

"It's good to finally meet you," Paul said, turning to Frank. "I've heard a lot about you."

"If it came from Megan, the description probably wasn't too flattering." Frank laughed.

"Oh, I'd say you pretty much live up to your advance billing," Paul replied.

"Megan mentioned you were a doctor," Frank responded. "Somehow I pictured you as being older."

"Really?" Paul retorted. "I envisioned you as being younger."

What's going on here? Megan wondered, glancing from Paul to Frank and back again. The two of them were obviously not hitting it off. While she had complained long and hard to Paul about Frank's conduct in the AIDS case, Paul's normal response was to pooh-pooh her remarks and say that she must be exaggerating because *nobody* could be that bad. And in public, Paul was usually courteous to a fault, no matter how much he privately disliked someone. Megan enjoyed witty repartee, but this exchange was getting nasty.

"What do you do, Madeline?" Megan asked, trying to defuse whatever was going on between the men.

Madeline tossed her head and shook back her thick mane of blond hair. "I'm in advertising," she said in a husky voice.

"That must be interesting," Megan said gamely.

"I think so," Madeline answered, smiling down at Megan solicitously. "It's a very creative field. There's always something new. Personally, I've always thought that law would be rather dull."

"That's funny, I've often thought the same thing," Paul chimed in.

Who the hell asked you? Megan thought, frowning. "I guess any career is what you care to make of it," she said lightly.

Madeline pursed her lips. "I suppose so." She seductively ran her hand up and down Frank's arm. "I will admit that Frank does make some of his cases sound exciting." Frank smiled at her.

Exciting? Megan thought. Oh, God. They probably discussed his cases while they were in bed. She could see it now. "Oh, Frank, tell me again how you utterly destroyed the doctor's credibility at the deposition. Oh, that's so wonderful! Oh, yes! Harder! Oh, yes! Oh! Oh!"

As Megan came back to reality, Madeline was asking Paul what his area of specialty was. "Plastic surgery," Paul answered. Seeing a slight smirk on Madeline's face, he quickly added, "I specialize in reconstruction of accident victims. I'm not the kind of doctor who tries to rejuvenate society women's sagging bodies. Not that you'll ever need to know anything about that type of practice," he added, grinning at her boyishly. Madeline rewarded him with another big smile.

"And if you botch one of your surgeries, how convenient it will be for you to have a lawyer in the house," Frank said. "Although Megan's firm isn't generally known for handling defense matters."

Before Paul could retort, Madeline spoke up. "I'd love another drink," she said, looking directly at Paul.

"I'd be happy to get you one," Paul said, a bit too eagerly for Megan's comfort. "What would you like?"

"Oh, I'm not sure," Madeline said, fidgeting with her evening bag. "Maybe I'd better come with you while I decide."

"All right," Paul said happily. "Would you two like something?"

"Yes. Glenfiddich on the rocks," Megan said tersely.

"Make that two," Frank added.

Megan and Frank watched their partners edging their way toward the nearest bar, Madeline walking a bit closer to Paul than was necessary. "That's quite a dress your friend is wearing," Megan said, keeping her eyes on Madeline's softly swaying derriere.

"Mmm, yes, isn't it though?" Frank agreed.

"In fact," Megan continued, still keeping her gaze fixed on Madeline, "as Dorothy Parker might have said, 'She's positively scrofulous with beading.' "

There was a moment of silence. Megan slowly turned and innocently looked up at Frank. There was a slightly shocked expression on his face, then he burst out laughing—a deep hearty laugh. Megan allowed herself a slight smile. Maybe the guy wasn't entirely a stuffed shirt after all.

Paul and Madeline returned with the drinks. As Megan and Frank took theirs, Frank raised his glass to Megan, said, "Cheers," and winked at her. She smiled back.

People were slowly being seated. "We should probably find our table," Frank said. "Do you know where you're sitting?"

"Yes, we're at table fifteen, over on that side," Paul said, motioning.

"We're at table thirty-two," Frank said. "I think it's the other way." He turned to Madeline. "Are you ready?"

"Of course," she replied. "It was *very* nice meeting you," she said to Paul.

"Same here," Paul responded.

"Enjoy your dinner," Frank said to Megan.

"You, too," Megan replied.

The two couples drifted off toward their tables. "I see now why you can't stand that SOB," Paul said when they were out of earshot. "What a jerk he is."

"I thought he was being very polite tonight," Megan retorted. "But his friend is certainly the original ice queen."

"What do you mean?" Paul said, surprised. "She was delightful."

Megan snorted. "If you like that type."

"What's that supposed to mean?"

Megan turned to face him, her eyes flashing. "I mean if you happen to like big-breasted, airheaded blondes who probably slept their way into whatever job they have. I just never thought you went for that sort."

"What are you talking about?" Paul flushed slightly.

"Oh, never mind," Megan grumbled. "Let's just forget it."

They found their seats. Paul quickly slipped into an animated conversation with Reggie Stroheim, and Megan managed to make small talk with Margie Washburn. As the waiters began to distribute the hearts of palm salads, she discreetly turned around and looked across the room. She could see Frank and Madeline's backs. Frank had his arm around Madeline's chair, and their heads were close together, as though they were sharing some secret. I wonder if they're talking about us, Megan thought sullenly. She didn't know why that prospect should bother her, but it did.

Megan's thoughts were interrupted by the ringing of

a knife against a crystal goblet at the head table. She
turned back. The Seventh Circuit Bar Association's
president was on his feet, calling for silence. "Good
evening, ladies and gentlemen. On behalf of the Ronald McDonald Foundation, we'd like to welcome you
all here tonight. Before we partake of the delicious dinner that has been prepared for us, Father William
Gillespie of the First Episcopal Church will say grace."

Father Gillespie stood up. "Let us bow our heads
and give thanks . . ."

Megan bowed her head, but was lost in her own
thoughts and paid no attention to the minister's words.
What the hell went wrong tonight? Why had Paul and
Frank been circling each other like a couple of young
rams trying to stake out their territory? Why had Paul
acted like a lovesick puppy around Madeline? And
why had she herself blown up at Paul?

She sighed. She'd been putting in awfully long
hours lately. She must just be overtired. In five months
the AIDS trial would be over and she'd be a partner.
Then things could get back to normal, and she and
Paul could devote some time to planning their future.
Until then, they'd just have to try to tread water, and
Paul would have to make some allowances for her. After all, he knew she was under a lot of strain. She
slipped her right hand into his lap, found his hand and
squeezed it. He squeezed back. She smiled. She was
forgiven. Things were going to be all right.

CHAPTER 16

Mike O'Riley whistled as he sat at his desk, sorting through papers. He skimmed some reports he'd just received from the FBI, detailing their most recent unsolved crimes. Predictably seeing none that even remotely matched the MO of the killer they were hunting, he added them to a pile of like reports. Next he flipped through a lengthy article that Dr. Sheridan had copied from a psychiatric journal containing a prototype psychological profile of a serial killer. Worthless, as usual, O'Riley muttered, stashing it in a brown expandable folder that contained all the materials received from the team's experts. Then he began to scrutinize summaries of a couple more interviews Greg Jablonski had conducted of Mary Collins's acquaintances and fellow church members.

As he read, O'Riley began humming "If I Were a Rich Man" softly under his breath. His indigestion had gone away, and his spirits were higher than they had been in months. The reason for the abrupt change in his mood was the fact that two weeks had now passed since he'd had the premonition that another murder was imminent. With each passing day, the dark cloud that had been hanging over him had started to lift little by little until today he felt almost giddy.

Maybe he'd been wrong. Maybe there never would be another killing. O'Riley fervently hoped that was the case. And though he still wanted to find the man responsible for the four women's deaths, he'd be willing to forgo that achievement as long as no one else was killed.

Every day that went by made that outcome seem

more and more possible. The first murder had been in mid-February, Julie Santini in March, the unidentified girl in early April, and Mary later that month. O'Riley knew that once they got a taste for blood, serial killers would usually claim their victims at increasingly short intervals. It was now the first week in August, so their man should have struck again by now. There were several possible reasons why he hadn't. Maybe he'd gotten his psychosis under control. Or maybe he was smart enough to know the police would be likely to catch him if he killed again. Maybe he was in jail or institutionalized. Maybe he was dead. Hell, maybe he found religion and became a practicing Buddhist. O'Riley didn't give a damn which of these alternatives applied. As long as there were no more murders, he was a happy camper.

In the past week he'd allowed himself to daydream about his retirement. Just a bit. He didn't want to get his hopes up too high. Well actually, a couple of times he had gone so far as to pick up the phone to call the mayor and hand in his resignation, but then he'd pulled back. He didn't want to rush things. He'd give it another month. But he'd already made up his mind. The day after Labor Day he was all through. If they weren't any closer to finding the murderer, and there hadn't been any more slayings by then, he was gonna hang it up.

Retirement. The word brought a smile to his lips. He'd managed to stash away a couple grand out of his overtime pay. The weather was still usually pretty nice in September and October. He might just have enough time to build that deck in back of the house before winter set in. There were so many things to look forward to. Being able to spend time with the grandkids. Being able to help Anne around the house. Not having a chill run through him every time the phone rang, wondering what sort of murder scene he'd be dispatched to this time.

O'Riley rolled up the sleeves of his blue-and-white-striped shirt and lit a cigarette. Maybe he'd go to one of those classes where they taught you how to quit smoking. Or maybe he'd ask his doctor about getting a prescription for those nicotine patches. He had managed to cut back a bit in the last week. He'd been up to over two packs a day. Now he was back down to a pack and a half. He'd really like to quit, but there was no point trying while he was still part of this cuckoo's nest. If he hadn't had his smokes to pacify him, *he* probably would've murdered somebody by now. He didn't want off the case quite that badly.

As he went back to looking over Jablonski's notes, he unconsciously began to sing in a low voice. "Tonight, tonight won't be just any night . . ." He was so wrapped up in his own thoughts that he didn't notice the young detective standing in the doorway.

"Let me give you some free advice, Mike," Jablonski said with a laugh. "Don't give up your day job."

O'Riley looked up with a start. "Didn't your mother ever tell you it's not nice to sneak up on old people?"

"You're not old," Jablonski said, crossing the room and taking a seat in the vinyl chair in front of O'Riley's desk. "You're just well seasoned. But I am curious. To what do we owe your unusually mellow mood?"

O'Riley stubbed out his cigarette. "What's the matter, isn't a man entitled to make a few happy sounds once in a while without his colleagues feeling the need to psychoanalyze him? I think you've been hangin' around those shrinks too long."

Jablonski shrugged. "I didn't mean any offense. I've just never seen you this laid back before."

O'Riley leaned back in his chair, causing the ancient springs to squeak. "Up till now we've been too busy for you to get to know the real me. I'm a laid-back kind of guy." Ignoring Jablonski's smirk, he said, "As to the reason for my particularly fine mood today, well for starters, the damn heat wave finally broke and I don't feel like I'm living in a steam bath twenty-four hours a day. And secondly, my wife is meeting me here in about twenty minutes and I'm taking her to lunch. It may not sound like anything special to you, but in my book both of those events are cause for celebration."

Jablonski nodded. "I've been giving thanks for the cooler weather, too," he said, running his hand through his blond hair. "Carol's been just miserable. She couldn't sleep, and her feet swelled up so bad that she's had to wear tennis shoes to work for the last month. If it hadn't cooled off, I think we might've ended up in divorce court before she had the baby."

"I warned you, kid," O'Riley said with a grin. "Women turn into total strangers when they're pregnant. You never know what they're gonna do next. How much longer has she got to go?"

"About six weeks," Jablonski said, yawning. "Then we'll be able to get back to normal." He crossed his legs and smoothed out the crease in his dark gray slacks.

"Normal!" O'Riley guffawed. "Boy, have you got a lot to learn. You better rest up while you can, both of you. Believe me, the fun is just about to start."

"Aw, you're just trying to scare me," Jablonski said, waving his hand in a gesture of dismissal. "Having a baby can't be all that bad. Hell, look at you. Don't tell me you would've had four of 'em if it'd been that awful."

"In case it hasn't occurred to you," O'Riley shot back, "in my day birth control wasn't all that reliable, and of course, Anne being a strict Catholic didn't exactly help the cause any."

Jablonski laughed. "Okay, now you've got my curiosity up. How many of the four were mistakes?"

"That's not what I meant!" O'Riley sputtered. He lit up another cigarette. "Did you want something or did you just wander in here to harass me?"

Jablonski crossed his arms. "I wanted to let you know that we got a couple calls on the hotline that sound like they're worth following up. One was from a guy who says he was driving in the area near St. Michael's on the night Mary Collins was killed and thought he saw a man dressed in dark clothing running south."

"Where the hell has he been all this time?" O'Riley said. "On the moon?"

Jablonski sighed patiently. "No. He doesn't live in the city. He's from northern Wisconsin and only comes down here every few months to visit an elderly relative. He headed north the morning Mary's body was found and just got back to Chicago two days ago. He said he'd read about the murder, but wasn't aware where it took place till now. He sounds legit."

O'Riley grunted. "Who's the other one?"

"A woman who said her dog was rooting around on the riverbank last week and found part of a hymnal, the kind the choir at St. Michael's uses. You know we wondered what happened to Mary's belongings. It's possible the killer tossed them in the river to make it harder for us to identify her. I know both of these are long shots as far as helping figure out who did it, but I'm gonna check it out."

O'Riley's stomach churned a bit as it suddenly hit him how much he'd been counting on there not being any more leads. "Sure, follow up on 'em," he said quickly, taking a long drag on his cigarette. "I doubt they'll amount to much, but you never know."

"One of these days, when we least expect it, this thing is gonna break wide open," Jablonski predicted confidently. "Mark my words."

O'Riley exhaled and began to cough. "I don't know, kid. I sure as hell wouldn't bet the farm on it."

"Do the two of you have so little to keep you occupied these days that you've taken up gambling?" Anne O'Riley chided from the doorway. She looked cool and fresh in a short-sleeved, mint-green, cotton dress.

"There's my sweetheart," O'Riley said jovially, grinding out his cigarette. "Right on time."

"Hello, Greg," Anne said, walking over to Jablonski's chair and extending her hand. "It's nice to see you. How's Carol?"

"She's hanging in there," Jablonski replied, giving Anne's hand a warm squeeze. "In fact, before you got here, Mike was just giving me some tips on how I can help her make it through the delivery."

"Well, you forget everything he told you," Anne said with a laugh, "and you and Carol will do just fine."

"Wait just a minute," O'Riley protested, getting to his feet. "Are you implying that I was of no use in helping you get through labor?"

"Let me put it this way, dear," Anne said, taking her husband's arm, "the most useful thing you did for me each time was to sit out the vigil at Rob Clancy's bar." She leaned toward Jablonski and said confidentially, "For someone who makes a living looking at lots of blood, he's always been awfully squeamish when it comes to childbirth." Before O'Riley could lodge a protest, Anne pulled him toward the door saying, "But I love you just the same. Now let's go. I'm starving."

"Have a nice lunch," Jablonski said, trying unsuccessfully not to laugh.

As they got into the car, O'Riley looked at Anne lovingly. *I know I've put you through a lot over the years*, he told her silently. *But I promise things are going to be different real soon.* As he started the car and headed toward the restaurant, he reached over and squeezed her hand. She smiled at him in reply.

Just hang on a few more weeks, sweetheart, he thought. *This whole damn mess will be over before we know it.*

PART TWO

CHAPTER 17

Megan was seated at a large table in a sparsely furnished conference room at Johns Hopkins medical complex in Bethesda, Maryland, and her head was pounding. It was a hot Thursday morning in mid-August. Ron Johnson was in his second day of questioning Dr. Jay Gillian, Chicago Memorial's expert witness. Dr. Gillian, a fifty-something bioethicist, was a graduate of Cornell Medical School and had completed a residency in internal medicine. The doctor was short and squat with salt-and-pepper hair, an oversized nose, and wide-set blue eyes.

As Megan surreptitiously reached under the table and felt for her white leather bag, she inadvertently caught Dr. Lenz's eye. He was seated across the table, next to Parks, taking copious notes. He gave her an icy stare, and she quickly dropped her glance. Bastard! she cursed to herself. She had not forgiven him for trying to intimidate Claudia Hartley. Finding her bag at last, she unzipped it and groped around inside until her hand closed over a bottle of Extra-Strength Tylenol. Bringing the bottle up into her lap, she unscrewed the cap and shook out three tablets. She quickly popped them into her mouth one by one, and washed them down with big gulps of water from a glass in front of her.

As she was downing the last tablet, she tipped the glass up too far, spilling water down the front of her red-and-white silk dress. Damn it! she thought, dabbing at the spot with her hand. It would probably leave a stain. She deftly replaced the bottle's cap, and dropped it back into her bag. Hoping that the pain reliever would kick in fast, she tried to turn her attention back to the proceedings going on around her. With all the squabbling that had taken place in the last two days, it was no wonder her head hurt.

"So, Doctor, are you saying that the particular symptoms Dr. Morris exhibited at the time of his annual examination should not have been a cause for concern?" Ron asked.

"Object to the form of the question," Frank cut in. "Please identify which symptoms you are referring to and clarify what you mean by 'cause for concern.' "

"All right," Ron said patiently. "Let me try it again."

Megan lightly rubbed her index fingers over her temples. This was turning out to be the deposition from hell. Parks was in rare form, objecting right and left. So much for Megan's hope that he might be getting more reasonable. She was glad she had insisted that Ron take the deposition. He was handling Parks's theatrics very well. She would have probably thrown a pitcher of water at him by now. She leaned back in her chair and flexed her shoulder muscles. At least the continuation of Dr. Leibowitz's deposition on Monday and Tuesday at NIH had gone very smoothly. In fact, it had gone so well, that Megan had come away feeling much more upbeat about the case.

Dr. Leibowitz was an old hand, both at giving depositions and at defending novel medical theories. Parks had spent two days trying to shake the doctor's opinions, but he couldn't be budged.

"Isn't it true that a person could have all the symptoms Dr. Morris exhibited and still be suffering only from a very minor ailment?" Parks had asked.

"Ya, that is possible," Dr. Leibowitz had answered patiently in his richly accented voice, "but that is not the point here."

"And what, in your opinion, is the point?" Parks had inquired.

"The point is that the hospital should haf done follow-up tests to find out what was wrong with Dr. Morris. It is true that less serious ailments cause the same kind of symptoms, and follow-up tests vould haf shown that. The problem is that no tests were run, and if they had been, then I think it vould haf been apparent that Dr. Morris was suffering from AIDS."

Dr. Lenz had sat in on the deposition, too, and had frequently passed Parks bits of paper on which he had jotted down new avenues of questioning. But even with Lenz's assistance, Parks had been unable to sway Dr. Leibowitz from his conclusions. Megan suspected that his inability to make any points with her doctor had contributed substantially to Parks's display of ill humor during Ron's questioning of Parks's own expert.

"Dr. Gillian, you are aware that at the time of his medical exam four years ago, Dr. Morris was suffering from swollen glands, oral thrush, and a low-grade fever, are you not?" Ron asked.

"Yes."

"If a patient came to you exhibiting those symptoms, what would you suggest? Would you prescribe some medication or order further tests?"

"Objection," Parks said. "Compound question."

Ron sighed. "What would you suggest for a patient with those symptoms?"

"I would probably prescribe a course of antibiotics."

"Let's say the patient takes the antibiotics for the prescribed period with no improvement. Then what would you do?"

"Objection," Parks said again.

"What, *if anything*, would you do?" Ron quickly corrected himself.

"It would depend on the history of the particular patient," Dr. Gillian said, unbuttoning his brown linen sports coat. "In some circumstances I might tell him to come back in a few weeks to see if the symptoms improved. In other cases, I might order further tests."

"So you agree that in some cases it would be appropriate to order more tests?"

"It's possible," Dr. Gillian said grudgingly. "As I said, the proper handling of these matters will necessarily vary from case to case."

"Excuse me," Frank interrupted. "I need to make

some phone calls. Perhaps this would be a good time
to take a ten-minute break."

Frank and Drs. Lenz and Gillian left the conference
room at once. The court reporter stood up and poured
herself a glass of water. Ron got up, walked over to a
window, and stretched. Megan rubbed the back of her
neck.

"You don't feel good, do you?" Ron asked sympathetically.

Megan shook her head. "Do I look that bad?"

"You look uncomfortable," he replied, tugging on
the diamond stud he wore in his left ear.

"It feels like somebody rammed an ax between my
eyes." She took a sip of water.

"It's no wonder you have eyestrain, after all the
hours we've spent going through the hospital's staff
files. We'll probably both end up needing bifocals. Personally, I was thinking of putting in for combat pay."

Megan squeezed her eyes tightly shut. To her surprise, Parks had given them access to the files soon after the hearing with Judge Edwards. Megan and Ron
had spent countless hours plowing through them, so far
to no avail. "Yeah, and to think that we haven't come
up with one useful piece of information. I can't believe
the hospital would have fought so hard to keep us from
getting access to the documents if there was nothing
there."

"Maybe they were just trying to throw us off the
track," Ron suggested.

"Maybe." Megan opened her eyes. "God, I feel
lousy. I'm so grateful you're handling this deposition."

"You shouldn't be," Ron snorted. "I'm doing a
shitty job." He removed his navy blue suit jacket and
tossed it over an unused chair. Then he straightened his
red-and-white tie flecked with small blue stars. "I'm
getting absolutely nowhere."

"You're doing fine," Megan said encouragingly. "In
fact, you're doing great, under the circumstances."

"You *must* be sick, if you really believe that," Ron
sighed. "I don't know why Parks won't let the guy answer a few questions now and then without making an

objection every damn time. At this rate we won't finish till next week."

"Oh, that reminds me," Megan said, pushing back the brown swivel chair and getting to her feet. "I'd better call Paul and tell him I probably won't make it back for his birthday party tomorrow night." They had made plans to celebrate Paul's thirty-sixth birthday by joining a group of friends for dinner and maybe some bar hopping afterward.

"I told you I can handle things here," Ron said, as he returned to his place at the table. "There's no reason for both of us to hang around, and I'm sure Paul would appreciate your help blowing out all those candles. How old did you say he is? Forty-two?"

"Thirty-six," Megan said reproachfully. "But I don't want to stick you with weekend duty. This is my case, remember?"

"It's my case and I'll cry if I want to, cry if I want to, cry if I want to. You would cry too if it happened to you," Ron sang.

"Shut up," Megan said as good-naturedly as possible given the throbbing in her head. "I'm in too much pain to laugh." She walked over to a nearby credenza and picked up the phone. In a few moments she'd reached the nurse at the appointment desk of Paul's group.

"Hi, Phyllis. This is Megan Lansdorf. Would Paul be free by any chance?"

"You're in luck, Ms. Lansdorf," the nurse replied cordially. "He's between patients. Hold on just a minute and I'll get him."

"Hi, kid, how are you doing?" Paul said brightly when he came on the phone.

"Not so good," Megan lamented, rubbing the bridge of her nose with her index finger. "It's going even worse than yesterday, if that's possible, and to top things off, I have a terrible headache."

"That's too bad," Paul said sympathetically. "Maybe tomorrow will be better."

"That's why I'm calling," Megan said, switching the phone to her other ear. "I'm not sure we're going to get everything finished tomorrow. After we're done

with the deposition, there are some documents we want
to look through at NIH, so I might have to stay over
till Saturday."

"Oh," Paul said. There was a slight pause. "Well,
that's okay. If you have to stay, I understand."

"But it means I might miss your party," Megan reminded him.

"I know," Paul said reasonably. "Don't worry about
it. Birthdays are no big deal anymore. If you don't get
back, I'll just make it an early night and then you and
I can have a private celebration next week."

"I'm glad you're so understanding," Megan said. "I
really want to be there, but right now it doesn't look
very promising."

"Let me know if your plans change," Paul said.

"I will. I'll call you tomorrow."

"Good luck. And I hope you feel better," Paul said.

"Thanks. Talk to you tomorrow."

"I love you, Meg. 'Bye."

" 'Bye." Megan hung up the phone.

"Was the birthday boy terribly disappointed you
might miss the big shindig?" Ron asked.

Megan ignored the note of sarcasm in Ron's voice
and shook her head. "No, he's always real good about
scheduling conflicts. He says that's just the price we
have to pay for both of us having demanding careers."

"How very big of him," Ron said. Before Megan
had a chance to retort, he quickly added, "Career demands have screwed up lots of good relationships for
me. Take Margery, for instance. She didn't like it that
I had to cancel out on going to the Florentine Opera after she'd dropped a bundle for tickets, so we decided it
was time to start seeing other people."

"Strange girl," Megan murmured. "So are you seeing anyone now?"

"Oh, sure. Her name's Susan. She's a friend of
Margery's. Say, I'm gonna go down the hall to the
soda machine. Do you want something?"

"Yeah. Would you bring me a Diet Pepsi? Maybe
the caffeine will help my head."

"Sure thing. Be right back." He walked briskly out the door.

The court reporter had left the room. Megan walked back to her chair and sat down. Her head was still throbbing. She leaned back and closed her eyes. Maybe she'd feel better after a few minutes of quiet meditation. And if that didn't work, she'd just have to take some more drugs.

Frank Parks was seated in a vacant office adjacent to Dr. Gillian's. Dr. Lenz was next-door giving Dr. Gillian pointers on how to handle troublesome deposition questions, and Frank was completing his phone calls. He traveled a lot, and Lucille, his secretary, was well trained in knowing which messages were important enough to be passed on immediately and which could wait until he was back in the office.

She'd had some good news to report today. Frank had won an appeal in a case in which a stockbroker had sued his former employer for wrongful discharge. Frank had represented the firm, and the win had saved them several million dollars. Not bad for a day's work. Frank would be able to pad his bill a bit, something he did only when he'd been able to achieve a particularly favorable result. He routinely cut bills when he felt he hadn't been able to accomplish much for the client. He instructed Lucille to have a younger partner who'd been working on the case convey the good news.

"Any other messages?" Frank asked.

"Just one," Lucille replied. "Ms. Winters asked that you call her as soon as possible."

"Oh?" Madeline had his number at the hotel, and he'd talked to her the night before. He wondered what could be so urgent. "She didn't say what she wanted?"

"No, sir. Just that I should tell you to call her."

"All right. Thanks, Lucille. If there are any emergencies, you know how to reach me. Otherwise, I'll talk to you in the morning."

Frank pushed the reset button on the phone and dialed Madeline's office, punching in his Illinois Bell Calling Card number at the tone.

"Hi. What's up?" he asked when she came on the line.

"I'm sorry to bother you there, Frank," Madeline said in her throaty voice, "but Clay Parrish said he just got two cancellations for his deep-sea fishing charter and he wondered if we'd like to fill in."

"When is it?" Frank asked.

"Next weekend. We'd leave Friday night and come back Sunday afternoon. It sounds fabulous. A fifty-foot yacht. Our own chef. Who knows, I might even be persuaded to try my hand at fishing." She laughed.

"Well . . ." Frank hesitated. He'd promised Jack they could go to a Cubs game next weekend, but since his discussion with Madeline a few weeks earlier, he'd been trying to spend more time alone with her and to include her in more activities with the kids. He'd been working awfully hard lately. A weekend on Lake Michigan sounded very relaxing. Dammit, he deserved to do what he wanted once in a while.

"I have to let him know today," Madeline went on. "Oh, please say you can go."

"All right," Frank said. "If you really want to, we'll go." There would be lots more Cubs home games before the end of the season. Jack would understand.

"That's great!" Madeline said exuberantly. "You are a darling."

"Yeah? Well, you're not too bad yourself."

"You say the nicest things," Madeline said seductively.

"I'd really like to continue this conversation, but unfortunately I have work to do here," Frank said. "Maybe we can pick it up again when I get back."

"When will that be?"

"Tomorrow night. I'm not sure what time. It might be late. I'll call you from the airport."

"I'll be waiting," Madeline purred. "How does caviar, chilled champagne, and cool satin sheets sound?"

"Deliciously decadent. See you then."

" 'Bye."

Frank was tingling as he hung up the phone. He sometimes wondered if Madeline fully realized the effect she had on him. Probably. She was a very smart woman, besides being the most luscious thing he'd ever gotten his hands on.

Frank glanced at his watch. His ten-minute break had stretched into twenty. The others would be waiting for him. Good. Let 'em wait. He knew the hospital had come out the loser at Dr. Leibowitz's deposition, and it was quickly becoming apparent that the case was going to be tougher to win than he'd originally thought. But Dr. Gillian was his expert, and he was going to make Megan and Ron earn any concessions they might be able to pry out of him. He got up, straightened his tie, and walked briskly back to the conference room.

CHAPTER 18

"What a week," Megan murmured, leaning back in the plush leather seat on Midwest Express flight 1093 from Washington's National Airport to Chicago's Midway. It was eleven P.M., and as she glanced out the window, Megan could see the lights of the greater District of Columbia metropolitan area fading behind them.

"It's been quite a marathon," Ron Johnson agreed, settling into the adjacent seat. "I'm glad it's over."

"You're a doll for helping me speed through those documents," Megan said. "I thought for sure we'd be at it all day tomorrow."

"As long as we finished Dr. Gillian's deposition early—or should I say we abandoned it as a lost cause after Parks set a new world record for the number of objections—I figured we might as well try to wrap things up today and get the hell out of town," Ron replied. "I've seen enough of both NIH and Johns Hopkins to last me a while. Besides, I knew how anxious you were to get back to the birthday boy."

"In spite of the problems you had with Dr. Gillian, I still say Dr. Leibowitz put us out in front," Megan said encouragingly. Then she smiled and added, "It will be nice to get back to town a day early, even if I did miss the party."

"Does lover boy know you're coming in tonight?"

"No. I thought I'd surprise him."

Ron looked at his watch. "Let's see. If we're on time, I'd estimate that you should be crawling into bed with him around one-thirty. I hope he's appropriately grateful."

With the strain of the past week now behind her, Megan felt relaxed and more like her old self rather than the uptight harpy she seemed to become when Parks was around. Ron had never made any real effort to hide his dislike for Paul, but Megan could never get him to tell her why he felt that way. She was feeling mellow enough now to try one more time.

"You don't like Paul, do you?" she asked bluntly.

Ron turned and looked directly at her. "I've never said that," he answered obliquely.

"You don't really have to say it. It's pretty obvious you don't like him, and I just wondered why."

Ron looked uncomfortable about being pinned down, but he tried to answer honestly. "I guess I just don't think he's worthy of you."

Megan wrinkled her nose. "Don't be silly. He's a brilliant surgeon. He'll probably be head of his department in a few years. He makes four times as much money as you and I do. How can you say he's not worthy of me?"

"I wasn't using the term in a monetary sense," Ron explained. "I just don't think he deserves you."

"Why not?" Megan pressed.

Ron squirmed a little in his seat. "It's hard to explain. He's just always struck me as being a little too cocky. Whenever I talk to him, he's always bragging about the latest miracle surgery he's performed, or about how fast he ran five miles, or about some obscure Asian food store he just discovered where they sell eight kinds of imported dried mushrooms. I always feel like I'm on the receiving end of a self-aggrandizing lecture."

"He *does* perform miracles," Megan protested, "and he does know a great deal about a lot of different things. I don't think he brags."

"That's not all," Ron went on, warming to the topic. "Sometimes I think he treats you in a condescending way."

"What do you mean?"

"Well, for instance, I don't like the way he lectures you about eating junk food, or about driving an American car. Besides that, you know he hates lawyers. I swear if I hear him tell one more lawyer joke I'm going to choke him."

"I can't believe you're talking about my Paul," Megan said, looking at Ron in astonishment. "He's not like that at all. As far as not liking lawyers, can you really blame him? Do you realize that malpractice insurance for doctors has gone up about a thousand percent in the last ten years, mainly because of the huge verdicts plaintiffs' lawyers like us have been winning? I'd be hopping mad, too." Megan's face was flushed. "And I don't think he lectures me or acts condescending," she continued. "He's always been very sensitive about my career and my needs, and besides that, he's very thoughtful and very romantic. He's constantly sending me neat cards with love poems or writing verses and leaving them where I'll find them. You know, real mushy stuff that he either composes himself or copies from a book. So I'm having a hard time understanding where you're coming from."

"Look," Ron said, putting his hand up defensively, "I didn't want to get into this discussion. You're the one who insisted on pursuing it. The last thing in the world I want to do is make you mad. It's just"—he pursed his lips and searched for the right words.—"It's just that I love you like a sister and I can't stand the thought of you being compromised in any way. Am I making any sense?" he asked, looking down at her with warm, caring eyes.

Megan shook her head emphatically. "No, you're not," she answered. "And don't give me that bullshit about loving me like a sister. You are not capable of loving any woman like a sister. I don't even think you love your *sister* like a sister."

"All right. I admit it," Ron said. "It's just possible that I have to fight off some incestuous impulses about you now and then." He paused. "But seriously, Megan, I think you're wonderful and I think you're much too good for him, but then again what the hell do I know?" He raised his hands in a gesture of futility. "All I care about is that you're happy, and you obviously are, so you go right ahead and rush back to Chicago and forget everything I just said. I just hope he appreciates what he's got. 'Cuz believe me, having you slide into bed unexpectedly would be the nicest birthday present I could ever think of."

Megan smiled and nudged him in the side with her elbow. "No lewd comments, please. I appreciate your brotherly concern for my well-being, but there's no need to worry. I think I've made a very good choice."

"Good," Ron said, smiling down at her, glad the discussion was at an end. "So, did you get him a present? What's an appropriate gift these days for an up-and-coming, though aging, surgeon?"

"I got him a pair of gold cuff links. He's not big on jewelry, but he admired a pair that Reggie Stroheim was wearing a few months ago. I hope he likes them."

"Hey, anybody who didn't absolutely love whatever gift you picked out for him doesn't deserve to have you," Ron said sincerely. "So let me give you one last little piece of advice: If he isn't properly appreciative, ditch him."

Megan laughed. "I think that's a little drastic. If he doesn't like them, I'm sure Bailey, Banks & Biddle will exchange them." She activated the lever on the armrest to make her seat recline a bit.

"You look tired," Ron said.

"I'm beat," Megan admitted. "I didn't sleep very well last night."

"That's too bad," Ron said sympathetically. "Couldn't you get rid of your headache?"

"It wasn't that," Megan replied. She glanced up, wondering whether she should confide in him.

"Then what was it?" Ron prodded gently.

"Well . . ." Megan hesitated. "This is probably gonna sound silly, but I went out for a walk around ten o'clock, and on the way back, when I was a couple blocks from the hotel, I suddenly had this weird feeling that I was being followed."

"What?" Ron exclaimed. "Why didn't you tell me this before? What happened?"

"Nothing happened," Megan assured him. "Like I

said, I was walking along and all of a sudden my skin
started to prickle and I got this really creepy feeling that
someone was following me. I glanced back and there
wasn't a soul in sight. I was the only person on the
sidewalk, which in itself was a little unnerving. So then
I started walking faster, and pretty soon I ended up running full speed till I made it back to the hotel."

"What made you feel that you were being followed?"

"I'm not even sure anymore," she admitted. "I guess
I thought I heard something."

"You mean like footsteps?"

"No, it was more of a rustling sound, like the way
your pant legs rub together when you walk."

"And you're positive you didn't see anyone?"

Megan shook her head. "No. Well," she admitted,
"for a minute there, when I looked back, I thought I
saw shadows, but I'm sure now it was nothing. This
case just has me so stressed that I guess I started imagining things. Plus, I took so many pain pills yesterday
to try to get rid of my headache that I was feeling a little woozy. That's why I went out for a walk in the first
place. I thought the fresh air might do me good."

"What did you do when you got back to the hotel?"

"I went to my room and took a bath and watched TV
a while, but I was pretty keyed up all night."

"I'll bet you were. Why didn't you call me? I
would've come right down."

"I didn't want to bother you, and besides, I figured
you'd just laugh at my overactive imagination."

"I would never laugh at you," Ron said, giving her
a quick hug. "I wish you'd learn to lean on people a
little more. You don't have to take on all of life's problems alone."

"I know."

"It's no wonder the case has you stressed out.
You've been working yourself into the ground. But if
it's any consolation, I think you're doing an outstanding job. Much better than I could do."

"You'll get your chance in another year or so,"

Megan said. Ron was the next associate in line for partnership at the firm.

"I'll have a tough act to follow."

"Thanks," Megan patted his hand. "I appreciate the vote of confidence. And I do have a favor to ask you."

"Name it."

"Please don't tell Rita what I just told you about last night. She gets so upset every time she hears about any threat to women. This might just send her over the edge. She's been feeding my cat while I'm gone, and I wouldn't be surprised if she carries a baseball bat with her for protection when she leaves her apartment."

"I don't blame her for being concerned. I think I'd be a little paranoid if I were a woman living alone. And Megan," he added tactfully, "if you don't mind my saying so, it's not real smart to go walking around a city alone at night. There are a lot of weirdos wandering around."

"I appreciate your concern, but the odds are greater that I'll win thirty million in the Illinois lottery tomorrow night than they are that I'll be accosted by a weirdo."

"I admire your plucky attitude, but like that sergeant used to say on *Hill Street Blues,* 'Be careful out there.' "

"I know, I know," Megan assured him. "Now, if you don't mind," she said, putting her seat into the full reclining position, "I'm gonna try to take a nap. Wake me up when we get to Chicago."

"Will do."

They landed on schedule, and Ron and Megan shared a cab downtown. As the cab driver hefted Megan's brown Hartmann bag and briefcase out of the trunk in front of Paul's high rise, Megan said, "Maybe I'll see you later on today. I don't plan on coming in very early, but there are some things I'd like to take care of."

"I'll be there with bells on," Ron said, as he walked her to the door. "But don't hurry on my account. I'm sure you'll want to spend some time with the good doctor."

"I *will* see you later," she promised. "And thanks for being so much help on this trip. I don't know what I would've done without you." She reached up and kissed him on the cheek.

Ron rubbed his cheek. "Wow. I'm not gonna wash for a week." He grinned at her. "I was happy to be of some help. Good night and sweet dreams." He got back into the cab and waved as it pulled away from the curb.

Megan walked inside the building's spacious art deco lobby. "Hello, Mr. Godfrey," she greeted the night doorman.

" 'Evening, Miss Lansdorf," the roly-poly old gentleman responded. "You working late again?"

Megan nodded. "I've been out of town all week and missed Dr. Finley's birthday party tonight, but thought I'd put in a late appearance anyway."

"I'm sure he'll be happy to see you," Mr. Godfrey replied jovially. "Dr. Finley brought a group of people back here with him around nine, but I think they've all left by now."

"I'm sure they have," Megan said. "Dr. Finley is a fanatic about getting enough sleep." She walked over to the elevators and pressed the UP button. The doors opened immediately and she stepped inside. "Good night, Mr. Godfrey."

" 'Night, Miss Lansdorf," he replied.

In the half a minute it took for the elevator to reach Paul's floor, Megan realized just how bone-tired she was. It was going to feel heavenly to sleep in a familiar bed. And after the scare she'd had the night before, it was going to feel even better not to be sleeping alone.

When the elevator doors opened, she picked up her bags and walked down the hall. Upon reaching Paul's door, she set her baggage down again while she fumbled in her purse and pulled out her key ring. She slipped the key into the lock and turned it. Then, picking up her bags, she quietly pushed the door open and stepped inside.

It was close to one-thirty, and the lights were all off. Megan set her bags down next to the couch in the living room. She noticed three empty wine bottles on a table. Must've been quite a celebration. She was glad Paul had had a good time. She tiptoed toward the bedroom, intending to undress and slip into bed without waking him. The bedroom door was open, as usual. But as she stood in the doorway, she suddenly sensed that something was amiss.

A small sliver of moonlight peeped through the window opposite the bed. This, combined with the light from the digital clock on the nightstand, gave the room a murky illumination. She could see Paul curled up on his side of the bed, his face turned away from her. Megan took a step inside the room, then froze in horror. Paul wasn't alone. There was a woman in bed with him.

Feeling like a voyeur, Megan stared hard at the two figures in front of her. The woman was lying on her side, one arm touching Paul's back. In the dim light, Megan could see her long blond hair fanned out across the pillows. Just then the woman stirred slightly and rolled onto her back. Oh, God! Megan thought. It's Paul's chief surgical nurse, Rhonda Benet.

For one long moment, Megan was riveted to the spot, illogical thoughts running through her head. Rhonda has much bigger breasts than me, she thought. Paul always claimed he wasn't a breast man, but I guess he must've just been saying that to make me feel good. My body probably revolted him. Looking at Rhonda, I can see I'd never be able to satisfy him. I drove him to this.

Megan's stomach began churning. I have to get out of here or I'll throw up, she thought, panicking. She wheeled around and ran back to the living room. In her haste, she stubbed her toe on the couch and cried out involuntarily. She immediately heard sounds of stirring from the bedroom.

"What's going on? Who's there?" she heard Paul ask sleepily.

Struggling to control her breathing, Megan picked

up her bags and ran toward the door. She hurriedly let herself out and sprinted down the hall to the elevators where she frantically pushed the DOWN button over and over. Come on, come on, she silently urged. She heard a door open behind her but willed herself not to look back.

"Megan!" She heard Paul's voice but tried to ignore it, still leaning on the DOWN button.

"Megan!" Her self-control faded and she turned. Paul, who had pulled on a pair of red jockey shorts, was racing toward her. It was like a scene out of a bedroom farce: A well-respected young doctor running down the hall of an exclusive high rise in his underwear trying to persuade his lady friend that things weren't as bad as they looked. Too bad there was no director to yell "cut and print."

The elevator doors finally opened at the same moment that Paul reached Megan's side. She rushed inside, dropped her bags on the floor and simultaneously punched the buttons for GROUND FLOOR and DOOR CLOSE.

"Megan, wait!" Paul put his hand on the door to prevent it from shutting. His hair was disheveled, and it looked like there were scratches on his chest. Rhonda must be a wild one, Megan thought.

"Let me go!" she hissed.

"I can explain!"

"No, you can't!" Megan said, her eyes flashing. "Now let go of the door." She slapped his hand.

"Meg, please. Listen to me. I had too much to drink . . ."

"Stop it!" she cut him off. "I don't want to hear your explanations. There *is* no explanation for what you did. Now get your lousy hands off the door. I want to go home!"

"Meg, I'm sorry," he started again, his eyes pleading.

"I mean it!" Megan said in a louder voice. "Let go of the door or I'll scream and wake up all your neighbors and you can explain it to them!"

Seeing that her face was contorted with rage, Paul

let go of the door and stepped back. "I'll call you in the morning," he mumbled as the doors closed in front of him.

As the elevator descended, Megan fought to remain calm. Her heart was pounding, and she felt faint. She took several deep breaths. When she reached the lobby, she rushed past a startled Mr. Godfrey, murmuring something about not feeling well.

She raced out into the warm, still night and was fortunate enough to immediately find a cab. Only when she was safely settled in the backseat and the driver had pulled away from the curb, did she allow herself to break down into great, gut-wrenching sobs.

CHAPTER 19

Mike O'Riley cradled the telephone between his chin and shoulder and rapidly jotted down some notes on a sheet of white notebook paper. "What was the nature of the sexual assault?"

"Anal and vaginal penetration," the clipped voice on the other end of the line answered.

"Did you find seminal fluid?"

"Yes, in both places."

"Any signs of strangulation?" O'Riley asked.

"Negative," the voice answered. "The victim did suffer a concussion; probably a blow to the head before she was carved up."

"Mmm-hmm," O'Riley responded, jotting down some more notes. "And you said she was five foot three and had blond hair?"

"Correct."

"It wasn't our man. Wrong MO. All of our victims were tall with long red hair. And they were all strangled—throttled from behind and either stunned or rendered unconscious before they were stabbed. And the last one was assaulted rectally and vaginally, but there was no ejaculate. The guy used a broom handle or something similar on her."

"I didn't think our victim fit the bill, but I know you guys are leaving no stone unturned, so I thought I'd touch base with you," Sergeant Alan Wilkins, of the Milwaukee Police Department Homicide Division said. Wilkins's department was investigating the recent sexual assault and stabbing murder of a young woman.

"We appreciate that," O'Riley said. "We sure need all the help we can get. Say, you don't by any chance have a line on any psychos or sex offenders that have been released from your prison system in the last six months?"

" 'Fraid not," Sergeant Wilkins replied. "We ran a check and came up cold."

"Same here," O'Riley said. "We tried to do a nation-wide cross-check of nut cases that've recently gotten out of the pen or out of mental wards, but not much came of it. I tend to think our guy is a local, and probably has a clean record."

"These serial killings are a bitch, aren't they?" Wilkins said. "I hope to hell I never see another one."

"Amen to that," O'Riley said. "Well, nice talking to you and good luck on your manhunt. Oh, and I'd be grateful if you'd fax us a copy of your pathology report for our files."

"No problem. I'll send it right out. Hope you catch your guy soon."

"That makes two of us."

O'Riley hung up the phone and jotted down a few more lines. When he'd finished, he added the sheet of paper to a three-ring notebook that contained notes of his conversations with law enforcement authorities all over the country. He lit a cigarette, then leaned back in his chair and leisurely stretched. He inhaled, then blew a couple of smoke rings. Another dead end. A slight smile played around the corners of his mouth. He'd never admit it to anyone, but that suited him just fine. He hoped there'd be two more weeks of no progress. Then it'd be Labor Day, and he'd retire.

As O'Riley had expected, Jablonski's follow-up interviews with the two hotline callers had not yielded any fruit.

The man from Wisconsin *thought* he remembered seeing a tall man dressed in dark clothes running down a sidewalk the night of Mary's murder. But when Jablonski drove him around the dozen square blocks surrounding St. Michael's, the man had become disoriented and was unable to say for sure which street he'd been on.

The fragment of the hymnal found on the river bank

might have belonged to Mary, but it was in a sorry
state and there were no prints or marks of any kind to
help determine who might have handled it. While
Jablonski doggedly kept beating the bushes, hoping for
a miracle, none had been forthcoming.

All in all, in O'Riley's opinion, things were going
exactly according to plan. Each day when he woke up
he did a silent countdown of the days remaining until
Labor Day. The count now stood at sixteen.

He had slacked off on the hours he'd been putting
in. He pretty much worked nine to five now, doing a
lot of mundane paper work. In fact, things were so
slow and the rest of the department was so stretched,
that a few days ago O'Riley had taken a break from the
case and helped out his brethren by responding to
the scene of another late-night stabbing. Even though
the victim had been a young woman in her twenties, it
was clearly not the work of the serial killer. The girl
had been petite, with shoulder-length, brown hair, and
she'd been found completely nude with vicious multiple stab wounds. It was always sad to see violent acts
played out on attractive young people, and once again,
O'Riley had been damn thankful that he'd soon be getting out of this rotten business.

He'd played hookey the preceding day in order to
take Billy to a Cubs game. He superstitiously viewed
the fact that the Cubs had won as another good omen.
Not wanting to look like he'd completely lost interest
in the investigation, he had come down to headquarters
on this bright Saturday morning to make a few calls.

O'Riley had told no one about his new retirement
plans, not even Anne. In the back of his mind was the
notion that if he shared his happiness with anyone, it'd
blow up in his face. He did feel a bit guilty about not
confiding in Jablonski. He knew how gung ho the
young man still was about the investigation, and he
knew Greg would be devastated if it were terminated.
He also knew that would be the likely result if nothing
had broken by Labor Day. He glanced over by the window where the computer sat, silent and unused. Al-

ways cost conscious, he hoped the department would be able to return it and get a refund.

As O'Riley began to daydream about the design he wanted to use for his new deck, Officer Marge Petronek, one of the first women to be assigned to the homicide division, rapped on the door and stepped inside the office. She was carrying a stack of folders.

In her mid-thirties, tall, big-boned, with short dark hair and dark expressive eyes, Marge was attractive in a strapping, farm-girl kind of way. Back in the late sixties when women libbers first became intent on breaking into all the professions, O'Riley had been opposed to the idea of having women on the force. "Unless they're dykes, they're not cut out for it, and they'll be a distraction," he'd said chauvinistically. He now admitted that he'd been wrong. Women made up nearly one quarter of the Chicago PD. They did a hell of a job, although police work still wasn't a career O'Riley would choose for his daughters.

"Whatcha got for me, Margie?" O'Riley asked warmly.

"Hot off the press: the latest report from Dr. Sheridan." Petronek handed him a manila envelope and sat down in the green vinyl chair in front of O'Riley's desk. O'Riley began to cough. He put out the cigarette and reached into his pocket for a throat lozenge. "Those cancer sticks are bad for you, you know," Petronek said.

"Don't you start lecturing me, Margie," O'Riley chided. "I get enough of that from Gregarious." He reached into the envelope, extracted several pieces of paper, and scanned the report which contained the doctor's latest thoughts on the murders.

"Very helpful, as usual," O'Riley grunted. "Just full of pearls of wisdom." He screwed up his face and mimicked the doctor's rather high-pitched voice. " 'In my opinion, whoever killed all of the young women was probably a loner. In my research I have found that stress sometimes brings about sadistic impulses that can lead to violent acts. Loss of a family member, being fired from a job, anything that results in loss of

self-esteem, could trigger such an act of violence.' "
O'Riley looked up. "What's he saying, that the killer
got fired from his job by a tall, redheaded woman and
that drove him to kill other women who look like her?"
He snorted. "I'm under a hell of a lot of stress, and
I've lost lots of jobs in my day, but it never occurred
to me that wasting somebody might make me feel better." He threw the report down on his desk. "Shrinks
are great at bullshit and double-talk. Why can't any of
them come up with something concrete?"

"Probably for the same reason we can't," Petronek
replied. "Because the killer was smart enough not to
leave us any real clues."

O'Riley shrugged. She was right about that. "Why is
Sheridan wasting his time and the city's money getting
out more reports?" he asked. "There hasn't been any
new evidence since Mary Collins was killed. We might
as well consult the Delphi Oracle as ask that smart ass
to tell us anything about the killer."

"I still think it could be a cop," Greg Jablonski said
from the doorway. "I don't know why you don't want
to listen to me."

"I've been listening all along," O'Riley said patiently. "Why haven't you brought me some proof?"

"Don't give up on me yet," Jablonski retorted. "I'm
still looking."

O'Riley rubbed his thigh. "Well, I hate to burst your
bubble, kid, but I don't think you're gonna find anything."

"Don't be such a pessimist," Jablonski chided.
"How about a little brainstorming session? Let's pretend we're the high-priced experts for a minute," he
suggested. "What do we know about the guy? Give me
some characteristics."

O'Riley groaned. The exercise would be a complete
waste of time, but he knew he'd better humor the lad
and play along. It wouldn't do to have the team know
that the commanding officer hoped the investigation
wouldn't uncover anything.

"He obviously has a thing for tall redheads," Marge

began. "And he has physical strength. He's able to strangle his victims with his hands."

"He's probably average-looking, polished, and well-spoken," Jablonski offered. "Since he apparently talked the women into voluntarily going to a secluded area with him."

"He's cautious and he thinks ahead. And he must wear gloves, since there's no prints," Marge said.

"He either has some sexual problems or he's into kinky sex acts," Jablonski said.

"He's methodical and consistent," Marge put in.

"Right you are, Margie," O'Riley said, pretending to get into the spirit of the game. "The two lethal wounds were identical in all cases. Now, I've got a question for you two hotshots," he said impulsively, deciding to show his hand just a bit. "Why hasn't he killed again?"

"He knows we're looking for him," Jablonski said.

"Well, of course, he knows we're looking for him," O'Riley said crossly. "Anyone this side of the planet Mongo knows that. But serial killers usually think they're the smartest people in the world, that they can't get caught. So why hasn't our guy killed in almost four months?"

"Maybe he has inside information about the investigation," Jablonski replied.

O'Riley frowned. "How could he?"

"He could if he was a cop," Jablonski said doggedly.

"Oh, for Christ's sake, will you lay off that idea?" O'Riley said crossly. "I know you think it's a cop. The whole department knows you think it's a cop. The question is, what do you propose we do about it: haul every member of the force in for questioning? Try to convince a judge to give us thousands of search warrants to go through thousands of homes to look for photos of redheaded women or knives or brooms or God knows what? I'm no lawyer, but I do know the judiciary frowns on those kinds of fishing expeditions." He rubbed his hand over his face. "Look, I appreciate how strongly you hold to your gut feelings, Jablonski, but if you want to be helpful, what we need here are some concrete ideas on how to proceed."

"I'm glad you said that, because I've been thinking we should consider retaining a couple more experts," Jablonski said. "I was just reading an article about a psychiatrist in L.A. who specializes in deviant sex crimes—"

"No!" O'Riley cut him off. "We've already got experts up the yazoo. You're the one that hand-picked Dr. Sheridan. We'll have to make do with him." Jesus! he cursed to himself. The case would be put on the back burner soon. This was a time for winding down. The last thing they needed was more experts.

"I just thought this other doctor might be able to give us a different perspective," Jablonski said.

"I said *no.*" O'Riley's tone was firm. "If you'd do your homework, you'd know that studies have shown experts are of limited use in solving murders anyway. Good old-fashioned police work is still what makes it in the long run. I probably should've put my foot down before you signed on the bunch of bloodsuckers we've already got, but I guess we're stuck with them. But that's it. Read my lips. *No more whores.* Now, any other bright ideas?" O'Riley ground out his cigarette. "How did I get stuck with help like you two? Go on, get out of here. I've got work to do."

The two detectives left quickly, closing the door behind them. When he was alone, O'Riley looked at his "To do" list and smiled. He had two more calls to return. Then he was going home. Maybe he'd stop at a lumber company on the way and pick up some plans for building his deck. It had been a long time since he'd worked with his hands. It would feel damn good to be physically active again. Only sixteen more days till Labor Day.

You have a delicious secret that no one else in the whole world knows. Especially not your stupid alter ego. If he knew what you've done, he would be very, very upset.

There's a new entry in the scrapbook, complete with new clippings and a new photo. Such a pretty girl, though not at all like the others. That's why no one would guess you've done it. At least not right away.

You've put that tragic episode from your past behind you, just as you'd always known you would. But at the same time you've come to realize that there is another evil woman in your life who needs to be dealt with, and you've hatched a brilliant plan to take care of her. Wouldn't the police be surprised if they knew what you have in mind now? If they thought you were clever before, they haven't seen anything yet.

CHAPTER 20

Megan held her engagement ring between her thumb and forefinger. The morning sunlight streaming through her office window danced off the facets of the diamonds. It was a beautiful ring, the kind she had dreamed about having when she was a little girl. It had symbolized so many of her hopes for the future: a husband, a home of her own, a family. What a crock of shit all that had turned out to be. She ran her hands through her hair and stared at the wall. Who would've ever thought it would end like this?

She carefully slipped the ring into the slot in the blue velvet box sitting on her desk and gave it one last parting glance before she snapped the lid shut. Even the sound of it closing had an air of finality about it. Then she gently set the box inside a larger, blue cardboard one labeled TIFFANY & COMPANY, and placed it on the corner of her desk. Opening a desk drawer, she took out a manila mailing envelope and carefully printed Paul's name and office address. As she finished the last line, several large tears ran down her cheeks and fell onto the envelope. Damn it! I'm not going to cry anymore, she thought fiercely. She reached for a tissue and blotted the tears away. She wiped her eyes, slid the box into the envelope, licked the flap and sealed it. There, it was done.

Megan sat back in her chair, picked up a mug full of cold coffee, and took a sip. She felt like a zombie. After spending a number of wretched, sleepless hours wandering around her apartment, weeping and feeling sorry for herself, she had come down to the office at six o'clock, hoping that being in a public place would force her to maintain her composure. It was now after eight, and so far the plan wasn't working too well. She'd already gone through half a box of Kleenex. She looked at the empty spot on her desk where the picture of her and Paul had stood. It was now stowed away, face down, at the bottom of a desk drawer underneath several years' worth of old appointment books. Oh, God, she thought, biting her lower lip, I feel so alone.

She blew her nose again, then took another sip of coffee and managed to spill some on her jeans. As she was attempting to wipe it up, there was a knock on her door. Oh, shit! She didn't want anyone to see her like this. "Come in," she said in a low voice. The door opened and Rita Montenero stepped inside. "How are you?" Rita asked anxiously, closing the door behind her and walking quickly over to Megan's desk.

Megan shrugged. "I don't know. Not too good, I guess."

While home alone in the middle of the night, crying uncontrollably, Megan had felt the need to confide in someone and had called Rita. Her friend had offered to rush over immediately to console her, but Megan had suggested they meet at the office in the morning.

"What time did you get here?" Rita asked, settling into a chair next to the desk. Like Megan, she was dressed in jeans and a T-shirt.

"I'm not sure. I think it was sometime around six."

"Why didn't you call me?" Rita scolded. "I would've come right down."

Megan shook her head. "There was no reason for both of us to lose out on a night's sleep."

"Do you really think I went back to sleep after talking to you?" Rita ran her hands through her thick black hair. "My God, I was pacing around all night thinking of the most devious means of torture that we could use on Paul."

Megan blew her nose again. "Did you come up with any good ones?"

"No," Rita shook her head. "I was sort of keen on drawing and quartering, but then I decided that was too humane. What did you do with the ring?" she asked, suddenly noticing its absence from Megan's finger.

Megan patted the manila envelope on the corner of the desk.

Rita rotated the envelope a half turn and looked at it. "You're going to *mail* it back to him?" she asked incredulously.

"No, I'm going to have one of the messengers deliver it," Megan explained.

Rita nodded. "Oh, yeah, that's probably a good idea. Has he tried to call you yet?"

"I don't know. I have the phone and the answering machine at home unplugged, and I programmed this phone to transfer all calls back to the reception desk."

"You're gonna have to face him eventually, Meg. I don't think he's just going to fade quietly out of sight."

Megan sighed. "I'll worry about that later. I just can't handle a big scene right now." She rubbed her eyes. They were bloodshot and had dark circles under them. "I look like hell, don't I?" she asked.

"Of course not," Rita lied. "You just look a little tired. How about some more coffee? That'll perk you up."

"Okay."

"I'll go get it. I could use a cup myself." Rita scooped up Megan's cup and quickly walked out of the office, again closing the door as she left. During her absence, Megan blew her nose again and then cradled her head in her hands. I have to try to think positive, she thought. Let's see. There must be something pleasant I can think about. But the only image that came to mind was the sight of Rhonda in Paul's bed.

There was a short rap at the door. Before Megan could respond, it was opened and Rita stepped inside, carrying two cups of coffee. "Are you up to having another visitor?" she asked.

"Depends on who it is," Megan replied warily.

"It's just me," Ron said, stepping into the room and closing the door behind him.

"I ran into him in the workroom," Rita explained.

Megan looked up at Ron, and his expression told her that Rita had explained everything.

Ron swiftly strode across the room and enveloped Megan in a bear hug. She put her arms around his neck and squeezed him tightly. "You okay?" he asked as he released her.

"Not really, but I guess I'll make it," she answered.

"If you want me to leave, I will," Ron offered.

Megan shook her head. "No, you can stay." She sniffed and wiped her nose with another tissue. "On one condition."

"Name it."

"If you start singing 'Love is Blue,' I'm going to push you out the window."

"Agreed," Ron said, settling down in the chair next to Rita. "Anyway, I think that song sucks. If I were going to sing, it would be something like 'It Keeps Right On A-hurtin'.' But don't worry, I won't sing anything."

Megan managed a wan smile.

After a moment of rather awkward silence, Ron said, "Gee, what do you guys think about that new pitcher the Cubs are recruiting?"

Rita made a face. "Just like a man. In times of crisis, all they can think about is sports."

"All right, then *you* come up with a topic of conversation," Ron challenged.

"Okay. I will," Rita said. "Megan's sending her ring back via messenger." She patted the manila envelope. "Personally, I think she should do something more dramatic, like tossing it into the river while we all chant 'Down with male pigs' or some other appropriate slogan."

"You're giving the ring back?" Ron asked, aghast. "Meg, that's stupid. It was a *gift*. It's your *property*. Trust me. There's case law on this." He put his head back and looked up at the ceiling. "That reminds me of a great song. 1965. Gary Lewis and the Playboys. 'This Diamond Ring.'" He closed his eyes and began to hum the tune, then looked back at Megan. "Sorry. I got carried away. Where was I? Oh, yeah. Why don't you sell the ring? I'll bet that baby is worth some bucks and let's face it, Meg, you could use a new car."

In spite of herself, Megan chuckled. "I don't want the ring or any benefits derived from it. He can shove it up his ass or take it to Tiffany's and get his money back or give it to Nurse Feelgood for all I care."

"That's pretty direct. You know, though, Meg," Ron began delicately, "have you stopped to consider that maybe Paul *was* drunk and got carried away?"

"If you're going to talk like that, you can get the hell out of here," Rita said angrily.

"Yeah. Last night you made it very clear that you don't like Paul," Megan said incredulously. "Why in the world would you be defending him all of a sudden?"

"I don't particularly like him," Ron admitted, "but I guess I feel some teeny-tiny obligation to stick up for my fellow man, no matter how big a gigolo he might be."

"Well, don't bother," Megan cut in. "There's nothing you can possibly say that would make me change my mind. For starters, Paul does *not* get drunk. He's scrupulous about everything he consumes. And I guarantee he was most definitely sober when he chased me down the hallway in his undies." Her eyes flashed, and she pushed her hair behind her ears. "He got carried away all right, but not with booze. Obviously this is something that's been building up for a while. He is not a very spontaneous person."

"Yeah, Ron, stop defending the louse," Rita chimed in. "He deserves to be vivisected—whatever that is—or, at the very least, castrated."

"Ouch." Ron made a face. "I'm not trying to defend him," he said seriously. "I just wondered if you're not being a little hasty."

"I am *not* being hasty." Megan shook her head adamantly. "Believe me, I've had plenty of time to think this through. Maybe some women could overlook an incident like this and give him another chance, but I can't. To me, what he did is the ultimate betrayal. I can't forgive and forget. I'm just glad I found out his true colors before we were married." She sipped her coffee and looked up.

"Good for you," Rita said. "He's scum."

"I agree completely," Ron said. "He's scum. So, would you like me to go shoot him?"

Megan sniffed. "You don't have a gun."

"No, but there's one in the exhibit room. Don't you remember the case I'm working on where a kid accidentally shot his cousin because the sight was so far out of whack? There's a box of ammo, too, so just say the word and I'll rub him out." He pointed the index finger of one hand and said, "Pow! Take that, you cad."

Megan smiled. "I don't think that's necessary." She paused. "But there *is* something you guys can do for me, though."

"Name it," Ron said.

"Look," Megan said earnestly. "I'd just as soon not have the details of this get around the office, okay? I mean, I know I'm going to have to tell people that we split up, but I'd rather make it sound like it was by mutual agreement. Can I count on you two?" Rita and Ron both nodded. "Good. It'll help a lot if I don't have to deal with a bunch of people making sympathetic noises."

"If you want to take a couple days off, I'll be glad to cover for you," Ron offered.

"Take time off?" Megan said in a startled tone. "That's the last thing I want to do. I intend to spend as much time here as I can. I never thought I'd say it, but I'm actually glad I've got the AIDS case to work on. God knows there's an endless amount of work to be done on it. And Roger Barrett's historic preservation case is going to demand a lot of hours in the next few weeks, too, so hopefully I won't have much time to feel sorry for myself."

"Don't push yourself too hard," Ron cautioned. "You've suffered a major blow here. You can't expect to get over it in a day."

"I know that," Megan agreed. "But work has always

been the best therapy for me. Don't worry," she said, seeing their looks of concern, "I'll be okay."

"Of course, you will," Rita said encouragingly. "Now, you look like you could use a good breakfast. Something healthier than a chocolate donut. How about the three of us getting out of here for an hour or so. We're not dressed too great, but I think the coffee shop at the Drake would probably let us in. I could really go for eggs Benedict and some quality coffee with real cream."

"Great idea," Ron seconded. "I'm starving. How about it, Meg?"

Megan considered the suggestion. Although she had no appetite, she realized that she needed to eat something. "Okay," she said. "That sounds good. I need to stop at the restroom first. I must've had two pots of coffee in the last few hours." She stood up, picked up the manila envelope, and handed it to Rita. "Would you mind giving this to the messenger and explaining that it's very important it get delivered this morning? I'd rather not have to deal with it."

"Sure thing," Rita said, taking the envelope. "I'll meet you at the front door in five minutes." She looked back wickedly. "Think of which client we can stick the Drake bill on." She turned again and quickly walked out of the office.

CHAPTER 21

Mike O'Riley was dreaming about fishing.

The Labor Day weekend weather was unusually balmy for the midwest, as if the dog days of summer were unwilling to relinquish their grasp on the region. O'Riley had spent a few hours at headquarters on Saturday, and as he'd expected, accomplished nothing. With the prospects of finding the killer looking as bleak as ever, he decided to take Sunday and Monday off and ordered the rest of the team to do the same.

Everyone else thought they were just getting a two-day hiatus. Only O'Riley knew that this probably marked the end of the road for the investigation. Bright and early on Tuesday morning he was going to city hall to give the mayor his resignation.

He knew the mayor might balk a bit, but this time O'Riley was going to stick to his guns. He intended to preface his remarks by telling his old friend that since he hadn't been able to find the killer, of course there would be no need to follow through on the promised bonus of a new dinghy. The mayor had a good sense of humor. That should make him laugh.

On Sunday, O'Riley had taken Billy fishing. They'd driven to a clear lake near the Wisconsin border where they'd spent a tranquil few hours. They hadn't caught much, but God, had it ever felt good being out in the fresh air without a care in the world. Soon every day would be like that.

O'Riley planned to spend Labor Day doing some preliminary work on the site where he was going to build his deck. There were a couple of bushes that needed to be dug out and a load of gravel to be spread.

That'd keep him busy for a good share of the day. Then maybe he'd take Anne someplace nice for supper to spring the retirement news on her and to thank her for putting up with the long hours he'd had to work on this case.

His fishing trip with Billy must have influenced his dreams, because in the early hours of Labor Day morning he dreamed he was on a deep-sea fishing expedition. He seemed to be on an ocean-going vessel. Its deck appeared to stretch for miles. O'Riley noticed he was wearing dress clothes. When he asked someone why, he replied, "Because you were invited to sit at the captain's table for lunch."

Of course. Lunch. Just then he heard the tinkling of a bell. Ah. It must be the signal that lunch was being served. O'Riley began to wander around the deck, trying to determine where the captain's quarters might be. He walked and walked, never seeing a soul he could ask for directions. And all the while, the bell's tinkling grew more insistent.

"Mike, the telephone!" Anne gave him a sharp jab in the ribs with her arm.

"What?" he said groggily. He propped himself up on one elbow and looked at the clock. 5:55, Labor Day morning. Suddenly he was wide awake. He looked at the phone with sheer terror running through his veins, then snatched up the receiver.

"O'Riley," he barked.

"Lieutenant, this is Norm Carruthers at dispatch. Sorry to bother you on a holiday, sir, but a woman's body was just found at the Oak Street Beach. She's cut up really bad."

"Oh, God!" O'Riley said aloud. To himself he added, Oh shit! Why couldn't this have waited two more days? Just two more lousy days. Was that so much to ask for? "Has she got long red hair?" he asked, his heart pounding.

"No, sir, she doesn't, but she looks just like the woman that was found on Damen a couple weeks back. Do you remember the one I mean? Lieutenant Reeser says you came by to help 'em out."

O'Riley tried to process what he was hearing.

"Sir?" Carruthers prompted.

"Yeah, I remember. I'll be right there."

Feeling like he'd been hit on the head with a hammer, O'Riley got up and hurriedly threw on his clothes.

O'Riley and Greg Jablonski stood quietly together, staring down at the bloody mess that had, hours before, been a vibrant young woman. A short distance away, O'Riley could hear the sounds of retching. One of the uniformed officers had lost his breakfast. O'Riley didn't blame him. This was one of the most gruesome sights he'd ever encountered. He tried to recall his knowledge of basic anatomy. How much blood was there in a human body anyway? This looked like gallons.

Carruthers was right: This girl sure looked like the one O'Riley had seen on Damen. She was in her late twenties, probably five-foot-three or five-foot-four, with shoulder-length, brown hair and a slight build. Like the girl on Damen, she was completely nude. Her neck showed signs of strangulation, and her body was covered with dozens of stab wounds.

"Jesus Christ!" Jablonski groaned. "What kind of animal could do this?"

O'Riley looked away and shook his head. "I'll be goddamned if I know." His stomach was churning, and he reached into his pocket for some antacids.

"What do you make of it, Mike? Think our man did it?"

O'Riley slowly shook his head. "If you ask me, it looks more like we've got a second wacko on the loose."

"You mean a copy-cat killer?" Jablonski asked incredulously.

"It happens," O'Riley replied grimly. Christ, he hoped he was wrong. They hadn't been able to find one serial killer. The thought of having to mount a search for a second one was more than he could bear.

O'Riley squinted in the sunlight and looked over to the west, where a hefty contingent of uniformed officers was keeping the press and other thrill seekers at bay. He shook his head in wonder at human nature. At times like these it was bad enough being in his line of work, where you had to endure scenes of grotesque mutilation in the hope that you'd be able to catch whoever was responsible before they did the same thing to someone else. It must really be dismal to be a reporter, where you actually got brownie points for being the first to report a tragedy.

A young uniformed officer sprinted up to O'Riley. "Lieutenant, we found one of her running shoes and her sweat pants."

"Good work," O'Riley said. "Where were they?"

"The shoe was in a garbage can a hundred yards south of here, and the pants must've been tossed in the lake. They got hung up on a pier."

"Tell your men to keep looking for the rest of her clothes," O'Riley barked.

"Yes, sir," the young officer said, hurrying off.

Dr. Packard, the assistant medical examiner, brushed past on his way back to his van to get more equipment. "Jesus, Mike," he said softly, his face ashen. "What's going on here?"

"I'm hoping you'll be able to tell me, Randy," O'Riley responded. "We think we might have a copycat killer. When you get back to the lab, I'd like you to pull the file on a woman named Candy Wells. I don't know who did the autopsy, but she was found stabbed over on Damen about two and a half weeks ago, and she looked just like this gal."

"Gotcha," Packard said, moving on.

In a few moments, O'Riley saw Marge Petronek making her way through the crowd. She was carrying several folded pieces of paper. "I hope you got good news for us, Margie," O'Riley said as she reached his side. "We sure as hell can use some."

"It's too early to tell," she replied, glancing over at the body and grimacing, "but it might be something." She unfolded the papers in her hand. "Around ten-thirty last night dispatch took a call from an older gentleman who'd been out for a walk in this area. He said he was heading back to his apartment building and was crossing the street down there," she said, pointing to the south. "Anyway, he claims he was halfway across, minding his own business, when a squad car suddenly pulled out of the beach parking area and almost ran him over. The guy had to jump back and fell down and hurt his ankle. He was so shook up that, after he limped home and had a couple drinks, he called in to report it."

O'Riley and Jablonski were both listening intently. O'Riley drew in his breath. "The guy didn't by any chance get a license number, did he?" he asked.

Marge gave him a broad smile. "You bet your life he did. Well, part of one anyway. He says it was definitely a Chicago PD squad, and the first three numbers on the plate were 1-0-9."

"Margie, I love ya!" O'Riley exclaimed, hugging her.

"I love you, too, Mike," Marge replied. She referred to her papers once again. "I checked it out, and squad car number 0-1-9-3-2, license plate number 1-0-9-4, was assigned to patrolman Roy Buenzli last night during the three-to-eleven shift."

"What've you got on Buenzli?" Jablonski asked eagerly.

Marge flipped to the next sheet. "Thirty-eight-year-old white Caucasian. Six-feet, one and a half inches tall. One hundred ninety-five pounds. Was a weight lifter in college. Been with the department eight years. Suspended without pay for five days two years ago for using excessive force during an arrest. Two other similar complaints received in past five years, but both of those were dropped after the complainants suddenly changed their stories."

Jablonski gripped O'Riley's arm. "This sounds like our man, Mike! See, I told you it was a cop! Maybe he was responsible for the other four murders, too."

O'Riley gritted his teeth. Jesus, he hoped Greg was right. "What's this witness's name and where does he live?" he asked Petronek.

"Cyril Ferguson. Floor twenty-two of Lake Point Tower."

O'Riley put his arms around Jablonski's and Petronek's shoulders. "Come on, both of you. Let's pay a call on Mr. Ferguson and make sure he didn't start hitting the hootch until after he got home last night."

Cyril Ferguson was a seventy-five-year-old, retired art dealer. He greeted the three detectives at the door to his exclusive high-rise apartment, wearing white cotton pants and a navy-and-white-striped T-shirt. He was barefoot and an Ace bandage encircled his left ankle. O'Riley eyed Ferguson, then glanced around him. The three detectives in their rumpled work clothes looked horribly out of place in the expensively furnished apartment. O'Riley looked back at Ferguson. The old guy was obviously a flaming fag, but he had an eye for detail. That should make him a good witness. When his offer of tea and cookies was politely refused, Ferguson settled himself on an antique Biedermeier sofa, propped his foot up on a needlepoint footstool and answered their inquiries with the grace and aplomb of a reclusive celebrity granting a rare interview to the press.

What was he doing walking around at night? "Although I am aged, I am neither feeble of form nor senile of mind," Ferguson said with amusement. "I underwent triple-bypass surgery in May, and my doctors informed me that walking was the best exercise to keep my newly cleansed arteries unclogged. So I normally walk two miles in the morning and another two miles in the evening." He put his head back and reminisced. "Being somewhat of a romantic, evenings have always been my favorite time of day. I left here around eight, just as the sun was setting. If I go out after dark, I always carry a flashlight with me, and I had it along last night. Eddie Bauer super-lightweight model, in case that's of any importance."

"And you were on your way back here when you injured your ankle?" Jablonski asked.

"*I* did not injure my ankle," Ferguson replied, a bit

haughtily. "One of your fine men in uniform was responsible for that."

"Can you tell us what happened, sir," O'Riley
prompted.

"Of course, I can. I'm afraid the experience is indelibly etched in my memory. I had walked north along
the beach as far as North Avenue. You should be able
to pick out my footprints. I was wearing a pair of Nike
Air, cross-training shoes. Size ten, medium. I left the
lakeshore at the south end of Oak Street Beach and
walked west. It was around nine-twenty-five. I began
to cross the street. It was a quiet night, with it being
Sunday and the long holiday weekend and all. There
was no traffic in sight. I had extinguished my flashlight, as the area is quite well lit. I was halfway across
the intersection when suddenly I heard a great squeal
of tires from behind me. I turned and saw a squad car
careening toward me. I jumped backward and in the
process, lost my balance, and down I went like a sack
of potatoes. As I was lying there in the street, cursing
at the imbecile who would be in such a hurry as to
drive like that, I was able to make out the first three
numbers of the car's license plate. They were 1-0-9.
That's all I had a chance to observe before the car sped
out of sight."

"Did you get a look at the person driving the car?"
O'Riley asked.

Ferguson shook his head. "Sadly, I did not. I have an
image in my mind of seeing a shock of dark wavy hair,
but I cannot attest to that fact. I am, however, certain
of the three numbers on the license plate."

"What did you do after you saw the license plate?"
Petronek asked.

"Well, my immediate concern was to get back up off
the street before another car came along and finished
me off. I got to my feet with some difficulty and discovered, much to my dismay, that my ankle was not
functioning properly. The lens of my flashlight was
also cracked in the fall. It's over there on the table, in
case you wish to inspect it. Luckily there were no other
cars coming, and I managed to limp across the rest of

the way. When I'd gained the other side, I sat down on the curb for a few minutes to catch my breath, ensure that there was nothing broken, and just generally get a grip on myself. Then I slowly made my way back here."

"What time did you get here?" Jablonski asked.

"My grandfather clock was striking quarter past ten as I came in the door," Ferguson replied. "I realize that is a long time to cover two blocks, but I was moving very slowly and cautiously. I did not want to do my ankle any further damage."

"Then what did you do?" O'Riley asked.

Ferguson sighed. "I went straight to my bar, over there," he motioned to his left, "and poured myself a goodly helping of Courvoisier. After I'd downed that glass, I poured out another. As I was sipping on that, I decided to call the police dispatcher and make a report of the incident while it was still fresh in my mind."

Petronek nodded. The dispatcher's report indicated that Ferguson's call had come in at ten-twenty-four.

"Could you see if there was anyone in the squad car besides the driver?" O'Riley asked.

Ferguson shook his head. "Not unless the other person was lying down."

"While you were on your walk, did you see or hear anything unusual along the beach?" Jablonski asked.

Ferguson again shook his head. "Not at all. It was a perfect night for a walk, quiet, warm, nearly a full moon. A superb night for outdoor activities." He rubbed his ankle through the Ace bandage. "Unfortunately, I'm afraid I'm going to have to curtail my walking excursions for a while."

"I don't mean to be impertinent, sir," O'Riley said, "but had you had anything of an alcoholic nature to drink prior to your walk?"

Ferguson smiled, and his blue eyes lit up. "Do you mean is it possible that my story is merely the overactive imagination of a drunken old sot?" He chuckled. "Don't worry, Lieutenant. I assure you my version of the evening's events is quite accurate. But in answer to your question, yes, I had two glasses of wine with dinner. Chateau Lafite-Rothschild, 1977. A superb wine. I highly recommend it. I have been drinking two glasses of wine at dinner for sixty years, and I can state most assuredly it does not impair my faculties in any respect."

"Thank you for your time, Mr. Ferguson," O'Riley said smoothly. "We would be very grateful if you would be willing to sign a statement outlining what you just told us. I realize you have some problems getting around at the moment, so if it's all right with you, sir, we'll have it typed up and send someone round with it this afternoon to get your signature. That will save you the trouble of having to go out."

"I would be most happy to oblige," Ferguson responded. "I can only hope that my reporting this unfortunate experience may save some other poor bloke's life."

"Believe me, we're hoping the same thing," O'Riley murmured.

When they were back down on the street moments later, O'Riley instructed Petronek, "Have somebody get that statement typed and back here right away."

"Will do," she said.

O'Riley turned to Jablonski. "Get on the horn and have somebody bring Buenzli in for questioning ASAP."

Jablonski grinned. "Buenzli's gonna crack this thing wide open, Mike. I can feel it. You're gonna be retired before you know what hit you."

"I hope you're right," O'Riley said, grinding his teeth. He was dying for a cigarette, but was trying hard to refrain in the presence of these two rabid antismokers. " 'Cuz if we don't arrest somebody, the whole city's gonna be after my ass. Now let's go. Something tells me it's gonna be a long day."

CHAPTER 22

Officer Roy Buenzli swaggered into the interrogation room. "Somebody mind telling me what this is all about?" he asked brashly.

The room was sparsely furnished—a beat-up, rectangular, wood table, four metal chairs, and drab olive paint peeling off the walls. There was dirty gray linoleum on the floor. No windows. No pictures. No clock. The idea was that questioning sometimes went more smoothly if the suspect didn't feel too comfortable.

O'Riley was seated at the head of the table, with Jablonski on the side facing the door. The younger man's jaw was clenched. O'Riley had told him to sit there and be quiet until he got the high sign that it was his turn to say something. Those instructions hadn't set too well. If there was a confession to be had here, Jablonski was salivating to be the one to get it. But O'Riley couldn't be swayed. In the past he'd given the young detective plenty of leeway, but if an arrest was imminent, O'Riley was going to be the one to administer the coup de grace.

"Have a seat," O'Riley said brusquely to Buenzli, motioning to the chair across from Jablonski.

Buenzli was tall, and had dark, curly hair and heavy-lidded dark eyes. A small scar extended from his left lower lip to his chin. He was wearing faded jeans and a red T-shirt with a hole in the pocket. The sleeves of the shirt had been cut out, showing off his muscular arms. His lips curled in a sardonic grin. "This is my day off, guys," he said. "I figure if I was good enough to come all the way down here voluntarily, the least you can do is tell me what's going on."

"Would you like some coffee?" O'Riley asked, ignoring the question.

Buenzli flashed that dark grin again. "Yeah, sure. I'll take some coffee. With plenty of cream and sugar." O'Riley motioned to Jablonski, who scowled openly at O'Riley before getting up and striding out of the room. During Jablonski's absence, O'Riley and Buenzli both remained silent. Buenzli leaned against the wall next to the door, staring unconcernedly at the ceiling.

O'Riley sat motionless at the table. Although he was trying not to get his hopes up about this suspect, he could almost feel his stomach pumping out acid. In the three hours since they'd left Cyril Ferguson, O'Riley had replayed the same scenario over and over in his mind. Buenzli would either confess to all the murders or he'd confess to the last two and miraculously turn over an accomplice who was responsible for the first four. O'Riley would phone the mayor with the good news. The mayor would call a press conference praising O'Riley and would see to it that the city issued him a commendation and a hefty cash bonus for a job well done. O'Riley would be retired as soon as the paperwork on the last killing was completed, and he would be able to start on his deck this week as planned. He knew it was all a pipe dream, but at the moment he desperately needed to grasp on to something.

In a few moments Jablonski returned with the coffee. Buenzli chuckled as he took it, then quickly took the two steps from the spot where he'd been standing to the table. He pulled out the rigid metal chair and letting it scrape across the linoleum, casually sat down. After taking a sip of the coffee, he said, "Okay, guys. See, I'm a good boy. I can follow instructions. Now it's your turn. What the hell is this about?"

"You worked the three-to-eleven shift last night," O'Riley said.

"Yeah," Buenzli answered easily. He took another sip of coffee, then folded his hands in front of him on the table. His hands were large and calloused like a manual laborer's. O'Riley caught himself staring at them. They could easily crush a woman's throat.

"Anything out of the ordinary happen during your shift?" O'Riley went on.

"Nah." Buenzli shook his head. "It was real dead. I guess all the loonies left town for the weekend. The eight hours really dragged. Personally, I prefer nights when there's a little more action."

"Did you make any stops while you were on patrol?" O'Riley asked.

Buenzli put his head back and thought for a moment. "Yeah. A few."

"When and where?"

"Oh, gee, lemme think." Buenzli drummed the fingers of his big right hand on the table. "Well, I issued a couple traffic tickets in the late afternoon, one for speeding and one for running a red light. I had a Big Mac and fries at McDonald's on Michigan Avenue around six-thirty. About seven-thirty there were a couple of black kids nosing around a BMW parked on Chestnut Street. They looked kinda suspicious, so I stopped and talked to them. They claimed they were just admiring the car. I gave them a little pep talk about how I better not ever catch 'em doing anything more than admiring nice vehicles." He took another sip of coffee. "About forty-five minutes after that I got a call from dispatch to check out an alarm that had gone off at a jewelry store on Michigan. It turned out to be a malfunction. After that, let's see, ah ... oh yeah, around nine I had to take a leak, so I stopped at a bar on Rush Street."

"Which bar?" O'Riley prompted.

"Hanrahan's. The bartender's a buddy of mine, so I shot the shit with him for a few minutes."

"What's his name?"

"Josh Rogers." Buenzli ran a hand through his thick hair. "What is this, guys, twenty questions? I can see you're driving at something here, but I'll be damned if I can figure out what the hell it is. You wanna maybe give me a hint?"

O'Riley's face displayed no emotion. "Are those all the stops you made before logging out for the night?"

"Yeah, I think so.... Yeah, that's it. Like I said, things were real dead."

"Did you drive past the Oak Street Beach at any time last night?"

"Yeah. A couple times."

"How many times?" O'Riley pressed.

"I don't know. Two or three, I s'pose."

"What time would that have been?"

Buenzli scratched his head. "I don't know. The first time was probably around four and then I think I swung by there again right after I left McDonald's."

"Those the only times you went by the beach?"

"As far as I remember, yeah."

"You never stopped there, you just drove by."

"Yeah, that's right."

"And you didn't make any other stops besides the ones you've already told us about?"

Buenzli shook his head. "Not that I remember, no."

"Are you in the habit of recording in your log stops that you make while on patrol?" O'Riley asked.

"Yeah, sure. That's standard operating procedure, right?" He drained the rest of the coffee.

O'Riley had reviewed Buenzli's log for the previous evening, and the stops he had mentioned had all been reported. "You're sure you weren't anywhere near the Oak Street Beach around nine-twenty-five last night?"

"No. By that time I'd left the bar, but I was still somewhere in the Rush Street area."

This guy was cool as a slab of ice in January, O'Riley thought. He hadn't batted an eye. If he had something to hide, he sure hadn't shown it. Maybe it was time to start being a little more direct.

"Officer Buenzli, dispatch took a call last night from a man who claims he was crossing the street at the south end of the Oak Street Beach when he was nearly run down by a squad car. Fortunately he was able to jump back out of the way, but he did fall and injure his ankle. He was obviously quite shaken, and so he wanted to report it to the department." O'Riley paused and waited for a response.

"Yeah?" Buenzli said after a moment of silence. "What's that got to do with me?"

"The man said he saw the first three numbers of the squad's license plate. They were 1-0-9. What were the numbers on the squad you were driving last night?"

Still not a glimmer of response from Buenzli. "You know as well as I do, Lieutenant, that the vehicle I was assigned to has license number 1-0-9-4. Is that why you hauled me down here? Because somebody claims I was driving erratically? So give me a warning and I'll be on my way."

"Do you recall having a near miss with a pedestrian at any time during last night's shift?" O'Riley asked.

Buenzli shook his head emphatically. "No. The guy was probably drunker than a skunk and was looking for an excuse to explain to his missus why he fell down and dirtied himself on a nice clear night."

O'Riley ran a hand through his hair. "The caller was an older gentleman who lives alone, and he didn't sound drunk. He also did hurt his ankle and he was quite definite about the license number on the car. But since you're telling us you were nowhere near the Oak Street Beach just before nine-thirty last night and that you don't remember almost running down an old man, maybe his knowing three digits of your license number was just a lucky guess."

Buenzli pushed his chair back. The metal feet made a sharp scraping sound on the linoleum floor. "That's right. That's exactly what I'm telling you. The old fart could've seen that license number anytime. The car's out on the street every day, with lots of different drivers. Now it's been fun spending Labor Day afternoon talking to you two fellows, but I really have some things I'd rather be doing than sitting here being accused of being a bad driver, so unless you're planning to give me a traffic ticket or something, I think I'll be shoving off."

"Have you heard any news reports today?" O'Riley asked.

Buenzli looked O'Riley in the eye. "Can't say that I have. I was getting some well-deserved shut-eye until your people so rudely interrupted me. Why?"

"There was a nasty slashing murder," O'Riley said coldly. "A very nice-looking, brown-haired girl met up with a psycho with a very sharp knife. Believe me, it wasn't a pretty sight."

For the first time during the interview, Buenzli flinched. "Jesus!" he said. "Where'd it happen?"

O'Riley paused. "Near Oak Street Beach."

Buenzli bolted upright in his chair and his face grew flushed. "Shit!" he spat out. "Is that what you hauled me down here for? I've heard the stories about you guys thinkin' the guy who killed those other girls was a cop. You're lookin' for somebody to take a fall 'cuz you can't find the real killer. But lemme tell you somethin' right now. You ain't gonna pin no murder rap on me! No fuckin' way, man!"

After receiving a nod from O'Riley, Jablonski spoke up for the first time. "Do yourself a favor, Buenzli. We all know you were speeding away from the beach about nine-thirty. If you weren't slicing up that woman, tell us what you *were* doing there."

Buenzli's left eye began to twitch, and he nervously rubbed his palms together. "I didn't slice up nobody," he said tersely.

"Then tell us what happened," Jablonski urged. "What were you doing at the beach?"

"I met a friend," Buenzli said slowly.

"What for?" Jablonski asked. "A social call?"

"Yeah," Buenzli said unconvincingly.

"What's your friend's name?" Jablonski asked. "Come on, Buenzli. What were you up to? You meet a prostitute for a quick blow job?"

There was no response.

"Or maybe your friend did the killing while you watched, is that it?" Jablonski pressed.

More silence.

"It wasn't exactly a social call, was it?" O'Riley asked, acting on a hunch. "Maybe it was more like a business transaction. Tell me, how much does good coke go for these days?"

Buenzli ran his tongue nervously around his lips.

"That's it, isn't it?" O'Riley raised his voice for the first time. "You're supplementing your income with a little dealin', aren't you? Well, aren't you, Buenzli? I'm talkin' to you, boy. Answer me!"

Buenzli swallowed hard and finally nodded.

"So you were dealing drugs at the beach," O'Riley said triumphantly. "What time was that?"

"Between nine-fifteen and nine-thirty," Buenzli admitted.

"And as long as you were in the area, you decided to take a few minutes out to hack up that girl." O'Riley was shouting now.

"No way, man." Buenzli was regaining his courage. "I didn't hurt anybody. I didn't see any girl. I was only at the beach five minutes, tops. Then I got back to my beat."

"You're a pretty powerful guy, aren't you?" O'Riley said in a calmer tone. "Just look at them muscles. I hear you were a weight lifter. Looks like you still work out pretty regular. You've had a few problems with roughing people up when you make arrests, haven't you? But then, I s'pose a big guy like you tends to get a little carried away with his authority."

"I was only suspended once," Buenzli said hotly. "Those other charges were dropped."

"Yeah, I heard the complainants suddenly changed their story for some reason. What happened? Did you convince them it'd be in their best interest not to pursue it?"

"You've got no proof of that," Buenzli slammed his big fist down on the table. "And you sure as hell got no proof that I killed anybody."

O'Riley leaned forward in his chair. "We've got eyewitnesses that saw a tall, dark-haired guy in a police uniform at the scene of at least one other murder. We got an eyewitness who you damn near ran over in your eagerness to get away from the beach last night. Now that might be circumstantial evidence, but I'd say it's a damn good start. I'd be willing to bet it's enough to get us a search warrant for your apartment. And once we get in there, who knows what we might find. More drugs, maybe some illegal weapons. Maybe some bloody clothes. Maybe some nice sharp knives."

Buenzli's nostrils flared. "You're fuckin' crazy."

"Am I?" O'Riley said coolly.

"Yeah, you are." Buenzli got to his feet. "Are you gonna arrest me or can I leave?"

O'Riley knew they didn't have probable cause to make an arrest. "You're not under arrest, but we're entitled to hold you for further questioning in last night's murder. Like Detective Jablonski said a minute ago, even if you didn't do the actual killing, maybe your customer did it, or maybe one of you saw something. I'll just bet you could provide us with lots of useful information once you've had a little time to think things over."

Buenzli turned and looked at the door. For a moment O'Riley thought he was going to bolt, but he turned back. "I'm not answerin' no more questions till I talk to my lawyer."

"All right," O'Riley said reasonably. "Detective Jablonski, would you escort the officer to a phone."

When the two men had left the room, O'Riley cursed to himself. Shit! Why couldn't anything go according to plan? He stood up. His leg was as stiff as a goddamn poker. Being under stress was sure as hell hard on a guy. He tapped his foot on the floor. Buenzli looked like he was capable of murder, but O'Riley's gut told him he hadn't killed this girl—or any of the other ones. And once Buenzli's lawyer showed up, they'd probably never get another word out of him.

O'Riley looked at his watch. Three-thirty. It would take a while for Buenzli's mouthpiece to get there. O'Riley was badly in need of a cigarette. What he could really use was a stiff drink, but he guessed he'd have to settle for a smoke. He shuffled down the hall to his office. He supposed he'd better call Anne and tell her he didn't know when he'd be home.

* * *

Sheldon Cohen, Esquire, didn't arrive until almost six. In the meantime, in an effort to be a hospitable host, O'Riley had sent Jablonski to a nearby deli for some sandwiches and chips for themselves and Buenzli. While Cohen and Buenzli spent the better part of an hour closeted in the interrogation room, O'Riley and Jablonski sat in O'Riley's office. Or, more precisely, O'Riley sat behind his desk popping antacids while Jablonski paced back and forth in the small confines of the room.

"Stop that goddamned pacing," O'Riley finally said. "You're making me dizzy. What the hell do you think you're doing, practicing waitin' around for your kid to be born?"

Jablonski came to a halt in front of the window, then spun around on his heel and finally sat down in the empty chair. "This morning, after we talked to Ferguson, I would've bet anything that Buenzli had killed all of 'em. He fit the profile to a tee. But now," he said, shaking his head, "it sure as shit isn't looking good. What do you think?"

"I think you and I were both so desperate to be done with the case that we deluded ourselves into believing that Buenzli might be responsible for all the murders." O'Riley heaved a great sigh. "Unfortunately, things don't usually work out that neatly. Even if Buenzli did kill the girl we found today, there's no way the D.A. would issue a warrant based on what we've got so far," he said, chomping down another handful of antacids. "And if I were a betting man, I'd say Buenzli's clean, and once we get Dr. Packard's report, we're probably going to find that we're looking for two different killers, just like I told you this morning."

Jablonski snorted. "Clean? How can you say Buenzli's clean? He's already admitted to dealing drugs while on duty. I wouldn't say that entitles him to a merit badge."

O'Riley shrugged. "Compared to facing a bunch of murder charges, drug dealing is a fairly minor offense."

"Shit!" Jablonski growled. "I was so sure we'd be

able to make an arrest today. God, how I wish this whole damn thing were over with. Hunting for one killer was bad enough. Now you're tellin' me we're probably looking for two. Fuck! What did I do to deserve this?"

In spite of himself, O'Riley couldn't help but be amused. "What's the matter, kid? Your boundless enthusiasm finally wearing a little thin?"

"Stop patronizing me." Jablonski bristled. His face was flushed. "Why the hell did you ever take this case anyway? I'm tired of listening to your bellyaching about how you could've spent the summer fishing. Well why didn't you? Maybe if you'd been man enough to turn down the assignment, the mayor could've appointed somebody with the balls to run this investigation right instead of going with a drunken old has-been who should've hung up his badge years ago!"

"Listen here, you dumb Polack!" O'Riley exploded, finally giving into his pent-up rage at once again having his retirement snatched away from him. "I don't see anybody holding your feet to the fire. If you don't like the way I'm handling the investigation, then I suggest you ask for a reassignment. Because, like it or not, I *am* in charge here. And some days I don't feel like listening to you crowing about what great things cracking this case is going to do for your career. I'd like to have a little more action and a lot less talk out of you. You got that?"

"Yeah, I got it," Jablonski answered sullenly.

"Good. I'm glad we understand each other."

There was a knock at the door. "Come in," O'Riley yelled brusquely.

Sheldon Cohen stepped inside. "Gentlemen, could I have a word with you?"

"Sure, counselor," O'Riley replied. "I'm afraid we're a little short on chairs here. Greg, would you let the man sit down?" Jablonski started to get to his feet.

"That's quite all right," Cohen said. "I'll stand." He walked over toward the window and leaned against one of the file cabinets. "First of all, I have instructed my client not to answer any further questions. If you want to try to get an arrest warrant, be my guest, but I don't think you've got a snowball's chance in hell of getting one. And even if you do, I guarantee I'll get a judge to dismiss any charges that are brought. Besides, for what it's worth, I believe him when he says that he has no knowledge of last night's murder or any other murder."

Cohen took a handkerchief out of his pocket and loudly blew his nose. "Excuse me," he said. "Hay fever." He put the handkerchief back in his pocket. "Now then, unfortunately for him, my client did make certain incriminating statements before I arrived, and you will no doubt be referring those to Internal Affairs for further investigation. Being a good citizen, my client would be willing to provide you with additional information regarding—how shall I say it—extracurricular activities engaged in by other members of the department, in exchange for a grant of immunity. Are you interested?"

O'Riley ground his teeth together. "I'll have to consult with the D.A. before agreeing to any deals."

"That's fine," Cohen said amicably. "I assume you won't be able to do that until tomorrow sometime, and I also assume you'll have no objection to releasing my client tonight. I will guarantee he won't leave the city."

"All right," O'Riley said. "Tell him he's suspended, with pay, until we get this resolved."

"He'll be very pleased to hear that," Cohen said, smiling. "Lieutenant, it's been a pleasure meeting you," he said as he headed for the door. "I assume you'll be in touch, Detective." He nodded to Jablonski as he walked out into the hall.

"Oh, shit!" Jablonski exclaimed when he was sure Cohen was out of earshot. "Why did you agree to that?"

"Because we have no case, and if we tried to pursue it, we'd look like laughingstocks."

"Now what do we do?" Jablonski asked dejectedly.

"I don't know what you're going to do," O'Riley said, standing up, "but I am going to go home and get very drunk. And tomorrow morning we're both going to come back in here, try to put our differences behind us, and keep looking for the killer, or killers, as the case may be. Unless, of course, you've decided you'd like to be reassigned."

Jablonski looked down at the floor, then met O'Riley's steady gaze and shook his head.

O'Riley nodded. "Try to get a good night's sleep. Believe me, you're gonna need it. 'Cuz when the mayor and the superintendent find out we had a viable suspect and had to let him go, *and* that we might now be hunting for two maniacs instead of one, there's gonna be some major ass-chewing going on. Now scram. I'll see you in the morning."

CHAPTER 23

The last month had been the most depressing time of Megan's life. After Paul received delivery of the engagement ring, he had sent her dozens of roses accompanied by soulful pleas that they meet and talk things out. After about ten days of vacillating, Megan had reluctantly agreed to meet him for drinks after work in a crowded, well-lit bar.

Megan had been very jittery about the meeting and was proud of the fact that she'd been able to maintain her composure. She'd arrived at the bar fifteen minutes early and was on her second scotch and water before Paul even arrived, in a somewhat futile attempt to calm her nerves.

She'd taken pains to dress up, wearing a new lavender linen dress accented with a striking, gold-and-purple necklace and matching earrings. She'd paid an exorbitant sum to have her hair and nails done that morning at Elizabeth Arden.

When Paul had walked in, she saw that he, too, must've been concerned about his appearance since he was wearing his best suit—a conservative, black-wool number—with a crisp white shirt and subdued blue-and-white tie. While Megan had always thought the outfit made him look very distinguished, Paul used to laugh and call it his funeral suit. Watching him walk toward her, it occurred to Megan that it was appropriate attire in which to officially end their relationship, though she doubted that was what Paul had in mind.

Paul joined Megan at the small table she'd chosen near the back. He ordered a bourbon and water, and after they each commented how good the other looked,

they managed to make small talk until his drink arrived. Paul must've needed some liquid courage, too,
because he immediately took a couple big gulps. He
managed to dribble some down his chin, and he
quickly wiped it away with his napkin.

Megan waited patiently, until he'd cupped his hands
around the glass and seemed to be on the verge of saying something, before taking the offensive. "So, how
long has it been going on?" she'd asked. Happily her
voice sounded steady.

Paul looked like she'd punched him in the stomach.
"What?" he gasped.

"How long have you been screwing Brenda?"

Paul took another big swallow of his drink before
answering. "That was the only time. I swear."

"Really? Well, then how many others were there before her?"

"Please, Meggie, don't do this," he begged.

"You're the one that insisted on this meeting,"
Megan responded. "You said you wanted to clear the
air. Well, go ahead. I want all the lurid details."

Paul swallowed hard. "I swear that was the only
time I was ever unfaithful."

Megan looked at him intently. Even though she
tended to believe him, she said, "That's nice to know,
but in my book that was one time too many."

"I don't blame you," Paul said, leaning forward
across the table. She knew he would like to hold her
hand, but she had primly folded them in her lap so he
wouldn't be able to see that they were shaking. "I
know what I did was unforgivable, but I don't want to
lose you. Please give me another chance." His eyes
were sad and imploring. "I love you."

Megan tried not to look at him. He was so handsome. She'd almost forgotten his nice long eyelashes,
the curve of his mouth. A host of memories came
flooding back. The way he tasted when she kissed him.
The soothing way he used to rub her back. The way his
skin felt when she was lying next to him in bed. Stop
that! she scolded herself.

She knew Paul was waiting for an answer, but she

made him sweat it out, chewing on her lower lip before
firmly shaking her head. "I can't," she said. "I'm
afraid I never was much good at forgiving and forgetting. And after all, what you did wasn't exactly a minor slipup."

"I know. You're absolutely right." Paul nodded his
head in agreement. "But I promise I'll make it up to
you. We can go slow for a while. Just don't give up on
us."

Megan was surprised at how tempted she was. She'd
been prepared to tell him to go to hell, maybe throw
her drink in his face for good measure, and then walk
out. But it wasn't so simple. They'd been through so
much together. She felt so lonely without him. Sometimes she'd wake up in the night from a bad dream and
long to be able to have him hold her and tell her not to
be scared, that she was safe with him. Maybe they
could work things out in time. But she took a deep
breath and shook her head again. "I can't," she repeated. "Believe me, I'm not being rash. I've had
plenty of time to think this through. As you can imagine, I haven't thought of much else, and I'm positive I
don't want to see you anymore."

Paul looked like he might cry. "Please," he repeated
sorrowfully.

Megan finished her drink, holding the glass firmly in
both hands to prevent them from trembling, then she
pushed back her chair and stood up. "If you'll excuse
me, I have another appointment," she lied. "Good-bye,
Paul." She turned and quickly left the bar, leaving Paul
sitting there open-mouthed. Then she walked back to
her car and threw up on the parking ramp.

What have I done? she thought as she wiped her
mouth with a tissue. Was this a mistake? No, damn it.
This was how it had to be, even though seeing Paul in
person had been rough.

Although she might be having second thoughts, evidently she must have convinced Paul that she'd meant
what she said, because she hadn't heard from him
since.

She'd been reasonably successful in convincing people that the breakup had been mutual. She'd had to tell Michael Gillette that they wouldn't be needing the Yacht Club for the wedding reception. Gillette had looked at her a bit quizzically and said he was sorry to hear that, but he hadn't pressed.

Megan had been a bit more candid with her parents, although she hadn't told them the whole story, and they had been unfailingly supportive. Her dad had quoted Edna St. Vincent Millay—" 'Tis not love's going hurts my days, but that it went in little ways"—and her mother had asked if she'd seen the latest issue of *Money* magazine because it had a very good article on diversifying your investments. Megan had confided the whole awful story to her brother, Jim, and he had invited her to come to Houston to spend some time with him and his live-in girlfriend. Although Megan had had to decline because of demands at work, it had made her feel better knowing that she had a safe harbor waiting if she needed it.

To take her mind off her breakup with Paul, Megan threw herself into her work with a vengeance, although most days she felt like she was just going through the motions without having any real interest in what she was doing. She and Ron spent countless hours going through the hospital's staff medical records and hadn't found anything useful. It seemed like the hospital's doctors were an incredibly healthy bunch and if they were sick, they were scrupulous about voluntarily absenting themselves from their practice until they'd recovered. While skimming through the files, Megan noted in passing that Dr. Lenz had taken a couple months' bereavement leave when his wife and sons were killed in a car accident. She'd been surprised that the doctor would have allowed the event to disrupt his life. He struck Megan as being the stoic type, who would've been back on the job within hours after the funerals.

Luckily, thanks to Dr. Leibowitz, things in the AIDS case did seem to be going well. The doctor had followed up his resounding success at his deposition by issuing another lengthy report, explaining in greater detail why he believed the hospital was at fault. As a result, Megan was feeling cautiously optimistic about the case.

And she'd had a big success recently when she'd won a temporary injunction stopping the demolition of a historic building near city hall. George Barrett had loudly praised her work on the case, and she knew that victory would mean an important mark in her favor when the vote on her partnership came around. It was ironic that just when her career was going great guns, her personal life was so lousy that she wasn't even sure partnership was what she wanted. The problem was she didn't know what the hell she *did* want.

Although Megan had thought keeping busy would be beneficial, deep down she knew she'd been over-doing it. She had no appetite and had dropped ten pounds, which she could ill afford to lose. She had circles under her eyes from lack of sleep, and lately she'd been feeling really run-down. Ron and Rita watched over her like concerned siblings. They prodded her to eat properly and to get enough rest. She knew they were very worried about her, and they kept urging her to take a few days off. She had promised them that she'd try to get more sleep, but the truth was that for her, keeping busy was the best medicine.

Megan and Ron entered the main door of the federal center and walked silently toward the elevators. As he pushed the UP button, Ron said, "Penny for your thoughts."

Megan looked up. "I'm sorry. My mind was wander-ing. What did you say?"

Ron smiled kindly. "You're awfully quiet this morn-ing. I just wondered if something was wrong."

Megan switched her brown leather briefcase to her other hand, buttoned the jacket of her black-and-white suit, and tossed her hair. "Wrong?" she snorted. "Re-mind me: Has anything gone right in the last six months? God, this has sure turned out to be a shitty year. I can't wait till it's over."

Ron nodded. "Hang in there, kid. You'll make it."

He paused, then added softly, "I know how bad you feel about Edna."

The elevator doors opened and they stepped inside. It was the second week in September, and they were on their way to a settlement conference with Judge Edwards. Although Megan didn't harbor any illusions that the hospital would want to settle, the timing of the conference was apropos.

Edna Randolph had paid Megan a visit the day after Labor Day. Edna said she'd been feeling awfully tired recently and had lost some weight and had lingering flulike symptoms, so she'd gone to the doctor and had just learned that she, too, now had full-blown AIDS.

Megan had been devastated, but Edna handled the news with her usual wry good humor. "Better me than Sam or Claudia," she'd said philosophically. "I've had a good life, and I won't be leaving anybody behind. Sam has younger kids who need him and Claudia's just a young chick herself."

"You make it sound like you're ready to give up," Megan had said in disbelief.

Edna had laughed. "Don't you worry about that, honey. I'm not just gonna lay down and die. If the Grim Reaper wants me, he's gonna have to fight like hell to get me."

Megan had been moved to tears. She'd come around her desk and embraced Edna, and the older woman had consoled her. She'd crushed Megan against her ample bosom and said, "Hey, cheer up. I'm a tough old broad. That bonehead Parks hasn't seen the last of me. But maybe this will make the bastards pony up some money. What do you think?"

Megan was skeptical. She had immediately sent Parks a letter informing him of this new wrinkle in the case. He hadn't responded yet. It would be interesting to see what he had to say today. Megan knew it was foolish, but she took Edna's decline as another personal failure.

When Megan and Ron reached Judge Edwards's outer office, they found that Frank and Dr. Lenz were already there, both attired in dark gray suits. Oh, shit!

Megan thought. Parks alone was hard enough to stomach. With the mood she was in, trying to remain civil to that egomaniac Lenz was going to be next to impossible.

Dr. Lenz completely ignored Megan and Ron. He continued jotting some notes on a legal pad, but Frank greeted them brightly. "Good morning. How are you two today?"

"Not so bad. How about yourself?" Ron answered jovially, setting his briefcase down and taking a seat next to Frank.

"Have you had a chance to go over my letter about Mrs. Randolph's condition?" Megan interrupted. She, too, had set her briefcase on the floor, but rather than occupying the empty chair next to the doctor, she elected to stand near the doorway.

"Yes, I got your letter," Frank answered easily. "I was sorry to hear about Mrs. Randolph, and I did discuss it with the hospital board. But why don't we wait until the judge calls us in before we get into a protracted discussion about it."

In a few moments the four of them were seated in the judge's office. Several days earlier Megan had furnished the judge with a synopsis of the evidence she intended to introduce at trial regarding damages. In the report, Megan had informed the judge that her clients had authorized her to settle the case now for five million dollars.

"This is a tough case, for both sides," Judge Edwards said, looking first at Megan and Ron. "In my opinion, the plaintiffs are going to have an uphill battle convincing a jury that the hospital should have required Dr. Morris to undergo further testing. However," he went on, turning to Frank and Dr. Lenz and rubbing the bridge of his nose with his thumb and forefinger, "if they make it past that hurdle, a jury is likely to award them a lot of money, particularly in light of the recent revelation that a second plaintiff also has AIDS. Doctor, Mr. Parks, I know in the past the hospital has been steadfast in its insistence that it wants to see this thing through and have its innocence proven and publicized, but I wonder if it hasn't had second thoughts about staying that course."

"May I address that question, Your Honor?" Dr. Lenz jumped in before Frank had a chance to speak.

The judge nodded. "Of course, Doctor. That's why you're here."

Dr. Lenz flashed the briefest of smiles in acknowledgment and shifted in his chair. "Your Honor, the hospital is just as much a victim here as the plaintiffs. Since news of Dr. Morris's condition was released, the hospital's revenues have dropped ten percent. Its reputation has been tarnished. So while I am sympathetic to the plaintiffs' plight, since the hospital bears no responsibility for causing their condition, it would be inappropriate for us to offer them any type of settlement."

Megan shot the doctor a nasty look, but he pretended not to notice.

The judge turned back to Frank. "Mr. Parks, do you have anything to add?"

"No, Your Honor," Frank replied.

"Well," the judge continued, "since we're obviously not going to be able to dispose of the case today, I want to reaffirm that we're set for a bifurcated trial with the liability phase starting on December first. Anyone have any questions or comments? Okay, thanks for coming in, folks." He closed his file.

As the lawyers were stowing their files in their briefcases, Frank said to the judge, "That murder last week was pretty close to your old stomping ground, wasn't it? Didn't you used to live near the beach?"

"Yes, we did, until about five years ago," Judge Edwards replied, opening a desk drawer and taking out a fresh legal pad. "And believe me, after hearing the news, my wife was extremely glad that we moved to the suburbs."

"I've heard rumors that it's the same guy who killed a number of women in the spring," Ron said. "If that's true, I can't believe they haven't caught him yet."

The judge shrugged. "I know it's not a pleasant

thought, but sometimes serial killers are never found. Look at Jack the Ripper."

"That's different," Megan put in. "The investigative techniques available a hundred years ago weren't very sophisticated. But now, when they can determine blood type from a hair follicle, it is amazing that they haven't been able to find him."

"Yes, but apparently that's the problem," Dr. Lenz put in. "I read someplace that the Oak Street Beach killer left no clues whatsoever. Apparently the police are marveling at how clever he is. Not to mention the fact that if he's willing to risk murdering someone in such an upscale area, he's obviously not afraid of the devil himself."

"So maybe your wife shouldn't feel so safe out there in the suburbs," Ron said to Judge Edwards.

The judge smiled. "I don't think I'll tell her that." Turning to Megan, he said, "Let's get a woman's perspective here. Have the killings made you feel more unsafe about living in the city?"

Megan bristled a bit. She was getting tired of being asked that same question by every man she talked to. She resented it when men assumed all women were terrified to be alone. Of course, some women did fit that mold. Rita Montenaro had been so rattled by the latest murder that she had encouraged Megan to carry a can of mace in her purse and was talking about taking a self-defense class. And Megan had to admit that, for a few nights after the murder, she hadn't slept so well herself. But she'd largely been successful in conquering her uneasiness and she'd be damned if she'd give this roomful of men the satisfaction of knowing that in her heart she would feel safer if she were still spending her nights with Paul.

She shook her head firmly in response to the judge's question. "No. I live on a well-lit street, and I feel safe enough there. I mean, you have to use your head walking to the car at night, but you've got to do that just about anywhere in the country these days. I guess my feeling has always been that if something's gonna happen, then it's gonna happen. It's the price we pay for being part of modern society. After all, what's the alternative? You can't very well inter yourself in a tomb."

The judge nodded. "That's probably a sensible attitude, but I don't mind saying that I'm a little more concerned about leaving my wife home alone at night than I used to be." He jotted a few notes on his legal pad, then looked up. "Well, let's hope the police will catch the guy soon so that discussions like this will go back to being strictly academic."

" 'Truth will come to light; murder cannot be hid long,' " Frank said brightly. "I think they'll catch him eventually."

"Amen to that," Megan said.

As Ron and Megan were waiting for the elevator, Frank and Dr. Lenz breezed by them, heading for the stairway. Even though she knew there was nothing to be gained by antagonizing them, Megan was in a foul mood and needed to vent her spleen on someone. Ignoring the hand Ron had placed on her arm, she called after the two men, "If the hospital comes to its senses and decides it wants to settle, you know where to find us."

Never breaking stride, Dr. Lenz merely looked over his shoulder and gave her one of his icy looks, but Frank stopped and turned, a slight smile on his face. He looked Megan in the eye and said, "You're right about that. I do know where to find you." Then he turned on his heel and hurried off after his client.

CHAPTER 24

Frank pressed his head back into the buttery-soft, brown leather of the sofa and closed his eyes for a moment. He was seated in the library at his home, preparing for an oral argument before the Illinois Supreme Court in one of his malpractice cases. It was a chilly September evening, and a fire crackled in the marble fireplace. The library had a complete set of *Illinois Appellate Reporters,* and the floor in front of him was littered with books. He'd been researching for a solid two hours and was beginning to get eyestrain. It felt good to be able to relax for a few minutes and enjoy the warmth of the fire.

Although Frank had always thrived on activity, the last couple months had been unusually hectic, even for him. It seemed that every few days he was flying someplace or other. The next day he had to go to Springfield. Next week he'd be back in Bethesda for the continuation of Dr. Gillian's deposition. The week after that he had three days of depositions in Boston. At the end of the month he had a two-day trial in Chicago. And the trial in the AIDS case was now less than three months off. His schedule showed no sign of easing up until after the first of the year.

At the thought of the AIDS case, Frank frowned and rubbed his right palm over his forehead. He usually had a fairly happy-go-lucky attitude about lawsuits. He always gave his client his best effort and then let the chips fall where they may. He had to admit, though, that this case had him worried.

It wasn't that he disagreed with Dr. Lenz's reasoning behind the directive not to offer the plaintiffs a settlement. There was a chance the hospital would come out of the trial with a finding of no liability. What bothered Frank was Dr. Lenz's unwillingness to even consider the possibility that they might lose. And the potential for a loss was always there in every case, and it loomed particularly large in cases like this one, where the jurors' emotions would so obviously come into play.

Frank would do everything in his power to see that they won, but he knew it was going to be an uphill battle. While Drs. Lenz and Gillian were both good witnesses, they paled in comparison to the charismatic Dr. Leibowitz. A loss would be a bitter pill to swallow and could be potentially devastating to Frank's hefty medical-malpractice-defense business. He was looking forward to having the trial behind him and getting some well-deserved rest.

He tugged at the sleeve of his cream-colored, fisherman's knit sweater and crossed his left leg over his right knee. Maybe he could sneak some time off in January. Madeline had been dropping hints about wanting to go someplace warm. In fact, she'd brought the subject up again the night before, when they'd been in bed. She'd been giving him a blow job—an activity that she had elevated to an art form—when she'd gotten chilled. As she'd scooted back under the covers to continue her ministrations, she had said in a sultry voice, "Don't you wish we were doing this on a nice warm beach somewhere?" He'd agreed, but the truth was she made him so hot they could be going at it on an ice flow in the Arctic Circle and he probably wouldn't notice the temperature.

Frank smiled. Madeline was a treasure. She had brought him ecstasy beyond his wildest dreams. She deserved a vacation in the sun. Maybe he'd surprise her with a trip to Aruba. That would make a nice Christmas present. She was impossible to buy for anyway. He usually got her a nice piece of jewelry or an accessory like an expensive handbag. She always claimed to adore whatever he selected, but he had a feeling a trip to the tropics would really excite her.

Since Madeline had expressed the opinion that Frank seemed to be keeping her isolated from the kids, he had made an effort to include her in more family activities. She and Jack hit it off real well. Madeline liked sports and fast cars, two of Jack's favorite things, so they always had plenty to talk about. Of course, Jack could charm a smile out of the Sphinx.

Getting Kate to loosen up was taking a bit longer, but Madeline seemed to be making some progress there, too. She had quite an extensive collection of classical music on CD's and had loaned Kate some of them. Kate had thanked her politely, and Frank was quite sure the girl had listened to the recordings. Maybe the time had come for the kids to understand the depth of their dad's relationship with his friend. Yes, a winter trip might be just the ticket.

Frank opened his eyes and looked around him as though he were seeing his library for the first time. This was his favorite room in the house, especially in cool weather when he could light a fire. The twelve-foot, vaulted ceiling featured a hand-painted mural depicting the nine muses. The home's original owner had not been a true bibliophile, and the finely bound leather books that had graced his shelves had been mainly for show.

Frank, on the other hand, had been an avid book collector all his life, and the room now boasted countless yards of books, some of them extremely rare and valuable. Frank's special area of interest was eighteenth-century English authors, and the jewel in his collection was a first edition of Dr. Johnson's 1755 dictionary, a bequest from Frank's grandfather.

As Frank momentarily lost himself in admiring his possessions, Cleopatra, Kate's gray, long-haired cat, came bounding into the room. As she turned the corner, her feet hit the highly polished parquet floor, and she began to slide. Although she had no front claws, she tried to brace herself with her back feet. The effort failed and she went on skidding until her momentum was finally slowed when she hit the edge of one of the room's thick Oriental rugs. Having regained control of her movements, she ran under a walnut table and hid.

Frank sat up straight. "Damn it, Cleo! You're going to put more scratches in the floor." He stood up and went to the door to see if he could determine the cause for the animal's haste. Looking down the hall, he saw Jack standing outside the dining room, a sheepish expression on his face.

"Were you teasing Cleo again?" Frank asked sternly as he stepped out of the room.

The boy shook his head. "No." He was wearing black jeans and a Chicago Bears sweatshirt.

"Then why did she come running into the library like a bat out of hell?" Frank asked.

"I wasn't teasing her," Jack explained seriously. "I was only trying to play with her."

"I don't know why you keep trying to be friendly with her," Frank said. "You know Kate is the only person in the house she likes. I would think you'd get tired of always being rejected. Why don't you just play with Marc?"

"What good is having a cat you can't play with?" Jack asked reasonably.

Frank rolled his eyes toward the ceiling, knowing it was futile to argue with the indisputable logic of a nine-year-old. "Are you finished with your homework?" he asked instead.

Jack started down the hall toward Frank, shuffling his feet, the soles of his black sneakers squeaking on the marble floor. "Some of it," he replied.

"Which part isn't done?" Frank inquired.

"Well, I don't think I'm done with all of my algebra problems."

"How many do you think you have left to do?" his father asked patiently.

Jack curled up his lip. "I dunno, maybe twelve or so."

"Well, I'll tell you what," Frank said, walking over to the boy and putting his arm around his shoulder. "Why don't you try to finish them up and when you're done, bring them to me and I'll look them over."

Jack smiled. "That'd be awesome," he said happily.

"I don't know if it'll be awesome or not." Frank laughed. "It's been a long time since I had an algebra class, but I'll see what I can do. Now, why don't we both get back to work, and you come see me in an hour or so."

"Okay, Dad," Jack said, skipping happily down the hall.

Frank had no more settled himself back down on the library sofa when Kate burst in. "Dad, I really need to talk to you," she said.

Frank put down his law book and looked up. "What's the matter?"

Kate walked over to the sofa and sat down beside him. She was wearing stone-washed jeans and a red-and-white sweater. Frank looked at her proudly. She was a very pretty girl. She was going to be a beautiful woman. Just like her mother, he thought with a pang. Long-buried memories came back. The library had been Caroline's favorite room, too. On more than one occasion they had made love in front of the fire. What had gone wrong? he wondered.

As soon as Kate was seated, Cleo came out of her hiding place under the table, jumped up on Kate's lap, and began to purr contentedly. "My recital is coming up in two weeks," Kate said, stroking the cat's head.

"Yes, I know," Frank said. "Two weeks from Saturday. And you're going to be absolutely brilliant."

Kate stopped petting the cat and began to twist her long hair nervously. "You keep saying that, but I know I'm going to embarrass myself. There are going to be a lot of important people there, instructors from Juilliard. I know I'm going to flub up and ruin my chances of ever getting accepted."

Frank smiled. How he'd ended up with two children with such totally opposite dispositions he'd never know. Jack was a social creature, easygoing almost to the point of laziness when it came to his schoolwork. The boy was bright enough and did fairly well in school, but he needed to be continually prodded in order to achieve.

By contrast, from the time Kate had started pre-school, teachers had termed her "brilliant" and "a prodigy." She always excelled scholastically and was doing very well in an accelerated junior high school program. She'd begun playing the piano at age five and it had quickly become her all-consuming passion. She practiced incessantly, always worrying that she wasn't good enough. From the time she was eight, she'd had her heart set on Juilliard. There was no doubt in anyone's mind—except Kate's—that she would be accepted. The girl was convinced that every wrong note she ever played, whether in recital or while she was at home practicing, would mean the end of her dream. Frank often thought it was a shame there wasn't some way to blend the children's personalities and come up with two equally bright but well-adjusted kids.

"So what's worrying you about the recital?" Frank asked.

"Everything!" Kate exclaimed. "But the reason I wanted to talk to you is that I really need a new dress. My dressy fall things don't fit me anymore, and I want something more grown-up."

Frank smiled again. Kate's body had sprouted womanly curves in the last year. It was no wonder her old dresses didn't fit. "I don't think getting you a new dress will present any problem," he said warmly.

Kate's face brightened for the first time. "Great!" she said. "Will you come with me either this weekend or early next week to pick something out?"

Frank sighed. "I'm sorry, honey, but my schedule is just awful right now. The soonest I'd be able to take you is next weekend."

"I can't wait that long!" Kate exclaimed.

"I know you can't, but I have a good idea," Frank said hastily.

"What is it?" Kate said suspiciously, a frown creasing her face.

"I'll bet Madeline would love to take you shopping."

Kate's frown turned into a scowl. "No!" she

exclaimed. She stomped her feet on the floor, causing the cat to yowl.

"What's wrong with that idea?" Frank asked, surprised at her reaction.

"I don't like her, that's what's wrong with it," Kate said forcefully.

"You barely know her," Frank said. "This would be a good chance for the two of you to get better acquainted. She's told me she'd like to spend more time with you."

"I'll bet!" Kate said haughtily. "I *know* what she wants, and it has nothing to do with spending time with me."

"Katharine!" Frank rebuked her sharply.

Kate bristled, but then said in a calmer voice, "If you're going to be busy, why can't Mrs. Gurney take me? I like shopping with her."

The more Frank thought about the idea of Kate and Madeline going on an outing, the more it appealed to him. Even though Kate was worked up about it now, he was sure she would thank him for it later. "Honey, you've seen how Madeline dresses. She has wonderful taste. I'm sure the two of you will be able to come up with a knockout dress."

"I hate the way she dresses! All those super-short skirts." Kate made a face. "I don't want to look like her."

"Of course, you don't," Frank said patiently. "I never implied that you should. I just think she has very good clothes sense and will be able to help you pick out something nice."

"Well, maybe she'll be too busy, too," Kate said hopefully.

"Oh, I'm sure she'll be able to find the time," Frank said. "I'll call her tonight and ask her."

Kate's expression turned soft. "Please don't make me go with her, Daddy," she pleaded. "I really don't want to."

"You'll have a good time," Frank said soothingly. "I promise."

"No, I won't," Kate said angrily, her eyes flashing.

"I'm going to hate every minute of it. You'll see." With that threat, she brushed Cleo off her lap and quickly strode out of the room.

Frank considered going after her, but then decided against it. Kate had a stubborn streak, and he had learned from experience that he could often win her over to his way of thinking simply by leaving her alone. Once she'd had a little time to think about one of his suggestions, she would frequently agree it sounded reasonable. He was confident that this time would be no different.

He looked at his watch. If he hurried, he should have just enough time to finish preparing his argument before he had to plumb the mysteries of square roots and exponents.

CHAPTER 25

Mike O'Riley took a swallow from his mug of strong black coffee and looked out the window of the bare-bones conference room down the hall from his office. The weather had abruptly turned cool right after Labor Day, and the leaves were starting to turn color. It was now mid-September. Officer Buenzli's fate was in the hands of Internal Affairs.

O'Riley had gone home that night so depressed that he'd drunk steadily until early the next morning. Anne had been worried and had sat up with him, but surprisingly the booze had little effect. He had been disappointed. He wanted to be blitzed. He wanted to forget, but try as he might, he couldn't get the newly discovered body, Officer Buenzli, or any other part of the whole goddamned case out of his mind.

In the morning, Anne had made him some strong coffee, packed his lunch, and sent him off again to do battle. He had been unable to tell her how close he'd come to retirement, but somehow he sensed that she knew. She'd kissed him and said, "I have faith in you, Mike. You just need to have faith in yourself."

The murdered woman had been a thirty-year-old buyer for Bloomingdale's named Tammy Clemment. She and her husband, Rick, lived in a swank high rise near the Oak Street Beach. Tammy was a fitness nut and had left the apartment at seven o'clock to go for a run along the lake.

O'Riley had attended Tammy's autopsy. God he hated those things. It was one thing to look at an intact dead body—not that Tammy's had been all that intact when they'd found her. It was something else again to watch one being methodically dissected. He didn't know how much money forensic pathologists made, but if they got five times that amount, it still wouldn't be enough.

He was always taken a bit aback by the lighthearted atmosphere that seemed to prevail at postmortems. Talk about graveyard humor. The pathologist and his assistants were always unfailingly respectful toward the deceased, but inevitably cracked jokes while they went about their business. "Did you hear about the cannibal that rented a new apartment? . . . It cost him an arm and a leg." "Why did they have to stop the leper hockey game? . . . There was a face off in the corner." Of course when your entire job description consisted of taking dead bodies apart, you probably had to take your humor where you could find it.

There had been little levity at Tammy's autopsy. Everyone in attendance had been visibly moved, particularly when Dr. Packard announced that there was no doubt Tammy's wounds had been inflicted with the same knife used on the four redheaded women. A quick check of the file on the victim found on Damen showed that her wounds matched up as well.

"Are you sure?" O'Riley had gasped.

"I'm positive," Dr. Packard had responded. "The two lethal wounds are identical in all cases: one to the heart and one to the left lung. The massive abdominal cutting on the last two victims occurred after death and possibly was done to throw us off the scent."

Goddamn it! O'Riley had sworn under his breath. He'd made certain that the unique wound pattern had never been reported in the press, so there was no doubt that the killer had now claimed six victims. And to think he'd seen the fifth one with his own eyes and had been too damn stupid to connect her with the earlier murders. He should have suspected there was a link, but with his arrogance and his fervent desire to quit the department, he'd seen only what he'd wanted to see. As a result, a different team of detectives had been following up on that slaying, and O'Riley's people had lost valuable investigative time.

To make matters even worse, Rick Clemment's family was socially prominent in Chicago, and O'Riley had received a terse phone call from the senior Mr. Clemment, saying he expected immediate action on finding his daughter-in-law's killer. O'Riley had resisted the temptation to tell the old fart to go screw himself. Instead, he'd politely assured him that everything humanly possible was being done to track down the assailant.

To that end, O'Riley had assembled the team's group of experts on this crisp fall morning to discuss this latest slaying. As he glanced around the table where they all sat patiently, waiting for him to get the show on the road, O'Riley mentally ticked off their hourly rates and calculated how much this meeting was costing the city. It was totally exorbitant, but screw it. At this point he'd be willing to auction off city hall to the highest bidder if he thought it'd help catch the murderer. He took another swallow of coffee and took a closer look at the cast of characters.

To O'Riley's left was Dr. Sheridan, the psychiatrist with a background in sex crimes. The doctor was in his early fifties, tall, with thinning brown hair. He wore horn-rims and a pained expression. No doubt he was recalling O'Riley's outburst at their earlier meeting. If that pompous ass didn't start coming up with some answers, he was really going to see some fireworks.

Next to Dr. Sheridan was Dr. Elizabeth Monson, a clinical psychologist. The doctor was an attractive blond woman in her late forties. O'Riley was no expert on women's fashions, but he could recognize expensive clothes when he saw them, and Dr. Monson's clearly fit the bill. She was wearing a simple, two-piece, navy knit dress with a wide, red leather belt that accentuated her still small waist. Although he couldn't identify her red-and-blue leather Vuitton Noé bag or her floral Hermés scarf by name, O'Riley knew they probably cost as much as he made in a month. He wished he had the money to buy Anne an outfit like that.

To Dr. Monson's left sat a very weary-looking Greg

Jablonski. His eyes were bloodshot and were ringed by dark circles. His obvious exhaustion was due to the months of long hours finally catching up with him, coupled with the fact that his wife had given birth to a baby girl four days after Tammy Clemment's slaying. The baby's arrival had kept Jablonski away from his desk only thirty-six hours. O'Riley had heard from Marge Petronek that the delivery had been a difficult one, and that the baby was unusually fussy. As a result, Marge reported, Greg's wife was none too happy that he was still working on this case. O'Riley had resisted the temptation to gloat, since he had told the young man back in May that his wife's unflagging support for his career might very well run out once the child had arrived.

O'Riley and the young detective seemed to have reached a rapprochement about the handling of the investigation. The morning after the debacle with Officer Buenzli, both men had arrived at work bright and early. Jablonski had started to apologize, but O'Riley had cut him off, saying they had to direct their full energies toward the case and not waste time on petty personal squabbles. Their tiff had brought home to each of them the need to be a little more tolerant and to keep an open mind.

Next to Jablonski was Dr. Randall Packard. He'd been a real godsend throughout the investigation. During Tammy's autopsy, Dr. Packard's voice had cracked several times as he reported his findings. O'Riley had always known that Packard was a hell of a good guy, but that small humanizing gesture had won him O'Riley's highest respect.

Rounding out the group was Dr. Douglas Mandrake, a white-haired, retired medical examiner in his late sixties, who had been called in to review the autopsy reports on all of the victims.

O'Riley called the meeting to order. "I trust that by now you have all had a chance to review the results of the postmortem on Tammy Clemment." His comment was met by nods from all present. "Good," O'Riley continued. "I asked you to come in today so that we could have a chance to share our views about this murder all at once, rather than waiting for each of you to prepare your own separate reports."

"Excuse me a minute, Lieutenant," Jablonski interrupted. He looked like he'd just come out of a coma. He sat up straighter in his chair and dug into a manila folder. "That reminds me. As long as you're all here, I'd like to hand out the updated computer discs with all relevant data we've received up through last Friday." He passed out the discs to the four doctors.

"Thanks, Greg," O'Riley said. "I'm sure all of you will want to review that information carefully." He scratched the back of his head with his ballpoint pen. "Now I'm sure it goes without saying that we've got a couple of new issues to address. First, the last two killings were much more brutal than the first four. As we all know, the trend toward escalating violence is common in serial killings, but why was there such a marked increase in carnage all at once? Second, after killing four tall, thin redheads, why would our man suddenly have opted to go after short brunettes?" He looked around the table expectantly. "Well, who'd like to start?"

Dr. Monson spoke first. "The utter brutality of the last two killings was something the rest of us were discussing before you arrived, Lieutenant," she said, brushing a strand of well-coiffed hair out of her face. "In fact, it looks like the killer was trying to obliterate the victim's sex organs."

"And why would he do that?" O'Riley asked.

"Frankly, we don't know," Dr. Monson admitted. "It's possible, as you and Dr. Packard suggested, that the mutilation was done to make it look like someone else was responsible for the murders."

"It's very common for serial killers to become emboldened and embellish their techniques," Dr. Mandrake said. "Thus with each successive killing there may be more mutilation, or the killer might strike in areas where there is a greater risk of detection. For some of these people, apparently just getting away with a run-of-the-mill murder no longer provides the rush they need to stimulate them. A case in point is that the last two victims were nude. The killer took the time to undress them and dispose of their clothing. The extra time required for that endeavor substantially increases the risk of being caught."

O'Riley looked around the table. "Any other ideas?"

"It's possible that the killer's new prototype, the shorter, dark-haired woman, represents someone toward whom the killer is directing even greater anger than he displayed with the red-haired women," Dr. Sheridan put in.

O'Riley rubbed his eyes. "The switch to an entirely different type of woman baffles me more than anything. As long as the guy was consistent in picking out tall redheads, I was willing to go along with the idea that what he was doing was getting revenge on a real, live woman who looked like the victims. But for me that theory goes completely to hell when he, number one, doesn't kill anybody for four months, and number two, then suddenly starts targeting women who bear no resemblance at all to the first group."

"Maybe the killer suffered harm at the hands of two separate women, and first he gained revenge on one, and now he's striking back at the second," Dr. Packard suggested.

"I just don't buy that scenario," O'Riley said. "If he wanted revenge on two women, why didn't he alternate and first kill a red-haired one, and the next time kill a brown-haired one? And what was going on during the four months there weren't any killings?"

"Maybe he was hospitalized or incarcerated during that time," Dr. Mandrake opined.

"We've checked on that angle and came up cold," O'Riley replied. "Anybody got any other thoughts?"

"Not along that line," Dr. Mandrake went on, "but in my experience it is very unusual that there was no sign of seminal fluid in any of the murders, despite the fact that all the victims showed evidence of vaginal and anal penetration with a blunt object."

"What do the rest of you think of that?" O'Riley asked.

Dr. Sheridan spoke up. "I agree with Dr. Mandrake that normally, in sexually motivated slayings, there will be semen—if not deposited in the victims themselves, then nearby, the result of masturbatory effort," the doctor said in his high pitched voice.

"Okay," O'Riley said. "Any ideas why there has been no semen? Do you think the killer is impotent?"

"That is possible," Dr. Sheridan said. "Obviously, in cases of this type, the perpetrator has very deep feelings of resentment toward women. Many sex offenders are incapable of consummating the sex act with a female partner, at least with a live one. But most of them are perfectly able to achieve an erection and ejaculate through masturbatory means, particularly after they have rendered their victim unconscious."

O'Riley stared at the doctor, a slight smirk on his face. "So what you're saying in plain English, Doc, is that these guys may not be able to perform normally with a living, breathing woman but they're able to jack off over her body after they've killed her."

Dr. Sheridan didn't bat an eye. "Yes, Lieutenant, I guess that is a fair paraphrase of my statement."

"Okay," O'Riley said, pursing his lips. "Another issue we need to talk about is how you think the killer selects his victims. If he's targeting a certain physical type, he can't just go out and be guaranteed he'll find a woman who looks the way she's supposed to. How do you think he finds someone appropriate for his needs?"

"We certainly haven't been able to find any connection between any of the victims," Jablonski said.

"From the information we have so far, I'm afraid it's impossible to say how the victims are selected," Dr. Monson said. The others nodded in agreement.

"Wonderful," O'Riley grunted. "So what do you think we can expect to see next?" O'Riley asked, rubbing his eyes. "I don't know about any of you, but I sure as hell don't want to imagine anybody attacked more violently than Tammy Clement was. I mean, what else could the guy do, unless he starts cannibalizing the bodies?"

Dr. Sheridan shook his head. "I'd be very surprised if we'd see that. The kind of person who is predisposed to cannibalism needs more time to harvest body parts, so generally those types of crimes take place in the killer's home, not in public places."

"That's the first good news I've heard all morning," O'Riley said. His remark was met by small smiles from all present.

"I know we talked about this before, but I'm still wondering if there isn't some chance there could be two men working together?" Jablonski posited. "Maybe one helps lure the women to a secluded area, where the other one kills them? And wouldn't that maybe explain the two different types of women who were killed? Maybe each of the two men have a vendetta against a different woman."

"Well, I suppose anything's possible," Dr. Sheridan admitted, "but, generally, serial killers are loners, distrustful of other people, so they're not likely to enlist another person's help."

"Let's go back to a subject we've discussed in our previous meetings," O'Riley said. "The fact that the two chest wounds, to the heart and left lung, have been absolutely uniform in all six victims. Do you think the killer has some special skill or is he just lucky enough to be able to hit the same two spots time after time?"

"The autopsies revealed that all of the victims were rendered unconscious before they were stabbed," Dr. Packard said, "so the killer has the luxury of working on a stationary victim rather than having to deal with someone who's thrashing about. And since the murders all took place in rather secluded areas, the killer is able to take a little extra time to make sure that the thrusts with the knife are just right."

"The last two victims were nude, but he stabbed the first four through their clothing," O'Riley said. "Don't you think that takes a little more savvy than the average joe would possess?"

"Not necessarily," Dr. Mandrake replied. "I'd be willing to bet that most folks could hit the heart and lungs of another person, if they were so inclined. As

Dr. Packard inferred from his earlier comments, we're dealing with a very methodical killer. He's no doubt driven to kill by highly explosive forces within him. But once he begins to carry out the act, he is deliberate and takes his time."

O'Riley nodded, but this was one area where his views diverged from those of the medical examiners. He still had a feeling there was something significant about the pattern of the victims' wounds. "Do any of you have any other ideas about what kind of bird we're looking for? I mean, I understand you think he's an intelligent loner who probably has a good job and has had some kind of major trauma in his life involving one or more women. But are there any other ideas you can give us?"

After a moment of silence, Dr. Sheridan spoke up again. "The biggest problem you're facing, Lieutenant, is that oftentimes serial killers have something akin to split personalities. They are, in effect, Dr. Jekyll and Mr. Hyde. I'd be willing to bet that if you could watch the person at work, interview his coworkers, you'd never know there was anything amiss in his life. I've even read of instances in which the 'good' person part of the killer's personality is unaware of the existence of the 'bad' guy, where the 'bad' half only comes out when the 'good' guy blacks out. Although a serial killer's mode of operation is likely to remain the same, there is little else predictable about their behavior. That's what makes them so dangerous and so hard to catch."

"That's a chilling portrait." O'Riley shuddered. He pushed back his chair to signal the end of the meeting. "Well, okay, why don't you all go over the new information Greg gave you, think for a day or so about the things we've covered and then get back to us. The way I see it, we can't afford not to consider any possibility, no matter how harebrained it might seem at first glance, because I've got a feeling that while we're sitting here, time is already running out for another woman."

* * *

The scrapbook is growing heavier by the day. The press loved Tammy Clemment and are making quite a fuss over her.

As you'd suspected, it has taken the police a while to figure out that the same person who dispatched Tammy—and pretty Candy Wells over on Damen—has also been responsible for sending those four redheaded women to their final rewards. It was comical to see the speculation. Would the next victim be tall and red-haired or short and brunette? Not even their hair-dresser knows for sure.

Yes, you are leading the police on quite a chase. Only you know that the real victim, the ultimate victim, is yet to come. In a way, it would be a shame to do it. But if it happens, she has no one to blame but her-self. After all, you tried to warn her, hoping to get her out of your life—that is, your alter ego's life—in a less drastic way, but so far she has chosen to ignore the warnings. You will give her one more chance, and if she ignores that final omen, well, let's just say that could turn out to be a fatal mistake.

CHAPTER 26

Megan wished to God she were back in Chicago. Here she was, stuck in Bethesda for the continuation of Dr. Gillian's deposition, while at home her friend Rita lay in a hospital bed, having been run down by a crazed driver as she'd emerged from Megan's apartment after stopping by to feed her cat.

Megan had flown east the previous morning to meet with Dr. Leibowitz in preparation for Gillian's deposition. Ron Johnson was in Phoenix, and Megan had been dreading spending two days alone in Bethesda, since Ron always did wonders to keep her spirits up and her temper in check. The deposition was supposed to start at nine o'clock, but it was delayed by the late arrival of Parks's early morning flight.

While waiting for Parks to get there, Megan had gotten a call from Rita's sister telling her about the accident. Rita had driven over to Megan's place around nine P.M. She'd spent twenty minutes or so playing with Andy and feeding him. She had then turned out all the lights in the apartment, locked the door, and stepped outside.

In the time Rita had been indoors, a driving, cold rain had started to fall. She hadn't brought an umbrella, so she'd paused at the top of the landing and pulled her jacket up over her head before she ran down the steps toward her car, which was parked across the street about a block away. About halfway to the car, she'd stepped off the sidewalk and began to run in the street, close to a line of parked cars, because it seemed to be a bit drier there. The street had seemed deserted when suddenly, Rita had heard a noise behind her.

She'd glanced back just in time to see a car with no lights careening straight toward her at a high rate of speed. Rita had screamed and tried to jump out of the way. She had hurled herself toward the nearest parked car and managed to get her torso and left leg onto the hood. The passing vehicle had struck her right leg, breaking her ankle. The driver of the car had never even slowed down.

Fortunately for Rita, the owner of one of the nearby parked cars had arrived moments later and had conveyed her to the hospital where they'd set her ankle and treated her for shock. Rita hadn't gotten a good look at the car, although her impression was that it was dark in color and full size. She had not seen the driver. So far the police had found no one else who might have witnessed the incident. They suspected a drunk driver. After all, who else would be so oblivious to their surroundings that they'd drive without lights and apparently not even realize they'd hit someone?

Although Rita's sister assured Meg that everything was fine and Rita would be released later that day, Megan was very distraught over the situation. Megan had always prided herself on living in a nice, safe neighborhood. How the hell could something like that have happened on her street? And wasn't it ironic that it had happened to Rita, who was always overly conscious of her own safety? It should've been me, Megan mused forlornly. And at that thought, a great chill had come over her and her stomach had started to churn.

By the time Megan had returned to the conference room where the deposition was to be held, Parks had arrived. "Good morning," he'd said cheerfully. "Was your plane late, too?"

Megan had shook her head. "I got here yesterday."

"Oh. For some reason I thought you were coming in this morning." When there was no response, Frank had looked up and noticed Megan's pallor. "Is something wrong?"

"I just got word that my best friend was in an accident."

"I'm sorry to hear that. I hope she's all right."

"They tell me she'll be fine."

"I'd have no objection if you'd rather not start the deposition just yet," Frank had offered.

Megan had shook her head again. "No. Let's get it over with so I can get home tonight."

Megan wasn't sure if Parks felt sorry for her or if it was because Dr. Lenz wasn't along on this trip, but whatever the reason, the deposition was going smoothly and Parks seemed to be in an unusually good mood. During a break, he asked, "Say, were you the person who got the injunction stopping the city from tearing down the old Randolph Building?"

"Yes," Megan replied. "I'd never done any work in that area, and we didn't have much time to put it all together, but I was real pleased with the outcome."

"You should be," Frank said. "I've worked on some of those cases, and they're tough ones to win."

"I hope I get the chance to work on more of them," Megan said. "Our society is just too eager to tear down beautiful pieces of the past and replace them with high-rise parking ramps."

"I quite agree," Frank said. "I live in Kenwood, and when I see other areas sinking deeper into squalor, I'm so thankful the city designated us a historic district before all our old homes were turned into Baptist churches."

"I love Kenwood," Megan said. "The houses are so majestic."

"So are the heating bills and the upkeep costs." Frank laughed. "But I do enjoy living there, even though I sometimes think it'd make more sense for me to have something smaller." He looked at his watch. "I have to make a quick phone call. Let's say we resume in ten minutes."

The remainder of Dr. Gillian's deposition went off without a hitch, and at four-thirty, Megan was at National Airport waiting to board the Northwest Airlines flight back to Chicago. She had just talked to Rita, who was now at home resting comfortably. Her sister was going to be staying with her for a few days. Their chat had made Megan feel much better. She'd bought some popcorn and was munching away and reading a popular mystery writer's latest novel when she heard a familiar voice.

"Is that book any good? I see it's still on the bestseller list."

Megan looked up. There was Parks, holding his briefcase and a brown leather, carry-on bag. Megan hurriedly swallowed her mouthful of popcorn before replying. "It's okay. His books are really all alike, but I like mysteries and these read fast. Which is a plus because I don't get a lot of time for pleasure reading, except on planes."

"I'm on this flight, too," Frank said. "Mind if I sit there?" He motioned to the seat next to Megan.

"No, go ahead," Megan replied unenthusiastically.

"Have you heard how your friend who was in the accident is doing?" he asked.

"Yes. I just talked to her, and she'll be okay."

"Good," Frank said, shrugging off his Burberry trench coat and draping it over the seat. "So, how do you think things went today?"

"Fine," Megan replied noncommittally. Then she added, "I have noticed that things move along much more smoothly when Dr. Lenz isn't here."

Frank smiled. He couldn't disagree with her on that point. "How do you think Dr. Gillian rates as an expert witness?"

"He's good. I think a jury will like him."

Frank nodded. "I think so, too. Of course, your Dr. Leibowitz is going to be a tough act to follow."

Megan smiled. "He's one of a kind, isn't he?"

"He sure is," Frank said, with a chuckle. "The first time I met him I thought he must be pulling my leg, with that accent and all, but the more I talked to him, the more respect I found I had for the guy. Where in the world did you come up with him? I've done a lot of work in med-mal cases, and I've never run into him before."

Megan's face clouded over for a moment. "My boyfriend had read about him in one of his medical journals and suggested I give him a call," she said smoothly.

"I see," Frank nodded. "I met your boyfriend at that fund-raiser, didn't I?"

"I think so, yes," Megan replied vaguely. Met him? The two men had looked like they wanted to punch each other after Paul started acting like he might jump Parks's companion's bones right in the middle of the Ritz-Carlton's grand ballroom. Who knows? Given Paul's proclivity for buxom blondes, maybe he had connected with her by now. Megan smiled to herself at the thought. That would serve Parks right.

Frank's gaze shifted to Megan's left hand which was clutching her book. "I'm probably out of line for asking, but I couldn't help but notice that the Hope Diamond seems to be missing. What happened?"

Megan bristled. "You're right. You *are* out of line. But to answer your question, I guess it just wasn't making me feel very hopeful anymore, so I gave it back," she said fliply.

Frank smiled but didn't press. He snapped open his briefcase. "Well, I'll let you get back to your story. I've got depositions in another case tomorrow. I guess there *is* no rest for the wicked."

Although Frank quickly became engrossed in his other case, Megan's mind was wandering. She found herself flipping pages in the book, even though she couldn't remember what she'd just read. It had been almost two months since she'd split up with Paul. How long was it going to take before she felt comfortable talking about him?

A soft feminine voice came over the intercom. "Good afternoon, ladies and gentlemen. We're now ready to begin boarding Flight 1223 nonstop to Chicago's O'Hare. At this time would all of our first-class passengers, and any passengers traveling with small children, or anyone who needs a little extra time boarding the aircraft please come forward."

Frank stashed his paperwork in his briefcase and stood up. "I got an upgrade to first class," he explained. "It's one of the few benefits that comes from traveling so much."

Megan nodded, seemingly occupied with her book, and Frank stepped over to the gate.

By the time it was Megan's turn to board, Frank had already settled himself into the plush leather seat and was back reviewing his paperwork. He looked up as Megan passed, lugging her own briefcase and carryon behind her.

"Hard at it already?" she asked. "You're very efficient."

Frank smiled. "Actually I'm as lazy as the next guy. I'm just trying to get a head start on this because I'm dead tired and I'm looking forward to taking a hot shower and going straight to bed when I get home."

Megan smiled back. "Have a nice flight," she said.

"Thanks. Catch you later," Frank replied.

Megan trudged back to her assigned seat, stowed her bags in the overhead compartment, and fastened her seatbelt. Maybe Parks wasn't all bad, once you got him away from his horrid client, that is. She hoped the flight back wouldn't be delayed. She'd told Rita she'd stop by if it wasn't too late. She yawned. God, she was beat. She closed her eyes and immediately drifted off to sleep.

CHAPTER 27

Frank pulled his Mercedes into the garage at seven-forty-five. Suppressing a yawn, he retrieved his bags from the passenger seat, shut the car door, closed the garage door behind him, and headed toward the house.

It had been a productive flight. He'd managed to finish his preparations for the next day's deposition. He'd eaten a snack. All he wanted to do now was skim through the mail, maybe have a leisurely drink, and go to bed.

He had no sooner stepped inside the foyer than Mrs. Gurney came rushing down the stairs. "Oh, Mr. Parks, I'm so glad you're home," she said as she reached the bottom. Her face was flushed, and she sounded out of breath. "I tried to have you paged at the airport, but you must have already left."

Frank hastily dropped his bags on the floor. "What is it, Mrs. Gurney?" he asked anxiously.

"It's Kate," the woman began.

"Kate?" Frank echoed. "What's wrong with Kate? Madeline was supposed to take her shopping after school."

Mrs. Gurney nodded. "That's the problem," she said. "Miss Winters dropped her off about an hour ago, and Kate has been hysterical ever since."

"What happened?" Frank asked.

Mrs. Gurney shook her head. "I don't know. Kate won't tell me. She burst in here crying like the world was going to end, then raced up to her room and locked the door. I tried to coax her into letting me in, but I couldn't get any response out of her."

"She didn't say anything?" Frank pressed. "Nothing at all?"

"Well ..." Mrs. Gurney swallowed hard. "I think I heard her say something about wishing she were dead. That's what really scared me, Mr. Parks. That's when I tried to call you at the airport."

Frank gazed up at the staircase landing. "Did you talk to Miss Winters when she brought Kate home?"

"No, sir. She didn't come in."

"I see." Frank sighed. So much for his plans to make it an early night. "Well, I'd better try to find out what's wrong." He slipped out of his trench coat and tossed it on top of his bags.

In spite of his weariness, Frank climbed the stairs quickly. His mind was spinning. What the hell could have gone wrong on a shopping trip? Kate's bedroom was at the far end of the hall. When he reached the door, he rapped on it lightly. "Kate, I'm home." There was no answer. "Kate, honey, let me in. I want to talk to you."

"Go away," a muffled voice replied.

"I'm not going to go away, sweetie," Frank said warmly. "I know you're upset, but I can't help you unless I know what's wrong."

"I don't want your help," Kate responded in a weak voice.

"Kate, please," Frank said patiently. "I'm going to stand out here until you let me in. I think it would help if we talked about whatever is bothering you."

There was a long pause, then Frank heard the lock being drawn back, and the door slowly opened. He stepped inside.

Kate's room was a young teenage girl's dream, an explosion of lace and blue-and-white floral chintz. On the window seat a family of velvet-clad teddy bears regally held court, a holdover from Kate's younger years.

The girl was sprawled facedown on the white crocheted bedspread of her canopy bed, her face buried in a pillow. She was wearing black stirrup pants and an oversized white sweatshirt. Frank walked over and lightly touched her on the shoulder. "Thanks for letting me in. Now, do you want to tell me what's the matter?"

Kate shook her head.

Frank walked around the bed and sat down in the blue velvet chair next to the dressing table. "Are you sure you don't want to talk about it? I think it might make you feel better."

Kate shook her head again.

"Come on, Katie, what is it? There's nothing so awful that you can't tell me about it."

The girl slowly picked her head up off the pillow. It was obvious she'd been crying. Her hair was matted, and her eyes were red and watery.

"Come on, honey. Tell me. Did something happen to upset you while you were shopping with Madeline?"

Kate looked at her father with her wide dark eyes. She sniffed loudly several times.

"Well," Frank pressed. "Is that it? Something happened while you were shopping?"

Kate nodded slowly.

"Go on. You can tell me."

Kate slowly sat up and took a deep breath. "I told you I didn't want to go shopping with her," she said in a whisper. "I told you I didn't like her. You said I'd have a good time, but I told you I'd hate it." Her sniffling increased.

Frank reached over and pulled several Kleenex out of a box on the dressing table. As he handed them to Kate, he said, "It's okay. Take your time."

Kate blew her nose and continued in a stronger voice. "Madeline picked me up after school. I told her we didn't have to spend a lot of time shopping because I'd already seen a dress I liked at Laura Ashley when I was with Clara last week and I said we could just go there and get it." She blew her nose again and brushed her hair out of her face. "But Madeline wouldn't listen to me. She said Laura Ashley had childish clothes and I should have something more grown-up. So she made me go to all these other stores and try on all these awful dresses."

Kate began to sniffle again. "Go on," Frank said softly.

Kate looked down at the floor and said in a whisper, "Then she . . . she said that I was a spoiled brat, and that after you were married, I'd have to learn how to behave."

"What?" Frank's head snapped up. "She said that?" Jesus Christ! he thought. What in the hell could have gotten into Madeline?

Kate nodded. "And I said it wasn't true, that you weren't ever going to marry her, that there was no way you'd marry somebody so hateful. She just laughed and said that you were." The girl began to sob harder.

"Was there anything else?" Frank asked.

Kate nodded again. "She said I was so unmanageable that it was no wonder my mother left us, and that if I didn't shape up, I was going to turn out to be crazy and a slut just like she was."

Frank could feel the blood rush to his face. His heart began to pound. For a moment he was so blinded with rage that he was frozen to the spot. Kate was now crying uncontrollably. Frank forced himself to remain outwardly calm to avoid upsetting her further. He quickly moved over to the bed and took her in his arms. Pressing her head to his chest, he nuzzled her soft hair. "Shhh. It's okay, honey. Everything's gonna be all right."

When her sobs had subsided somewhat, Kate raised her head. "She said something else, Daddy," she whispered.

"What's that?"

"She said if I told you any of this she'd deny it, and that you'd never believe me and you'd be really mad at me for making up stories."

"Oh, she did, did she?" Frank said. "Well, she was wrong. I do believe you, and I'm certainly not mad at you."

Kate relaxed a bit in his arms, and Frank relaxed as well.

"Now, Kitten, is that all? Have you told me everything that happened?"

Kate nodded.

"Good," Frank said soothingly. "Do you feel a little better?"

Kate nodded again. Frank rocked her for a few moments, then Kate spoke up in a weak voice. "Daddy, can I ask you something?"

"Of course you can."

Kate swallowed hard. "Mom wasn't crazy, was she?"

Frank had a lump in his throat. Over the years he had tried many times to talk to Kate about her mother, but the girl had never shown any interest. "Of course she wasn't crazy," he answered at once. "Your mother was a beautiful and kind woman. You remember her, don't you?"

Kate shrugged. "I don't know. I think I do, but sometimes I'm not sure what really happened and what I made up."

"You are a lot like her, you know," Frank said, rubbing Kate's back. "In lots of nice ways. Your mother played the piano, too. Not as well as you do, but pretty well. And she loved growing flowers. The house was always full of them. We didn't need a gardener when your mom was around."

"Why did she leave?" Kate asked.

Frank fought to find the right words. "I'm not sure, Kitten. I guess she left because she didn't want to be married to me anymore. But there's one thing I'm absolutely sure of," he said, raising Kate's chin with one hand so he could look into her eyes. "She did not leave because of you or Jack. She loved you both very much. You believe that, don't you?"

Kate nodded, reassured.

"Now," Frank said, "would you like something to eat or maybe something to drink?"

Kate blew her nose again. "I'm thirsty. I'd like some lemonade."

"Okay, lemonade it is. I'll be right back."

He returned in a few minutes with a large glass of lemonade and a plate with two of Mrs. Gurney's homemade chocolate chip cookies. "In case you decide you'd like a snack later on," he said, setting the cookies down on the dressing table and handing Kate the lemonade. She took a big swallow. "Is that better?" Frank asked.

Kate nodded.

"Good." Frank smiled at her. "Say, I just had an idea. How about if I pick you up after school tomorrow and we go to Laura Ashley and get you that dress you want?"

"I thought you had to work late tomorrow," Kate said cautiously.

"I'll stop what I'm doing at three-thirty and come get you. That is, if you want me to."

"Would you really go with me?" Kate asked softly.

"Of course, I will." Frank took a deep breath and put his arms around her. "Kate, I'm very sorry for what happened today," he said contritely, "and I hope you'll be able to forgive me for making you do something you didn't want to do."

"It wasn't your fault," Kate murmured.

"Yes, it was," Frank said, "but I'm gonna try very, very hard to make it up to you." He gave her a big hug. "Now, why don't you try to get some rest." He headed toward the door.

"Thanks, Daddy. I love you."

"Good night, honey. I love you, too."

CHAPTER 28

The drive from Frank's home to Madeline's apartment normally took him twenty minutes. That evening he made it in twelve.

He had a vague notion that someone in his mental state had no business behind the wheel of an automobile. He drove like a professional race-car driver, weaving in and out of traffic on Lake Shore Drive, sounding the horn when a slow-moving vehicle had the audacity to get in his way. His hands were clamped so firmly on the steering wheel that he had to flex his fingers a few times to get the blood circulating once he screeched to a halt in front of Madeline's building.

He ignored the doorman's cheery greeting and raced to the elevators. As he leaned on the buzzer outside Madeline's door, he could hear movement inside. "Just a minute. I'm coming," Madeline's low voice announced.

When she opened the door, she didn't seem surprised to see him. "Hi," she said brightly. "Welcome home."

Madeline was wearing a white pant suit, accented with a bright red-and-blue floral scarf, and looked even lovelier than ever, but Frank brusquely pushed past her and walked into the living room. He had left the house in such haste that he'd forgotten to put on his coat, and a sudden chill came over him. He rubbed his hands together. He'd give anything to be sitting at home in front of the fire rather than here.

"Would you like something to drink?" Madeline asked, following him inside. "Or maybe some coffee?"

"No, I would not like something to drink," Frank

said, fighting to keep his voice calm. "What I would like is an explanation of your behavior."

"Why don't you sit down?" Madeline said, settling herself into a rose-colored velvet chair and tucking her legs under her. Scowling, Frank sat down on a cream-colored sofa opposite her.

"Now, what's this all about?" Madeline asked. Then, in answer to her own question, she said, "I assume you've been talking to Kate."

"Yes, I've been talking to Kate," Frank replied in a hoarse voice. "And she's been telling me how abominably you treated her today. What the hell did you think you were doing, telling her we were getting married? You know damn well we've never discussed marriage!"

Madeline shook her head. "I don't remember saying any such thing. Kate must have misunderstood."

"Like hell she did!" Frank snapped. "And I suppose she also misunderstood your calling her mother a crazy person and a slut?"

Madeline's eyes opened wide, as if in amazement. "Is that what she told you? Oh, Frank, you know how she carries on. She's jealous of me, you know," she said, shifting in her chair. "She doesn't want to share you with anyone. If you ask me, you're much too lenient with that girl. She's a bright young woman, and she ought to start acting like one instead of carrying on like a spoiled child."

"She *is* a child, Madeline," Frank shot back. "And a high-strung one at that. I thought I'd made that clear to you. Why do you think I insisted that we take it slow in introducing you to Kate and Jack? I wanted to give them time to get to know you, hopefully to get to like you. But what happens? I turn my back for one minute and you manage to fuck everything up."

"Frank, calm down. It's not as bad as you're making out," Madeline said, fidgeting with the ends of her scarf.

"You've been complaining for months that I've been hiding you from the children, that you'd really like to get to know them better," Frank rattled on. "So when

I was too busy to take Kate shopping, I asked you to take her."

"I did take her—" Madeline protested.

"Will you let me finish?" Frank snapped. "I thought that would be the perfect opportunity for the two of you to get better acquainted. So I went off to Bethesda without a care in the world, thinking that Kate was in your able hands. But what happens? I get home and find not only does Kate not have a new dress, she is on the verge of hysteria because of the things you said to her."

"What did I supposedly say?" Although Madeline continued to feign ignorance, her face was flushed.

"Let's not play games," Frank shot back. "We both know what you said. What I want to know is why you said it."

Madeline took a deep breath. "Maybe things *did* get a little heated for a minute," she admitted, "but it wasn't as one-sided as you've been led to believe."

"Oh? How was it?" Frank challenged. "Please enlighten me. I want to hear what *really* happened."

Madeline licked her lips. "Well, I tried to give Kate some guidance on what kind of dress to buy, but she just wasn't interested. It was obvious she didn't want to be with me and felt she'd been coerced into the whole thing. She said she'd already picked out a dress and we could just go pick it up so she could go home." Madeline's lips felt parched and she ran her tongue over them again. "I said that was silly, that as long as we were out shopping, we should look at a lot of different dresses to make sure she got the best one. Well, that set her off. She stomped her feet and said she didn't want to look at any dresses."

"So you're saying the whole thing was Kate's fault," Frank interjected.

Madeline started to get flustered. "Well, not the whole thing, but ... She was impossible, Frank," she said, throwing up her hands. "I tried my best to be nice, but no matter how hard I tried, no matter what I suggested, she wouldn't hear of it. She sassed me at every turn—"

"And you thought you could turn things around by telling her that her mother was a crazy whore. That makes perfect sense to me! You missed your calling, Madeline. You should have been a child psychologist!" Frank got up from the chair and began to pace back and forth on the thick, blue-and-cream Oriental rug.

"Frank, it wasn't that bad," Madeline said. She got up from the couch and walked over to him. "All right, I'll admit we did have words. As I recall Kate started it, but it's just possible I overreacted because I had an absolutely shitty day at work. Frank, I lost the Anderfang Beverage account." She sighed and threw up her hands in despair. "It was one of our biggest, and it was totally unexpected. So obviously I wasn't in the best mood. Anyway, yes, things got a bit tense for a minute, but let's call it a mutual mistake. 'Cuz believe me, it was really no big deal." She put her hand on Frank's arm.

"No big deal!" Frank echoed incredulously, brushing her hand away. "Jesus Christ, woman, what is the matter with you?" He grabbed her by the shoulders and shook her hard. "I never thought your maternal instincts were particularly well developed, but a guppy would have more compassion than you showed today."

"You're hurting me!" Madeline cried, pushing him away. "All right, you want to hear the truth? I'll tell you the truth. I've been trying to tell you for two years that those kids have you wrapped around their little fingers," she said, her eyes flashing, "but you'd never listen to me. So let me make it a little plainer: The two of them are spoiled brats. Well, maybe Jack isn't so bad," she conceded, "but you're going to have big problems with Kate, unless you take matters in hand, and soon. As long as she was in my charge today, I guess I thought I'd take the opportunity to try to get her behavior in line."

"There is nothing wrong with Kate's behavior," Frank retorted. "Now tell me straight. What was that crap you told her about us getting married?" His dark eyes bored into her.

Madeline looked at the carpet. "Well, I guess I just

assumed . . ." She looked up at him, her face taking on a softer look.

"Well, you assumed *wrong,*" Frank shot back. "I've *been* married, and it is *not* an experience I'm eager to recreate, especially with someone who thinks my children are degenerate monsters. And while we're on the subject, where in hell did you get the idea that my ex-wife was either mentally off balance or of loose moral character? I certainly never said any such thing. In fact, I don't remember ever discussing her with you."

"You didn't need to discuss her. Caroline's problems are common knowledge," Madeline said, bristling. She tossed back her hair. "You must be the only person in Chicago who didn't realize what they were."

"In addition to being mean and vindictive, you're a damn liar!" Frank shouted.

"Don't call me names, you bastard!" Madeline shouted back.

Frank was so angry he was shaking, and he unconsciously found himself balling his right hand into a fist. Suddenly realizing what he was doing, he unclenched his hand and, in an effort to keep his temper in check, stepped back a couple paces and took some deep breaths. Then he said in a somewhat calmer voice, "I have never in my life hit a woman, and in order to keep that record intact, I think I'd better go."

"I think that would be a good idea," Madeline agreed. "And then maybe tomorrow, after you've calmed down, we can have a rational conversation about this."

Frank was already heading toward the door, but he turned and faced her again. "I don't think you understand what's happened tonight. We won't be having any more conversations, ever. It's over, Madeline."

"What?" she asked incredulously.

"You heard me," he said evenly. "What you did to Kate is unforgivable. I thought I meant something to you, but obviously I was wrong. Good-bye."

As he began to turn again, Madeline grabbed his elbow. "Frank, you can't be serious. Do you mean to say you're actually going to throw away what we had because of some little misunderstanding?"

Frank moved away and looked at her coldly. "I realize now that the only thing you and I ever had going for us was overheated genitalia. And in the long run that doesn't count for much."

He turned quickly and walked out the door, leaving Madeline standing there with her mouth agape. As he closed the door behind him, the shock of what he'd said finally hit her. "Fuck you, Frank Parks!" she shouted. "If you're actually so stupid as to let your kids run your life, then you're not the man I thought you were. I hope you get what you deserve!"

Frank walked down the hall to the elevators and after he had pushed the DOWN button, he leaned against the wall and took deep breaths to control the churning in his stomach. When the elevator came, he stepped inside and automatically pushed the button for GROUND FLOOR. I've already gotten exactly what I deserve, he thought. I just hope it's not too late to make amends. With that, he buried his head in his hands and wept.

CHAPTER 29

Mike O'Riley stood at the front of the fourth grade classroom, leaning against the corner of the teacher's desk. It was mid-October, and the walls of the room were covered with handcrafted ghosts, skeletons, black cats, and pumpkins, as the children eagerly awaited Halloween.

Back in August, at the beginning of the school year, O'Riley had agreed to speak to his grandson Billy's class about careers in law enforcement. Although that was only two months ago, to O'Riley it seemed like a lifetime. Since Tammy Clemment's murder, the department had pulled out all the stops trying to hunt down the killer. O'Riley and his team had been working very long hours, usually seven days a week. He would have liked to beg off from this speaking engagement, but he knew Billy would be heartbroken if he did, so here he was, trying his best to muster up some enthusiasm for his chosen profession, when all he could think about was how much he wanted to get the hell out of it.

O'Riley was wearing his full-dress uniform for the first time since that fine spring day when he had gone to the mayor's office and agreed to head up the search for the killer. He'd only spoken to his old friend, the mayor, once since then. Shortly after the interrogation of Officer Buenzli, the mayor had called. Not to complain, he'd hastened to say, but merely to ask if there was any additional assistance, manpower, equipment, or funding that O'Riley needed for his team.

O'Riley had offered to resign his post. "What you need is somebody with some brains heading this thing," he'd said.

But the mayor wouldn't hear of it. "Nonsense, Mike," he'd replied. "I told you last spring you were the right man for the job, and I stand by my decision."

"I think you're making a big mistake, Richie," O'Riley had said. "I read the papers. I know the press is calling for my resignation. I suspect the Clemments have something to do with that. I know they're well connected. If you don't get rid of me, they're going to start coming down hard on you, too."

"I don't give a damn about the press or the Clemments," the mayor had scoffed. "I've got all the confidence in the world in you. We both knew this was gonna be a tough case. It's just turned out to be a little tougher than either of us thought, that's all. I know you're gonna catch him. It's just a matter of time."

Time, and how many more mutilated bodies? O'Riley had wanted to ask, but he'd restrained himself. "All right, Richie," he'd said. "I'll stay on as long as you want me to, but if there ever comes a time when you think somebody else would be better qualified to handle the job, you just say the word and I'll step aside."

"In that case, you're gonna be waitin' till hell freezes over," Mayor Daley had said cheerfully.

At least something good had come out of the Buenzli fiasco. While Internal Affairs was far from finished with its investigation, so far Buenzli had fingered eight other officers who were involved in schemes ranging from stealing and reselling department property to drug dealing to extorting protection money from local businesses. The superintendent had congratulated O'Riley for bringing these activities to light. It was a far cry from finding the serial killer, but the praise had helped bolster O'Riley's sagging ego just a bit.

So that's how he found himself on a crisp October morning, telling a group of twenty-five nine-year-olds what a rewarding profession law enforcement was. He'd explained that he was a second-generation cop and that the O'Rileys had been involved in police work in Chicago for sixty years. He told them how when his

Uncle Marty was a rookie he'd been involved in helping the G-men hunt for Public Enemy Number One, and how Marty had been one of the local policemen stationed outside the Biograph Theater on that fateful day when John Dillinger's luck finally ran out.

A stocky black boy at the back of the room raised his hand. O'Riley nodded to him. "Yes, son. Do you have a question?"

"Did you really get shot once when you were chasing a criminal?" the boy asked.

O'Riley looked toward the back of the room where Billy sat, beaming with pride. The boy loved to tell his friends about Grandpa's near brush with death. O'Riley nodded. "Yes, I did."

Another boy waved his hand in the air. O'Riley nodded at him. "Did it hurt to get shot?" the boy asked.

O'Riley smiled. "Yes, it hurt. It hurt a lot, as a matter of fact. But I was young, and I had good doctors. They got the bullets out, and after some physical therapy, I healed up again, almost as good as new."

"I'll bet that was sore," a little girl murmured. O'Riley winked at her.

"Do you have a scar?" the black boy asked.

"Yes. I've got a pretty good-sized scar."

"Wow! Can we see it?"

O'Riley laughed. "I think I'll have to pass on that request." The teacher, a middle-aged woman who was sitting at the back of the room, nodded in appreciation. "Are there any other questions?"

"Why did you become a detective?" a small Hispanic boy asked. "Didn't you like being a patrolman?"

"It was a promotion, and I thought it'd be more challenging," O'Riley replied, moving over to the side of the room where the questioner sat. "Detectives get to work on more serious crimes, and I guess I thought I'd be able to do more good for more people if I got into that division."

A girl with black pigtails raised her hand. "How many women are on the police force?"

"That's a good question," O'Riley said. "About one out of four officers on the force are women, and that number is growing all the time. And the women I've worked with have all done an excellent job."

"Are there any women detectives?" the girl asked.

O'Riley nodded. "Yes, there are some. Not as many as there are on patrol, but you have to be on the force a while before you can be a detective, and women are just now working their way up the ranks, so I'm sure in time there will be lots more women detectives."

"If I were a policeman, I'd want to be a detective," the girl said seriously, "so I could catch really bad criminals."

"The department could use you right now," O'Riley said with a smile. "Actually," he added, "there's a woman detective in homicide named Marge that I've been working with a lot lately. She's going to be taking the sergeant's exam soon, and I'm sure she'll pass, 'cuz she's real smart. A lot smarter than most of the men in the department, in fact." Several girls snickered. "Anybody else got a question?"

"Yeah." Another black boy waved his hand. "Don't cops sometimes hurt innocent people? How come that happens?"

That was a tough one. O'Riley chose his words carefully. "It's true that sometimes when police officers are in pursuit of a criminal, innocent people will be hurt, but that happens very seldom."

"That's not what I meant," the boy continued, a hint of anger in his voice. "I mean sometimes cops beat up people that didn't do nothin' wrong or break into their house and trash the place for no reason at all."

The boy's face was flushed. O'Riley wondered if the scenario he was describing had happened to someone in his family. "I won't tell you those things never happen," O'Riley said gravely, "but they *shouldn't* happen. And if they do, the officers involved should be reported immediately and should be punished." He looked around the room. "I mean that sincerely. If any of you or anybody in your family feels they've been mistreated by the police, you report it right away. If you don't know who to call, you can call me. My number's in the phone book, and I promise I'll look into it. Now, are there any more questions?"

A dark-haired boy spoke up. "Billy says you're in charge of finding the guy who killed all those women. Is that true?"

O'Riley flinched ever so slightly. These kids were a tough audience. He'd been hoping he could get through his appearance without having to discuss the murders. He nodded at the boy. "Yes, son, that's true."

"Why haven't you caught the killer yet?" another boy asked.

"You've got to remember that the police aren't ever going to be able to solve every crime. We do solve most of them, but there are always going to be some crimes where, no matter how hard we try, we never find out who did it. The truth is that so far in this murder case, we just haven't found many clues to work with. But we do have a lot of people helping us on the case, and I feel certain that in time we're going to catch the person responsible."

"Do you think there's going to be more killings?" a red-haired girl asked.

How could he answer that? Even if they caught this murderer, it wouldn't stop the two or three other killings that took place in the city every day. "I wish I could tell you that there won't be more murders," O'Riley answered, "but if I said that, I'm afraid I'd be lying. What I can tell you, though, is that there are a lot of very good and devoted men and women working on the Chicago Police Department that are doing everything they can to make sure the city is a safe place to live."

A hush fell over the class as the students took that information in. "Any more questions?" O'Riley asked. "No? Then I'd like to thank Mrs. Logan for inviting me here today."

The teacher stood up. "Thank you very much for coming, Lieutenant O'Riley. Class, why don't we give the lieutenant a big hand before we break for lunch." The students burst into applause.

As the boys and girls began to file out of the classroom toward the cafeteria, Mrs. Logan came up and shook O'Riley's hand warmly. "I know how busy you are, Lieutenant, and we appreciate your taking the time to come talk to us. I think the students really enjoyed having you."

"It was my pleasure, Mrs. Logan," O'Riley replied.

"I'd better get down to the cafeteria. I'm a lunchroom monitor today," Mrs. Logan said. "Good-bye and good luck on your case. No running in the halls!" she admonished the students as she stepped out of the room.

As the classroom emptied, Billy came striding up from the back. A tall, towheaded youngster, he was obviously proud of his grandpa. O'Riley put his arm around the boy. "Well, Billy, how did I do? Did I pass the test?"

"You were great, Grandpa," the boy responded happily. "I'm glad you came."

"I'm glad I came, too," O'Riley replied, hugging the boy tightly. "Now you'd better hurry up, or you'll be late for lunch."

CHAPTER 30

Megan snapped the deadbolt on her front door into place, switched on the overhead light in the living room, and walked slowly to her bedroom. She slipped out of her black heels and pulled on a pair of thick blue socks. As she padded back to the living room, her cat emerged from the kitchen.

"Hi, Andy, I'm back," she said, leaning down and scooping him up in her arms. At thirteen pounds, he was quite a handful. She cradled him on his back and tickled his belly. The cat purred briefly, then began to squirm. "Okay, be antisocial," Megan said, setting him down again. "To tell you the truth, I'm not in the best mood myself."

It was nine o'clock on a Saturday night, and Megan had just returned from her first date since her breakup with Paul. Ron had arranged the outing, and Megan had gone under protest. "I don't want to go on a date. I'm too busy," she'd said when Ron had first suggested the idea.

"You're not that busy," Ron had said patiently. "I'm not asking you to take two weeks off. It'd just be for a few hours on Saturday night. Even *you* can spare that much time."

"I'm not ready. I have no interest in dating," she'd said.

"You're as ready as you're ever gonna be," Ron had said. "It's been over two months. It's time to test the water."

"Maybe I've forgotten how to swim."

Ron had smiled. "Joe is a good friend of mine. He's

a nice guy. I promise." Megan had looked skeptical. "Come on. Would I set you up with a jerk?"

"I don't know. Would you?" Megan had countered.

"Of course I wouldn't," Ron had said, giving her a pained look.

"If this guy's so great, why is he unattached?"

"He's recently divorced—" Ron began.

"Forget it." Megan had shook her head firmly. "That's even worse than my situation. I'm harboring a great deal of hostility toward men right now, and he's going to be death on women. We'd probably kill each other in the first five minutes."

"There's not a hostile bone in Joe's body," Ron had assured her. "Come on, what have you got to lose?"

Megan had sighed. "Oh, all right. I'll try it. But I'm warning you, if this is a total bomb, I'm not ever going to let you set me up with anybody again."

"It's a deal," Ron had agreed. "I'll have Joe call you."

The evening hadn't exactly been a bomb. It just hadn't been much of anything. Megan was willing to wager that a month from now both she and Joe would have forgotten the event ever took place.

Joe Altouros had pretty much lived up to Ron's advance billing. He was perfectly average. They'd gone to an early show at the Biograph Theater. It was a re-release of *Citizen Kane,* one of Megan's favorite movies. She'd always found movies to be safe fare for blind dates because you didn't have to worry about making conversation. Afterward, they'd gone to a small Italian restaurant nearby. The conversation hadn't been too strained. As they dug into hearty salads, Joe had talked about his company, how fast it had grown, the long hours he needed to put in, how competitive the software market was. He told her they had just patented a new antivirus program that they hoped would be a big seller. Megan didn't know much about the computer field and had found the discussion interesting.

When the waiter brought their main courses, Joe asked Meg about her job. She described some of the more challenging cases she'd had over the years and told him about the AIDS case. Joe listened attentively and, when she was done, said, "That does sound like a fascinating case. It's obvious the doctor is responsible for what happened, but gee, I really can't see that the hospital did anything wrong."

Megan laughed and said, "I'm real glad you aren't going to be on the jury."

By the time they'd finished the wine and were sipping espresso and nibbling on biscotti, Joe was talking about his ex-wife, how glad he was they hadn't gotten around to having kids, how bitter the divorce was, how she'd tried to take him to the cleaners, how he would have to pay her alimony for five years. Megan just nodded a few times, realizing that he probably wasn't really looking for a response; he just needed to unload on someone.

Joe was a nice enough guy, Megan had reflected on the short ride from the restaurant back to her place. There just wasn't any chemistry between them. Maybe if they weren't both just coming off of failed relationships, there might have been some spark. But as things were, she'd found the date about as exciting as going out with her short, fat cousin Arnold.

During the drive, Megan reluctantly admitted to herself that Joe's biggest failing was that he just didn't measure up to Paul—in looks, in charm, in any way. Megan was sorry she'd let Ron talk her into going on a date. It was obvious she wasn't ready for a new relationship.

When Joe turned onto Megan's block, she told him that she had some work she needed to do yet that night and he could just drop her off in front. He did so without protest. Megan patted him on the arm and thanked him for the nice evening. Joe said it had been fun and that he'd call her. They both knew it hadn't been and he wouldn't. Megan got out of the car, walked up the steps, and briefly turned and waved when she reached the top. Joe waved back and then drove off. They would never see each other again.

Megan walked into the kitchen, opened up a cabinet

and took out a bottle of Chivas Regal. She took a glass out of another cabinet and poured out a generous amount of booze. As she took a sip, her cat rubbed himself against her legs. "Still hungry, huh?" she asked. "Okay. How'd you like a treat?" She opened the refrigerator and reached for a package of dried beef. She slit it open with a knife, took out several slices, ripped them into small pieces, and put them in the aluminum pie tin that served as the cat's dish. He sniffed at the meat, then wolfed it down hungrily. "Don't eat so fast or you'll throw up," she scolded. When the cat had finished eating, he loudly lapped water out of a white bowl with the words TUNA BREATH spelled out in blue letters on the side.

Andy was a lot of fun, Megan thought as she watched him while she leaned against the counter and sipped her drink. Maybe she should get him a companion. She'd like to have a kitten around again. They were so cute and cuddly. Then she shook her head and made a clucking sound with her tongue. Geez, get a grip on yourself, she scolded. If she didn't watch out, she'd end up one of those pathetic old women who died with no family and left all their money to their pets. Honestly!

Brushing black cat hair off her mauve sweater dress, Megan carried the glass of scotch back to the living room and sat down on the blue-striped chintz couch. She tucked her feet up under her and reached down on the floor to pick up a notebook and a stack of deposition transcripts. She was working on witness outlines for the trial. She'd pretty much finished formulating the questions she wanted to ask her own witnesses and was now working on cross-examination of the hospital's witnesses, which was much more time consuming.

For what had to be at least the tenth time, she carefully paged through the transcripts of Drs. Lenz and Gillian's depositions, marking certain lines with a yellow highlighter, trying to get it clear in her mind just what they had said on key points. Dr. Lenz had contradicted himself on a number of occasions. She jotted down some ideas in her notebook that she might be able to use when she was cross-examining him, then set the whole stack of materials back down on the floor in disgust. She just couldn't seem to concentrate. She took another sip of scotch. It probably wasn't a good idea to drink while she was trying to work.

Megan stood up and walked around the room, still carrying the glass of liquor. She chewed on her lower lip. Her apartment was really too crowded. And after what had happened to Rita, she was no longer sure how safe the neighborhood was. Rita was well on the way to recovery, and psychologically she had handled the accident much better than Megan had expected. Still, police had no clues who the phantom driver might have been, and whenever Megan walked to her car, she thought of how close her friend had come to being killed. Megan had to admit she would feel safer living somewhere else. Maybe when she made partner—*if* she made partner—she quickly corrected herself, she'd think about moving. There was no reason she couldn't have a house if she wanted one. She had quite a bit of money saved that she could use for a down payment. After all, she thought morosely, she wouldn't be spending it on a lavish wedding. A house would be more work than an apartment, but she'd manage. Besides, everyone was always telling her what a good investment real estate was. She nodded. That settled it. In the spring she would definitely go house hunting. It would be something to look forward to. She sure as hell needed that.

Megan padded into the bedroom, still carrying her drink. She looked at the picture of her grandmother staring defiantly into the camera. "All of a sudden, my life's an awful mess, Grandma," Megan said out loud. "I wish you were here to straighten me out."

Do I really want to make partner? she mused, taking another sip of scotch. She looked back at the picture and closed her eyes. She could almost hear Hallie say, "Well, of course, that's what you want, Megan. That's been your goal for years. Why should the fact that your fiancé turned out to be a two-timer change anything? Remember what I always told you. You've got to look

out for yourself in this life. 'Cuz if you don't, it's for
damn sure nobody else will."

Megan nodded. She did enjoy her work and knew
she was good at it. The money was certainly nice and
besides, what else did she know how to do? If she
could just get this damn trial behind her and be voted
into the partnership, she could start calling some of the
shots as far as what cases she worked on. That would
be a welcome change.

She went back to the living room, switched on the
TV and plopped down on the couch to watch the ten
o'clock news. She needed to focus on preparing for the
trial. She knew she had a good case, but she was starting to get nervous about it. You could never tell what
a jury was going to do. And as much as she hated to
admit it, Frank Parks was a very good lawyer and had
a delivery that was smooth as glass. Megan had had a
new associate spend a day sitting in on a trial Parks
had recently handled. The young lawyer had come
back with positively glowing reports. "He had the jury
eating right out of his hand," he'd said with admira-
tion.

Great. That was the last thing Megan needed to hear.
She had to think positive. She'd just have to beat him
by being more persuasive than he was, by making the
jury care about her clients.

The case was going to get national press and media
coverage. A reporter from the *Tribune* had been in
touch and said she'd be following it closely, as had As-
sociated Press and a number of television stations. It
was bad enough to lose a case where nobody outside of
the parties was paying any attention. It was something
else again to lose one when the whole country was
watching.

The news was over, and Megan got up and flipped
off the TV. She had finished her drink and set it down
on a coffee table. She sat back down and picked up the
depositions again, but it was useless. She just couldn't
concentrate. She looked across the room at the piano.
Playing used to relax her. She wondered if it still
would. She hadn't played in God knew how long.

What the hell. It was supposed to be like riding a bicycle. Once you knew how, you never really forgot.

Megan got up, walked over to the piano, and stood in front of it for a moment. Then she decisively cleared the clutter off the bench so she could sit down. She folded back the cover to reveal the keys. She leaned her head back and closed her eyes. Let's see. What did she remember how to play? The last time she'd played regularly was about ten years ago in college, when she'd taken a performance class. What had she played then? Oh, yes. Gershwin. *Porgy and Bess.* She'd gotten an "A-" on her recital, as she recalled. Might as well give that a try.

She was very rusty and played haltingly at first, making lots of mistakes. But then it started to come back to her and she began to play with feeling. She played for more than an hour. After she made partner, she thought, she was going to somehow find the time to play more often. Maybe she'd even splurge and get a better piano. She'd always wanted a baby grand. Once she had her house, she'd have room for one.

Feeling suddenly energized, she closed the lid over the keys and went back to the couch. Once again she picked up the depositions and began to read. Andy jumped up on the other end of the couch and purred himself to sleep. After about ten minutes, Megan's burst of energy completely evaporated and she nodded off, dreaming that the jury awarded her clients so much money that she was able to give up practicing law and devoted the rest of her life to studying music and furnishing her lavish new home with priceless antiques.

CHAPTER 31

Frank reached over and picked up the can of Diet Pepsi from the walnut table next to him and took a swallow. As he set the can down again, he looked at the stacks of books and papers filling the library's leather sofa and spilling over onto the floor and laughed out loud. What a mess. He bent down and picked up the pile of documents next to his right foot and rapidly sorted through them. Where was that diagram? He could have sworn he'd seen it fifteen minutes ago. He set that stack of papers down and reached for the one next to it.

The following morning Frank was flying to New York for depositions in a patent infringement case. It was one of his infrequent plaintiff's cases. He was representing a company that manufactured components that went into fax machines. His client claimed that another company had pirated its designs. Both sides' expert witnesses were going to be deposed, and Frank was struggling to understand the makeup of the machines and the chronology of the industry's development.

He was beginning to feel like his work schedule was mushrooming out of control. The AIDS trial wasn't that far off, and he hadn't begun to prepare for it. Thinking of the case made his head hurt. Dr. Lenz was starting to become a bit of a pest, calling frequently to offer suggestions on trial strategy. Frank had to admit that a lot of the ideas were good ones, but it pissed him off royally to have a layman think he might need advice on how to handle a case. If the hospital weren't such a good client, Frank would've told the doctor to back off. But knowing what side his bread was buttered on, he held his tongue and thanked Lenz profusely for his insights.

Aha! he said to himself triumphantly as he located the missing diagram. I knew it was here someplace. He scrutinized it carefully and jotted some notes on a legal pad balanced on his lap.

"Dad?" Jack's voice broke his concentration.

Frank looked up. His son was standing in the doorway, a notebook under one arm. "What is it, Sport?" Frank asked.

"I was wondering if maybe you could look at my math homework," Jack said hopefully.

"Oh, I guess maybe I could do that," Frank answered, "but it'll have to be a little bit later, okay? I want to finish going through these documents or I'll lose my train of thought."

Jack walked over to the sofa, leaned down, and picked up the top couple of pages from one of the stacks. "What is all this stuff?" he asked.

"Don't get them mixed up," Frank cautioned. The boy set the papers down again. "This is all information on how fax machines are put together," Frank explained.

"What do you have to know about that for?" the boy asked.

"Remember I told you I'm going to New York tomorrow?" Jack nodded. "Well, the case is about fax machines and who has the patent rights to certain parts that go into them."

"Oh." Jack wrinkled his nose. "Doesn't sound very interesting."

Frank smiled. "Just between us, it doesn't sound too interesting to me, either, but I have to try to figure it out anyway." He turned back to the documents.

"Dad?"

"What?"

"You're going to be back for Halloween, aren't you?" Jack asked in a concerned tone.

Frank looked up again. "I sure will. Halloween's not till Thursday. I'm only going to be gone tomorrow and

Wednesday. I'll be back home sometime Wednesday night."

"That's good," Jack said, relieved. He was counting the days until he could wear his new Captain Hook costume and wanted to be sure Frank would be there to accompany him on his rounds.

"Dad?"

Frank sighed. "Now what?"

"Do you think maybe we could get a dog for Christmas?"

"A dog?" Frank asked in surprise. Jack had never shown any interest in dogs before. "Why do you want a dog all of a sudden?"

"Well, see, Henry Sager's family just got two new puppies." The words came out in a rush. "They're King Charles spaniels, and they're really a lot of fun. They're real furry and cute and Henry says they don't get very big, so they wouldn't take up much room in the house. And I was just wondering if maybe we could get one, too."

"I don't know that we need any more animals in the house," Frank said. "I think two cats are really enough. In fact, sometimes I think two cats are too much."

"I'd take care of him," Jack assured him. "Really, I would. And I don't think he'd eat much, being as how they're really small and all."

Frank laughed. "I don't know how the cats would take to having a puppy around. Cleo would probably scare the poor thing to death. Or maybe eat it for dinner, if she was having a particularly bad day."

"Will you at least think about it?" Jack asked.

"All right," Frank agreed. "I'll think about it. But I'm not making any promises."

"That's okay." Jack nodded his approval that the topic hadn't been dismissed out of hand.

"Are you all done with your math homework?" Frank asked.

Jack nodded.

"Then why don't you leave it here with me and I'll look it over just as soon as I'm done with my work. Okay?"

"Okay," Jack said agreeably. He set the notebook down on the table next to Frank's can of soda and headed back to the living room.

Frank turned back to his documents, but found he couldn't concentrate. The last few weeks had been sort of a blur. He hadn't heard a word from Madeline since the night he'd gone to her apartment. He'd been expecting her to call to apologize and ask his forgiveness, and frankly there were times when he wasn't sure what his response would be to such an entreaty. In spite of what she had done, he still missed her terribly.

He rubbed the heel of his hand against the back of his neck. Admit it, old man, he chided himself. What you miss is getting laid three times a week by a woman who could probably teach professionals a thing or two. But it went beyond that. It really did. He missed going to dinner with her. He missed the closeness he'd felt with her. Sometimes he woke up in the middle of the night and reached for her. She'd been an important part of his life for two and a half years. He wondered how long it would be before he got over her. Probably a very long time.

Anyway, speculating about what he'd do if she begged him to take her back was academic, because she hadn't called. Countless times he had reached for the phone, but had always pulled back. He had his pride. If there was going to be any communication between them, she would have to be the one to initiate it.

Frank was damned if he could figure the situation out. Madeline was the consummate career woman. One of the things that had immediately endeared her to him was her lack of the game playing that had colored so many of his past relationships. Most women seemed to have a not-so-hidden agenda. They might tell you they loved being single and didn't want kids, but that was all an act. They'd go home and secretly pore over women's magazines and listen to their biological clocks ticking away and try to figure out how to trap themselves a husband so they could quit their jobs and stay home, raise kids, and watch soap operas.

But Madeline had been different. From the begin-

ning she'd made it clear that she loved to go out and
a have a good time and she loved to come home and
have sex. Frank had thought it was a match made in
heaven. If she'd been interested in marriage, she sure
hadn't given off any discernible signs. What would he
have done if she'd openly broached the topic? Frank
stroked the bridge of his nose.

Even though his failure with Caroline had left him
spooked, he supposed he wasn't inherently averse to
getting married again. It's just that ... His thought
process stopped cold for a moment. Go on, he silently
urged himself. It's just that Madeline wasn't someone
he ever would've married. As a lover and companion
she was without peer. But as a wife and stepmother to
Jack and Kate? ... No, it would never have worked.
But then again, maybe her comment about marriage
was just a ruse. Maybe Madeline had been tired of the
relationship and had been looking for a way to get him
to end it. If so, she'd certainly done a bang-up job.

Frank's efforts to find solace in his work had only
been marginally successful. A lot of the time he just
plain felt like shit. For the first time in his life his
nearly photographic memory failed him, and sometimes during crucial meetings or in depositions, he'd
find his mind wandering. He knew this was a perfectly
normal reaction for someone who'd been through a
personal crisis, but he had to admit it had him a little
uneasy. He had been trying hard to focus on the good
things that had come from the breakup with Madeline.
He was able to spend more time at home with the kids.
He enjoyed that, and his relationship with Kate seemed
to have improved.

Kate's recital had gone flawlessly. Not only had she
looked beautiful and very grown-up in her green-satin,
Laura Ashley dress, she had played brilliantly and received many favorable comments from those in attendance. The admissions director at Juilliard had made a
point of talking to Kate and Frank afterward and said
he was looking forward to seeing her perform again.
Kate had been walking on air ever since.

Although Frank had never again mentioned the ill-fated shopping trip with Madeline, Kate seemed to have gotten over the incident. Frank had had a discussion with Mrs. Gurney a few days later in which he'd pointedly asked if Mrs. Gurney thought he was a bad father. The older woman had smiled warmly, shook her head, and said that Frank was one of the best fathers she knew—that he ranked right up there with her own dear father and her late husband. Then she had hesitated a moment before admitting that she had never cared for Madeline.

"I know it's not my place to say anything," she'd said, rubbing her hands together a bit nervously, "but it just always seemed to me that there was something cold about that woman, like she was an ice queen or something."

Frank had nodded. "You know how much I value your opinion, Mrs. Gurney," he'd said. "Thinking back, I guess I can understand how you might have formed that impression. Obviously Madeline had very little interest in children, and fewer skills in dealing with them. But she wasn't entirely without feeling." He'd found himself blushing at that statement.

Mrs. Gurney had looked at him with amusement. "I'm sure she wasn't, sir," she had answered, with a smile.

"Dad?"

Once again Frank found himself jolted back to reality. He looked up and saw that Kate was standing in front of him, with Cleo at her heels.

"What can I do for you, my dear?" he asked warmly.

"Do you think you'd have time to proofread my history paper? It's not due until Friday, but since you're going to be gone the next two days, I hurried up to finish it so you could look at it before you go." She held out a sheaf of papers.

Frank took them and read the title. " 'The Effect of the French Revolution on the Peasantry.' Sounds like a pretty heavy-duty topic." He flipped through the paper. "Twenty typed pages. I'm impressed. Of course I'll proofread it for you. Just let me finish what I'm doing here first, okay?"

"Okay." Kate nodded and turned to go.

"How are you coming on the Mozart?"

Kate was trying to perfect her rendition of one of the sonatas. "Slowly," she said, making a face. "I'm going to go practice some more now."

Frank nodded. "I'd like to hear it. Maybe you could play it for me later. That is, if you want to."

Kate cocked her head. She didn't like to perform for anyone, even Frank, until she could play a piece with precision. "All right," she said.

"Great. I'll look forward to it."

Cleo was rubbing herself against Kate's legs, and the girl bent down and scooped the animal up in her arms. "I'll see you later," she said as she left the room.

Frank managed a brief smile. He was a lucky bastard, he reflected. He had two great kids, a top-notch job, a mid-six-figure income, a beautiful house. Most men would kill to trade places with him. Then why the hell did he feel so empty? He sighed. He knew the answer.

He had lulled himself into thinking his idyllic relationship with Madeline could go on forever, and he blamed himself for its abrupt end. By ignoring signs that must have been there all along, he had hurt Kate deeply, something he would never be able to forgive himself for.

And in a way, he knew he had hurt Madeline, too. He feared that maybe he had somehow been the cause of her behavior, just as he feared he was the one responsible for Caroline's fragile mental state. Maybe there was some flaw in his character that jinxed his chances of having a long-term relationship with any woman.

He squeezed his eyes shut tightly, then opened them again. He had better things to do than to get into psychological dialogues with himself, although he realized this was an issue he was going to have to confront eventually. But that would have to wait. For now, he was almost grateful he could turn back to reviewing his documents.

CHAPTER 32

Megan slouched in her seat at the United Airlines gate at LaGuardia airport and pulled her tan trenchcoat around her, waiting for the seven P.M. flight to Chicago to be called. She had been so successful in getting an injunction in the historic preservation case that she'd been asked to come to New York to lend her expertise to a group of attorneys and local preservationists, who were planning to mount a similar challenge to the destruction of a venerable old Manhattan building. Megan had demurred, citing her busy schedule, and had suggested that possibly the matter could be handled by phone. The New York group had insisted on meeting with her in person, so she had left home at four in the morning, met with the preservationists for most of the day and was now looking forward to zonking out on the flight home.

Megan reached into the skirt pocket of her red suit and pulled out a peppermint candy. As she unwrapped it and popped it into her mouth, she paged through an article in *Flying* magazine that praised her brother, James Lansdorf, for his innovative design in developing a new type of airfoil that streamlined the design of small planes. Jim, as always, was very modest and credited other members of his team for their work on the project, but his supervisor at NASA had confirmed that it was largely Jim's efforts that resulted in the new development. Megan swelled with pride as she read the article. Although Jim lived in Houston and she only saw him a couple times a year now, they remained close. She had called on his expertise numerous times when she'd been working on the plane crash case. He was a brilliant engineer, and she was glad he was getting the accolades he so richly deserved.

"Well, what do you know. A familiar face." A low, cheerful voice broke Megan's concentration. She looked up and groaned silently. It was Frank Parks. "Mind if I sit down?"

Megan shrugged noncommittally and continued looking at the magazine.

Frank draped his Burberry trench coat over the back of the seat next to Megan, set his briefcase and carry-on bag on the floor, and sat down. "Anything interesting in there?" he asked, pointing to her magazine.

Megan shut the magazine and set it on her lap. "As a matter of fact there is," she said coolly. "There's an article about my brother inventing something revolutionary."

"Your brother is a pilot?" Frank asked with interest.

Megan shook her head. "An aeronautical engineer. He's with NASA."

"Older or younger brother?"

"Two years older."

"Any other siblings?" Frank asked.

Megan shook her head.

"What line of work is your father in?"

Megan squirmed in irritation. What was this, a game of twenty questions? "He's a college English professor."

"Really? I sort of figured you probably came from a long line of attorneys."

"Well, you figured wrong," Megan said sweetly. "How about you? Are there lots of lawyers in your bloodline?" Two could play at being nosy.

Frank smiled. "Not a one."

"Brothers or sisters?"

"One brother, three years older than me. He went into the family business, but I declined. Sort of makes me the black sheep, I guess."

Megan raised her eyebrows. "*Family* business?" She had always thought Parks looked like Mafia.

Frank caught her drift and laughed. "Nothing that sinister, I'm afraid. I come from a long line of stockbrokers. My grandfather started a firm in the twenties, before the crash. My dad just retired from it last year, and my brother is also a member of the firm."

Megan cocked her head. "No, I don't think being a broker would have suited you at all."

"And why is that?" Frank challenged.

"Because you wouldn't have the opportunity to be flamboyant."

Frank laughed again. "I never thought of it quite that way, but I suppose you're right. What brought you to New York?"

"I was asked to consult on a historic preservation case. How about you?"

"Depositions in a patent infringement action. And I'm happy to report that things went exceptionally well."

Megan made a face. "I hate those things. They're too technical to suit me."

"And how," Frank agreed. "I now know everything you always wanted to know about the insides of fax machines but were afraid to ask. Were you just here for the day?" he asked, noticing her lack of baggage.

Megan nodded. "A very *long* day. I wonder why they haven't started boarding the flight," she said, craning her neck to look over at the desk where a member of United's ground crew was talking on the phone.

"Haven't you heard?" Frank asked. "O'Hare is fogged in. They don't know when we'll be able to take off."

"Oh, no," Megan groaned. "Are you sure about that?" Just as she was about to get up and go over to the desk, the ground crew member hung up the phone and picked up a microphone.

"Good evening, ladies and gentlemen. This is United flight 1403, nonstop to Chicago's O'Hare. We've just been informed that the Chicago area is experiencing some dense fog and O'Hare has temporarily suspended operations. As a result, flight 1403 is going to be delayed. Unfortunately, at this time we are unable to give you any estimate as to when the flight might be able to depart. We suggest that you remain in the gate area and check the monitors for updated information. We apologize for the delay, and we thank you for choosing United."

"Shit!" Megan said crossly. "Just what I want. Getting stuck at an airport all night."

Frank smiled. She was a stubborn one, obviously used to getting her way. "I don't think it'll be all night. I'm no meteorologist, but I think once the temperature drops a few degrees, the fog should lift and we can get under way."

"But that could be hours," Megan grumbled.

"I suppose it could," Frank agreed. He looked at her closely and hesitated just an instant before continuing. "Say, I have an idea. Why don't you let me buy you a drink? There's a bar right over there, and you look like you could use one."

Megan eyed him suspiciously. "I don't know."

"Come on," Frank urged. "You might as well do something to help pass the time. Unless, of course, you're afraid of me." He grinned sardonically.

Megan rose to the bait. "I'm not afraid of anyone," she said, standing up. "Let's go." What harm could come from having a drink with him? Maybe she'd be able to gain some insight into his character that she could use to her advantage during the trial.

They picked up their bags and coats and walked over to the bar, called Any Port in a Storm, a dimly lit place with an island theme. "How's this?" Frank asked, walking to a table near the back festooned with a yellow-and-orange-flowered beach umbrella. "We can see the monitor from here."

"Fine," Megan said, tossing her coat across an empty chair and sitting down.

"What would you like to drink?" Frank asked. "White wine?"

Megan bristled. "No, I would *not* like white wine. Whatever gave you that idea?"

"Oh, I don't know," Frank said innocently. "I guess in my somewhat limited experience, white wine seems to be the drink of choice for most women."

Megan glared at him. Patronizing bastard! Limited experience, indeed! "I am *not* most women," she snarled.

"You certainly are not," he agreed. "Well, then, what *would* you like?"

"I'll have whatever you're having," Megan responded.

Frank's eyes twinkled mischievously. "You got it. Be right back."

He walked up to the bar and returned in a few moments with two glasses of clear liquid with an olive perched on the bottom. Megan eyed hers cautiously. "What is it?" she asked.

"Gin martini, extra dry," Frank answered. He lifted his glass. "Cheers," he said, taking a big swallow.

Megan picked up her drink. She hated martinis, but she'd be damned if she'd give Parks the satisfaction of saying so. She took a small sip, and felt her stomach lurch. She prayed that the horrid concoction wouldn't come back up.

"Well, are you all prepared for the trial?" Frank asked.

"If you don't mind, I'd rather not talk about the trial," Megan said. She wished she had some popcorn or some crackers to wash the godawful taste out of her mouth. Why had she agreed to have a drink with him anyway? She must have a masochistic streak.

"As you wish," Frank said easily. "So, are you going to become a historic preservation expert? That'd be an interesting field, though probably not a very lucrative one."

"Is that all you defense types think about is money?" Megan snapped. Her mouth tasted like raw sewage. "Doesn't it ever occur to you that sometimes there are good causes out there worth taking on, even if you don't get paid to do it?"

"Wait just a minute," Frank protested, shaking his finger at her. "I'll have you know that in the patent infringement case I was telling you about, I'm on the side of the angels." Megan gave him a blank look.

"I'm representing the plaintiff," Frank said triumphantly.

"Big deal!" Megan shot back. "What is this, your token plaintiff's case of the decade?"

"That's not fair," Frank said. "Our firm does handle some plaintiff's work. I think you misjudge us. We're not the bunch of conservative old fogies you seem to think we are."

"Is that so?" Megan scoffed, taking another sip of her drink. The taste was getting worse, if that was possible. "How many women partners does your firm have?"

"Four," Frank answered.

"Four? Out of how many? A hundred? I'd say those aren't very good percentages. How many black partners do you have? How many other minorities?"

Hagenkord & Phillips had no minority partners. "Hold on," Frank said heatedly. "Why can't you liberals ever understand that the fact a firm doesn't have a whole slew of women or minority partners does not necessarily mean that it is prejudiced against non-WASP's. Did it ever occur to you that maybe our white male associates are more qualified—"

"Spare me!" Megan snapped back. "If you actually believe that drivel, then you really *are* from the Middle Ages." She tossed back her hair. "God, I don't know how you can spout such nonsense with a straight face."

"Hey, just because you happen to work for the Rainbow Coalition doesn't mean you have the right to criticize the rest of the legal community!"

Megan stared at him a moment, open-mouthed, then suddenly began to laugh. At first, Frank was surprised by her response, but then he, too, started to chortle. He composed himself and said, "Okay, time out. Can we declare a truce here?"

Megan wiped her eyes and nodded. "I think that's a great idea."

"Are you ready for another drink?"

"I'll have another one if you will," she said gamely.

"Do you like martinis?" Frank asked.

Megan smiled. "No. Do you?"

"I think they're disgusting," Frank admitted. "What would you really like?"

"How about scotch and water?"

Frank grinned. "Sounds good to me. Let me get rid of these." He picked up the two unfinished martinis and took them back to the bar.

"Here, this should be more to your liking," he said as he returned and set the fresh drink down in front of Megan.

"Thanks." She squinted to see the departing flights' monitor. "I wonder how much longer it'll be."

"I don't know," Frank said. "I just hope I get back before tomorrow night. My son gave me explicit instructions that I had to be home for Halloween."

Megan smiled and took a sip of her drink. "Mmmm. Much better. How old is your son?"

"Nine and a half. He's Captain Hook this year. The hook is a bit too realistic for my tastes. Hopefully he won't impale any little girls with it."

Megan laughed. "What's his name?"

"Jonathan Edward Parks. Although if I called him that, I doubt he'd know who I was talking to. He's been Jack since he was a baby."

Megan nodded. "And I suppose he's already a budding lawyer."

Frank chuckled. "Jack? I think not. Of course it's a little early to tell, but I'd say his interests run more toward developing new video games."

"Do you have other children?"

Frank nodded. "A daughter. Kate. Actually Katharine Marie, but I only call her that when I'm especially trying to get a point across. She'll be fourteen in December."

"Is she interested in law?"

Frank shook his head. "No, she wants to be a concert pianist. If she can't make it as a soloist—and she just might, she's awfully good, and I'm not just saying that because I'm her father—then I think she'll probably teach music."

Megan remembered Rita's story about how Parks's wife had taken off and left him with the children. "It must be hard to be a single parent," she said. "I mean, with all the traveling you do."

"It's a challenge," Frank agreed. "Fortunately we have a wonderful live-in housekeeper. She's been with us since Jack was a baby, and she's an absolute godsend. The kids love her, and she runs the house very efficiently. Probably more efficiently than I would if I were there all the time. I sometimes feel like I get in her way. Are you ready for another drink?"

"Sure," Megan replied. "I've almost managed to get the taste of that wretched martini out of my mouth."

Frank fetched another round. After taking a big swallow of his new drink, he said boldly, "I know it's none of my business, but I didn't get a very satisfactory answer the last time I asked you what happened to young Dr. Kildaire."

Megan looked him in the eye. "And as I told you the last time, it *is* none of your business." She paused a moment, then added, "But what the hell, I'll tell you anyway. I caught him playing doctor with his nurse."

Frank whistled. "That must have been unpleasant."

"Very," Megan agreed, taking another sip of her scotch. "But I'm glad I found out his peccadilloes before I married him. I saved the costs of both a wedding and a divorce." She hoped her voice sounded more confident than she felt.

"A very practical attitude," Frank commended her.

"Since we're talking about personal matters," Megan said coyly, "how is your friend? What was her name, Martha?"

"Madeline." Frank finished his drink in one long swallow. "She's history, too."

"Really? What was the problem?"

"Let's just call it a personality conflict," Frank said evasively.

"That's not good enough," Megan taunted, emboldened by the liquor. "I want a full disclosure, just like you got from me."

"Oh, all right." Frank felt himself flush slightly. It was still difficult for him to talk about Madeline. "She had a great deal of animosity toward my kids, especially Kate. I guess I'd always known that, but in the beginning she managed to keep it somewhat under wraps. Things came to a head about a month ago. We had a rather ugly scene and, well, I guess it made me see how important my family is."

"That's too bad," Megan said, finishing her drink. "You know, she and Paul seemed to hit it off pretty well at that fund-raiser. Now that they're both unattached, maybe they'll find each other."

Frank pursed his lips. "It'd serve them both right." He picked up his empty glass. "One more for the road?" he asked.

"Why not? And while you're ordering, would you mind getting me a sandwich? Roast beef with lots of mustard, if they've got it. Otherwise a hamburger. I'm starving."

"Coming right up."

As Frank went to the bar to get the drinks, Megan leaned back in her chair and stretched. What an odd evening this was turning out to be. Who would have thought she'd be having drinks with Frank Parks and actually having a good time. What was the world coming to?

In minutes Frank was back carrying a tray with two roast beef sandwiches, a large order of fries, and two more drinks.

"This is great," Megan said, bitting into her sandwich ravenously. "I didn't realize how hungry I was. I had a roll on the plane this morning and a bowl of soup at noon, but all of a sudden I felt like I was going into hypoglycemic shock."

"We couldn't have that," Frank said, chomping down some fries. "You have to keep up your strength for the trial."

"I told you I don't want to talk about that," Megan scolded.

"Don't talk with your mouth full," Frank countered. "Let's have a toast." He raised his glass.

"To what?" Megan asked warily.

"Oh, I don't know." Frank put his head back and

thought a moment. "How about 'To stellar legal careers for both of us'?"

"How about 'To the fog lifting in Chicago so we can get the hell out of this airport'?" Megan lifted her glass.

"I'll drink to that." They touched glasses and took big swallows of their drinks.

As they were finishing their sandwiches, Frank said, "Look. I think they've posted a flight time for us."

"Really?" Megan looked up. "You're right. They have. Eight-forty-five." She looked at her watch. "That's in fifteen minutes. Thank God. I'm ready to go."

"Me, too. And I'm certain that Captain Hook will be eternally grateful."

They finished their drinks and walked leisurely back to the boarding area. A flight attendant picked up the microphone and announced that first-class passengers and anyone who needed extra boarding time should proceed to the gate. Frank stepped forward.

"Another first-class upgrade?" Megan asked.

" 'Fraid so," Frank replied.

"Well, while you're eating lobster and drinking champagne, I hope you'll think of the rest of us miserable wretches fighting over crumbs of dry bread back in tourist."

Frank laughed. "If you'd like, I'll save you some lobster."

Megan shook her head. "Don't bother. That sandwich really hit the spot. And after that much scotch, I think I'll sleep like a log all the way home."

"Have a good flight."

"You, too. And thanks a lot for the drinks and the snack."

"My pleasure," Frank said, smiling down at her. "I enjoyed the company." In fact, for the first time in ages he felt like maybe he was finally ready to shake off the doldrums that had been plaguing him and rejoin the land of the living.

"So did I," Megan said in a tone that barely concealed her surprise. As Frank headed toward the gate, she thought to herself again, who would have ever believed it?

CHAPTER 33

Halloween was one of Mike O'Riley's favorite days. It wasn't a religious holiday, so Anne didn't pressure him into accompanying her to mass like she did on Christmas and Easter. He liked being around children, and it was a great time for that. He always made it a point to knock off work early so he'd be sure not to miss any of the night's activities.

This year he'd had another reason for wanting to leave work early. In the midafternoon he'd gotten a phone call from Richard Clemment, Sr., demanding to know why his daughter-in-law's killer had not yet been brought to justice.

"As I told you the last time you called," O'Riley had replied through clenched teeth, "we're doing everything we can."

"If that were true, you would have caught the man by now," Clemment had retorted.

"I can understand your frustration, Mr. Clemment, but sometimes these things take time."

"Perhaps if you told me what leads you are pursuing, I could make my own judgment on whether your investigation is as thorough as it should be," Clemment had suggested.

O'Riley had rolled his eyes. "I'm afraid I can't do that sir."

"And why not?" Clemment had demanded indignantly.

"Because this is an ongoing investigation, and all of our files are privileged police business."

There was a short, angry pause. "I've tried to be patient, Lieutenant O'Riley," Clemment had continued coldly, "but in my opinion your investigation has been *ongoing* for an unacceptable length of time. I'm putting you on notice that if some progress is not made in the next few days, I am going to retain my own investigator to look into the matter. Perhaps an independent professional may be able to provide a fresh slant on the case."

The blood had risen to O'Riley's face. If that SOB had been in his office, he would've knocked him on his pedigreed ass. "You listen to me, you pompous bag of wind," he'd shouted. "You can go right ahead and hire Sherlock Holmes, Sam Spade, Mike Hammer, and Colombo for all I care. That's your prerogative. But I'm warning you, if your private dick hinders this investigation in any way, or if you divulge any information about the details of your daughter-in-law's murder without my okay, I'll slap you both in jail for obstruction of justice faster than you can wind your Rolex. And the next time you talk to the press, you can quote me on that!"

O'Riley had slammed the phone down so hard it knocked a Styrofoam cup half full of coffee into his lap. He'd be damned if he was gonna sit around the rest of the afternoon looking like he'd peed his pants, so he'd packed up and gone home.

Two large jack-o'-lanterns with fierce visages decorated O'Riley's front stoop. His wife had invested in two strings of white skull-shaped lights, and they were draped eerily on the two yews on either side of the entrance. A plastic skeleton dangled from the front door.

It was a cool, dry night, with a touch of ground fog. Just enough to silhouette the youngsters as they made their rounds, but nothing like the all-encompassing murk of the night before.

O'Riley's grandson Billy, decked out as Robin Hood, and his six-year-old brother, Jimmy, outfitted in a Batman costume, were the year's first trick or treaters. O'Riley had pretended not to recognize them, a ploy which fooled little Jimmy, although Billy was much too sophisticated to fall for it.

After the boys had been given a double helping of

treats, they ran inside to show Grandma their costumes, and O'Riley spent a few minutes talking to their mother.

Just as Billy's position as the oldest grandchild had earned him a special place in O'Riley's heart, his relationship with his firstborn had always been a close one. At thirty-four, Colleen O'Riley Sowatzki was a slender, petite woman with shoulder-length auburn hair and sparkling green eyes. She bore little resemblance to the grubby tomboy she'd been at Billy's age.

To Anne's eternal consternation, the child had showed no interest in dolls, preferring instead to go fishing with her dad or help him fix things around the house. She had been utterly fearless and had a hair-trigger temper. In other words, she had been a miniature version of Mike himself.

One day when Colleen was seven, her second grade teacher had called to inform Anne that the little girl had punched a boy in the face, giving him a bloody nose. When asked to explain her actions, Colleen had replied, "He called me a dumb potato eater. I said I was *not* a potato eater; I was Irish. Then I hit him." She'd paused a moment and then added proudly, "I may be small, but I'm mighty!" and had smacked her balled-up right fist into her left palm for emphasis. O'Riley thought the little twerp she'd decked had gotten exactly what he deserved, but he'd dutifully explained to Colleen that in the future she should try to win her battles with words rather than muscle.

Father and daughter remained close. With the boys safely out of earshot, Colleen leaned against the side of the house, stuck her hands in the pocket of her jeans jacket, and looked up at her dad with caring eyes. "So how goes the war?"

O'Riley shrugged. "About the same." He told her about his phone call from Clemment.

"Dumb jackass!" Colleen spat. "Too bad somebody didn't off him instead of his daughter-in-law." She linked her arm in O'Riley's. "Hang in there, Dad. You'll find him."

"I hope you're right," Mike replied, kissing the top of his daughter's head. "And I hope it's soon."

By this time the boys had come barreling out of the front door, eager to show off the special treats Grandma had given them. "Remember, we're going to ration the candy out over the next few weeks," Colleen cautioned. "Otherwise you'll end up getting sick." The boys had already scampered down the sidewalk toward the next house. "Hey, wait up!" Colleen hollered, racing after them. " 'Bye, Dad. Good luck," she called back over her shoulder.

After the grandchildren had departed, O'Riley had donned a gorilla mask and handed out Reese's peanut butter cups and bite-sized Snickers to eighty or so small ghouls. He always selected his favorite candies as treats and bought large enough quantities to ensure that there would be some left over for him to munch on at the office.

The stream of children had dried up around eight-thirty. O'Riley had turned off the porch light, gone inside, put his feet up, and had a beer while going over the latest round of communiqués received from law enforcement agencies around the country. By ten o'clock, he was beat and decided to call it a night.

He was still sleeping peacefully when the insistent ringing of the telephone next to his bed jarred him awake. He sat up and looked at the clock. It was five A.M. and still pitch-dark out.

He snatched up the phone's receiver. "Mike O'Riley."

"Mike, this is Stan Dubrovnik down at headquarters. Sorry to wake you."

An image of Dubrovnik's corpulent figure flashed through O'Riley's mind. "Yeah, Stan," O'Riley said sleepily. "What is it?"

"I'm afraid the slasher struck again," Dubrovnik began. "Another brown-haired girl, just like the last two."

"Shit!" O'Riley was fully awake now, his stomach churning. "Son of a bitch!"

"No, Mike, hold on a minute," Dubrovnik interrupted. "This might be the break you guys have been waiting for."

"What do you mean?" O'Riley demanded.

"This victim is alive."

"What?" The hair on the back of O'Riley's neck stood on end. "Where is she?"

"She got cut up pretty bad. She's in surgery right now at Northwestern Memorial, but you should be able to talk to her later this morning."

"That's great!" O'Riley exclaimed. "If you were here right now, Stan, I'd kiss you."

"I appreciate the thought, Mike," Dubrovnik said with a chuckle, "but I'm not sure my wife would understand. Hey, lots of luck, buddy. I'll be thinking of you. I know how bad you wanna wrap this thing up."

"Thanks for the call, Stan. This is the best news I've had all year."

O'Riley hung up the phone and carefully got out of bed, trying not to disturb Anne. He felt like singing.

Anne stirred. "Who was that?" she asked sleepily.

"We might have a break in the case," he replied, quickly pulling on a pair of tan perma-press slacks and a brown-and-tan plaid shirt. "We have a victim who got away. Hopefully she can give us a description."

"Oh, Mike, wouldn't that be wonderful!" Anne murmured. "I'll pray that you're right."

"You do that," O'Riley said, patting his wife on the shoulder. "We can certainly use all the help we can get. I don't know when I'll be home," he added, slipping into his brown loafers. "I'll call you later on. Why don't you try to go back to sleep."

"Good luck, dear," Anne replied.

O'Riley raced down the stairs, retrieved a jacket from the hall closet, and headed out to the garage. He didn't bother to take the time to shave. He wanted to get to headquarters as quickly as he could. He had an electric razor in his desk, and he'd try to pretty himself up a bit before he headed over to the hospital to talk to the victim. He'd call Jablonski from his car phone on the way.

As he got in the car and started the engine, Mike repeated to himself over and over, please let this be it. Please, please. He backed the car out of the garage and floored it. For the first time in a long time, he couldn't wait to get to work.

PART THREE

CHAPTER 34

James P. (Jocko) Vandermere was the head of a multimillion-dollar, real-estate-development empire headquartered in Denver. The eldest son of a Texas oil-and-cattle baron, Jocko had been educated in eastern prep schools and had an M.B.A. from Wharton. When he got the word that his daughter Judy, a VP in one of his companies who was in Chicago on business, had been viciously assaulted in the parking ramp of the Ritz-Carlton, Jocko immediately got on the phone to his old prep-school buddy George Barrett and asked that someone from George's firm be present when Judy was questioned by the police.

Barrett reached Megan just as she was stepping out of the shower. When she heard the phone's insistent ringing, she cursed under her breath, hastily dried off, and wrapped a towel around herself before sprinting to her bedroom to answer it.

Barrett explained the situation and concluded by saying, "Jim is chartering a jet and will be here later this morning, but he probably won't make it in time to be there when the police talk to Judy. I'd go down to the hospital myself, but I've got a feeling Judy would be more comfortable with a woman close to her own age."

Megan shivered and pulled the towel tighter around her with her left hand while holding the phone in her right. "You're probably right," she said, her teeth chattering. "I can't believe something like that could happen at the Ritz. Do the police think it's the same guy who killed those other women?"

"It sounds like that's what they suspect," Barrett replied. "That's why they're so eager to talk to Judy. If it *is* the same guy, she's the first woman to get away from him alive."

Megan's shivering grew more intense. God, when were they going to catch that psycho? She glanced over at the clock next to her bed. It was six-thirty. "I'll be on my way within half an hour," she promised.

"That's great," Barrett said. "Judy should be out of surgery now. Jim called the hospital and left instructions that no one was to talk to her until someone from our firm arrived. I'll call him back and tell him you'll be handling it."

"I'll let you know what happens," Megan said.

"Thanks, Megan. I appreciate it. Oh," he added, "the name of the policeman who will be meeting you is Detective Mike O'Riley."

"Gotcha," Megan replied, hanging up the phone and rushing back to the bathroom to dry her hair.

Megan arrived at the hospital at seven-fifteen wearing her most conservative black suit and a white silk blouse. She'd been in the hospital often enough with Paul to know her way around, and went directly to the nurses' station in the surgical ward. After she had identified herself, the young nurse on duty said, "Yes, Ms. Lansdorf. We've been expecting you. Ms. Vandermere was just transferred back to her room about fifteen minutes ago. That's room 1041, straight down the hall. She's conscious but still pretty groggy."

"So she came through the surgery okay?" Megan asked. "How extensive were her injuries?"

"I'm really not sure," the nurse replied. "One of the surgical nurses is with her, and she should be able to answer your questions. And her doctor is currently in surgery with another patient, but he should be available later this morning."

Megan nodded, and had already started down the hall when a sinking feeling in the pit of her stomach caused her to turn back. "Who is her doctor?"

"Dr. Paul Finley," the nurse answered brightly.

Megan stumbled and nearly lost her balance. Jesus! What were the odds of this happening?

"Are you okay?" the nurse asked anxiously.

"I'm fine," Megan replied automatically, her heart pounding wildly. I can't face him. I'm not ready for this. "I'm going to puke," she muttered under her breath. Right here in the middle of the hallway. Get a grip, she rebuked herself. You knew you'd run into him sooner or later. You're both professionals. You'll get through it just fine. Take deep breaths. In. Out. In. Out. There. That's better. She swallowed hard. "A couple of police officers are going to be arriving shortly," she said in an even tone. "Please ask them to wait here. I'll come out when Judy is ready to talk to them."

"Yes, Ms. Lansford," the nurse replied.

When Megan reached the door of Judy's room, she knocked lightly, and then stepped inside. Upon seeing Megan, the nurse seated at the side of the bed got up and walked over to meet her. Megan explained who she was and asked about Judy's condition.

"She's doing pretty good, considering," the nurse, a black woman about Megan's age, answered softly. "She was really lucky. She's got some bad bruises around her neck, and some pretty deep slashes on her forehead and on the right side of her face, and some more on her hands where she must've tried to fight the guy off. But luckily he missed her eyes. She might need some follow-up surgery, but she shouldn't have any permanent scars. Dr. Finley is a wizard in cases like this."

Megan ignored the reference to Paul and ran her tongue over her lips. "Has she said anything?" she asked, motioning to the bed.

The nurse shook her head. "Nothing coherent. She's just starting to come out of the anesthetic. Come on. We can try to talk to her."

Megan followed the nurse over to the bed. Judy Vandermere was in her mid-twenties. Her wavy brown hair was fanned out over the pillow. There were ugly black-and-blue marks around her throat. Large bandages covered her forehead and her right cheek. Both hands were also encased in bandages, giving her a mummylike aspect.

The nurse leaned down and touched Judy's shoulder. "Judy? Can you hear me? Are you awake?"

Judy moaned slightly in response.

"Judy?" The nurse applied firmer pressure on her shoulder. "Can you hear me?"

Judy's deep-green eyes slowly fluttered open. She blinked several times, struggling to bring the room into focus. She saw the nurse and moaned again.

"Judy, do you know where you are?" the nurse asked.

Judy swallowed and answered in a hoarse whisper, "Chicago. Hospital."

"That's right," the nurse said soothingly. "My name is Mary, and I'm going to be sitting with you this morning. And there's someone else here to see you." She put her hand on Megan's arm and indicated that she should move closer to the bed.

Megan took a step forward. "Hi, Judy. My name is Megan Lansdorf. I'm a lawyer. One of the men I work with is a good friend of your dad, and they asked me to come over and make sure you're okay. How are you feeling?"

Judy swallowed again. "Thirsty," she whispered.

Megan looked at the nurse. "Can she have some water?"

"Sure." The nurse reached over to a nearby table and picked up a small plastic glass with a bent straw in it. "Here," she said, directing the straw to Judy's lips. "Just take small sips." Judy raised her head slightly off the pillow and managed to take several swallows. Then she put her head back down, clearly exhausted from the effort.

"Judy," Megan continued, "the police are going to want to ask you some questions about what happened last night. Do you feel strong enough to talk to them this morning?"

"Now?" Judy asked, her eyes widening.

"As soon as you feel up to it," Megan replied.

"Do I have to?"

"I'm afraid you do," Megan answered softly. "The

sooner you talk to them, the quicker they can catch whoever did this to you."

Judy closed her eyes for a moment and took several deep breaths. "I can't remember much," she said.

"Don't worry about that," Megan said. "All you have to do is tell them whatever you do remember."

"Will you be here?"

"You bet I will," Megan said reassuringly. "I'll be right here the whole time and I'll make sure they're nice to you."

Judy looked down at her hands. "I look awful, don't I?"

"Of course you don't look awful," Megan said, patting her on the shoulder. "And don't worry about your face. I know Dr. Finley, and he's the best. You're gonna be just fine."

"Really?"

"Really," Megan said sincerely. "Now, should I go see if the police are here?"

"Okay," Judy answered. "Can I have more water?"

"You sure can," the nurse said.

Megan walked back out to the nurses' station where the two detectives were waiting. "I'm Megan Lansdorf," she said, extending her hand to the older one.

O'Riley stared at her, riveted to the spot. Holy shit! he thought to himself. What the hell was going on here? Megan looked enough like Tammy Clemment and Candy Wells to be their sister.

"Is something wrong?" Megan asked sharply.

"I'm sorry," O'Riley replied, catching himself. His eyes must be playing tricks on him. He glanced over at Jablonski and found that he, too, was gawking at Megan. So it's not just me, O'Riley thought. He quickly took her outstretched hand. "I had a momentary lapse. I'm Lieutenant Mike O'Riley, and this is Detective Greg Jablonski."

Megan tried hard not to frown as she shook hands with both men. What the hell was the matter with these two? Hadn't they ever seen a female attorney before?

"How is Miss Vandermere doing?" O'Riley asked.

"She's gonna be okay. Her throat is real bruised and

it's kind of hard for her to talk, but she's ready for you. She says she can't remember much, though."

"She might be surprised what she remembers once she starts talking about it," Jablonski replied.

Megan brushed her hair out of her face. "Do you think Judy's attacker was the same person who killed those other women?"

"I think it's a good possibility," O'Riley responded, continuing to scrutinize Megan closely. The resemblance really was uncanny. Same hair. Same build. Same mouth.

"I wonder why he let her go?" Megan queried.

"What did you say?" O'Riley blinked a couple times to clear his head. "Oh, well, apparently he either didn't get a good enough grip on her or she was just tougher to subdue than he expected, because several people in the parking ramp reported hearing her scream a couple times. I guess the guy figured it'd be smart to get out of there before help arrived, so he just sliced up her face instead of doing more serious damage."

"How thoughtful of him," Megan murmured. "Well, let's get this over with so Judy can get some rest."

The three walked into Judy's room, and Megan introduced the two detectives. O'Riley stood next to the bed and motioned to Jablonski to keep his distance.

O'Riley looked down at Judy. With all those bandages it was hard to tell what she looked like, but her hair was certainly similar to Candy's and Tammy's. And Megan's, too, he thought, giving her another quick glance. He cleared his throat. "I know this is hard for you, Judy," he said quietly, "but it's real important that you tell us anything you can remember about what happened last night, okay? Even little trivial things that you might think aren't important could be, so we need to try to be thorough."

Judy nodded and wet her lips nervously.

"Good," O'Riley said. "I have a tape recorder with me, and if it's all right with you, I'd like to record our conversation so I'm sure I don't miss anything. Do I have your permission to do that?"

Judy nodded again.

"Great," O'Riley said, motioning to Jablonski to start the tape recorder. "Now, when did you arrive in Chicago?"

"Yesterday morning," Judy answered in her hoarse whisper. "About eleven o'clock."

"And you're staying at the Ritz-Carlton?"

"Yes."

"Can you tell us what you did yesterday after you got to town?"

"I rented a car at Midway airport and drove downtown. I checked in at the hotel around eleven-thirty. Then I had a luncheon meeting at Cricket's."

"Who was that with?" O'Riley asked.

Judy sighed. "Six people. I can't remember all the names. I have them in my briefcase, if it's important. It's in my room at the hotel."

O'Riley looked over at Megan. "I can go get that later, if you need it," Megan said.

"I'd appreciate that. It might be useful," O'Riley said. He turned back to Judy. "What did you do after lunch?"

"I had a meeting at two-thirty at First National Bank of Chicago, with a Mr. Long in the trust department. One of their trusts owns some land near Denver, and we talked about a possible sale."

"Did you talk to anyone else at the bank?"

"No."

"Did you go anyplace or talk to anyone between the time you left Cricket's and the time you went to the bank?"

"No. I took a cab right from the restaurant."

"How long were you at the bank?"

"Till about four."

"Did you see anyone who looked suspicious, anybody who seemed to be watching you or following you at any time during the day?"

"No."

"Then what did you do?"

"I took a cab back to the hotel and took a bath and changed clothes. Then I drove out to the Marriott in Oak Park for another meeting."

"Who was that with?"

"A man named Joe Evans from the commodities exchange and his wife. I forgot her name. And Wilbur Rentmeester from the Harris Bank."

"What time did you leave the Marriott?"

"About nine-thirty."

"And you drove directly back to the Ritz-Carlton?"

"Yes."

"Then what happened?"

Judy took a couple of deep breaths. "I got back to the hotel around ten-fifteen. I drove into the parking ramp, parked the car and got out. The ramp was pretty full, so I was quite a ways away from the elevators. I didn't see anyone around. I started walking and all of a sudden somebody grabbed me."

"How did he grab you?" O'Riley asked.

"Around the neck. From behind," Judy whispered. "Can I have more water?" she asked.

Megan stepped forward and handed her the glass. As Judy greedily took a couple of sips, Megan could feel O'Riley's eyes on her again. Jesus, she thought, what is he looking at?

"Take your time," O'Riley said, turning back to Judy. "You're doing great. So someone grabbed you from behind. Then what happened?"

Judy swallowed hard. "He had his hands around my neck. I couldn't breathe. I had heels on and I stomped on his feet, and he let go just a little, enough so I could get my breath, and I screamed. I tried to get away, but then he grabbed me tighter. I put my hands up to try to pry him off."

"Then what happened?"

Judy shook her head. "I don't know. The next thing I remember, I was in the ambulance."

"It's very important, Judy," O'Riley said. "Are you sure you can't remember anything else?"

She shook her head again. "I don't think so. I—" Judy broke off in midsentence and turned her head toward the door.

Megan turned, too, and involuntarily groaned. Paul was standing in the open doorway. He smiled broadly as he caught Megan's eye. He was wearing surgical gloves, and as he approached the bed, he pulled the right one off.

Megan heard a strangling sound, and she turned back to look at Judy. The young woman's face was purple, her eyes rolled around in her head, and her tongue protruded from her mouth. "Oh, my God, what's the matter?" Megan asked, rushing to her side.

Judy raised one bandaged hand and attempted to point. "It's him!" she whispered. "It's him! He did it!" She began to hyperventilate, and put both hands over her face. Paul's mouth dropped open in amazement.

The nurse sprang to the bed to try to calm Judy down, and O'Riley glared at the new arrival. "Doctor, would you please step back outside," he ordered, his eyes flashing. "I'll be with you shortly."

In a few moments, O'Riley stepped out into the hallway. Paul was standing right outside the door.

"Would you mind telling me what was going on in there?" Paul asked the lieutenant crossly. "Does this patient need a psychiatric referral?"

"That won't be necessary, Doctor," O'Riley replied. "Ms. Vandermere's outburst was caused by seeing your gloves. That triggered a recollection that the person who attacked her was wearing surgical gloves."

"Thank God for that," Paul replied.

Just then, Megan and Jablonski walked out of Judy's room. Paul immediately rushed up to Megan and took her hand. "Meggie," he said tenderly, "I'm so glad to see you."

At his touch, Megan felt a jolt, as though she had come in contact with a live electric wire. She looked up at Paul and felt her insides turn to mush. His hair was tousled, and she had a sudden urge to reach up and caress his cheek.

Before she could respond, Paul continued, "I'm so glad you're safe! When I first saw that girl in the ER, I was afraid it was you."

Megan felt a chill run down her spine, and she angrily pulled her hand away. "What are you talking about?"

"I was afraid it was you," Paul repeated. "You can't tell it so much now with all the bandages, but she looked just like you. Her hair, her cheekbones, everything. I was really scared there for a minute."

As Megan stood there with her mouth agape, O'Riley spoke up. "That's a very interesting comment, Doctor. When I first saw Ms. Lansdorf, my first reaction was that by some coincidence she looked an awful lot like the last two slashing victims. Don't you agree, Greg?"

"Yes, I do," Jablonski replied. "Very much."

"That's ridiculous!" Megan exclaimed, but she could feel herself breaking out in a cold sweat.

"I didn't mean to upset you," O'Riley said soothingly. "As I said, it's obviously just a coincidence."

"I'm *not* upset!" Megan replied, turning back toward Judy's room. "I'm sure Ms. Vandermere would appreciate getting this over with so she can get some rest. Shall we continue?"

"All right, Judy," O'Riley said a moment later, when they had all reassembled in her room. "Now you've told us you remember that the person who attacked you was wearing surgical gloves. Is that right?"

"Yes," Judy whispered.

"When did you see the gloves?"

"Right before he grabbed me. I saw them out of the corner of my eye."

"Do you remember anything about the person's hands? Were they big, small, average size?"

Judy thought a moment. "I can't remember."

"Did you get an impression of the person's height?"

"No."

"Do you remember whether the person's arms were angled down toward you, like they might be if the person were taller than you, or pretty much straight out, like if he were close to your size?"

"I don't know."

"Think hard," O'Riley urged. "Try to remember."

Judy shook her head again. "I'm sorry. I can't."

"That's okay," O'Riley said soothingly. "You indicated earlier that after you managed to scream, the attacker tightened his hold on you again and then the next thing you recall was being in the ambulance. Have you thought of anything else that happened in between?"

"No," Judy whispered. "Nothing."

"All right. You've been very helpful, Judy. I'm going to leave you my card. It has my phone numbers, both at the office and at home. It's possible that you might remember something else about what happened last night. In case you do think of anything, no matter how trivial you might feel it is, I'd appreciate it if you'd call me, okay?"

Judy nodded.

O'Riley turned to Megan. "Do you think it'd be possible to get me that list of names from Judy's briefcase later today?"

By this time Megan had gotten her emotions under control. "Sure," she replied. "I'll go over to the hotel from here and have a copy delivered to you later this morning."

"I appreciate your help," O'Riley said, handing Megan one of his cards. "It was nice meeting you." Turning back to Judy, he said, "Maybe you can get some rest now. We'll get your statement transcribed and I'll stop back tomorrow so you can look it over and sign it."

Judy was exhausted from the interview and merely nodded, her eyes already closing.

God, what a morning, Megan thought to herself as she rode down to the lobby. She felt completely drained and more than a little shaky. She looked at her watch. It was only ten o'clock. Maybe she'd stop by the hospital cafeteria. She hadn't eaten anything and she was badly in need of some caffeine.

As Megan reached the ground floor, she tried to make sense out of the jumbled thoughts that kept popping through her head. Why had seeing Paul put her into a state of emotional overload? And why had it upset her so much to hear that she looked like a couple of dead girls? After all, the lieutenant had said it was just a coincidence.

She headed toward the cafeteria, disparate images running through her mind. Her car window being demolished. Thinking that someone was following her down that deserted street in Bethesda. Rita being the hapless victim of a hit-and-run driver. They were all coincidences ... weren't they?

CHAPTER 35

Shit! Mike O'Riley cursed silently as the computer flashed an error message for the umpteenth time. O'Riley took a puff of his cigarette, bounced his right leg up and down in nervous irritation and reread the instructions Jablonski had so painstakingly prepared on how to access the various parts of the elaborate computer database.

It was mid November, two weeks after the attack on Judy Vandermere. As O'Riley had expected, forensics had confirmed that the knife used on Judy was the same one that had killed the other six women. As a result, the investigation had reached a fever pitch. Everyone on the team realized they were working against the clock, that every night that passed was one more step on the countdown to another murder attempt.

That was why O'Riley was spending this blustery evening in his office trying to master the rudiments of computer operation. No one realized more than he that time was of the essence. He could no longer afford the luxury of manually leafing through the reams of papers in his office when he needed to put his finger on a particular fact.

Jablonski's instructions were pretty straightforward, and O'Riley had managed to access the bank of interview transcripts with little difficulty. For the last twenty minutes, though, he'd been stymied over how to get into the physical diagrams of the crime scenes.

He looked at the instructions again. They said to go back to the main menu. He punched the ESCAPE key and the menu appeared. So far, so good. It was after that point that he ran into trouble. The instructions said to scroll down to the desired category of information and press ENTER. O'Riley could've sworn he'd tried all of the categories and still couldn't find where the diagrams might be hiding. He guessed he'd have to start at the top and try them all again.

The first category was INTERVIEWS. He knew there were no charts there. He tried FACTS. No, that was just a bunch of lists of physical facts relating to each crime. How about MEDICAL. No, that was a synopsis of the experts' reports. HOTLINE was a list of all calls received on the toll-free phone line. CRIMINALS was a listing of known sex offenders and their current whereabouts.

O'Riley gritted his teeth. Goddamn it! He knew the information he wanted was in there someplace, and he was going to find it if he had to sit here all night.

Judy Vandermere's attack and survival had been a breakthrough. Judy was now back in Denver recuperating from her ordeal. O'Riley had interviewed her three more times while she was still in the hospital. Unfortunately, she hadn't been able to remember anything else about the attack or her assailant. O'Riley hadn't given up hope on that front, though. Victims of violent crimes often blotted out the details as a defense mechanism. They sometimes remembered important bits of information weeks after the event.

O'Riley had personally interviewed everyone Judy had met during her brief stay in Chicago as well as countless Ritz-Carlton guests and employees. The people's backgrounds and alibis had all checked out, and O'Riley believed they were clean. Because Judy wasn't from the city, O'Riley was almost certain that her attacker had been a stranger and that she'd just been unlucky enough to have been in the right place at the wrong time. However, though the assailant couldn't have known Judy would come along when she did, because her looks matched those of the two previous victims, that meant the attacker must have lain in wait, ready to pounce on the first lone female who fit his physical requirements.

The entire mode of Judy's attack had raised a number of new questions. First, although all of the victims had been strangled from behind, in the earlier attacks there was evidence the women had first been lured to a secluded place where the killer could work on them with some privacy. Judy had not had the benefit of any such preliminary niceties. Was there a reason why the killer had apparently abandoned his earlier technique? And why had he only sliced up Judy's face? Even though his attempt to render her unconscious had failed, he obviously had his trusty knife with him and could have struck a mortal blow.

Then there was the location of the attack. If someone was planning to strangle, stab, and sexually assault a woman, why in hell would he pick the well-lit parking ramp of a major downtown hotel to do it? No matter how fucked up the guy's mind was, he surely ought to have realized that his chances of escaping detection there would be small. Could that mean he was ready to get caught?

This was by far the goddamnest case O'Riley had ever worked on. Generally speaking, you needed three things to solve a crime: physical evidence, eyewitnesses, and a motive. Here, they had no physical evidence beyond the fact that the guy always used the same knife and always struck the mortal wounds in the same way. They had no eyewitnesses, except for a couple of vague, unconfirmed reports that a tall, dark-haired cop might have been spotted near two of the crime scenes. And they had no motive except for their shrinks' theory that the guy was seeking revenge on both a tall redhead and a short brunette.

And all of that seemed to lead them absolutely nowhere. No matter how smart the killer was, O'Riley couldn't help but think that he must have left *some* sort of clue that they hadn't picked up yet. And if it was there, by God, he was going to find it if he had to sit and stare at this miserable computer screen all night.

As O'Riley continued fumbling with the computer, Greg Jablonski stood in the doorway, smiling to himself. So the old man had finally come around. Jablonski had known it would just be a matter of time.

"Oh, shit!" O'Riley exclaimed out loud when yet another attempt to access the diagrams failed.

Jablonski stepped into the office. "Can I give you a hand with something, Mike?" he asked.

O'Riley's head snapped up, and he swung around in his chair. "How long have you been standing there?" he demanded.

"I just got here right now," Jablonski replied.

O'Riley eyed him suspiciously. "Yeah? Well, as long as you're here, maybe you can show me how to find the damn crime-scene diagrams."

"Sure thing," Jablonski said, walking over the computer. "It's a little tricky to get to them because they're considered a graphic. So the instructions you're looking at don't apply. The explanation about graphics is on this other sheet." He reached into the folder to O'Riley's right and pulled out the correct page. "See, here it is." Leaning over O'Riley's right shoulder, he deftly punched in the appropriate codes and, like magic, a diagram showing the layout of the spot in the parking ramp where Judy had been attacked appeared on the screen.

"Well, I'll be damned," O'Riley said. "I knew it was there someplace."

"Then if you want to move to another diagram, just press 'page up' or 'page down.' They're loaded in here chronologically."

"Thanks for the help," O'Riley said. "I appreciate it."

"No problem," Jablonski replied. "If you ever have trouble finding something, just holler."

O'Riley grunted and scanned the crime-scene graphics.

"Looking for anything in particular?" Jablonski asked, peering over his shoulder.

O'Riley shook his head. "No I just thought if I go over these enough times, eventually something's gonna jump out at me."

Jablonski snorted. "I used to think that, too, but I'm not so sure anymore." He leaned against one of the file cabinets and rubbed his eyes.

"How are Carol and the baby doing?" O'Riley asked, continuing to stare at the computer screen.

Jablonski yawned. "Melissa is sleeping a little better at night, but if she only wakes up once, we think it's an event worth celebrating. Carol is holding up pretty well, considering. Why doesn't anybody ever tell you how exhausting babies are?" He ran his hand through his hair. "I'm not home much, but after a couple hours of feeding her, changing her, and trying to get her to sleep, I'm ready to collapse. I don't know how women do it."

O'Riley smiled. "You think you got it bad. You haven't lived till you've had two kids under age two, both in diapers, and both waking you up every night. That's a real picnic."

Jablonski shook his head. "We've already had serious discussions about being a one-child family. Carol has four more weeks of maternity leave, but I think part of her would like to go back to work tomorrow just to have some peace and quiet."

"It'll get better soon," O'Riley predicted, still flipping through the crime scenes. "By the time Melissa's three months she'll be sleeping all night, and she'll start smiling at you and making little noises like she's trying to tell you something. That's when you'll start thinking being a dad is the neatest thing since sliced bread, and you'll wonder why you waited so long to do it."

"Really?" Jablonski asked hopefully. "You promise?"

O'Riley nodded. "If your kid doesn't turn out like that, it'll be the first one in history."

Jablonski chuckled. "I sure hope you're right. And I hope Carol and I can hang on that long." He scratched his chin. "Say, Mike, there's something I've been meaning to ask you."

"What's that?"

"Well, um . . . you see . . ." Jablonski paused.

O'Riley turned around and looked at the younger man with amusement. Greg Jablonski hard up for words? What the hell was this all about? "Yes?" he asked expectantly.

Jablonski took a deep breath. "I've been meaning to

tell you that I registered to take the sergeant's exam next month, and I was wondering if you'd be willing to write a recommendation for me." The words came out in a rush. "I know there's been a freeze on promotions, so this whole discussion is probably pointless, but I just wondered . . ." His voice trailed off.

O'Riley hesitated a moment, as though he needed to consider the request. He watched with satisfaction as a flush crept over Jablonski's face. "Of course, I'll write a recommendation for you," he said, grinning. "I've already written one for Margie. I think you'd both make good sergeants."

Jablonski, who had been holding his breath, exhaled loudly. "Thanks, Mike. I really appreciate it."

"No problem. Let me know when you need my comments and I'll have 'em ready for you. And I wouldn't be so sure the discussion is pointless. As you've pointed out to me many times, there are bound to be big promotional opportunities for the guy who cracks this case." O'Riley winked at him.

Jablonski's face flushed again. "Is that a hint that I ought to get back to work instead of standing around here flapping my gums?"

O'Riley shrugged. "You can do whatever you want, but I'm on a roll with this computer stuff, so I suggest you go do your thing someplace else."

"Yes, sir," Jablonski said, snapping his heels together smartly. "I'll be at my desk if you need me." He walked out of the office.

O'Riley shook his head ruefully. What a pleasant surprise. The kid was doing a good job of toning down his ego. Maybe you could teach an old dog new tricks. Smiling to himself at the irony of that concept, O'Riley turned back to his computer screen.

The scrapbook is in its place on the shelf. Looming. Laughing. Taunting.

Pace back and forth across the floor. Toward the window. Away from the window. Toward the window.

There is a full moon. It looks like a laughing face.

Taunting. Mocking. Pull the curtain shut. Walk away from the window.

The preparations had been so carefully made. The verse had been reverently chosen, lovingly inscribed in the book. Even the selection of the date had been given careful thought. All Hallows' Eve. Could there be a more appropriate time to carry out an act of retribution? Everything was in order. The girl had been just the right type. So what had gone wrong?

Walk toward the window. The girl had been surprisingly strong. She must have sensed your approach. It was her shoes that had ruined everything. Spike heels can inflict great pain. That was a contingency that you should have foreseen, but you didn't. Very sloppy. Have to be more careful in the future. You can't afford to make another mistake.

Walk away from the window. Once again you wonder whether your alter ego suspected what was happening, whether he had stopped you. He had been very agitated lately, under a lot of strain. But, of course, that was precisely the reason why you had to come to his rescue.

No, you are certain he is still in the dark, although he would try to stop you if he had any inkling what is going on. He thinks of himself as an honorable man. He would be appalled by what you were doing. Stupid sot. Allowing himself to be victimized, first by one woman, then by another. But never fear, you will help him, in spite of himself. You will put matters right.

Nearly every day the papers carry statements from the detective in charge of the investigation. Lieutenant Michael F. O'Riley. In today's paper O'Riley said he thought a break in the case was imminent. He was lying. He has no clues.

Walk toward the window. Stop pacing! This self-abasement is unproductive. Have to direct your energies toward positive thoughts. So many more lovely verses. All you have to do is choose one. You will make up for your failure very soon. Soon it will be time to claim your ultimate victim. And in that endeavor, you will not fail.

CHAPTER 36

"Did you ever stop to wonder how many trees gave their lives so we could have all these wonderful copies?" Ron Johnson asked reflectively.

Megan quickly shuffled through one of the large stacks of papers on the conference room table. "Damn!" she sputtered crossly, drumming the fingernails of her right hand on the tabletop in irritation. "No, I can't say I've ever pondered that particular question," she said to Ron. "The only thing I'm wondering right now is what the hell happened to the exhibits marked at Dr. Gillian's deposition."

Ron made a clucking sound with his tongue. "Don't know. You had them last."

It was a Saturday afternoon, and Megan and Ron were sorting through the tens of thousands of documents that had been produced by both sides in the AIDS case, trying to cull the ones they wanted to introduce as trial exhibits.

Megan had just started leafing through another stack of papers when her secretary, Karen, came into the room, looking chagrined. "I think I got to the bottom of what happened to the Gillian exhibits," she said. "And you're gonna be pissed."

"Why? What happened?" Megan asked warily.

Karen sighed. "The copy shop lost them when we sent over the last batch of stuff to be duplicated. They didn't want to admit it at first, but I finally wormed it out of them."

"What?" Megan exploded, throwing the papers back on the table. "Oh, shit! Those idiots! That's the second batch of documents they've lost this month. From now on I want all our copying done in-house. I don't care if it does tie up our copy machines. We're three weeks away from trial and we can't afford any more screwups."

"I'm sorry, Megan," Karen said contritely.

"It's not your fault," Megan said, slumping into a chair. She was wearing faded jeans and a hand-knit, wine-colored sweater with a tan turtleneck underneath. She leaned down and retied her left tennis shoe. "It's just that after five straight hours of sorting all this junk, I'm getting a little edgy. I was really hoping we could get through the rest of this today."

"See if you can reach Parks or someone at his office," Ron suggested. "If they're around, we could borrow a set of the exhibits and get them copied this afternoon." Karen nodded and headed back toward her desk. "If Parks isn't there, ask for Daniel Bartlett," Ron added. "He's the associate that's going to be second-chairing the trial."

"Can you imagine waiting until this late in the game to bring an associate in the case?" Megan said. "The poor guy is going to have to work day and night just to read the entire file by the time the trial starts."

Ron shrugged. "Obviously Parks intends to examine all the witnesses himself. Poor Bartlett will probably get stuck taking notes and pouring glasses of water."

Megan wrinkled her nose. "Sounds to me like a stupid way to do business."

In a few moments Karen returned, shaking her head ruefully. "Neither Parks nor Bartlett are in, and without their say-so, nobody is authorized to give us any documents."

"I've got it!" Ron exclaimed, smiling impishly. "We'll break into Parks's office and steal the exhibits. And while we're there, we'll rifle through all his files and find out his trial strategy. We'll need to get past building security, though. Let's see ... I know, we'll attach rubber suction cups to our feet and scale the outside of the building."

Megan made a face. "If you want to scale the outside of the Hancock Building, be my guest, but you'll

have to do it solo because I'm afraid of heights. Too
bad Parks's office isn't in this building. We don't have
any security people to worry about."

"Yeah. It wouldn't be too tough to sneak past old
Mr. Higgins," Ron said. "Especially after the cocktail
hour, which in his case I think starts at nine A.M."

Megan rubbed her middle finger over the beauty
spot next to her lip. "I really want to finish this job today," she said, standing up again. "I'm going to try to
reach Parks at home. He might have a set of exhibits
with him."

She walked over to the phone on the wall of the conference room, located Parks's number in the phone
book and dialed. After a brief conversation, she hung
up and turned around, a smug look on her face. "He *is*
home, he *does* have the exhibits with him, and he'd be
delighted to let us borrow them until Monday." She
turned to Ron. "You and Karen keep plugging away at
this while I go pick them up."

"Are you sure you don't want me to go get them?"
Ron asked.

"No, I'll go. I could use a break. If I'm not back in
a couple hours, call the police."

"Hey, with that slasher still on the loose, if you
don't come back pronto, you bet your life we'll call the
police," Karen said. "Maybe you should call us when
you get there to let us know you're okay."

"Yeah," Ron said. "And while you're at Parks's
house, take a good look around. Maybe you'll find
some evidence that *he's* the slasher. You know, look for
things like bloody knives lying around the living room
or a boxful of surgical gloves in the hall closet."

"Grow up!" Megan retorted as she walked out of the
conference room. "I'll be back before you know it, and
I expect you to have made lots of progress while I'm
gone." As she headed down the hall, she could hear
Ron belting out the chorus of "Monster Mash."

There was a reason for Meagan's dour mood and her
eagerness to get out of the office for a while, beyond
her exasperation with misplacing some documents.
Ever since she'd seen Paul at the hospital, she'd been

overwhelmed with an urge to call him. Just to chat, she'd told herself, maybe to talk about Judy's recovery.

The previous day she had summoned her courage and placed a discrete call to one of Paul's closest friends to see if she could learn whether Paul still mentioned her, whether he still missed her. To Megan's great surprise and disappointment, the friend had informed her that Paul was seeing someone steadily.

"Not Rhonda?" she'd asked anxiously.

"No. Her name's Nicole. She's a neurosurgery resident."

"Oh. I see," Megan had said, fighting to keep her voice calm. "Well, I'm glad to hear he's happy."

The news had hit her hard. It was almost like going through the breakup all over again. She knew it was childish of her. After all, she'd been the one who was so adamant about ending their relationship. But somehow, in the back of her mind, she'd always thought that she'd have the option to reconsider her decision. Well, this turn of events explained why Paul hadn't bothered to call her. He'd certainly wasted no time in finding a replacement. She supposed she should think about doing the same, but the idea was not at all appealing.

The funny thing was that things had been going very well for her professionally. She'd garnered a lot of accolades for her work on the historic preservation case, and was feeling pretty darn good about the AIDS trial, too. What a shame her private life was in such a mess. She sped toward Parks's house, hoping that a liberal dose of fresh air would clear her head. With a little effort, she could probably manage to pick a fight with Parks while she was there. That might make her feel better.

Megan had often driven through Kenwood admiring the architecture, but had never been inside any of the homes. She braked her Buick to a stop in front of the address Parks had given her, and let out a low whistle. God, the place was absolutely gorgeous!

She shivered slightly and pulled her ivory-and-brown Icelandic jacket tighter around her. She wished she'd dressed up. Owning a house like that, Parks would probably be lounging around in a red-silk smoking jacket. Courage, Megan, she thought, as she stepped on the accelerator and pulled the car into the brick driveway.

She stopped in front of the garage and took a deep breath before getting out of the car. She walked up the brick sidewalk to the front door and rang the doorbell, figuring a servant would answer it. To her surprise, Frank himself opened the door. "Come on in. Bit nippy out there, isn't it?"

Megan stepped inside. As she looked at the ornately carved open stairway, the fine oak paneling of the foyer, and the white-and-black Venetian marble in the hallway ahead of her, all her best intentions to remain aloof flew out the window and she exclaimed, "Wow! What a wonderful house!"

Frank smiled boyishly. "Thank you. We like it. As long as you're here, would you like me to show you around?"

Megan looked at him. He was wearing jeans and a forest-green sweater. So much for her theory about servants and smoking jackets. She nodded enthusiastically. "Yes, I'd love to see the house."

She followed Frank down the hallway. As they reached the door to the living room, Jack stepped out. "Megan, this is my son, Jack," Frank said, putting a hand on the boy's shoulder. "Jack, this is Megan Lansdorf. She's an attorney."

"Hello, Jack," Megan said warmly.

Jack cocked his head and looked at the visitor. "You don't look like an attorney," he said.

Megan laughed. "No? What do I look like?"

"Mmmm," Jack considered a moment. "You look kinda like my English teacher."

"You should consider that a compliment," Frank said. "Miss Watson is Jack's favorite teacher."

The house tour continued, with Jack tagging along behind them. Kate was sitting in a chair in the music room, reading. Frank introduced Megan, and Kate said a curt "hello" before turning her attention back to her book. Just then Cleopatra, Kate's snooty gray Persian, emerged from behind a table. Megan said, "Oh, what a nice kitty," and began to walk toward it.

"She doesn't like strangers," Kate said haughtily, looking up from her book.

Megan smiled to herself, suspecting that the remark reflected Kate's own attitude toward intruders as much as the cat's. Kate was a beautiful girl, Megan noted, with her long legs encased in tight black pants under a sweater with black-and-white geometric designs over it.

Megan turned her attention back to the cat. She stopped a few paces from it, bent down, and extended her hand. "Hi, sweetie. How are you?" Cleo pinned back her ears, but did not retreat. Megan inched forward. "You're very pretty. Can I pet you?" The cat stretched its head forward, allowing the tip of its nose to come in contact with Megan's outstretched fingers. After allowing the animal to sniff her for a moment, Megan patted it on the head, then reached down and carefully picked it up. Cleo stiffened a bit but made no attempt to escape.

"That's amazing," Frank said. "She never goes to anybody."

"She can probably sense I'm a cat lover," Megan explained. "What's her name?"

"Cleopatra," Kate said, watching the scene with astonishment.

"And that's Marc Antony over there," Jack added, pointing to the white ball of fur curled up on a corner of the sofa.

Cleopatra? Marc Antony? Megan thought. Whatever happened to names like Morris or Pumpkin? But then again, it should come as no surprise that someone living in a mansion like this would have highbrow names for their pets.

The cat sniffed Megan's sweater. "You probably smell my cat, don't you?" she asked the beast.

"What's your cat's name?" Jack inquired.

Megan had been afraid someone would ask that. "Andy," she replied. When Jack seemed to look quizzically at her, she explained, "You see, he was a stray, and when he arrived on my front steps, I was watching an old Andy Griffith show rerun." She shrugged. "Not very original, but it suits him." She set Cleo down. The animal stepped back several paces, and then reclined and began to groom itself.

Megan walked over to the piano. "I'm very jealous. I've always wanted a Steinway," she said, reverently touching the case. "Of course, I don't have room for anything this size right now, but I'd love to have one someday." She turned to Kate. "Your dad has told me what a wonderful pianist you are, and I'd love to hear you play sometime."

"I don't give command performances," Kate said in a frosty tone.

Out of the corner of her eye, Megan saw Frank frown at the girl, but he said nothing.

"I didn't expect you to play anything for me right now," Megan said smoothly. "I just meant that maybe sometime I could come to one of your recitals."

Kate turned back to her book without replying.

"Let's get out of here," Jack said, walking back toward the hall.

"My thoughts exactly," Megan murmured under her breath as she and Frank followed.

When they reached the library, Megan oohed and aahed over the first edition of Dr. Johnson's dictionary, saying, "My dad would kill to own this. When my brother and I were in junior high, our family went to London for the first time. Dad wouldn't even let us get settled in the hotel before taking us on a pilgrimage to see the house where Johnson worked on the dictionary. Here we were, ready to collapse from jet lag and Dad made us stand around in that damn garret for what seemed like an eternity, while he drank in the rarefied atmosphere where his idol had done this great creative work. The rest of us were ready to call the nearest mental-health ward and have Dad committed."

Frank laughed. "Well, you tell your dad that he's welcome to come and peruse my dictionary any time he likes."

"I'm sure he'd take you up on that offer," Megan said.

When Frank had finished showing Megan the first floor, Jack, who was still following close on his father's heels, said, "Now let's show her the basement."

"I don't know that she wants to see the basement," Frank protested.

"I'd be happy to look at the basement," Megan said, sensing that there must be something special down there that the boy wanted to show off.

It turned out she was right. In one corner of the great room, near the fireplace, was a jukebox full of classic hits from the 1950's and 1960's. "Ron Johnson would go nuts down here," Megan said. "You'd never get him out."

Jack put a dime in the machine and punched a couple of buttons to make his selection. In a moment he was gyrating around the floor while he lip-synched the words to "Jailhouse Rock." When the song was over, Megan applauded.

"With a little more practice, I'm hoping he'll be able to support me in my old age," Frank joked. "That is, if I can fatten him up a little."

"Now can we show her the garage?" Jack asked eagerly.

Frank laughed. "I think we'll save the garage for another time. Why don't you run along and play now?"

"It was nice meeting you, Jack," Megan said, shaking the boy's hand.

"I'm glad you came," Jack said. " 'Bye." He scurried up the stairs.

Frank and Megan walked back upstairs and went into the study, where Frank located the exhibits Megan had come to pick up. "Would you like a drink?" he asked as he handed her the documents. "Or maybe some hot chocolate before you go back out into the cold?"

Megan was tempted. She glanced down at her watch. My God! She'd been away from the office almost two hours. "Thanks," she said hastily, "but I'd better be getting back, or my secretary will be sending out a search party." As they walked down the long marble hallway toward the front door, she said, "We should probably set up a time to mark the exhibits we both agree should be admitted at trial. I know the judge wants a list of those ahead of time."

Frank nodded. "How does your schedule look for next Saturday?"

"Next Saturday would be fine. Do you want to come over to our office, say around ten?"

"Ten would be good."

They had reached the foyer. "I'll get these exhibits back to you first thing Monday morning," Megan said. "And thanks very much for the tour. I enjoyed it."

"I'm glad," Frank said, looking down at her. "I think you made quite a hit with all the members of the household." He paused a moment before adding, "At least almost all of them."

Megan shrugged, understanding that that was his way of apologizing for Kate's icy reception. "I'm generally a big hit with animals and children. It's adults I sometimes have a hard time dealing with."

Frank smiled. "Good-bye, Megan. I'll talk to you next week."

"Good-bye."

As she walked down the brick sidewalk, Megan realized with a start that she hadn't thought of Paul once since she'd arrived. And she'd managed to put herself in a better frame of mind without getting in a fight with Frank. Musing that life could sure as hell be strange sometimes, she got in her car and headed back to the office.

CHAPTER 37

Mike O'Riley cradled the telephone receiver under his chin as he lit a cigarette. He inhaled deeply, then exhaled the smoke through his nose. He rapidly scribbled some notes as he listened to the voice on the other end of the line. "Okay. So you say your guy got ten years for carving up his old lady with a fileting knife. Does he have any record for sexual assault or was he just knife happy?"

The superintendent of one of Indiana's maximum security prisons consulted his file. "No mention of prosecutions for sexual assault, but he was arrested twice for soliciting a prostitute, so he might be a little screwed up sexually."

"Umm-hmm," O'Riley grunted, puffing on his cigarette. "And when did he escape?"

"May fifteenth."

"He can't be our guy," O'Riley said ruefully. "We'd already had four murders by then."

"Sorry," the Indiana superintendent said. "Anyway, if Jack Morrison wanders into your bailiwick, watch out. We think he's probably left the state, and he's to be considered armed and dangerous."

"Okay. We'll keep an eye out for him. Thanks for calling."

O'Riley hung up the phone, finished jotting down some more notes, and ripped the page off the pad in front of him. One more useless piece of information for Jablonski to add to his data base. He started to get up from his chair when the phone rang again. "This is O'Riley," he said, snatching it up.

"Lieutenant O'Riley?" a soft voice asked. "This is Judy Vandermere."

O'Riley's face brightened. "Hi, Judy. How are you?" he asked warmly.

"Oh, pretty good, I guess. I'm still not sleeping all that well, but my sister's been staying with me, and that makes me feel a little safer."

"It takes time," O'Riley said. "You can't rush things. What can I do for you today?"

He heard Judy sigh. "Well, umm . . ." she hesitated a moment. "I talked to my attorney this morning. You know, Ms. Lansdorf, and she said I should call you right away. You see, I think I've remembered something."

The hair on the back of O'Riley's neck stood up. He ground out his cigarette in the green plastic ashtray on his desk and picked up a pen. "Go on," he prompted gently. "What do you remember?"

"Well, I was watching TV last night," Judy began, somewhat haltingly. "It was some dumb adventure movie where the hero was trying to rescue a bunch of people from a building that terrorists had under siege." She stopped and cleared her throat. "And the only way for the hero to get into the building was to climb up the side. And so he's climbing, and when he gets close to the top, he climbed up an old chimney, and I was looking at that and that's when I remembered."

"What did you remember?" O'Riley asked patiently.

"The guy that attacked me said something about a chimney."

O'Riley rubbed the bridge of his nose with the top of his Bic pen. "I'm not sure I'm following you, Judy. What did he say about a chimney?"

Judy sighed again. "I can't remember all of it, but when he first grabbed my neck and was squeezing me real tight, and I couldn't breathe and was just about ready to pass out, he said something like 'Boys and girls, like chimney sweepers, will go and dust.' And that's when I managed to stomp on his foot with my heel. But it was just like you said. I'd forgotten all about it until I saw the program last night. And then when I saw the chimney, I remembered."

O'Riley looked at the words he'd rapidly scribbled on the pad in front of him. " 'Boys and girls, like chimney sweepers, will go and dust,' " he repeated. "You're sure that's what he said?"

"I think that's how it went. I know it doesn't make any sense, but that's what I remember."

"Can you remember anything else?"

Judy sighed again. "No, I can't. I've thought and thought, and my sister and I tried word association and stuff like that, but it didn't help. So if he did say anything else, I can't remember it."

"Do you remember what his voice sounded like? Was it high-pitched, low, loud, soft? Did it sound like he had an accent of any kind?"

O'Riley could hear Judy grinding her teeth together. "It was a soft voice, not much above a whisper. And I think it was lower pitched, but I'm not sure. I was so scared, and I was trying to think how I could get away. . . ." Her voice trailed off.

"I understand," O'Riley said, tapping his pen against the pad of paper. "This is great, Judy," he said encouragingly. "I'm very proud of you. I want you to keep trying to remember anything else that the guy might have said or done. Don't force it. Just keep an open mind. You might be surprised what else you think of."

"I'll try," Judy said, "but I don't know if I'm going to be able to remember anything more."

"Well, if you *do* remember anything, and I mean *anything* at all, you call me right away. You've got my home number, don't you?"

"Yes."

"Okay, good. Don't be afraid to call anytime, day or night."

"I will," Judy promised. "Lieutenant?"

"Yes."

"Do you think it means anything? The stuff about the chimney, I mean."

"I don't know, Judy," O'Riley admitted, "but I'm gonna do my best to find out."

"Well, I hope it helps you catch him. I can't stand the thought that he's still running around loose there someplace."

"We'll catch him," O'Riley vowed. "If it's the last thing I do, we're gonna catch him."

"Good luck," Judy said.

"Thank you, Judy. Good luck to you, too. I really appreciate the call, and I'm glad to hear you're getting along so well."

"Thanks, Lieutenant. 'Bye."

"Good-bye, Judy."

O'Riley ripped the piece of paper from the pad, got up, and sprinted down the hall to the cramped office that Jablonski shared with three other detectives. The young man was busy entering information into his computer. "Stop whatever you're doing," O'Riley ordered as he walked in. "I've got a job for you."

Jablonski looked up. "What is it?"

"I just got a call from Judy Vandermere. She remembered something the attacker said as he was choking her. It doesn't make a hell of a lot of sense, but it might lead to something." He set the sheet of paper down on Jablonski's desk. "You're a college graduate. Does this ring a bell with you?'

Jablonski looked at the paper and shook his head. "No, it doesn't look familiar, but I'll call Ready Reference at the library and see if they can find it in *Bartlett's Quotations* or some such thing. I'll get right on it."

In half an hour, Jablonski walked into O'Riley's office, a smug look on his face. "Got it," he said triumphantly. He referred to the paper in his hand. " 'Golden lads and girls all must, as chimney-sweepers, come to dust.' It's Shakespeare. *Cymbeline*. Act Four, Scene Two. The librarian found it in a book of quotations under the heading 'death.' The entire verse is:

> Fear no more the heat o' th' sun,
>   Nor the furious winter's wages;
> Thou thy worldly task hast done,
>   Home art gone, and ta'en thy wages:

> Golden lads and girls all must,
> As chimney-sweepers, come to dust."

O'Riley scratched his head. "Shakespeare, huh? I had to read some of his plays in high school. Hated the damn things. Too highbrow for me. What do you s'pose it means?"

Jablonski shook his head. "I don't know. Death? The guy was telling her everybody has to die eventually and her time had come?"

"Maybe," O'Riley agreed, "but why didn't he just say 'You're gonna die, bitch?' Whoever heard of a killer reciting Shakespeare as he's in the middle of the crime?"

"It's a new one on me," Jablonski admitted. "Do you want me to run this by our experts?"

O'Riley made a spitting sound. "Yeah, go ahead," he said grudgingly. "I don't expect much help out of 'em, but might as well give them a shot at it. I suppose Dr. Sheridan will come back with some cockamamie intellectual profile." He screwed up his face and continued in sotto voice, " 'The killer's use of a quotation from the immortal Bard of Avon indicates that he has a higher than average IQ and his mother refused to breastfeed him.' "

Jablonski laughed. "While the experts are working on that valuable analysis, what do you suggest we do?"

O'Riley lit up a cigarette. "Keep mulling it over. Say, you don't happen to know any English professors, do you?"

"I have a passing acquaintance with one or two."

"Might not hurt to ask them what they think. And make it clear we just want an off-the-cuff answer. They're not gonna get paid for their thoughts unless one of 'em comes up with an idea so brilliant that it helps us solve the case. I know the mayor gave us free rein here, but I have a sneaking suspicion that for an investigation that's turned up absolutely nothing, we're running a little over budget."

Jablonski smiled. "Gotcha. I'll keep you posted."

As the young detective walked back to his desk,

O'Riley ran the quotation over and over in his mind. A Shakespearean killer? Obviously they were dealing with somebody considerably smarter than your average criminal. But who? "Aye, there's the rub." O'Riley smiled. See, he could be literary, too.

He took a drag on his cigarette and started to cough. The building's heating system was pumping out hot, dry air, and his office was awfully stuffy. A trip outside in the cold might clear his sinuses. He hadn't been to a library for a long time. Maybe it was time to bone up on his research skills. It might be interesting to take a look at some other quotes on death. It was a long shot, but then again, what wasn't? He stubbed out his cigarette in the ashtray, got up, and reached for his jacket.

CHAPTER 38

It was the Saturday before Thanksgiving, and Megan and Frank were seated on opposite sides of the table in one of Barrett, Gillette's conference rooms, going through the exhibits that each wanted to introduce at the trial, and marking and numbering those documents that both agreed on.

Megan rubbed her eyes. "I wonder why law schools don't warn you how much of your time is taken up in working with documents."

Frank laughed. "Because they'd have a mass exodus of students, that's why. People who go to law school are looking for excitement and high courtroom drama, not drudge work."

"I suppose that's true," Megan agreed, leaning back in her chair and stretching, "but all real lawyers know they spend a lot more time on shit jobs than on anything remotely exciting. I think the law schools should be charged with failing to disclose a material fact by not saying so."

Ron Johnson had been there helping them for the first few hours, but at one o'clock he'd had to leave to go to a wedding with his friend Jackie. Megan usually couldn't keep the names of Ron's revolving door of girlfriends straight, but she'd thought she'd remembered Ron saying that he was seeing someone named Jackie a while ago. So before Frank arrived, she'd asked Ron if this was someone new.

Ron had acted indignant. "No, it's still the same one. I've been seeing her for six weeks."

"Six weeks!" Megan had shot back. "That must be some kind of record for you. 'Fess up, Ron," she'd chided. "You're not thinking of turning monogamous on us, are you?"

Ron had laughed. "You never can tell."

"She's a social worker or something, right?"

"A psychologist."

"Oh, well that explains her interest in you. She's probably using you for some sort of clinical study." Megan had ducked just in time to miss the rubber band Ron had shot at her. "Well, when do I get to meet this miracle worker?"

"Soon. I'm going to bring her to the office Christmas party, and that's the week after the trial."

Megan had sighed. "What wonderful words: 'after the trial.' I can't believe the end is finally in sight."

"It's definitely in sight," Ron agreed. "Victory is within our grasp," he said in his best Winston Churchill voice. He held up the index and middle fingers of both hands and waved them over his head, playing to an imaginary crowd.

"Oh, you think so, do you? Well, I'll tell you, what I'm looking forward to grasping is a few days off."

"I told you to take it easy or you were going to burn out," Ron chided.

"I'm not burned out. Just sort of temporarily running out of steam."

" 'Running hard, running on empty,' " Ron crooned, clapping his hands together. "Anyway, Little Red Riding Hood," he joked, referring to the red, hooded sweatshirt Megan wore over her jeans, "I hate to leave you here alone with Big Bad Wolf Parks, but something tells me you can handle him." Then he added impishly, "Of course, now that you're on a first-name basis with his cats, you'll probably have him eating out of your hand."

"I'd feel a whole lot better if his cats were trying the case." Megan laughed. "But there's no need to worry. I'm not afraid of the Big Bad Wolf. If he gets out of line, I might just have *him* for lunch. And if that doesn't work, I'll have one of the messengers throw him out."

Megan had been pleased to find that Frank was in a

noncombative mood. Once again she suspected that since Dr. Lenz wasn't looking over his shoulder, there was no point for Frank to waste time on exaggerated posturing.

By two o'clock they had marked over six hundred documents that both agreed could be introduced at trial. After her comment that law schools should be cited for nondisclosure, Megan added, "It's bad enough that associates have to do this stuff, but it really adds insult to injury when even highly paid partners like you get stuck with document duty."

Frank shrugged. "It goes with the territory. Besides, I've been working on the case from the beginning, so it makes sense for me to be the one to go through the documents."

"Mmm," Megan said, narrowing her eyes. "You know, I have been wondering when your phantom associate, Mr. Bartlett, was going to make an appearance. Here we are, two weeks from trial, and I haven't met him yet."

"Are you questioning my game plan?" Frank asked, pretending to be hurt.

"It's your business how you run your case," Megan said, "but it seems a little odd to me."

"It's not odd," Frank replied. "This is my normal procedure. Dan Bartlett is a very capable associate, and I've given him every scrap of paper filed in this case from the beginning. I expect he will be very helpful to me at the trial. But on the other hand, I *am* in charge here, and being the egomaniac I am, in a high-profile case like this one, I insist on taking all of the depositions. As a result, if I were to drag poor Bartlett along, he'd be relegated to the role of note taker. That would be inefficient for several reasons." He then counted on his fingers. "First, I can take my own notes. Second, I would be taking Bartlett away from more useful duties. And last, but certainly not least, why should my client be charged for having two lawyers present at proceedings where one of them is just not needed?"

Megan shrugged. "Like I said, it's not my place to

criticize, but when I have someone second-chairing a case, I want them with me every step of the way."

"To each his own," Frank replied.

As Megan picked up the next stack of documents, Frank looked at his watch. "I don't know about you, but I'm hungry. If you'd like to stop for a snack, I'll buy."

Megan looked up. "Now that you mention it, that's a great idea. I'll have a ham and cheese on rye, with extra mustard. And some potato chips."

"Want something to drink?" Frank asked.

Megan shook her head. "We've got soda in the refrigerators here, so save your money."

Frank nodded. He stood up and stretched, then walked over to the chair where he'd casually thrown his brown-leather bomber jacket. He slipped the jacket over his gray wool pants and blue-and-gray herringbone sweater. "Be back in a jiff," he said.

While she waited for Frank to return, Megan leaned back in her chair and closed her eyes. It had been an emotional week. Several days earlier, Jeff Young had entered the hospital and no one expected him to leave. Then Judy Vandermere had called to report that weird verse the attacker had recited. Although she was glad that Judy had remembered something, the situation made her uneasy. A killer who knew Shakespeare? She'd always figured sex murderers would have to be mentally deficient. This seemed to prove otherwise.

The knowledge that the killer was probably educated and articulate was particularly unnerving, because it meant he was someone like her. The kind of person she saw every day. And try as she might, she hadn't been able to forget the comment both Paul and the detectives had made, that she looked like a couple of the victims. She'd tried to shrug it off, but she had to admit it was a little spooky.

Megan was still thinking about Judy when Frank returned carrying a large deli bag. He set the bag down on a chair while he shucked off his jacket. Megan looked around her. The table, credenza, and a good share of the floor were all covered with documents.

"I'd hate to spill food on any of this stuff," she said. "Why don't we go into my office? It's kind of cramped, but it's basically spill proof."

Frank followed her down the hall. When they came to one of the workrooms, she asked over her shoulder, "What kind of soda would you like?"

"Diet Pepsi if you've got it."

Megan stepped inside the workroom and opened the refrigerator. She took out a can of Diet Pepsi and an Orange Crush for herself. As they continued their trek down the hall, Frank peered into each of the offices they passed, with obvious interest. "I guess I've only been in a couple of your conference rooms," he said. "These offices are very nice. Who did your decorating?"

"Elizabeth Langley and Associates did the general decorating scheme," Megan replied. "But the partners can do whatever they want with their own offices."

"What's that?" Frank asked as they squeezed through an area sheathed from floor to ceiling with heavy plastic and tarps bearing the warning DANGER. HARD HAT AREA. KEEP OUT.

"We're going to take over some space on the eleventh floor next spring," Megan answered, pausing for a moment. "They're going to put in a spiral staircase here for easy access, and they need to run all kinds of wiring between the two floors. Some of our more curious associates have snuck through the barricades after hours, and they say there's a hole that looks like it goes into the bowels of the building. I'll have to take their word for it. I'm not fond of heights." She continued down the hall and around the corner. "Well, here we are," she said, stepping into her office. "Home sweet cubicle."

Frank followed her in. As he stood there holding the deli bag while she cleared off a corner of her desk, he gave the office the once-over. "It's nice," he said.

Megan shrugged noncommittally. "It's adequate. There," she said as she finished rearranging things, "have a seat." Frank sat down and unpacked the con-

tents of the bag while Megan popped the tops on the
two cans of soda.

"I hope I didn't go too heavy on the mustard," Frank
said as Megan peeled the plastic wrap off her sandwich.

Megan took a bite. "Perfect. I like lots of mustard."

"Me, too," Frank said as he bit into his rare roast
beef. "I like really strong horseradish, too. My kids
think it's disgusting."

Megan smiled. "How are your kids?" she asked,
wiping her mouth with a paper napkin.

"They're fine," Frank answered, his mouth full of
food. "Jack asked if maybe he could come visit your
cat sometime."

Megan laughed, reached in front of her, picked up
the photo of her cat, and handed it to Frank. "Here he
is," she said. "Andy and his pet bunny."

Frank looked at it and chuckled. "Cute," he said,
setting the picture down again.

"You tell Jack that I'm sure Andy would be very
pleased to meet him," Megan said. "Maybe after the
trial you can bring him over sometime."

"I know he'd like that. He's crazy about animals.
He's trying to convince me we should get a dog. So far
I've managed to stall him. Where do you live?"

Megan hesitated for a split second before answering.
She didn't like to give out her home address. "In a
town house just off Lincoln," she replied.

Frank nodded. "Great used-book stores in that area."

"Yeah, it's a good way to spend a Saturday afternoon," Megan agreed. She took the top slice of bread
off her sandwich, put a layer of potato chips on top of
the cheese, and replaced the bread. She bit down, making a crunching sound. Seeing Frank watching in
amusement, she said, "I've added chips to my sandwiches ever since I was a kid. It used to drive my mom
nuts."

"I think you and Jack have similar eating habits,"
Frank said, shaking his head. "Oh, thanks for sending
over the updated copy of Jeff Young's medical records
so promptly. How's he doing?"

Megan took a drink of her soda. "He went into a coma yesterday," she said quietly. "They don't expect him to come out of it."

"I'm sorry to hear that," Frank said. They'd both finished their sandwiches, and Frank pulled two chocolate chip cookies wrapped in plastic out of the deli bag. He handed one to Megan and unwrapped his own. "What are you doing for Thanksgiving?" he asked.

Megan unwrapped her cookie. "I'm going downstate to my parents' house Wednesday night, but I'm coming back Friday morning. With the trial this close, I just can't afford to take any more time off. I told my folks I should be able to hang around a bit longer at Christmas. How about you?"

Frank nibbled on his cookie. "My parents live at St. Charles, so we're going up there."

"Nice town," Megan said. "Lots of good antique shops."

Frank grinned. "My folks run one of them," he said proudly. "It's called 'Window to the Past.' My dad retired a couple years ago, and after about six months, he was real bored and he and my mom were getting on each other's nerves, so this is sort of a second career for them. I guess business has been pretty good."

"I get up there a few times a year," Megan said. "I'll have to look them up."

One of the pieces of plastic wrap had fallen on the floor, and as Frank bent down to retrieve it, he put his hand on his lower back and said, "Ow!"

"What's the matter?" Megan asked, looking at him sharply.

"I think I must've stretched too far and pulled something in my back," Frank said ruefully as he sat up and rubbed the heel of his hand over the tender spot. "Nothing to be concerned about. Just old age setting in before your eyes."

Megan laughed. "I really doubt that."

"It's true, I'm afraid," Frank said, nodding. "I turned forty-three this week. It's all downhill from here."

"You look like you probably have a few more good years left," Megan said.

"How chivalrous of you, young lady," Frank said, winking at her. Megan felt her face redden a bit, and she looked away.

"Have you decided in what order you're going to call your witnesses?" Frank asked, switching back to business.

Megan had finished her cookie and brushed the crumbs off her sweatshirt and jeans. "I think I'll call Sara Young first, then Edna, then Sam and Claudia. After that I'm going to introduce Dr. Morris's medical records, call the person from the hospital who did his medical workup, and finish up with Dr. Leibowitz."

Frank nodded. "That leaves me with Drs. Lenz and Gillian. Sounds pretty simple when you break it down in those terms, doesn't it. The whole thing shouldn't take much more than a week. Then another week for damages, assuming we get that far."

Megan took another drink of her orange soda. "I don't know about you, but I'll be very glad when it's over."

"Getting nervous?"

Megan glanced at Frank to see if he was being a smart ass, but his look and tone were sincere. She shrugged. "A little, I guess. Have the reporters been bugging you as much as they have me?"

"Yeah, but don't let that bother you," Frank said. "Just pretend they're not there."

"That's easier said than done," Megan retorted. "I'm not exactly used to trying cases on national TV."

He smiled. "Judging by the way you've handled things up to now, you'll do just fine."

Megan drummed the fingers of her right hand on the desk. "Thanks for the vote of confidence. Hope you're right."

Frank impulsively reached out and squeezed her hand. "I'm a pretty good judge of character, and believe me, you've got nothing to worry about. You're a good lawyer. This case is no different than any other. You just have to keep plugging away to get your points across to the jury." With his hand still on hers, he said, " 'And many strokes, though with a little axe, hew down and fell the hardiest timbered oak.' *Henry VI*," he added modestly.

Megan tensed a bit and pulled her hand away. She eyed him warily. "Are you in the habit of reciting Shakespeare?" she asked, a slight edge in her voice.

If Frank noticed the sudden chill in the air, he didn't let on. "Only when I want to sound intellectual," he replied with a laugh.

Megan drained the rest of her soda and tossed the can in the wastebasket, scolding herself for being so jittery. This damn case had her nerves all unraveled. She stood up. "Well, shall we get back to the salt mines?" she asked.

Frank got up, too, and bowed from the waist. "After you, m'lady." Megan followed him back to the conference room, unable to erase the frown from her face.

CHAPTER 39

Mike O'Riley turned his car south on Halstad. Traffic was horrendous. It was shortly before noon on the day after Thanksgiving, the traditional kickoff for the Christmas shopping season, and it looked like every person within fifty miles of Chicago who owned a vehicle was in it, speeding toward the nearest store. Anne and their two daughters were out there, too, running up their charge accounts with the best of them. It was cold and overcast and they'd had about a half inch of snow around dawn, too little to warrant calling out the street crews, but enough to make some of the lesser traveled streets a little slick.

O'Riley had spent an unproductive morning at his desk, going through the latest FBI reports on prison escapees. He'd tried to make a few phone calls, but found that most of his counterparts in other cities had taken the day off. His own department was operating with a skeleton crew. He'd told Jablonski to take a four-day weekend so he could spend some time with his family and study for the sergeant's exam. The young man had protested, but O'Riley had insisted. They'd made no real progress in the case in the last seven months. A few more days of inactivity weren't going to make much difference. When it became clear that O'Riley wasn't going to take no for an answer, Jablonski had grinned, pumped the older man's hand, and warmly wished him a happy Thanksgiving.

O'Riley lit up a cigarette and cracked the driver's side window. Overall, it had been a pleasant holiday. Anne had made Thanksgiving dinner—a lavish feast of roast turkey and dressing, sweet potatoes, creamed

corn, homemade rolls, relishes, and pumpkin and pe-
can pies. Colleen, Ruth, and Mike, Jr., and their families had all been there. The grandchildren were always
a delight.

On a negative note, he did have words with Colleen's husband, but that was par for the course. Chuck
Sowatzki, a tall, stocky man in his late thirties, was a
labor steward and had always been a bit of a redneck.
O'Riley had often wondered what his eldest child ever
saw in the guy. As Uncle Marty used to say, whatever
it was, you couldn't see it from the street. The women
had been serving the pies when Chuck, no doubt emboldened by the several glasses of wine he'd had with
dinner, said, "Well, Mike, when are you guys gonna
crack that murder case?"

Out of the corner of his eye, O'Riley saw young
Billy pause with his fork halfway to his mouth.

"Soon, I hope," O'Riley replied noncommittally.

"Whatcha waitin' for? Christmas?" Chuck chortled.
"You've been workin' on it since Easter, haven't ya?"

"Not quite," O'Riley demurred.

"Haven't you got any suspects?"

"Not at the moment, no."

"Hell, it sounds to me like the mayor should've let
you retire on schedule. Maybe then the damn case
would be closed by now."

Anne and Colleen had returned to the dining room in
time to hear this last remark. Anne frowned but said
nothing. Colleen wasn't so kind. "If you think you
could solve the case, why don't you join the force? I'm
sure Dad would put in a good word for you," she
snapped, drawing herself up to her full five feet, three
inches. "Till then, keep your comments to yourself so
the rest of us can enjoy our dessert."

Chuck's face reddened and his jaw tightened, but he
kept still, knowing full well that his wife could get the
better of him in any verbal sparring match. Billy's eyes
widened and his mouth gaped open. Then he grinned at
his mother and went back to attacking his pie.

Everyone had left around eight, and O'Riley had
spent a couple hours looking through files he'd

brought home. Then he'd gone to bed, feeling bloated and uncomfortable. He'd awakened early, downed half a bottle of Maalox, and finished reading his files before heading down to headquarters.

On his visit to the library, O'Riley had checked out a variety of reference books which contained the *Cymbeline* quote and had carefully pored over the sections on "death" in each one. He'd never realized how many literary references there were on the subject. As he paged through the various materials, he wondered if what had happened to Judy was a fluke or if the killer had recited similar verses to the other victims.

Over and over he tried to figure out what kind of person would recite lines from a play while he was strangling someone. What the hell kind of bird were they dealing with? An English teacher with a fetish for knives and broom handles? A frustrated actor? Jesus, what a thought. Maybe the guy they were looking for was a cross between Laurence Olivier and Jack the Ripper.

Around eleven-thirty the day after Thanksgiving, it felt like the hard plastic walls of his cubicle were starting to close in on him, and O'Riley had decided to take a drive. Originally he'd intended to visit each of the murder sites, but he'd forgotten about the barrage of shoppers, and once he got underway, he'd quickly abandoned plans to go downtown. They were predicting a flood of a million people rushing into the Loop. No sense for him to add to the congestion. Instead, he headed south and pulled over to the curb in front of St. Michael's school.

He got out of the car, dropped his cigarette on the snowy pavement, and ground it out with his foot. Then he walked around the corner into the alley where it had all started for him: the spot where Mary Collins's body had been found. He circled the Dumpster a few times, replaying the murder scene in his mind. The thick treads of his black athletic shoes left fresh prints in the snow. He inhaled deeply and then exhaled, watching his breath come out in a fog. He looked skyward, then shook his head. If he'd been expecting the heavens to open up and announce the name of the murderer, the gods didn't seem to be cooperating.

He looked at the school building. A color poster heralded the Christmas pageant on December nineteenth. Turkey decals adorned many of the windows. He walked back out of the alley and gazed at the church proper. On impulse, he crossed the street, walked up the steps, and tried the door. It was open. He shrugged. That probably shouldn't surprise him. Catholics had always been a trusting lot. It was no wonder so many of them had ended up as martyrs. A sign in the vestibule said that Father Joseph McIntyre would deliver Sunday's sermon on THE MEANING OF THE ADVENT SEASON IN THE NINETIES.

O'Riley stood quietly in the back and looked around him. St. Michael's had been built in the late 1960's and had high-beamed ceilings, light-colored wood pews, kneelers comfortably padded with fake, red leather, and a modern sound system. It had few of the trappings he remembered from the neighborhood parish of his childhood. No fancy altar. No communion rail. No marble statues. Nothing ostentatious. It looked like there was a confessional booth in a corner, but it had been covered up by a red velvet curtain. Anne had said the church now did some kind of communal penance service a couple times a year because no one, except doddering old ladies, was going to individual confession these days. O'Riley smiled. The ritual of confession brought back memories.

O'Riley slowly walked up the side aisle toward the front of the church. In the front right-hand side, opposite the altar, was a pipe organ. O'Riley looked at it, imagining Mary Collins sitting there, playing hymns, joking with the choir members, not knowing that when she walked out of the building that night in April, the next time she'd return would be for her funeral. A chill came over him, and his leg suddenly started to throb. He pried his gaze away from the organ.

In the center row of pews near the front of the church, two old women knelt with their rosaries, their gnarled, blue-veined hands caressing the beads. They wore brightly colored scarves on their heads. That brought back memories, too. O'Riley's mother wouldn't enter a church without some type of head-gear. If by chance she forgot to wear a hat or a lace mantilla, she would fish around in her big black hand-bag until she found a lace handkerchief that she would secure to her scalp with a couple of bobby pins. Another stupid rule. If a person came to worship with a sincere heart, who the hell cared what they had on their head?

Perpendicular to the altar, underneath a window depicting the young Jesus preaching in the temple, were rows of votive candles in red glass containers. Several of the candles were burning. O'Riley hesitated for a moment, then reached into his pocket and fished out three quarters and dropped them into the slot. In the stillness of the church, the coins made a loud clanking sound as they hit the bottom of the container. O'Riley picked up one of the matchbooks provided on a tray, pulled off a match, and struck it. The matches must have been old, because he had to make several attempts before it ignited. He lit one of the candles in the top row and blew out the match. The odor of sulfur lingered in the air. After standing there a moment watching the little flame, O'Riley walked back halfway down the side aisle, and sat in a pew.

He hadn't been in a church since Easter. He figured Anne's piety and devotion more than made up for his failings in that area. He had stopped being a regular churchgoer before they got married. He accompanied her to sunrise service on Easter and midnight mass at Christmas without complaint because he knew she expected it. The kids had been raised as Catholics, although only Colleen still attended Sunday mass regularly.

O'Riley looked back toward the front where the old ladies were still clutching their rosaries. He wondered what it would be like to have a strong faith. He wasn't even sure he believed in God.

He closed his eyes. He didn't really know how to pray either. Once in a while he'd mentally ask God to grant some request, but that was more a superstitious thing, akin to rubbing a lucky rabbit's foot. He fought to clear his mind of all extraneous thoughts, hoping that if he were clearheaded enough, he might gain some new insight into the murders. To his disgust he found that the more he tried, the more he saw in his mind's eye a row of mutilated female bodies, their arms outstretched, their mouths gaping open, shouting, "Help me! Help me!"

O'Riley felt his stomach churning. So much for the joys of meditation. He opened his eyes, reached in his pocket, found a couple of antacid tablets, and popped them into his mouth. A life-sized crucifix was suspended from the ceiling above the altar. His eyes focused on that. For a time, he sat there, transfixed. Then, without consciously realizing it at first, he began to repeat silently over and over, Please, God. Help me find the killer. If you grant me this one request, I won't ever ask for anything else. Please help me find him. Please. He became so engrossed in his entreaties that he didn't even notice the two old ladies pack their rosaries away in clear plastic cases and shuffle silently out of the church.

Poor Lieutenant O'Riley. So engrossed in his pursuit of justice that he's gotten sloppy. Wouldn't he be surprised to know he was being watched? Poor, washed-up old man. He should have retired. He's in over his head and he doesn't even know it. So he thinks that praying for guidance is going to help him in his quest, does he? Silly old man. Prayer will be of no use to him. He needs something far stronger than prayer if he is going to stop you.

Events are already in motion. Preparations have been made. A new verse has been selected. A special verse for a special target. The ultimate target. The one whose demise will put everything right.

Yes, it won't be long now before you carry out your final and most perfect act of revenge. And there is nothing Lieutenant Michael O'Riley or anyone else can do to stop you.

CHAPTER 40

"Ladies and gentlemen of the jury, we submit that the evidence will show that Chicago Memorial Hospital knew that Dr. Dan Morris was not in good health." Megan's stance was erect and confident as she delivered her opening argument. "At the time the hospital's representatives made this discovery, it would have been an easy task for them to prevent Dr. Morris from performing further surgical procedures until the cause of his malaise was determined. If they had done that, we wouldn't be here today." Megan took a step forward.

"But instead of curtailing Dr. Morris's surgical practice, the hospital chose to do nothing, chose to look the other way. As a result of this inaction, Dr. Morris continued to perform surgery and four of his patients became infected with the AIDS virus. We submit, ladies and gentlemen, that the hospital's failure to act in the face of what it should have seen was a potentially life-threatening situation, was a serious breach of the duty of care it owed to its patients."

Megan took a step backward, opened her mouth to continue, and froze. She stood there a moment, her mind a blank. She had completely lost her train of thought. "Oh, shit!" she said, stomping her foot on the floor.

She stuck out her tongue. She had been sucking on a cherry cough drop and the reflection from the mirror in her living room, where she had been practicing her opening statement, revealed a tongue and lips that were almost the same color as the bright pink sweater she wore over her jeans. She sighed, took another sip of water, and tossed back her hair. Once more, from the top.

It was eight P.M. on the Saturday after Thanksgiving. Only nine days left until the trial started. Megan's nerves were on edge. She and Ron had divided up the witnesses that each would examine, and Megan felt they were in pretty good shape on that front. For the last three hours she'd been working on her introductory statement to the jury, trying to synthesize mountains of notes into a concise, cohesive argument. Megan had never forgotten the advice Mike Gillette had given her five years earlier, as she'd been preparing for her first trial.

"Studies have shown that nearly seventy percent of jurors never sway from the impression of the case they form during opening statements," he'd said seriously, "so you gotta go in there and grab 'em by the balls early on." Definitely words to live by.

Megan knew her inability to concentrate was due in large part to a phone call she'd received on Wednesday afternoon. She and Ron had been in her office when Sara Young had called to tell them that Jeff was dead. Ron could tell what the call was about, and when Megan hung up, he'd come around the desk and hugged her. Megan had wiped her eyes, blown her nose, and told Ron she didn't feel like working anymore. He'd wished her a happy Thanksgiving and gone back to his office. After spending a few moments alone composing herself, Megan had walked down the hall to see Mike Gillette.

She managed to catch Gillette in one of his rare free moments, and he listened impassively as she sat down in one of the chairs in front of his desk and told him the news. He nodded, expressed his sympathy, and immediately picked up the phone and instructed his secretary to see that a large floral arrangement was delivered to the funeral home as a memorial from the firm. Then he hung up the phone and turned back to Megan. "I've been meaning to talk to you anyway," he said. "I looked over the draft of the trial brief and jury instructions you sent me, and they sound right on. Do you feel like you've got things in hand?"

Megan nodded. "I think so," she said, brushing her hair off her face. "I haven't written my opening statement yet. I'm going to work on that this weekend. I've got a bunch of notes, but I didn't want to put it together until close to the end when I had a pretty good idea of what everybody's testimony was likely to be."

Gillette's head bobbed up and down. "Good strategy. If you'd like to run it by me next week, I'd be happy to listen to what you've got, and maybe offer a few suggestions. When you've been so close to a case for so long it can be hard to be objective."

"Thanks. I might take you up on that."

"Is Frank Parks still giving you a hard time?" Gillette asked.

"Actually, he's been pretty friendly lately," Megan replied, "but that's probably just a ruse to get me off guard so he can try to stomp on me at the trial."

Gillette smiled. "You can handle him."

"That's what you said the day you assigned me the case," Megan reminded him.

"Did I? Well, it was true then and it's true now." He leaned across his desk. "I've been following your progress on the case, Megan, probably more closely than you know, and I like what I've seen. I know Jeff Young's death has cast a pall on the whole proceeding, but it was an event you all anticipated, and you'll just have to find a way to harness your feelings in a positive way."

Megan's eyes were bright. She sniffed, then nodded. "It's going to be tough, but I'll do my best."

"I know you will. And if you need help—paralegals, an extra associate, whatever—just holler and we'll take care of it. This case is to be given top priority by the entire firm."

"Thanks, Mike. I appreciate it." She stood up and started toward the door.

"Have a good Thanksgiving, Megan. Try not to think about the case for a couple days. It's amazing how much more clearly you'll see things after a little break."

Megan went back to her office, threw some things into her briefcase, and dictated a short note to Frank Parks informing him of Jeff Young's death. Thankfully, Sara Young said she'd take care of breaking the news to the other plaintiffs. Megan didn't think she could handle talking to them then. After wishing her secretary and a couple of colleagues a happy holiday, she drove back to her apartment.

She changed into jeans and a sweater, put out extra food for Andy, quickly packed her suitcase, and headed south out of the city. During the six-hour drive she listened to the radio and tried to put work out of her mind. The effort had only been minimally successful. She kept thinking of Sara Young and the three children who would grow up without a father.

She arrived at her parents' home at ten o'clock. Her brother and his girlfriend had arrived from Houston earlier in the day. Sally was also an engineer at NASA, and she and Jim had been living together for two years. If it bothered the Lansdorfs that neither of their children seemed interested in making them grandparents any time in the near future, they'd never let on. They all sat up until midnight, catching up on each other's activities and local gossip.

They had Thanksgiving dinner at a local restaurant—an intimate place housed in what had once been an elegant Victorian mansion. While everyone admired the ornately carved woodwork, leaded-glass windows, and crystal chandeliers, Megan thought fleetingly that it didn't hold a candle to Frank Parks's home.

A traditional turkey dinner with all the trimmings was served family-style, and as Professor Lansdorf was carving the bird, the conversation turned to the slashing murders. "So they haven't caught the guy yet, eh, Megan?" her father asked.

"I'm afraid not," Megan replied, nibbling on a rye roll. "The Shakespearean quote isn't much to go on."

"The last couple murders made the news in our neck

of the woods, too," Jim said, taking a sip of wine. "I didn't realize you were involved in the case."

"I'm not exactly *involved* in it," Megan protested. She wished someone would change the subject. Not wanting to worry her family, she hadn't told them that she resembled some of the victims, nor had she told them about the weird things that had happened to her, or about Rita's accident.

"It's frightening to think someone would be so bold as to lodge an attack in the Ritz-Carlton's parking ramp," Sally put in, helping herself to some candied yams. "You'd think their security people would have noticed a sleazy-looking guy lurking around."

"He's probably not sleazy looking," Megan replied, taking a drink of water. "Which makes it all the more frightening. It's probably someone who looks very mainstream, somebody who wouldn't stand out in a crowd. Maybe even someone from the upper class."

"Somebody who runs around quoting Shakespeare at the drop of a hat," mused Jim, reaching for another rye roll. "What kind of deviate would do such a thing?" He paused a moment. "Say, Dad, what were you doing the night of the attack?"

Professor Lansdorf flashed an evil grin and held up his carving knife menacingly. "Wouldn't you like to know?" he snarled fiendishly.

"Didn't you say there were rumors that a policeman had been sighted at one of the earlier crime scenes?" Mrs. Lansdorf asked, passing the dressing to Sally.

"There were rumors to that effect," Megan said, not wanting to add that Paul had been the source, "but never any official reports."

"Well, watch yourself," Jim cautioned her. "And if you see some guy running toward you with a knife yelling 'Et tu, Bruté,' get the hell out of his way."

Megan laughed. "Don't worry. If I saw someone coming toward me with a knife, I'd try to get out of his way even if he were reciting 'Mary had a little lamb.' "

By then Professor Lansdorf had finished carving the turkey and the subject was dropped as they all got down to some serious gorging. The five of them took in a movie that night, and Megan headed for home the following morning, after breakfast.

Jeff Young's funeral service had been held on Saturday afternoon in a large, cheerful Catholic church near the Youngs' westside home. The priest was a rotund, gray-haired man in his fifties, who spoke eloquently about Jeff's love for his family and the uncomplaining way in which he had endured his suffering. Ron had met her at the church, and the two of them had sat near the back with Edna, Claudia, and Sam and his wife.

Megan had found the service very moving and had to struggle to fight back tears, fearing that any outward expression of sentiment on her part might upset Edna, who was now also fighting full-blown AIDS.

Megan had skipped the trip to the cemetery and the reception in the church hall, coming home to work on her opening statement.

Her throat was a little scratchy, and after yet another aborted dry run, she walked back to the kitchen to get another cough drop. When she got there, she found Andy perched on the window sill, growling. She went over to him and attempted to pat his head. "What's the matter?" she asked. He turned and hissed at her in response, then turned his attention back to the window.

"That's not nice," she scolded. The animal wasn't particularly well behaved. It wasn't entirely his fault. After all, she wasn't home much. She could hardly expect him to learn good manners cooped up by himself. It was probably a good thing she didn't have kids. They'd undoubtedly be horrid little monsters. She was about to shoo the cat onto the floor when she heard a scratching noise on the brick wall outside the window. She involuntarily jumped back, and her first thought was, Oh God, there's someone out there!

Then she shrugged her shoulders. Don't be silly, she admonished herself. "What's the matter?" she asked the cat. "Is one of those neighborhood tom cats out there again?" There was a door off the kitchen leading to a small backyard, and in warm weather, Megan would sometimes go out and physically chase the offending beasts away. But after what had happened to

Rita, she was a bit more cautious about venturing outdoors at night if she didn't have to.

The window was frosted over, and she couldn't see out. She slapped the pane a couple times with the palm of her hand. "Shoo! Get away from there," she shouted. She listened a moment and heard nothing. "There. I think I got rid of him. It's safe now," she said, more to reassure herself than the cat. The animal obligingly jumped down and sauntered back to the living room.

Megan went to another cupboard, took a cherry-flavored cough drop out of a packet, and popped it in her mouth. She sat down at the table and wearily rubbed her eyes. She was beat, and her nerves were raw. She'd give anything if the damn trial were over and done with. The mounting suspense of these last few weeks was taking its toll. She was tired of practicing. She wanted to get into the courtroom and start the live performance.

Not much longer, she reminded herself, slowly getting to her feet. She'd soon know whether her carefully staged production was a hit or a flop.

CHAPTER 41

As Megan and Ron sat at one of the counsel tables, their heads close together, going over their notes, Megan tried to ignore the host of television cameras positioned around the room. Although the federal court system generally did not allow the use of cameras in their courtrooms, the Northern District of Illinois was one of several districts across the country participating in a two-year pilot project that permitted proceedings to be televised. As a result, the entire case would be broadcast live by both a local cable station and a national court TV station. A number of other channels would be taping selected segments to use during their news programs. Numerous print reporters were also in attendance, their tape recorders at the ready and note pads balanced on their laps.

The sixty prospective jurors, who had been ordered to report to Judge Edwards's courtroom, talked animatedly among themselves. They were a diverse group, running the gamut in age from college students in their early twenties to white-haired, senior citizens. There were great variations ethnically and professionally, too—with blacks, Hispanics, Orientals, business people dressed in expensive suits, and blue-collar workers in torn jeans and faded sweatshirts. The selection of six jurors and one alternate was expected to take the better part of a day.

Parks's associate, Dan Bartlett, had finally made an appearance. Megan had unobtrusively sized him up when he had walked in with Parks and Dr. Lenz. Bartlett was tall and blond and looked like he'd either just returned from a vacation in the sun, or made a

habit of frequenting a tanning salon, because his face
and hands were golden brown. Typical preppie, big-
firm lawyer, Megan thought with disdain. She wondered somewhat whimsically whether Hagenkord &
Phillips had a dress code for trials. Both Bartlett and
Parks were dressed in navy suits with white shirts, and
conservative navy-checked ties. Dr. Lenz, who was
seated to their right, was wearing dark-gray pinstripes
that complimented his gray hair. In Megan's opinion,
all three of them looked stiff and arrogant. By contrast,
the plaintiff's side strove for casual elegance, Megan
mused, pretending she was writing a fashion commen-
tary, with lead counsel Megan Lansdorf attired in an
attractive, powder-blue suit with a white silk blouse
and blue-flowered silk tie, and the always debonair
Ron Johnson dressed in gray wool-flannel, with a
yellow-dotted power tie.

The court clerk's office had made cards containing
information about prospective jurors available to the
attorneys the week before trial. Both Megan and Frank
had carefully scrutinized the information provided, and
had immediately identified some people whom they
knew they did not want as jurors. Megan wanted to
avoid people who worked for doctors, hospitals, or insurance companies, because they were more likely to
sympathize with Chicago Memorial. Frank favored jurors who were educated and had white-collar positions,
since lower-income people were sometimes more
swayed by emotionalism, and tended to award more
money in damages.

The din in the courtroom subsided as Judge
Edwards's bailiff, a former, marine drill sergeant in his
early fifties, entered the room through a rear door.
"Hear ye, hear ye. All rise," the stocky, short-haired
man barked authoritatively as he stood ramrod straight,
next to the bench. The crowd got to its feet as the
judge, dressed in his black robe, followed the bailiff
into the room and took his seat. The TV cameras began
to roll. "This court is now in session, Judge Alexander
Edwards presiding," the bailiff continued. "Your si-

lence is commanded. God save the United States and this honorable court."

"You may be seated," Judge Edwards said, adjusting the microphone in front of him. "Good morning, ladies and gentlemen." He smiled down at the assembled multitude. "We are here today to select a jury of six people and one alternate to serve in the case of *Young, et al.* v. *Chicago Memorial Hospital.* In a moment the bailiff will be conducting a random drawing of fifteen juror numbers. If your number is called, would you please come up and take a seat in the jury box. After fifteen numbers have been drawn, the attorneys for both sides will ask that group of people some questions. Please respond to those questions truthfully, to the best of your ability. While the questioning is going on, I would ask that the rest of you remain seated quietly in the courtroom. If we are unable to fill the jury panel from the first fifteen people drawn, the bailiff will draw some additional numbers. This process will continue until the jury has been impanelled. We appreciate your attendance here today, and we'll try to move the selection process along as quickly as we can so that those of you who aren't chosen can get about your business."

The judge leaned forward in his chair. "Before the bailiff begins to draw the numbers, I'm going to ask the entire group a few preliminary questions. Depending on your answers, I may let some of you go home right off the bat." The judge then asked the group if any of them were related to any of the plaintiffs; whether they were acquainted with any of the attorneys; whether any were employed by Chicago Memorial; and whether any of them had ever been involved in a lawsuit against their doctor or hospital. One man indicated that his wife had been employed in the hospital's records department several years ago, and the judge dismissed him.

Judge Edwards then instructed the bailiff to draw the first fifteen numbers. The bailiff moved to a small table at the side of the judge's bench that had a wire cage on it that looked like it could be used at bingo

games when court wasn't in session. The bailiff
cranked a handle, causing the cubes inside to tumble
about like popcorn. He then opened a trap door and
pulled out the first number. "Juror number forty-two,"
he called out. A middle-aged black man walked forward and took a seat in the jury box. When fifteen people had been seated, the judge nodded to Meg and
Frank that they should proceed. Matching the numbers
to the juror information cards they had previously received, the two attorneys spoke to each person in turn.
Each side was entitled to three peremptory challenges.
This meant they could strike three jurors without having to state a reason why they did not want the people
serving on the panel. In addition, if they could point to
a particular reason why a juror might be prejudiced
against them, they could ask the judge to remove the
person for cause.

Both started out with obvious questions: whether the
juror had any friends or family members with AIDS;
whether they felt any prejudice toward people who had
contracted AIDS; whether they had ever been involved
in a lawsuit; whether they knew any of the expert witnesses; whether they had ever been unhappy with the
care they'd received from a doctor; and whether they
had heard or read anything about the case.

If an answer sounded suspect, there would be
follow-up questions. Four out of the fifteen said they'd
been involved in lawsuits. Two of those turned out to
be divorce actions, one woman had sued for damages
she'd sustained in an auto accident, and one man had
started a suit to evict a tenant from rental property he
owned. The car accident victim said the case had gone
to trial, and Frank asked if she had been satisfied with
the amount the jury had awarded. When she said she
had, Frank decided to strike her. She might be tempted
to return the favor her jury had done her by finding the
hospital at fault.

As they proceeded, the questions got more subtle.
Megan asked if any of them had had disagreements
with their supervisors at work, and how they would
handle the situation if they thought a supervisor was

not following an established company rule. After consulting with Ron, she struck a man who seemed to think a subordinate should never question a supervisor's mandates. She wanted jurors who would have challenged Dr. Lenz's decision not to follow up on Dr. Morris's health problem.

Frank asked a number of jurors what books they had read lately, what movies they had seen. Finding out what people did in their spare time was a good way to get a feel for how they might judge a case. Defense attorneys wanted conservative, thoughtful types; plaintiffs were likely to have better luck with impetuous, free thinkers. Nobody wanted stupid or dull jurors. Frank struck a woman who said she hadn't been to a movie in fifteen years, never read anything, including the morning paper, and whose sole leisure activity was watching daytime soap operas and talking on the phone to her sister in Cleveland.

Megan frequently leaned over and asked Ron his impression of a particular person. From time to time, Frank would confer with Bartlett and Dr. Lenz, but when making a final decision, Frank went with his own instincts. On a couple of occasions his ideas diverged sharply from Lenz's, and when that happened, the doctor furrowed his brow and shot Frank a very icy glance. Frank ignored him. He'd patiently listened to Lenz's ideas all through trial preparation, but now that they were in court, Lenz would just have to learn who was in charge of the case.

As jurors were eliminated, the bailiff drew more numbers out of the squirrel cage. The judge ordered an hour-long break for lunch. By three P.M. they had their panel: four men and three women, one of whom would serve as the alternate. Megan had a hunch that women might be more sympathetic than men, but overall she was pleased with the group that had been chosen. Two of the men were black; one of the women was Hispanic. The rest were white. Out of the seven, two were professionals—one man an engineer and one woman a bank trust officer. There was a teacher, a student working toward a master's degree in European history, a housewife, a factory worker, and a hostess at a swank downtown restaurant.

After the jurors had taken an oath to discharge their duties fairly and to the best of their ability, Judge Edwards spent a few minutes informing them about how the case would be conducted. He told them that their most important function would be to weigh the credibility of the witnesses. There was no magical formula by which they could evaluate the testimony, and they should bring with them into the courtroom all of the experience and background from their own lives. He also admonished them to resist the temptation to discuss the case with anyone outside of the courtroom, since in no other way could the parties be assured of the absolute impartiality they were entitled to expect from jurors.

When he had finished his remarks, Judge Edwards said, "That's it for today, folks. We'll convene at nine o'clock tomorrow morning, at which time we'll hear opening statements. See you all then."

As the attorneys were packing up their briefcases for the trek back to their offices, Frank walked over to Megan and Ron's table. "Well, what do you think of our panel?" he asked.

Megan shrugged noncommittally. "I think they'll be fine."

Frank gave her an enigmatic smile and nodded. "Me, too. Well, see you tomorrow." He turned and walked out of the courtroom, with Dr. Lenz, Bartlett, and several reporters in close pursuit. He acts like he thinks he's the king with his court, Megan thought with disgust. What arrogance.

Megan shrugged off questions from reporters, merely saying she was sure the jurors would discharge their duties fairly. She walked back to where the plaintiffs were sitting in a group. Edna gave her a big hug and said, "I'm glad we're finally getting this show on the road."

Megan nodded. "Me, too." Turning to Sara Young, she asked quietly, "How are you doing?"

"Okay, I guess," Sara replied. Then she sighed. "Actually, I feel a little disoriented yet, but I know how happy Jeff would be that we're finally here, and I have a good feeling about it."

"So do we," Sam Gardner put in. "Monique and I both dreamt that we won."

"That's incredible," Claudia Hartley spoke up eagerly. "I had the same dream last night."

Megan smiled. "Here's hoping your dreams come true," she said, patting Sam on the arm. "Ron and I have to get back to the office now. We'll see you all tomorrow morning."

As Ron was driving back to the office, he asked, "Well, Chief, what do you think?"

Megan took a deep breath, held it a moment, then exhaled. "So far, so good. I agree with Edna. I'm glad we're underway."

"Still nervous?" Ron asked, glancing over at her.

"Yeah," she admitted. "What do you think Parks was getting at when he came over and asked what I thought about the jury?"

"What do you mean?"

Megan grimaced. "He looked like the cat that ate the canary, grinning at me like that. It was unnerving."

Ron shrugged. "You're imagining things. He was just making conversation. I think we did good," he added. "I've got a feeling this jury's gonna do all right for us."

"I sure hope you're right," Megan said. She reached into her purse and pulled out a cough drop, then stared out the window as the car crawled northward in the rush hour traffic.

"Is there anything you want to work on tonight?" Ron asked.

Megan shook her head and popped the cough drop in her mouth. "No. I'm just going to stop by the office long enough to check for messages and then go home and practice my opening a couple more times. We're going to be burning the midnight oil enough in the next couple weeks. There's no need for us to start tonight."

Ron nodded. "I'll be at home, too. If anything

comes up, give me a call. And try to get some rest. You look beat."

"I will," she promised. "I'll meet you at the office tomorrow at seven-fifteen."

Megan and Ron were back in the courtroom by eight-thirty the next morning. Megan had spent a largely sleepless night, too keyed up to drift off and afraid to employ her usual soporific of scotch for fear it would leave her feeling hung over and lethargic. After tossing and turning for several hours, she had finally gotten up at four o'clock and played the piano for an hour. With Andy sitting beside her on the floor, looking on quizzically, she'd pounded on the keys unmercifully and hoped that the sound wouldn't wake her neighbors. The effort had helped to relax her, and she'd then taken a leisurely bubble bath, pressed her black-and-white suit, drank half a pot of coffee, eaten a cinnamon-and-raisin bagel and half a muffin, and arrived at the office at six-forty-five.

Before taking their seats at the counsel table, Megan and Ron spent a few moments chatting with the plaintiffs. Sara Young would be the first witness to testify. She was dressed in a bright yellow wool dress and looked more rested than Megan had seen her in months. The strain of living with Jeff's illness had been so onerous that his passing had been a relief for the whole family.

Edna Randolph had splurged on a new rose-colored dress. When Megan complimented her on it, she'd said, "Yeah, it's nice, isn't it? I think I'd like to be buried in it." Sam Gardner looked distinguished in a dark suit. His wife, Monique, looked nervous but chic in a stylish black sheath. Claudia Hartley had toned down her makeup and hairstyle and looked almost demure. What a nice group of people, Megan thought to herself as she took her seat. She hoped she would be able to do them justice.

Frank Parks and his entourage arrived at eight-forty-five. Frank was wearing a black suit with a white shirt and a red-checked tie. He poured himself a glass of water and talked animatedly with Bartlett and Dr. Lenz. Megan noted somewhat jealously that he appeared not to have a care in the world.

On the stroke of nine, the bailiff performed the ritual of calling court into session. The jurors filed into their seats in the jury box. "Good morning, ladies and gentlemen," Judge Edwards said brightly. "We're going to start the day off by hearing opening statements." He looked down at Megan and smiled. "Ms. Lansdorf, you have the floor."

Megan took a deep breath, fighting hard to suppress the butterflies in her stomach. She picked up her handwritten notes and stepped up to the lectern that had been placed in front of the bench, facing the jury box. At first she was a bit disconcerted by the television cameras zooming in on her, but after a few moments she was so engrossed in her remarks that she was oblivious to what was going on around her.

She tried to keep her comments simple. You couldn't talk down to the jury or be condescending, but it was important to use language they would understand. She spoke for over an hour, referring to her notes only occasionally. She tried to make her remarks a flowing narrative story, with the four plaintiffs the stars of the action and the hospital the antagonist.

She told them about Dr. Morris's medical exam, the explanation he had given for his symptoms, and the hospital's decision not to follow up on the situation. She explained how the plaintiffs had contracted the AIDS virus, told them a little about each one, and told them about Jeff Young's death and Edna Randolph's recent diagnosis.

"We're not saying that the hospital knew for sure that allowing Dr. Morris to continue performing surgery would result in his transmitting the AIDS virus to his patients," Megan said. "It's not necessary that they did anything that blatant. What we submit the evidence will show the hospital *did* do was to ignore a situation that they knew *or should have known* might threaten the well-being of others. We submit that this act or omission on the part of Chicago Memorial resulted in a most grievous injury to the plaintiffs and their families." She spoke slowly and clearly, putting emphasis on certain key words that would be cropping up over and over in the witnesses' testimony and in the instructions the judge would give at the close of the case.

As Megan spoke, she tried to make eye contact with each of the jurors, and she was pleased to see that they all appeared to be giving her remarks careful attention. From time to time she would notice one or more of them nodding at something she'd said. She addressed what she knew would be the hospital's main line of defense early on.

"The hospital is going to tell you that because Dr. Morris lied, it was relieved of any obligation to check out the cause of his condition. There's no question that Dr. Morris *did* lie," she said earnestly. "But we submit the hospital also played a big part in the harm that befell the plaintiffs because it had the opportunity to stop Dr. Morris and it didn't." As she said this, she caught Dr. Lenz's eye. He was staring at her so hard he seemed to be looking right through her. She shuddered and looked away.

She concluded by saying, "Because of the hospital's inaction, one person is dead. Three more are going to die. Dying of AIDS is a slow, painful, gruesome process. The disease robs you of your dignity and your ability to care for yourself. We submit that after you've heard all of the evidence, you will conclude that the hospital possessed enough information to put it on notice that Dr. Morris suffered from a serious health problem and yet, in the face of this knowledge, the hospital chose to take no action. If you reach this conclusion, then you should find for the plaintiffs." She paused and looked at each of the jurors one more time. "Thank you very much for your attention." She picked up her notes from the lectern and walked back to her seat.

As Megan sat down, she caught Ron's eye. He nodded and gave her a quick smile. Megan poured herself a glass of water and took a sip. She thought it had gone pretty well, but how could you ever really tell? Frank was already standing at the lectern, and though Megan was spent from her effort, she picked up her pen and forced herself to listen attentively to his remarks and to jot some notes now and then.

Frank had a couple of pages of notes in front of him, but he never seemed to refer to them. Once again, Megan was aware of what an eloquent speaker he was. As she'd anticipated, he focused the bulk of his remarks on Dr. Morris's untruths. He also made the point that Dr. Morris's symptoms weren't that serious and that the explanation the doctor gave the examining physician was entirely plausible.

"Ladies and gentlemen, we're not talking about a kid fresh out of medical school. Dr. Morris was a well-respected surgeon with eighteen years' experience at Chicago Memorial. There was no reason in the world for the hospital to doubt his word when he told them that his symptoms were the result of antibiotics he had been taking to combat a minor infection that arose after a wisdom tooth extraction. The plaintiffs' argument that the hospital should have somehow known that Dr. Morris was lying, and should have seen that his ailment was in fact something serious, would require hospital personnel to be psychic. Not only is there no law requiring such a thing, the argument defies common sense."

Frank paused a moment, and his eyes rested on Megan. When she realized he was looking at her, a chill ran down her spine and she quickly dropped her glance. Frank gave a slight smile and went on. "What happened to the plaintiffs is a tragedy that should not have happened. But you must lay the blame where it belongs, squarely on Dr. Morris. Ladies and gentlemen, we submit that when the evidence has all been presented, you will agree that the hospital did all it was required to do to protect its patients' well-being, and if this is your conclusion, then you should find for the defendant. Thank you." He picked up his notes and returned to his chair.

Judge Edwards pulled his microphone toward him. "Thank you, counsel." He looked at the clock on the wall. "Why don't we take an early lunch and reconvene here in one hour, at which time the plaintiffs will call their first witness. Till then, court is adjourned."

"All rise," the bailiff intoned, as the judge exited. The television cameras ground to a halt and the courtroom quickly began to clear.

Megan leaned over to Ron. "Why don't you run down to the coffee shop and get us some sandwiches. Then let's try to find a quiet place to go over Sara's testimony one more time." Ron nodded and hurried off. Out of the corner of her eye, Megan saw Parks, Bartlett, and Dr. Lenz casually walk out of the courtroom. As the plaintiff's attorney, Megan would have the laboring oar in the first part of the case. Frank's role would be limited to cross-examination, trying to poke minute holes in her witnesses' stories, with the hope that by the end of the case there would be enough holes to sink the plaintiffs' chances of winning.

Megan sat quietly in her chair for a moment, trying not to think how much was riding on her ability to convince those jurors that her view of the case was the one they should believe. Was the hospital an innocent bystander or a truly culpable bad guy? So much depended on the answer to that question. Her stomach began to churn. Maybe eating something would help calm her down. She hoped so. She had to stay focused. She'd be no use to anyone if she couldn't concentrate on her presentation. She took a deep breath, then walked back to talk to her clients.

CHAPTER 42

Megan leaned over, reached into her briefcase, and took out a throat lozenge. Peeling off the foil wrapping, she popped it into her mouth. It was the seventh and final day of testimony in the liability phase of the trial. Frank had rested his case the previous afternoon, and Megan was going to call Dr. Leibowitz as her only rebuttal witness. After that, she and Frank would deliver their closing arguments and the jury would begin its deliberations.

Megan was exhausted and was fighting a cold. She had consumed the better part of a tin of throat lozenges in the last two days, praying that she could make it through her closing remarks without losing her voice. She had a vague notion that the trial was going well, but she was hardly an impartial bystander, so who could tell? Once in a while she'd see individual jurors nodding slightly as she was questioning witnesses, but for the most part they sat poker-faced, listening intently to the testimony, but giving no clue as to what they were thinking.

Frank had seemed distant and preoccupied throughout the trial, barely acknowledging her existence. The easy camaraderie they'd enjoyed on those couple occasions was gone. It was obvious to Megan that for all his pretrial posturing, when it counted, Frank took his work very seriously and as long as the trial lasted, she was his adversary and not someone to fraternize with. Megan told herself that that suited her just fine. After all, it was easier to deal with Parks when he was being cold and calculating. But deep down she couldn't help but feel a sense of loss, as though she had come close to winning a new friend, only to have him pull away.

The first phase of the trial, like everything that had gone before, had shaped up to be a battle between Drs. Lenz and Leibowitz, and in Megan's opinion, the white-haired German doctor stood triumphant. He had been on the witness stand for two days and never became flustered. On direct examination, Megan elicited the opinion that the hospital had breached the duty of care it owed to the plaintiffs by failing to follow up on Dr. Morris's health problems. Despite Parks's repeated pounding on cross-examination, the doctor remained steadfast in his conclusion that once it was put on notice of Dr. Morris's symptoms, the hospital should have suspended his surgical privileges pending further medical tests.

"But, Doctor, surely you would agree that Dr. Morris's symptoms were rather minor," Frank had persisted.

"No, I don't agree at all," the doctor had said, shaking his head vigorously from side to side. "I think the symptoms were serious enough to warrant further checking by the hospital."

"So you're saying if you had been in charge, you would have taken the drastic step of suspending Dr. Morris's surgical privileges?" Parks had hammered.

"Ya, I would," the doctor had replied.

"But Dr. Morris lied. Don't you think the hospital was entitled to rely on the doctor's explanation as to the reason for his symptoms?" Frank had asked, a deep frown creasing his brow.

"I don't think any trained medical professional should be entitled to ignore symptoms that were so clearly manifested as Dr. Morris's. I think a first-year medical student should have recognized that something was wrong, and that whatever it was, it was more serious than just an infection from wisdom teeth."

Frank was a master at cross-examination, but the harder he tried to find a weak spot in Dr. Leibowitz's testimony, the more the feisty old doctor dug in his heels. Megan had watched the parrying between the two men with considerable amusement. This was the first time she had seen Frank visibly rattled, and she loved it.

Dr. Lenz had also made a good witness, although Megan thought he was a little too aloof, and too sure of himself for the jury to really warm up to him.

Frank had been very direct in pointing out exactly what the hospital knew about Dr. Morris. "Dr. Lenz, were you aware that Dr. Morris was gay?"

"No."

"You never had occasion to discuss Dr. Morris's life-style either with him or with anyone else on staff?"

"Chicago Memorial's goal is to provide quality health care to our patients. Our physicians' life-styles are not our concern and are none of our business."

"How many doctors do you have on staff?"

"Approximately six hundred fifty."

"Do you personally review the results of the annual medical exams performed on all of those doctors?"

"I look them over, yes."

"And was there anything in Dr. Morris's exam results that caused you to think Dr. Morris might have a serious health problem?"

Dr. Lenz shook his head. "Nothing," he said, giving Megan an icy glance.

"You had no reason to believe that allowing Dr. Morris to continue his surgical practice might endanger the health of his patients?"

Dr. Lenz looked squarely at the jury. "Absolutely not. His symptoms were relatively minor, and he had a plausible explanation for them."

"Thank you, Doctor," Frank said, smiling slightly. "I have no further questions."

Megan had gotten Dr. Lenz to acknowledge that Dr. Morris's symptoms were consistent with the onset of AIDS. However, the doctor stated unequivocally that, given Dr. Morris's coverup, there was no reason for anyone at the hospital to suspect the real cause for Dr. Morris's malaise. Megan sat down from her cross-examination hoping that the jury would think Dr. Lenz had sounded just a tad too defensive and been just a little too quick to pooh-pooh all of her theories. Juries didn't like witnesses who talked down to them or acted condescending toward lawyers, and Dr. Lenz had come close to crossing the line in both respects.

Frank's final witness had been Dr. Gillian, the expert from Johns Hopkins. He was also an impressive witness, less dramatic than Dr. Leibowitz, but thoughtful and sincere. Frank had asked him more open-ended questions about how the medical profession policed itself. The doctor had expounded at length, opining that to require Chicago Memorial to distrust one of its best surgeons was a step down the path to requiring mandatory AIDS testing for all health-care workers, something the AMA had firmly rejected, and a policy that would ultimately set the entire medical profession on a downhill course.

"Let's assume, Dr. Gillian," Frank said, "that you were responsible for reviewing the results of all employee health exams at Chicago Memorial and that Dr. Morris's report came across your desk. What would you have done?"

"Exactly what Dr. Lenz did: accept Dr. Morris's explanation for his symptoms and move on to the next file."

Frank had nodded in satisfaction. "Thank you, Doctor. I have no further questions."

Megan had conducted a thorough cross-examination, but again had been unable to make any real points. By the time she had finished, it was late afternoon and Judge Edwards had called a recess for the day.

Jack and Kate had the day off from school, and Frank had brought them along to hear Drs. Lenz and Gillian testify. Before leaving for the day, Megan made a point to go over and talk to them. Jack was his usual outgoing self and asked Megan about her cat.

"He's fine," Megan answered with a smile. "Your dad told me you'd like to come visit him sometime."

Jack's face lit up. "Yeah! That'd be cool."

Megan patted him on the shoulder. "As soon as the trial's over, we'll see what we can do." Then she turned to Kate. "You're welcome to come along, too."

The girl had given Megan a look that indicated she thought she was far too sophisticated for such childish pursuits. Undaunted, Megan tried again. "There's a great store right on Lincoln that sells all kinds of sheet music. Maybe we could check that out."

Kate's expression seemed to soften a bit. "Maybe," she agreed noncommittally.

Megan smiled and took her leave.

She and Ron had taken Dr. Leibowitz and his wife, Marthe, to dinner at the Pump Room, and had gone over the doctor's rebuttal testimony. They had left the couple in their suite at the Ambassador East and had returned to the office where they'd worked on Megan's closing statement until one o'clock.

After the bailiff called the court into session on this overcast December morning, Judge Edwards motioned to Megan to present her rebuttal.

She recalled Dr. Leibowitz to the stand. "Doctor, were you present in the courtroom yesterday during Dr. Gillian's testimony?"

"Ya, I was," he answered.

"Then you heard Dr. Gillian express the concern that for the hospital to have questioned Dr. Morris's explanation for his symptoms would be a step toward mandatory AIDS testing and would throw the entire medical profession into chaos."

"Ya." Dr. Leibowitz nodded.

"How would you respond to the concerns expressed by Dr. Gillian?"

Dr. Leibowitz pursed his lips. "I agree that the medical profession should be able to police itself, but we haf to realize dat dis does not always work. In dis case, I believe that the hospital should haf recognized that der was something wrong with Dr. Morris and it should haf taken it upon itself to find out vat it was. Dis is not mandatory testing; dis is merely common sense."

"Thank you, Dr. Leibowitz," Megan said. "I have nothing further."

The judge looked at Frank.

"I have no questions," he replied.

"In that case," Judge Edwards said, "Dr. Leibowitz, you may step down, and at this time we will hear closing arguments. Ms. Lansdorf, the floor is again yours."

The doctor returned to his seat in the courtroom, next to his wife. The couple had indicated they would retire to their suite at the hotel until after the jury had returned its verdict, and they had invited the plaintiffs to keep the vigil with them.

Megan was wearing a white wool suit with a navy silk blouse and navy pumps. When they'd met at the court that morning, Ron had jokingly asked her where her white Stetson was, and had added that Frank, who was wearing a gray suit, had obviously not been told that the bad guy was supposed to wear black. Megan carried her notes and a glass of ice water, laced liberally with lemon, to the podium in front of the jury box. Taking a sip of water, she tried to weave the threads of the various witnesses' testimonies into a cohesive garment for the jury.

"Ladies and gentlemen, when we began this case I told you that this was going to be a story about four people who contracted the AIDS virus from their doctor and how this tragedy could have been prevented. You've heard Dr. Lenz explain that he didn't see any reason to question Dr. Morris's explanation about having some problems after a wisdom tooth extraction. The hospital's expert, Dr. Gillian, agreed with Dr. Lenz, in spite of the fact that Dr. Morris had symptoms that are readily identifiable as being AIDS related.

"You also heard Dr. Leibowitz testify that the hospital should have looked beyond Dr. Morris's simplistic explanation and required some concrete proof that things were as Dr. Morris said they were. Ladies and gentlemen, we are not asking you to establish a hard-and-fast rule that all doctors should be tested for AIDS. We are not saying that hospitals have to be suspicious or distrust their doctors. What we *are* saying is that the hospital had the obligation to make sure Dr. Morris's illness was as minor as he said it was. Until that had been checked out, the hospital should have prevented Dr. Morris from performing surgical procedures. If the hospital had done these things, the true cause for Dr. Morris's symptoms would have come to light and the four plaintiffs would not have been infected."

Megan paused and cleared her throat, then took a sip of water. "Ladies and gentlemen, when Mr. Parks and I have finished our remarks, the judge will be instructing you as to the law that is to be applied in this case. In his preliminary instructions, Judge Edwards told you that your most important function as jurors would be to weigh the credibility of witnesses. He also told you that while serving as jurors, you were to bring to bear all of your common sense and experiences in everyday life. We submit that when you think about the testimony the various witnesses have presented, when you think about what happened to the plaintiffs and why it happened, when you weigh all of the evidence, your common sense will tell you that the defendant, Chicago Memorial Hospital, made a conscious decision not to find out the cause for Dr. Morris's ill health, and that conscious decision caused grievous injury to the four plaintiffs. After weighing the evidence, we believe you will agree that you must find for the plaintiffs. Once again, thank you very much for your diligence and your attention." With that, Megan scooped up her papers and her glass of water. As she returned to the counsel table, she stole a look at the defense team. Bartlett smiled at her, Lenz was frowning, and Frank's face was completely devoid of expression.

Frank kept his closing remarks simple. "Dr. Morris had been a valuable member of Chicago Memorial's surgical team for over fifteen years. He was well-respected. His work was above reproach. Before he died, Dr. Morris stated emphatically that no one at the hospital knew he was suffering from AIDS because he told no one. He also made it clear that he deliberately lied to the doctor who conducted his medical exam.

"The plaintiffs are asking you, based on hindsight, to condemn the hospital's decision to accept Dr. Morris at his word. It's easy for all of us to be Monday-morning quarterbacks, but that is not your function as jurors. The only question you need to answer is whether the hospital, at the time of Dr. Morris's exam, should have questioned Dr. Morris's own explanation for his symptoms and should have suspended his surgical privileges pending further tests. Even though we know that Dr. Morris was in fact suffering from AIDS, his symptoms were not serious enough for the hospital to insist on the drastic response of suspending the doctor's surgical privileges."

Frank paused and looked intently at the jurors. "I'd like you to recall Dr. Gillian's testimony. Remember that he said the medical profession is, by and large, a self-policing profession. As such, it operates on a relationship of trust between its members and the patients they serve. Dr. Dan Morris breached that relationship of trust. He out and out lied to his employer and to his patients. His employer was entitled to believe Dr. Morris's lie because there was no reason not to.

"Ladies and gentlemen, we submit that when it comes time for you to weigh the evidence, you will conclude that the hospital did *not* play a part in causing the plaintiffs' injuries; that this was the sole province of Dr. Morris. We further submit that when reaching your verdict, you must find for the defendant. Thank you." Frank gave the jurors each a lingering look, then returned to his chair.

Megan returned to the podium for a short rebuttal. Then Judge Edwards read the jurors the instructions they were to follow in reaching their decision, and the bailiff escorted them to the jury room.

Megan glanced up at the clock on the wall. It was twelve-thirty. She took another drink of water. "Do you want to go back to the office or would you like to wait around here?" Ron asked.

Megan leaned over and put her hand on Ron's arm. "Let's go back to the office," she said in a hoarse voice. "I want to start looking over the witness outlines for the damage phase. I guess I might as well think positive."

Ron grinned at her. "Good girl. Let's go."

As they were packing up their briefcases, Frank

moved over to their table, flanked by Bartlett and Dr. Lenz. "Nice job," Frank said, nodding to Meg. His eyes looked distant, as though his mind was somewhere else.

"Thanks," Megan replied evenly. Why did she feel disappointed that he wasn't friendlier? What had she expected, that he'd ask her out for drinks?

"Yes, nice work," Bartlett echoed.

"Thank you," Megan said again. "See you later." Dr. Lenz brushed past her without speaking.

Ducking reporters, they all left the courtroom.

When she and Ron returned to the office, Megan realized she should have known better than to think she'd be able to get any work done. Everyone, from senior partners to messengers, swarmed around them, wanting to hear how things had gone. Several of the attorneys had brought in televisions so they could watch part of the proceedings when their time permitted.

Michael Gillette managed to catch Megan alone and made a point of congratulating her on a job well done.

"It's a little premature for that," Megan croaked. "The jury's still out."

Gillette shook his head. "I watched enough of it to know that you did a great job. Whatever the jury decides isn't going to sway my opinion."

"Thanks," Megan said. "Believe me, that means a lot."

"Are you taking something for that throat?" Gillette asked, concerned. "We don't want you trying the damage phase using sign language."

"I'll be fine," Megan assured him. "And Ron is very capable of taking over for me if my voice completely takes a holiday."

"Don't go away," Gillette said. "I'm going downstairs right now to get you some tea with honey."

Megan smiled, enjoying the attention. "That sounds good. Thanks."

By six o'clock the office had pretty much cleared out, and Megan was starting to get nervous. Ron had ordered a pizza and while he ate hungrily, Megan picked lethargically at one piece while going over her notes of questions she intended to ask each of the plaintiffs when they were recalled to the stand to present their testimony regarding damages. "It shouldn't be taking them this long," she said uneasily. "If they were going to find in our favor, they should've done it by now."

"They're probably just taking advantage of their chance to get one more free meal at taxpayer's expense," Ron said. "I'm sure it's nothing to worry about."

The call from Judge Edwards's clerk informing them that the jury had reached a verdict came in at six-forty-five. Megan gripped Ron's hand tightly. "I'm scared shitless," she said, looking up at him. "What if we lost?"

"If we lost, we'll appeal," Ron said pragmatically. "But I'll bet you twenty bucks we won."

Megan shook her head. "I can't bet on this. It'd be bad luck. You call Dr. Leibowitz and tell him to get everyone back down to the court. I have to go to the bathroom. I'll meet you by the elevator in five minutes."

Twenty minutes later they were back in their seats in the courtroom watching the jury file in. Megan tried to read the jurors' expressions, but none of them was looking her way. Oh, God, they must have found against us, she thought, swallowing hard. She could hear the TV cameras whirring behind her. She felt light-headed.

"Ladies and gentlemen, have you reached a verdict?" Judge Edwards asked.

"We have," the tall black man who had been elected the jury's foreman answered.

The bailiff stepped over to the jury box, took the folded paper containing the verdict from the foreman, and handed it to the judge. Judge Edwards unfolded the paper, looked at the contents, and handed it back to the bailiff. Megan's pulse was racing. Please, please, she thought. She had her hands in her lap and superstitiously crossed her fingers. A hush fell over the courtroom as the bailiff read: "In the matter of *Young, et al.* v. *Chicago Memorial Hospital,* we, the jury, find in favor of the plaintiffs."

Megan closed her eyes for a moment. Oh, my God! They'd won! She actually did it. She felt like jumping out of her seat and belting out the "Hallelujah Chorus," but she supposed that wouldn't be considered appropriate courtroom etiquette. She felt Ron's leg inch over and nudge her under the table. She turned slightly and saw him smile. She nodded in response.

The judge was thanking the jurors for their service in the first phase of the case and explaining that they would reconvene the following morning at ten o'clock to begin hearing testimony on damages. "Until then, court is adjourned," he said, banging his gavel. "Good night, everyone."

As soon as the judge exited the courtroom, Frank stepped over to Megan's table and extended his hand, first to her and then to Ron. "Congratulations," he said. "Good work." He looked a bit drawn.

"Thank you," Megan said politely, resisting the urge to gloat.

"You'd better get a good night's sleep and rest your voice," Frank added, his face expressionless.

Megan shook her head. "I'm afraid we've still got work to do tonight," she said. "Maybe I'll get a chance to rest when the damage phase is over."

Frank nodded. "See you tomorrow."

Bartlett also shook hands with Megan and Ron, and murmured a few words of congratulations before following Parks toward the door.

After the verdict was read, Dr. Lenz had remained slumped dejectedly in his chair. As he saw his attorneys exit the courtroom, he slowly got up and followed them. "So, Ms. Lansdorf, I guess you won this round," he said tersely as he passed her. "But don't forget: The war goes on." He made no move to shake her hand.

Megan tried not to frown. The doctor looked exhausted, and Megan realized that this loss might very well put his job in jeopardy. Even though she thought he was a real pain in the ass, she guessed, under the circumstances, she could forgive his bad manners.

"See you tomorrow," she said cheerfully. Dr. Lenz moved on without responding.

Megan and Ron walked back to where the Leibowitzes were sitting with the plaintiffs and their families. A beaming Megan hugged the white-haired doctor and kissed him on the cheek. "Thank you so much, Doctor," she exclaimed. "We couldn't have done it without you."

"It was a pleasure, Miz Lansdorf," the doctor said, beaming. "I vus happy I could be of service."

Megan hugged each of the plaintiffs in turn. They were all grinning broadly. "We knew you could do it," Edna Randolph said, summing up the feelings of the others. "There wasn't a doubt in our minds that you could beat those bastards."

Megan smiled broadly and hugged Edna again. "We've won one battle, but we're still not home free," she cautioned. "I hate to run out on you, but Ron and I have some things we need to work on yet tonight, so we'll see you all tomorrow at quarter to ten."

As Megan and Ron walked toward the door of the courtroom, they were deluged by reporters wanting them to comment on the verdict. "We're obviously very gratified that the jury agreed with our theory of the case," Megan responded in a weak voice. "We can only hope that they see the damage calculations our way as well." She declined further comment, saying, "I'm sorry, but we have work to do. Good night."

Ron and Megan walked sedately to Ron's car, with more reporters dogging them all the way. Only when they were safely inside, away from prying eyes and ears, did Ron grab Megan and give her a big kiss on the lips. "Way to go, darlin'," he shouted, tousling her hair.

Megan laughed. "You'd better watch out or you're going to catch my cold," she croaked. "But we did okay, didn't we?"

"We did better than that," Ron said, patting her on the knee. "Just a minute. Let me think of something appropriate," he said, throwing his head back. "Okay.

Got it." He began to sing in a loud falsetto. " 'Lightning is striking again.' "

Megan slapped him on the arm and laughed so hard she went into a coughing fit. "Stop it before I choke to death. Let's hurry up and get back to the office. I know Mike was watching us on cable. I can't wait to hear his reaction."

CHAPTER 43

Megan felt like she was on an emotional seesaw. One minute she was so euphoric about the verdict that she wanted to turn cartwheels. The next minute she was so depressed at the thought of having to go back to court the next day that she wanted to cry. Either way, her mood was hardly conducive to getting much work done.

She rubbed her neck and worked her shoulders up and down. It felt like she'd been hunched over a desk for her entire life. She glanced up at the clock on the wall of the conference room. Ten-fifteen. She'd give anything to be able to go home and soak in a hot bath, turn her electric blanket on high and climb into bed for an extended stay. Next week, she promised herself. Next week she was going to tell the firm to kiss off and do something for herself for a change. But for now she had to force herself to concentrate. She was struggling to put together her opening statement on damages. Ron had left the room about fifteen minutes ago to get her some more tea. She wondered what was taking him so long.

Mike Gillette had been ecstatic about the verdict. She could almost hear him jumping up and down in his living room when she called him. "It's wonderful, Megan! Just wonderful!" he'd said repeatedly. "I'm very, very proud of you."

"Thanks," she said, "but we're not home free yet."

"There's no question the jury is going to award substantial damages," Gillette assured her. "It's just a matter of *how* substantial. You know, I wouldn't be at all surprised if you got a call from Parks before the night is out saying the hospital is willing to settle."

Megan laughed. "You obviously don't know Frank Parks," she said in a raspy voice. "He'll never settle."

"But surely he realizes he's exposing his client to tremendous risk if he allows the question of damages to go to the jury," Gillette retorted.

"He'll never give any money away voluntarily," Megan said. "He'll make us earn every dime."

"That strategy is going to cost him dearly," Gillette predicted. "But I guess that's his funeral. Don't work too late," he counseled. "Why don't you go home and have a couple drinks. It'll help your throat and, besides, you deserve it."

"I can't celebrate till the whole thing is over," Megan said. "God, Mike, you don't know how much I'm looking forward to getting back into a normal, humdrum routine. I've had enough excitement to last me a long while."

Gillette laughed. "Trials *are* exciting," he agreed. "Hell, the most interesting thing that's happened in the office this week is that our computer system was apparently infected with some sort of virus."

"Really? What happened?"

"Didn't I mention it this afternoon? No? Well, for the last couple nights the word processing department noticed weird graphics suddenly appearing in the middle of their documents. We called in somebody from IBM, and they seem to think it's the work of a hacker, probably some hotshot, teenage computer whiz trying to see whose networks he can get into. They're coming to install some sort of virus repellant first thing in the morning."

"Was any damage done?"

"Not that we know of," Gillette replied. "It seems to be a harmless prank, at least so far. Anyway, those are the kinds of things you'll have to look forward to when you return to the everyday world of practicing law."

"I'll take it," Megan said. "Sounds relaxing."

"Seriously, Meg, don't work yourself too hard. Go

home and put your feet up. Tomorrow will take care of itself."

"I'll feel better if I stay here a while and try to get psyched up," Megan replied. "But we should be able to knock it off around midnight at the latest."

"You take care of yourself and get a good night's sleep," Gillette said. "That's an order. I don't want you getting pneumonia."

"Don't worry," Megan said with a laugh. "I'm pretty tough."

"I know you're tough," Gillette replied. "And you're also a damn fine lawyer. Thanks for calling, Meg. You made my day."

Rita, who was celebrating getting the cast removed from her ankle, had called to congratulate her and had promised her a steak dinner at Eli's as soon as the second phase of the trial was over. But the most unexpected call had come around nine o'clock.

Few people outside of the office knew Megan's direct-dial number, so when the phone rang, she expected it to be another one of her colleagues. To her extreme surprise, it was Paul.

"Umm ... I heard the news on the radio," he said haltingly, "and I just wanted to say congratulations. I know how hard you worked on the case, and nobody deserves a big win more than you do."

"Thank you," she replied, genuinely touched. "It's nice of you to call."

"So, how've you been?" Paul asked.

"Okay," Megan replied. Then she sighed. "Actually I've been tired and overworked. And as you can probably tell, I have a doozy of a cold."

"Yeah, I noticed," Paul said. After a slight hesitation, he added, "I talked to Judy Vandermere last week. She's coming into town next month for an appointment to see if she needs any follow-up surgery. She's doing just great. She's a nice girl. She still reminds me a lot of you."

"She is nice," Megan replied, once again ignoring his comparison of her and Judy. "I told her she was in good hands with you."

"Well, I'm sure you've got a million things to do, so I'll let you go. I just wanted to let you know I'm proud of you."

"Thanks, Paul. Have a good Christmas."

"You, too. Say hi to your folks."

"I will. 'Bye."

"Goodbye, Meggie."

Megan hung up the phone feeling that another milestone had been reached. She'd managed to have a polite conversation with Paul without getting weepy or wanting to scratch his eyes out. Maybe she had finally let go. Now if she could only keep her mind on the case. But damn it, why did an image of Frank Parks's face keep popping into her head?

As Megan went back to perusing the report submitted by one of the plaintiffs' economists, she found herself daydreaming about what life would be like after the trial. Having evenings to herself. Not having to work weekends. Putting in an eight-hour day. Okay, ten hours.

God, she couldn't believe it was already December ninth. A ten-foot-tall, elaborately decorated, fraser fir tree graced the firm's reception area. As usual, Megan hadn't been able to give any thought to Christmas shopping. That would be one of her first priorities next week. Look on the bright side, she thought wryly. Her breakup with Paul meant she had one less person to shop for. She idly wondered where Frank and the kids spent Christmas. Stop that! she ordered herself.

As she finally turned back to the economist's report, Ron walked back into the conference room. "Where were you?" she asked without looking up. "I was beginning to think you fell in somewhere."

"I sort of did," Ron replied weakly.

"So where's my tea?" Megan asked as she glanced up at him. "God, you look awful!" she exclaimed in her throaty voice. "What's the matter?"

Ron slumped into a chair. "I hate to tell you this, Meg, but I must have the flu. I've spent the last fifteen minutes in the bathroom puking my guts out."

"Oh, no!" Megan said, grimacing. "I told you not to eat all that pizza."

"I'm sorry," Ron said contritely. "I'm sure I'll be better in the morning."

"Oh, God! What great timing," Megan rasped, putting her hands to her face. "I've got laryngitis—not to mention the fact that I feel totally spaced out—and you've got the flu. We're quite a pair. At the rate we're going, they'll probably have to quarantine the jurors. Well, go on," she said, making a shooing motion with her hands. "Get out of here before you spread more germs around. I'll see you tomorrow at eight-thirty, unless you're still sick."

"I'll be here. I promise," Ron said, holding up one hand. "Scout's honor." He got up and dragged himself toward the door. "I hate to leave you here alone. Why don't you knock it off, too. We could both come back in early, say around seven."

Megan shook her head. "No. If I didn't go through all this stuff, I'd never be able to sleep anyway. You go ahead. This shouldn't take me more than a couple hours."

"Okay," Ron said. "See ya." As he reached the door, he suddenly doubled over and groaned. "Oh, oh," he moaned as he sprinted down the hall toward the men's restroom.

Megan doggedly plowed through her files. It was so quiet that she started to get sleepy. At eleven-fifteen she had a coughing spell and walked back to her office to get another packet of throat lozenges out of her purse. Feeling a little flushed, she slipped out of her white suit jacket and tossed it on a chair. As she sat down at her desk and unwrapped a lozenge, she suddenly heard a beeping sound coming from the computer on her secretary's desk. That was strange. She was quite sure there was no one else on the floor.

Remembering what Gillette had said about a computer virus, she got up and walked out to Karen's desk. Rubbing her eyes, she glanced down at the computer screen. A great chill came over her, and she was so startled that she swallowed the throat lozenge and nearly choked.

On the screen was a skull and crossbones with her name "MEGAN LANSDORF" printed in bold, capital letters underneath. As Megan stood there, transfixed, another graphic appeared. It was a knife with a long sharp blade. Then more words, this time in italics. *"To die, to sleep, perchance to dream."* She heard more beeping and looked up. All of the computer screens within view bore the same ghoulish message.

"Oh, my God!" Megan whispered aloud. Shakespeare. Judy Vandermere's assailant had spouted Shakespeare while he was strangling her. And she looked like Judy! Jesus Christ! The killer was after her!

She ran into her office, slammed the door, and leaned against it, shaking uncontrollably. Get a grip on yourself, she thought. There's no killer out there. There has to be a logical explanation for this. She clenched her teeth to keep them from chattering. It must be a sick practical joke. Yes, that was it. Somebody was playing a nasty trick on her. But who? She could've sworn she was the only person in the office. The elderly black couple who were responsible for cleaning had left while Ron was still around. She hadn't heard anyone else come in, although working in a back conference room, she knew it would be easy enough for someone to have entered without her knowing it.

Megan ran her index finger over the beauty mark near her lip. Although she knew next to nothing about computer viruses, she'd read that they could originate from a computer miles away. Maybe someone outside the office had tapped into the firm's computer network. Who knew she would still be in the office at this hour? Mike Gillette? He was completely ignorant about computers. Ron? While he was a practical joker and did have a PC at home, she doubted that he would broadcast such a malicious message. Besides, she was certain his illness had been genuine and he was probably sprawled on the floor of his bathroom with his head in the toilet, hardly a convenient position from which to operate a computer. Paul? He might have been unfaithful to her, but he wasn't malicious. He'd sounded genuinely friendly when they'd talked earlier. And besides, he'd already replaced her with a newer model. He had no ax to grind.

Megan pressed her hands against her sides to stop them from trembling. Who else knew she'd probably still be here? Who would benefit from scaring her out of her wits? She drew in her breath as the obvious answer flashed across her mind.

Frank Parks.

Megan pushed back her hair and tried to sort out her thoughts. At first view the possibility was too ridiculous to even consider. Why would a respected attorney do such a childish thing? On the other hand, what did Megan really know about the man? He was a mass of contradictions. He could be aggressive; he could be aloof; and he could be charming, if it suited his purposes. Could he be cruel and vindictive if it might give him the upper hand in winning a case? She didn't know. Maybe.

As much as Megan hated to admit it, Frank had been on her mind a lot lately. During the time they'd spent together at the airport, at this house, and at her office, she had begun to like him. They had some common interests: a love of antiques, an appreciation of historic architecture, a fondness for cats. And she liked his kids, too. At least she liked his son. She suspected it would take a lot of hard work to break his daughter's reserve. Although she'd tried to push such thoughts from her mind the instant they arose, more than once she had caught herself daydreaming about spending more time with Frank and his family.

A couple times, when this had happened, she'd asked herself angrily, what's the matter, are you so eager to show Paul that he's not the only one who can find a new companion that you grab the first available man you see? Well—it was true that finding a new romantic interest would definitely help her forget about Paul. But there was more to it than that. Megan had begun to feel that maybe she'd been wrong about Frank.

Maybe he wasn't an ogre after all. If he came across that way, maybe it was just because he was a top professional giving his best effort for his client. Underneath it all, though, he seemed to be a soft touch, especially with his kids. Megan admired him for that.

But the trial had changed everything. Frank had gone back to being distant. The dark shutters, which for a time had been raised to reveal his persona, had been pulled back down and latched tight, leaving Megan to wonder whether she had ever known him at all. Unfortunately, her daydreams and her curiosity about him were still there. Just who the hell was the real Frank Parks anyway? She realized uneasily that she had no idea.

What she *did* know was that this incident was the work of a sick mind, and if Frank Parks was behind it, Megan wasn't going to let it drop. It was better to meet the thing head on. By God, she'd let him know he couldn't scare her.

Megan walked over to her desk and flipped through her rolodex until she found Frank's direct-dial number. Taking a deep breath, she picked up the phone and rapidly punched the numbers. As it began to ring, she stood next to the desk, tapping her right foot on the floor.

As the phone kept ringing, unanswered, Megan's confidence began to waver. She'd been so sure Frank was in his office playing an elaborate trick on her. If he wasn't there, where was he? Was it possible he might be in *her* office? No, he just couldn't be. Because if he were in her office, then this wasn't a trick at all, it was the real thing. And that would mean Frank was . . .

Her eyes widened with fear as she remembered the night in Bethesda when she'd thought she was being followed. Frank had been there, too. And he'd been in Chicago the night Rita was run over and, in fact, he'd seemed surprised to learn Megan had flown out a day earlier. Rita had come out of Megan's apartment with her jacket over her head and had been hunched over so anyone watching from the street would've thought it was Megan. Oh, God. It all fit! He'd been after her all along!

Megan's hands were shaking so badly that she nearly dropped the phone. Just then a brusque voice came over the line. "Frank Parks." For a moment, Megan was so flustered she was unable to respond. "Hello?" she heard Frank bark with obvious irritation.

"Frank, this is Megan," she finally managed to choke out in her raspy voice. She took a deep breath and felt herself relax a bit. See, she scolded herself. Her imagination had been getting the better of her again. Of course Frank wasn't the killer, and of course the killer wasn't after her. This was all just a bad joke, and now she was going to get to the bottom of it.

"Megan, hi," Frank replied in a much softer tone. "God, your voice has really gotten a lot worse. What can I do for you?"

Megan cleared her throat. "I just wanted you to know that I don't find your little joke to be the least bit funny," she said, trying to harness her shaky voice into sounding stern.

"I beg your pardon?" Frank replied in a puzzled tone.

"You know very well what I'm referring to," Megan plunged on. "I can understand that you are unhappy about the verdict, but I would think you'd have better things to do with your time than trying to scare me. What did you think, that I was going to drop the case?"

There was a long pause. "Megan, I don't know what the hell you're talking about," Frank finally said.

"I mean, any reasonable person in your position would be thinking about trying to settle the case rather than playing childish games—"

"For your information," Frank cut in curtly, "if it were up to me, I probably would be talking settlement, but my client isn't interested. Now in case you haven't checked the time recently, it's very late, and I was just getting ready to leave, so I suggest you get to the point. Just what is it you're accusing me of?"

Megan was growing more confused by the minute,

but she kept her voice firm. "So you're denying that you tapped into our computer network?"

There was a pause. "What?" Frank finally asked indignantly. "I don't know anything about your computer network. I'm lucky to be able to type a few pages on my PC at home now and then. For Christ's sake, what's going on over there?"

Megan sat down in her chair. Holy shit! What *was* going on? "There's been some weird things happening with our computers the last couple nights," she blurted out. "They think a hacker has been tapping into our network. About ten minutes ago all of our machines started beeping, and when I went to check it out, there was a skull and crossbones on all the screens, with my name under it. And under that was a picture of a knife and the words 'To die, to sleep, perchance to dream.' "

"And you thought *I* was responsible for that?" Frank said angrily. "Jesus! Why would I do such a thing?"

"I thought you were trying to scare me into dropping the case."

"By quoting Shakespeare?" Frank said incredulously.

"Well ..." Megan hesitated. Then she said, "You see, the woman who was attacked by the slasher at the Ritz-Carlton on Halloween said the man quoted a verse from Shakespeare as he was choking her. I thought you somehow must've heard about that and were trying to scare me."

"Listen to me," Frank interrupted urgently. "You may be in great danger. Is there anyone else in the office?"

"Not that I know of," Megan replied. "Ron went home sick. But I guess someone could've gotten in without my seeing them."

She heard Frank draw in his breath. "Is there someplace you could hide? A storage room or something?" he asked.

The feeling of utter panic that she'd so successfully conquered moments before swept over her once again. "Frank, you don't really think the killer was responsible for the computer message, do you?" she gasped.

"I don't know what the hell to think," Frank replied, "but from what you've told me, I'd take this very seriously until somebody proves otherwise."

"Then why don't I just leave the office?" Megan asked. Her hands were shaking so badly she could barely hang on to the phone.

"No!" Frank yelled at her. "If there's someone in the building who's after you, you'd be an easy target in the elevator or the stairs. You're better off to find someplace safe and stay put. I want you to hang up right now. I'll call the police and then I'll come right over."

Megan hesitated a moment, then said, "Maybe you're right. I'll call Lieutenant O'Riley—"

"No!" Frank barked. "I said *I'll* call the police. If there's someone there, he might be monitoring the phone lines."

"Frank, you're scaring me," Megan whispered. "I'm sure there's some other explanation . . ."

"I hope so, too," Frank said fervently, "but we can't take any chances. Now hang up and sit tight. I'm on my way."

The line went dead. Megan sat there for a moment, still holding the receiver. This couldn't be happening. She got up from her desk as noiselessly as she could, walked over to the door, and switched off the light. Then she leaned against the door, closed her eyes and listened. The only thing she could hear was the sound of her own heart pounding.

CHAPTER 44

Megan took several deep breaths to try to calm herself. This must be a bad dream she told herself. She'd just had the best day of her legal career and was well on the way to winning a multimillion dollar verdict. What possible reason could someone have for wanting to harm her? She'd never hurt anyone in her life. She hated violence. She didn't even like to squish bugs.

Her knees grew weak as she allowed herself to seriously consider the possibility that the madman who had attacked Judy Vandermere and killed all those other women was now stalking her, that at this very moment he might be somewhere in the office, watching, waiting.

Megan thought of Judy's face, slashed to ribbons. She thought of the newspaper accounts of the murders. "The victim suffered multiple stab wounds. . . . The body was horribly mutilated. . . . Sources close to the investigation report that there was evidence of a vicious sexual assault." Then she thought of someone deliberately running Rita down with his car, possibly thinking it was Megan. Her first impulse was to run toward the lobby, screaming as loud as she could, and she had to continue her deep breathing to restrain herself.

Think, she ordered herself silently, still leaning against the door. She couldn't just go running through the office like a scared rabbit. She had to have a plan. Someplace safe to hide. Think. Her brain refused to cooperate. Assuming Frank was right and there *was* someone in the office looking for her, where wouldn't he look? She ground her teeth, then came up with an answer. The supply room on the opposite hall had a number of large cabinets that held Xerox paper. She'd been in there making some copies earlier in the evening and had noticed that the bottom shelves were empty. If she scrunched down, she'd probably fit inside.

Megan had her hand on the doorknob when she looked down at her feet. She was still wearing her navy leather pumps. Not exactly the best footgear for quick getaways. She moved noiselessly over to her desk, feeling her way in the darkness. She slipped out of her heels and, bending down, found her white Reeboks and white-cotton socks underneath her chair. She quickly pulled on the socks. There was no time to bother with the shoes.

Megan recalled Rita's concern for her safety and her suggestion that Megan carry a can of mace in her purse. She wished she'd taken Rita's advice. She'd give anything to have some type of weapon. She pulled open a desk drawer and reached inside. Her hand closed around a pair of scissors with a sterling handle, part of a desk set her brother had given her for her college graduation. Clutching the scissors close to her chest, she laughed mirthlessly to herself. This was great. There might be a crazy man with a machete out there. What did she think she was going to do, hold him at scissors' point until the police arrived? She took one more deep breath. She had to get going. There was no time to waste.

Megan walked back to the door, planning her movements. If there was someone looking for her, at least she had the advantage of knowing the office layout. She could find her way around in the dark. She nodded. Good idea. She'd shut off the lights as she went. Think positive, she told herself. If Frank had called the police right away, they should be here soon. Hold that thought. Help was on the way.

Megan slowly turned the doorknob, then eased the door open, first one inch, then two. She peered out into the hall. She couldn't see anything. Still clutching the scissors, she stepped out, not stopping to close the door. As she swiftly turned left and padded down the hallway, she noticed that the computer screens had all gone blank. She passed one bank of light switches and quickly snapped them off. She continued down the hall, past the construction project connecting their floor to the one below. Was it her imagination or did she hear something behind her? She picked up her pace. She came to another bank of light switches and turned them off as well. The entire hallway was now dark. That was definitely a point in her favor, but would it be enough? Not daring to consider the answer to that question, she kept moving.

Mike O'Riley sped along Lake Shore Drive. A wet, heavy snow was falling, and the streets were slick. The car began to fishtail.

"Son of a bitch!" O'Riley swore as he was forced to let up on the gas.

"Take it easy, Mike," Greg Jablonski cautioned. "We're not gonna be much use to anybody if we crash."

O'Riley again pressed down on the accelerator. Jablonski slapped the portable turret light onto the roof of the unmarked squad car while O'Riley radioed in to dispatch. "This is Lieutenant O'Riley," he barked. "I want a SWAT team and about ten uniformed officers at the Gilman Building in five minutes. Detective Jablonski and I are on our way. I want everyone to wait in the lobby until we arrive. The man who may be in that building is to be considered armed and extremely dangerous."

The hairs on the back of O'Riley's neck were standing up, and blue veins protruded from his big hands as he gripped the steering wheel tightly. "I had a feeling something weird was going on the first time I met Megan, but I talked myself into believing my imagination was getting the better of me. Christ! What a fool I was!" he berated himself.

"Are we gonna make it in time?" Jablonski asked anxiously.

"We'll make it," O'Riley answered tersely as the car

careened south. "You'll be getting your promotion before you know what hit you."

Jablonski ground his teeth and shook his head. "I just want to catch the SOB," he said. "Jesus, I can't believe that a professional person—" his voice trailed off.

"Me neither, kid," O'Riley said tersely.

He brought the car to a sliding stop in front of Megan's building. As he leapt out of the vehicle, O'Riley patted the shoulder holster that held his .38 caliber Colt revolver. In all his years as a detective, he had never once had to fire his weapon in the line of duty. But based on his performance at the practice range, he was still a pretty fair shot and if he got the chance, he'd happily blast this bastard to kingdom come.

The two detectives raced through the building's revolving doors and found the lobby already filled with cops. There were eight SWAT team members armed with assault rifles, backed up by a dozen uniformed officers.

Upon seeing the detectives, the SWAT team's commander, a sandy-haired, wiry man in his mid-thirties, stepped forward. "Lieutenant O'Riley, I'm Sergeant Wilkins."

O'Riley nodded in acknowledgement of the introduction. "Have you found out anything?"

Wilkins motioned to the far side of the lobby. "There's an old geezer over there says he's the night security guard. Looks like he's half soused. He says it's been a quiet night, not many people in and out, except a policeman came in about ten minutes ago claiming he had a late meeting with one of the lawyers in the building."

"What floor did he go to?" O'Riley asked.

"Twelve," Wilkins replied.

"Shit!" O'Riley spat out. He trotted across the lobby with Jablonski and Wilkins in close pursuit. Seated at a small wooden desk was a gray-haired man who looked to be in his late fifties. His face was puffy and flushed, his eyes a bit glassy. The hands that were folded in front of him were trembling.

"What's your name?" O'Riley demanded.

"Higgins. George Higgins," the man replied in a shaky voice.

"You're the security guard for this building?"

Higgins's head bobbed up and down nervously.

"This policeman that came in a little while ago—did you get his name or ask him for ID?"

"Ah . . . ah . . ." Higgins stammered, "no." He shook his head.

"What did he look like?"

"Ah . . . he was tall, over six feet, had dark hair and glasses."

"How do you know he went to the twelfth floor?"

Higgins swallowed hard. "He said he had a late meeting with one of the lawyers at the Barrett law firm, something about court testimony. He sounded like he'd been up there before, because he knew what floor they were on."

"Did you see him get in the elevator?"

"Yes."

"Did you watch to see what floor he got off on?"

"N-n-no," Higgins stuttered. "There was no reason for me to watch. He said he was going to twelve."

O'Riley looked around him. "Where's the stairway?" he asked.

Higgins's whole body was shaking. "Around the corner."

"Is there a way to shutoff the elevators?"

Higgins nodded.

"Give me the keys for the elevators and the stairwells," O'Riley demanded. "Hurry up!" he shouted as Higgins fumbled with his heavy key chain.

"This one is the elevators'," Higgins said nervously, handing the keys over.

O'Riley snatched the keys out of the man's hand. "Is there any other way to get from the eleventh floor to the twelfth?"

Higgins gulped and bobbed his head again. "The law firm is expanding onto the eleventh floor. I know they've been working on making an inner stairway between the two floors, but I don't know if it's finished. I've never been up there."

O'Riley tossed the keys to Sergeant Wilkins. "Shut off the elevators and get your men into position upstairs. Have the uniforms sweep the rest of the building and secure the exits and the building's perimeter. Detective Jablonski and I will secure the hallway on twelve."

As Wilkins prepared to give his men the order to move out, O'Riley called after him, "I want this guy, dead or alive. Do you understand? I don't care what it takes, but we can't let him get away."

Wilkins nodded and motioned the contingent of officers to move toward the stairs.

"I'm too fuckin old for this, Gregarious," O'Riley said ruefully as they, too, jogged toward the stairway. "No matter what happens here tonight, I'm hangin' it up."

"Don't talk like that, you crazy old man," Jablonski chided. "I'm not gonna let you quit now. You're gonna see this thing through whether you like it or not. Now get your tired old ass up those stairs."

O'Riley managed a low chuckle. "Yes, sir. Come on, hotshot. I'll race you to the top."

Megan reached the end of the hallway and rounded the corner, running now. The supply room was near the end of that hall. She snapped off another set of lights and kept moving. Not much farther. As she scurried along, an elusive thought tugged at her brain. She had a vague notion that she was missing something, but what was it? As she approached the exhibit room, she suddenly stopped short, then pushed in the swinging door, and ducked inside.

Snatches of a conversation she'd had with Ron were replaying themselves in her head.

"So would you like me to go shoot Paul?"

"You don't have a gun."

"No, but there's one in the exhibit room. Don't you remember the case I'm working on where a kid acci-

*dentally shot his cousin because the sight was so far
out of whack? There's a box of ammo, too, so just say
the word and I'll rub him out."*

Not long after Ron's flippant remark about shooting
Paul, Megan had passed the room one day when Ron
and an expert witness were examining the gun. Megan
had stopped in briefly to chat with them. They had explained it was a 20-gauge semiautomatic shotgun, and
Megan knew it was stored in the bottom of a cabinet in
the corner of the room.

Megan cautiously felt her way across the room. The
drapes were partially open, admitting enough outside
light to enable her to see where she was going. When
she reached the far wall, she knelt down and, setting
the scissors on the floor in front of her, tugged at the
cabinet door with both hands. The door opened with a
squeaking sound that she was certain must have carried
to the other side of the office. She stuck her hand inside and felt the leather gun case. She quickly lifted it
off the shelf. It was heavy. She set it on the floor and
fumbled for the tab on the zipper.

Running the zipper around the side of the case as
quietly as she could, Megan slid the shotgun out and
held it in her hands. The wood of the stock was smooth
as glass. When she was a kid, her dad and brother
would go pheasant or rabbit hunting once in a while.
On a couple of occasions they'd offered to take her
with them, but Megan had always been afraid of guns
and had declined. *Another mistake on my part,* she
thought ruefully.

She remembered her grandmother telling her that
she had shot a gun once. As a girl of fifteen, Hallie had
wanted to impress a neighborhood boy whose first love
was target practice. Figuring she'd never seen any boy
do something that she couldn't do right after him,
Hallie had tagged along to a field where her beau was
taking practice shots with a small rifle. The girl cajoled
him into letting her take a stab at it. She'd listened to
his instructions, carefully took aim, and pulled the trigger. But she hadn't been prepared for what happened
next.

"It knocked me right on my ass," the old woman had cackled sixty years later. "I was mortified. The only redeeming thing was that I *did* hit the target. Barely, just on the edge, but I did hit it. I never shot a gun again, and I wasn't too interested in that boy after that, either, come to think of it."

Why am I thinking of that story at a time like this? Megan wondered. It wasn't exactly a morale booster. Maybe it was true that in times of great danger your life did flash before your eyes. The weapon felt cold and foreign in her hands. She swallowed hard as for a fleeting moment she remembered that one person had already been killed because of the gun's defect. Oh, hell, she thought grimly. The accuracy of the sight wasn't going to make a bit of difference. She couldn't shoot straight anyway, but maybe she could scare the guy off by firing at the ceiling.

She slid her hand back inside the cabinet in search of the shells. Bullets came in a small cardboard box, didn't they? She leaned forward and reached way in, patting the shelf. Ah. There it was. She pulled the box out and lifted the lid, then nodded in satisfaction. Those little things looked like shells. Now how the hell did you get them into the gun?

Megan turned the weapon over, and in the dim light, saw what must be the chamber. She reached into the box and took out a shell. Her hands were shaking so badly that she dropped it on the floor. Calm down, she scolded herself, picking it up off of the thick tan carpet. She pushed it into the chamber. There seemed to be room for additional shells, so she shoved in two more. There. It was loaded. At least she hoped it was. Now how did you shoot the damn thing?

As she crouched on the floor, puzzling that question out, she suddenly thought she heard a crunching sound out in the hallway. She froze and listened. Nothing. Keep calm, she told herself again. If Frank had called the police right away, they were probably in the building now. They'd be there any minute.

If Frank had called . . . Megan frowned and sat back on her haunches, her back against the wall. Why had

Frank been so insistent that *he* call the police? Why had he asked if she was alone in the office? Why hadn't the police arrived yet? The obvious answer to all those questions hit her, and once again she began to tremble uncontrollably. You stupid shmuck, she said to herself wordlessly. You fell for his trap.

Fear washed over her. The police weren't coming. But *he* was out there right now, searching for her. And *he* had been in the office before, had been so interested in the layout. She'd given him a tour of the whole damn place. She wouldn't be able to hide from him. He'd find her. She was going to die. Megan's hands loosened their grip on the gun, and it slid to the floor.

Her back was pressed so tightly to the wall that she could feel the plaster scraping through her silk blouse. She sat motionless for what seemed like an eternity, but was probably only ninety seconds. Finally, she took a deep breath, raised her head toward the door, and listened intently. Nothing. The knots in her stomach began to unwind.

Look at me, she scolded herself. She was acting like a kid, thinking there was a bogeyman behind every door. It was ridiculous to believe Frank or anyone else was after her. Her resemblance to Judy Vandermere and those other women was probably just a coincidence. The business with the computers was probably just a hoax. Instead of cowering in a corner with a gun at her feet like a six-year-old playing cops and robbers, she was going to get up, walk across the room, and call the police. They would reassure her everything was okay and then she could go home and get some rest.

She put both hands on the floor to steady herself and began to stand up. It was then that she heard the voice out in the hall, low and melodic but vaguely familiar.

" 'But soft! What light through yonder window breaks? It is the east and Megan is the sun. Arise fair sun, and kill the envious moon, who is already sick and pale with grief.' "

Megan sank back to her knees.

"Megan?" the voice was getting closer. "Why are

you playing games with me? You know I'm going to
find you."

In the dim light, Megan saw the door open just a
crack. She tried to move, but found she was rooted to
the spot, paralyzed with fear.

"Megan?"

As if in a trance, Megan watched the door open
wider, then wider still.

"Are you in here?"

The silhouette of an outstretched hand came into
view. It was clutching something long and pointed.

"Megan?"

At the last possible moment, Megan sprang to life.
Snatching the gun up off the floor, she steadied the
stock against her shoulder, and pointed the barrel toward the door. Then, in a reflexive action born of des-
peration, she squeezed the trigger. In the stillness of
the office, the noise sounded like a cannon exploding,
and the recoil threw her off balance, knocking her on
her side. Although her ears were still ringing from the
shot, she heard a startled yelp and footsteps rapidly
moving away.

Detectives O'Riley and Jablonski were positioned at
opposite ends of the hallway on the twelfth floor, their
guns drawn. Two members of the SWAT team were inside the hard-hat area on eleven, in case the perpetrator
tried to make a quick getaway through there. The remaining SWAT team members had begun to sweep the
twelfth floor proper. The elevators had been shut
down. Additional backup units had arrived, and uniformed officers were canvassing the entire building. If
their man was inside, they had him trapped. Unless he
was able to vanish into thin air, they'd get him.

"Jesus, I'm too old for this!" O'Riley cursed as he
tried to catch his breath after running up twelve flights
of stairs. His leg was throbbing, and it felt as though
his lungs were going to burst. When this damn case
over, he was definitely going to join a health club. He
was turning into a pile of mush. He'd heard those stair-
climbing machines gave you a real good workout. If

only the case were over. When was it finally going to be over?

Please, God, he silently intoned, the veins on his right hand protruding as it clutched the revolver. Please let us catch him. Please. I'll never ask for anything again. I'll even start going to church more often. I'll help Anne around the house. I'll try to quit smoking. I'll do anything. Please. Please.

As O'Riley briefly leaned his head against the wall, trying to slow his racing pulse, the sound of a gunshot rang out from inside Barrett, Gillette's suite of offices. What the fuck was that? O'Riley swore to himself as he leaped toward the center of the hallway. He and an equally startled Greg Jablonski both stared at the heavy cherry-wood door with its fancy gold lettering, then looked at each other uneasily. What the hell was going on in there?

Megan struggled shakily to her feet. Had she hit him? She wasn't sure. All she knew was that she had to get out of that room. The attacker now knew for certain where she was, and there was always the chance he might come back after her. She abandoned all notions of making further use of the gun, which was now lying on the floor next to the discarded scissors. Her only thought was that she'd have to outrun him and find a new place to hide.

She went to the door and paused a moment to listen. As she did so, she glanced up. The shotgun blast had ripped a gaping hole in the wall and the oak crown molding. The firm's insurance carrier was going to have a conniption over the damage claim. After assuring herself that no sound was coming from the hall, she pushed the door open and stepped outside. For a moment she was afraid her legs were going to buckle, but then she managed to steady herself and took off in the direction of her office.

Megan sprinted down the hall and rounded the corner. Just then she heard a noise. Out of the corner of her eye she saw a dark figure emerge from the shadows.

She tore down the long hallway at top speed, all the while aware of pursuing footsteps. As she approached the construction area, her mind formed a plan. She'd duck into a conference room that was connected to two other offices. It had a means of egress to the opposite hall. If she could make it that far, she just might have a chance.

In her haste to get past the construction site, she rushed headlong into some of the heavy plastic sheets that shielded the opening to the floor below. Flailing wildly, she fought to escape the plastic tentacles that surrounded her.

Freeing herself at last, she was just about to make her dash across the hall toward the refuge of the conference room when she heard a noise right behind her. In spite of herself, she turned to look. Her heart rose in her throat as she saw a tall figure dressed in a policeman's uniform brandishing a large knife.

Before Megan could turn and run, the attacker leaped toward her. But in the darkness, he miscalculated the distance he needed to cover. Catapulting himself toward Megan, he landed instead in the middle of the construction area. As Megan stood there transfixed, she saw the knife fly out of his hand and watched him fall out of sight behind the plastic. A bloodcurdling scream was followed by a loud cracking sound. And then there was silence.

What happened? Megan wondered. She took a couple of steps forward, pushed the plastic aside, and peered down into the hole. She soon had the answer to her question. The lights from the floor below provided an eerie illumination to a macabre scene. The man was hanging by the neck from some electrical cords, his body swinging to and fro. For a fleeting moment Megan failed to comprehend what she was seeing. Then her brain began to process the ghoulish image, and she put her hands over her eyes and screamed at the top of her lungs.

CHAPTER 45

Greg Jablonski reached Megan first. She had stopped screaming, but was still standing perilously close to the opening between the floors, her trembling hands clasped close to her chest. As the young detective approached, he heard her moaning.

"Ms. Lansdorf, are you all right?" Jablonski asked in a soothing voice.

Megan didn't respond.

"Why don't we go to the lobby where you can sit down and be a little more comfortable," Jablonski suggested, putting his hand on Megan's arm.

Megan turned suddenly and flung herself against the detective's chest. "I killed him! I killed him! I killed him!" she sobbed hysterically, tears streaming down her face.

Jablonski put his arms around her and rocked her gently. "Shhh. It's okay. You're gonna be all right," he said in the same patient voice he used to calm his infant daughter when she cried. In a few moments he felt Megan's body begin to relax.

"I killed him," Megan said again, looking up at him, a helpless expression on her face.

"You didn't kill anyone," Jablonski assured her. "It was an accident. Now let's go to the lobby. Lieutenant O'Riley is very anxious to see for himself that you're all right."

Megan allowed herself to be led to one of the overstuffed navy-and-white-striped couches in the firm's reception area, next to the Christmas tree. Jablonski sat next to her and held her hand. The office was crawling with policemen, but Megan took little notice. Looking down, she saw with detachment that her white skirt was dirty and wrinkled, and the right knee had been ripped out of her pantyhose.

Her mind was reeling. Poor Frank. What a horrible end. In spite of what he did to those other women and in spite of what he'd tried to do to her, she was overwhelmed with guilt. And contrary to what Jablonski had said about his death being an accident, she firmly believed that she had killed him just as surely as if she'd shot him dead. After all, she was the one who had led him to the construction site.

Her mood darkened even further as she thought of his kids. What would happen to them? They'd probably end up living with their grandparents. Poor things. First their mother deserted them and now this. It would be devastating for them, particularly his daughter, with her already fragile emotional state. Megan couldn't bear to think of it.

She started to shake again and closing her eyes, she leaned her head back against the cushions of the couch. Just then the door from the outside hallway opened Megan's eyes fluttered open, and she saw Mike O'Riley step inside. Upon seeing Megan, he smiled broadly and said. "Young lady, you are a sight for sore eyes. I don't mind telling you that you had us all mighty worried for a while there."

"I'm sorry I caused you so much trouble," Megan replied contritely.

"No trouble at all," O'Riley said, "but you sure as hell got my attention when that gun went off."

"It got my attention, too," Megan said in a weak voice. "I didn't realize how much noise they make." She ran her hands through her hair. "So what happens now?" she asked hoarsely. "I suppose you'll want me to give a statement."

"There'll be plenty of time for that," O'Riley said. "But first, if you're up to it, there's someone outside who's very anxious to see you. In fact, he was downstairs and heard the gunshot and was so concerned about your well-being that he risked being charged with obstructing an officer by breaking away from my

men and running up twelve flights of stairs to make
sure you were okay."

Megan gave him a puzzled look, then decided that
Ron must have miraculously recovered from his bout
with the flu and come back downtown. He was probably beside himself with worry. "Sure," she said aloud.
"Let him in." Jablonski released her hand, and she
sluggishly got to her feet.

O'Riley walked over to the door and pushed it open
a crack. "All right," he said, "come on in."

Megan blinked, expecting to see Ron's blond head
and cheerful face. Instead, it was Frank Parks who appeared in the doorway. Megan gasped, opened her
mouth as if to say something, and then fainted dead
away.

When she came to, Megan was laid out on the
couch, her head resting on Jablonski's jacket. The first
face she saw was O'Riley's. He was kneeling next to
her and shaking her gently. "Are you all right? Should
we call a doctor?" His voice was full of concern.

Megan weakly raised a hand and rubbed her forehead. "I . . . I don't know," she said. Was she dreaming
or had she just seen a ghost? Turning her head, she decided the answer was neither. Frank was standing a
few paces away, next to Jablonski, looking uncharac-
teristically disheveled but very much alive. There was
a rip in the sleeve of his navy jacket where he'd caught
it on a nail in the stairwell, and his handmade, black
wing tips were wet from running across the slushy
streets. His face was flushed, and his usually fastidious
hairstyle was windblown and wet with snow.

Aided by O'Riley's strong arms, Megan slowly sat
up. She stared at Frank, then looked back at O'Riley.
"I don't understand," she rasped, shaking her head to
try to clear the cobwebs. "What is he . . . ? I mean, I
thought . . . I mean, if he's here, then who's dead?"

Frank looked perplexed, not grasping her meaning at
first. Suddenly it hit him. "You mean you thought *I*
was the killer?" he exclaimed. "You can't be serious!"

"Oh, my God!" Megan's pale face grew flushed.

"Oh, my God!" she repeated. "I'm sorry. I'm so sorry." She put her hands over her face and began to sob.

"Hey, the only thing that matters is that you're okay," Frank said. He quickly strode over to the couch and sat down next to Megan. She impulsively threw her arms around him and buried her face in his shoulder.

"You're alive, you're alive," she repeated over and over, her voice choked with emotion.

"Yes, I'm alive," Frank answered, holding her tightly. "You *are* okay, aren't you?"

Megan raised her head. "I think so," she sniffed. "I'm just very confused right now."

Frank looked down at her, flooded with relief that she hadn't been hurt. "I always knew you were a worthy opponent, but if I'd realized you made a habit of walking around armed, I would have treated you with a little more respect." With one hand he reached into his pocket, took out a white linen handkerchief, and handed it to her. "You look like you could use this."

Megan took it gratefully and blew her nose and wiped her eyes. "You have no idea how happy I was to see you come through the door." Once again she started to shiver.

"Are you cold?" Frank asked, rubbing her arms.

Megan nodded. "My jacket is back in my office." She looked down at her feet. "Along with my shoes."

"Here," Frank said, "take this." He slipped out of his jacket and wrapped it around her. "It's a little damp, but it should warm you up some."

"Thanks," she said, giving him a tentative smile.

O'Riley, who had moved a discreet distance away, walked back over and sat down on the other couch, facing them. Jablonski followed and stood behind him.

"You have to tell me who it was," Megan begged, wringing the handkerchief in her hands.

O'Riley and Frank exchanged looks. They had already had a discussion about the killer's identity. Frank nodded to the lieutenant and put his arm around Megan.

O'Riley answered without fanfare. "It was Dr. Lenz."

Megan stared at him in disbelief. "What?" she finally gasped. "I don't believe it. It can't be him."

"I'm afraid so," O'Riley said.

Megan turned to Frank, her eyes wide. He nodded.

"We don't have all the details yet," O'Riley explained, "but we ran a check and found out that Dr. Lenz suffered a nervous breakdown about six years ago, after his wife and twin sons were killed in a car accident."

"That's why he took two months' bereavement leave," Megan interrupted. "It was in his medical file."

O'Riley nodded. "A drunken woman driver ran them off an embankment. A jury acquitted the woman of vehicular manslaughter and only found her guilty of reckless driving. She got off with no jail time, just a fine.

"The driver was a very attractive woman in her late twenties who had worked for a time as a model," O'Riley continued. "She moved to the West Coast a few years ago, and one of the reasons she left Chicago was that she thought Lenz was harassing her. There was never any real proof it was him, but she'd get weird phone calls in the middle of the night, and she had the feeling someone was following her. She went so far as to swear out a complaint against him. The department looked into it, and talked to Lenz. Of course he denied it, and with his impressive professional credentials, the police figured the woman's imagination was just getting the better of her, and no charges were ever filed."

"But it wasn't her imagination," Frank put in.

O'Riley shook his head. "My people just conducted a search of Lenz's home. They found a scrapbook at Lenz's house with clippings about the accident and the trial. There were some photos of the driver. She had long red hair, just exactly like the first four women who were killed this spring."

"Oh, my God!" Megan exclaimed.

"We also found a handwritten address in San

Francisco where the woman driver now lives. The address was underlined three times in bold pen, so maybe Lenz or his alter ego was planning a trip west. That is, until his attention was diverted."

"By what?" Megan asked warily.

"By you," O'Riley replied.

"Oh, my God!" Megan moaned again.

"Or rather," O'Riley corrected himself, "by your case. I know this must sound incredible to you, but it all fits. There were four murders from mid-February until late April. All tall, thin women with long red hair, just like the woman who killed Lenz's family. Then the murders stopped completely until August, and when they did start up again, we didn't even realize at first it was him because the victims looked completely different." He paused a moment and looked at Meg solemnly. "They all looked just like you. Remember how I kept staring at you when we met at the hospital? Well, your resemblance to the two women who'd just been killed, and to Judy, really startled me, but I told myself I was imagining things, that there couldn't possibly be a connection. Turns out it was there all along, but of course there was no reason for anyone to suspect it."

"I should've suspected," Megan said softly.

"Why's that?" O'Riley asked with surprise.

Megan swallowed hard. "Because some weird things happened to me over the summer, before Judy was attacked."

"Like what?" Frank chimed in.

"First my car window was smashed in," she said, turning toward him. "Then, when Lenz and you and I were all in Bethesda, I went out for a walk and thought I was being followed. Then my best friend was struck by a hit-and-run driver when she came out of my building." She put her hands over her face. "It all fits."

"Why didn't you tell me all this when we met at the hospital?" O'Riley exclaimed. "We might've been able to piece things together sooner."

"Because I thought I was just being paranoid, and I

didn't want anybody to accuse me of being just another woman who was afraid of her own shadow."

"I'm still having a real hard time believing this," Frank said, "but the timing does fit. By summer we did know the plaintiffs had a real good case. But can you be certain Lenz was targeting Megan?"

"We're positive," O'Riley replied. "My men found a second scrapbook at Lenz's house where he'd been keeping press clippings about the murders. He'd started a new section of the book for each victim, each headed with a Shakespearean quote about death. The final section was headed with the quote 'To die, to sleep, perchance to dream,' and under that was Megan's name."

Megan shuddered and looked at Frank. "Oh, my God. The computer message."

O'Riley nodded.

"Why Shakespeare?" Frank asked.

"That threw me for a long time, too," O'Riley replied. "But it turns out there's a rather simple explanation. Lenz's wife was an English professor whose area of speciality was Shakespeare. Maybe Lenz thought that reciting verse during the attacks gave legitimacy to what he was doing, or maybe he thought his wife was listening to him. He evidently found the practice to be helpful, so he kept it up, even after he'd begun to focus on a set of victims who had nothing to do with his wife's death."

"I should've suspected something was wrong," Frank said in a self-reproachful tone. "Jesus! I did think he was strange duck. And come to think of it, he did show an unusual interest in Megan. Remember how he badgered your client to get information about you?"

Megan nodded.

"He kept telling me that the case was a matter of honor and he was positive we'd win," Frank went on. "And after the verdict came in, he became extremely withdrawn, but I just chalked it all up to a bad case of nerves. I should've paid more attention."

O'Riley shook his head. "There's no way you could

have known. People like Lenz are the original Dr. Jekyll and Mr. Hyde. I doubt very much that the Dr.
Lenz you knew was aware what was happening. I'd be
willing to bet the man doing the killing was a totally
distinct personality. And serial killers often function
quite normally in their everyday lives. Look at Ted
Bundy."

Frank looked at Megan with tenderness and compassion, and squeezed her tighter. "Still, if he'd hurt you,
I feel like it would've been my fault."

"How can you say that?" Megan exclaimed, looking
up at him. "You saved my life." Frank began to retort,
but she cut him off. "Yes, you did. I was too stubborn
to realize I was in danger. If I hadn't talked to you, I
would've gone back into the conference room and I'd
be mincemeat by now."

"Don't even think such a thing!" Frank ordered.

"Hey, you're not the only one here who missed a
bunch of clues," O'Riley said to Frank. "You know, I
had a feeling all along that the killer might have some
medical expertise. All of the victims' chest wounds
were absolutely identical. Mind you, I never suspected
it was a doctor, but I thought it might be someone with
an above-average knowledge of anatomy. I can see
now I should've pursued that angle a lot harder."

"So what happens now?" Megan asked.

"There are a few loose ends to wrap up," O'Riley
replied. "We still want to interview some of Lenz's
colleagues to see if anyone realized how unstable he
was. And we'll be checking into his background further. I wouldn't be surprised if we found some more
skeletons in his closet. But the case is just about over
with." Over with. What a joyous sound those words
had, and how long he'd waited to say them.

A young, uniformed officer emerged from around a
corner. "Lieutenant," he said as he walked up to them,
"sorry to interrupt, but we've finally been able to reach
Mayor Daley at the national mayor's conference in
New Orleans. I've got him on hold."

O'Riley got to his feet. "There's really no reason for
the two of you to hang around here any longer," he

said. "I'll stop by in the morning and get Megan's statement. We should be out of here in half an hour or so, and we'll take care of locking up. Why don't you guys go someplace and have a couple stiff drinks."

"Thank you for everything," Frank said, getting up and pumping both O'Riley's and Jablonski's hands vigorously.

"Yes, thanks a lot," Megan echoed. "I'll never forget you."

"Young lady," O'Riley said with a smile, "something tells me we're not going to forget you either. Good night. And happy holidays," he added as he followed Jablonski down the hall.

"Well, Mike," the mayor's voice crackled over the phone line, "it looks like this is going to be a very merry Christmas indeed."

"Sorry it took so long to wrap it up," O'Riley said ruefully, leaning against the table in the small conference room.

"I don't want to hear any apologies," the mayor interrupted. "You did an outstanding job, just like I knew you would."

"Thank you," O'Riley said in a heartfelt tone. "That means a lot to me."

"Now that the case is over, I don't suppose I can persuade you to delay your retirement any longer," the mayor chided.

"No way in hell," O'Riley shot back. "As soon as the paperwork is done, I'm outta here."

"In that case," the mayor continued, "how does your schedule look for the day after tomorrow?"

"Clear as a bell. What've you got in mind?"

"I'll be flying back from New Orleans tomorrow night, and I'd like to hold a press conference publicly commending you on a job well done."

"I think I can work that into my schedule," O'Riley said with a chuckle.

"Good. I'll have my office set it up and let you know about the time. Anne should be there, too."

"She wouldn't miss it for the world."

"And tell young Jablonski he should bring his wife," the mayor added.

"I will," O'Riley assured him.

"I know I should probably keep this a secret," the mayor went on confidentially, "but after all, this is the holidays, and I want you to know how much I appreciate all you've done. I plan to see to it that you get a nice cash bonus for your efforts."

O'Riley beamed. "Thank you, Richie," he said warmly. "And as long as we're on the subject of bonuses, when can I expect delivery of the dinghy you promised me?"

Frank returned to the couch and stood in front of Megan. "Would you like a ride home?"

The high Megan had felt after realizing Frank wasn't the killer was starting to wear off, and she felt like she was going into shock. "My car's over in the ramp," she replied vacantly.

"It's snowing and nasty out," Frank said gently. "And anyway, you're not exactly in any condition to drive. Why don't you let me give you a ride? I'll be happy to come pick you up again in the morning."

Frank's jacket started to slide off her shoulders. As Megan pulled it back around her, a sudden thought sprang into her mind. "What's going to happen to our case?" she asked.

"The judge will have to grant a mistrial. After all, the hospital isn't going to be able to get a fair trial on the issue of damages when it's splashed all over the media that their key witness was a murderer."

"Oh, no," Megan said forlornly, her eyes starting to tear up again. "I can't go through it again! I just can't!"

"You won't have to," Frank said kindly. "I promise that first thing tomorrow I'll see to it that the hospital pays your clients a good settlement."

"Promise?" Megan asked, brightening a bit.

"Scout's honor." Frank held up his hand. He smiled to himself. With his oversized jacket around her and her rumpled clothing, Megan looked like a poor waif sitting there. But a damn feisty one. She was holding up amazingly well, considering all that she'd been through.

"Come on. Let's go find your shoes and coat and take the lieutenant's advice and get something to drink. Could I interest you in some coffee with Bailey's?"

"Yes, you could," Megan said. "But let's get one thing straight first."

"What's that?"

"The next time we try a case against each other, you're not going to be able to take the easy way out and settle it like you did this time," she said, sticking out her chin. "I'm gonna see it all the way through and I'm gonna beat the pants off you."

"Really!" Frank said in a shocked tone. "Is that any way for a lady lawyer to talk?"

"A little respect, please!" Megan retorted. "Mike Gillette told me on the QT that I'm a shoe-in for partner."

"Well then," Frank said, "this calls for something stronger than Bailey's. I've got an idea."

"What's that?" Megan asked warily.

"How about a nice big pitcher of gin martinis? I remember how much you enjoyed the last one I bought you."

Megan tossed her hair back and stared up at him defiantly.

Frank smiled. This was the Megan he knew. "What's the matter? You lose your appetite for martinis?"

"Before you try to force me to drink a martini," she said, her eyes flashing, "I want to warn you that I know where there's a loaded gun. And now that I've had some target practice, you'd better watch out."

Frank shuddered. "Okay, okay. Motion withdrawn. The defense rests its case."

Megan wadded Frank's handkerchief into a ball and threw it at him. It bounced off his chest and landed on the floor. "Let's go, counselor," she said, getting to her feet. "You've got exactly fifteen minutes to buy me a drink before I find you in contempt of court."